The Blue Mage Raised by Dragons

by Virlyce

This book is dedicated to my HxC guild members.

Prologue

"Sh-shouldn't we stop her?" asked a red dragon. She sat on top of a boulder with her head raised, her reptilian eyes staring off at the rising smoke in the distance.

"No…. It should be fine. Probably." A puff of smoke flew out of a gold dragon's nostrils as he sighed. The dragon's paws covered his head as he lay on the ground beneath the boulder.

"But what if the humans come?" the red dragon asked, flapping her wings twice. Her tail hung off the boulder, swishing above the gold dragon's head.

A black dragon lying on his back, with his arms and legs splayed, snorted. He yawned and smacked his lips. "Then let them come."

"Grimmy! You can't solve everything with violence!" said the silver dragon who was sitting next to him.

"Of course not, dear," Grimmy said as he raised his head to nuzzle her neck with his dark snout. His head fell back to the ground, creating a web of cracks on the rock surface below.

"Oh, get a room, you two," the red dragon said, puffing her cheeks out while staring at the couple. She turned her head back to the gold dragon and asked, "Are you sure we shouldn't do anything, Vernon?"

"If you can stop her, be my guest," Vernon replied. "The only thing I'll be doing is praying I don't die when she returns." The gold dragon shuddered and closed his eyes. The other three dragons stared at him.

"He's whipped."

"Definitely whipped."

A chorus of agreement resounded throughout the valley.

1

***

"Your Majesty, the Red Blade Adventurers have returned and wish to seek an audience," a guard said with his head lowered and right arm across his chest. Across from him, sitting on a throne, there was a man with a crown.

"They may enter," the king said. A group of six people, four men and two women, walked through the metal doors towards the king. They stopped twenty steps away, with one man ahead of the others, and knelt while staring at the floor.

"Your Majesty," the man in front said. He wore a blue chainmail, and a red zweihander was strapped to his back. The blade of the sword extended from his shoulders to his knees while its hilt was slightly longer than his face.

"You may rise."

The leading man stood up and crossed one arm over his chest. "We have accomplished your request. After stealing the dragon's egg, we split up and entered six different towns before teleporting back to the capital. Sophie," he said. One of the women, wearing a red robe, rose and retrieved a watermelon-sized egg from her bag.

"Excellent. You have done very well. As promised, I'll send a word in to the adventurers' guild to increase your ranking. Each of you may also select a weapon from the royal armory. You are dismissed," the king said after taking the egg. The Red Blades stood up and bowed before turning around to leave.

"Won't the dragons retaliate, Your Majesty?" a man standing next to the king asked. He had a white robe and a silver cross necklace, the metal barely showing from under his beard.

"They will, but we'll only lose a few frontier towns at most. They wouldn't dare to attack the bigger cities. What is worth more, Gale? A town or a dragon?" the king asked before bursting out into laughter.

"Forgive me, I misspoke," Gale said while looking at the floor. He clenched his necklace until it cut into his palm and drew blood. *I'm sorry.*

2

Shrieks and screams resounded through the air. A man, wearing worn-out clothing, ran out the town gates with his wife. Tears streamed from the woman's eyes as she clutched the infant in her hands to her chest. Behind them was a sea of fire. The smell of burning wood and meat lingered in the air.

"Head towards the forest." The man had to shout over the roaring of the flames. The woman nodded and ran towards the woods. Before they even took ten steps, a shadow blotted out the sun and the earth shook as a sky-blue dragon landed in front of them. Its eyes, with golden irises and black slit pupils, stared at the two who had fallen over onto their butts. The dragon bared its fangs. Each tooth was the length of a man's forearm, and flecks of flesh were speckled throughout its mouth. The man's pants warmed up as a liquid passed through the cloth, but he couldn't move. He tried to scream, but no sound came out. The dragon arched its head up towards the sky and roared.

"Wh-why?" the woman asked. Her baby stirred in her arms, and her chest ached as fear gripped her.

The dragon glared at the woman.

"Vengeance," it said as it raised its leg into the air. The woman closed her eyes and hugged her baby tight while sobbing. The baby's eyes opened after a teardrop fell on its face. It made eye contact with the sky-blue dragon and opened its tiny mouth. The ground shook and shattered as a roar escaped from the baby's lips, eliciting a scream from the woman as she dropped the baby and dove to the side.

The dragon's claw stopped a foot above the dazed woman's head, and it blinked its eyes. A rumbling sound caused the earth beneath the woman to tremble. It took a second before she realized the dragon was laughing.

A blue mage? Interesting. If they take one of mine, then I'll take one of theirs, the dragon thought with a smile. She gently scooped up the infant with her claws. Her golden eyes stared at the woman who trembled beneath her. Her mouth opened, and the smell of carrion assaulted the woman's nostrils.

"What is his name?"

1

"Um, Sera, dear? What is that?" Vernon asked.

"It's your son." The sky-blue dragon stared at Vernon.

"I see. My son. Yes, of course. How could I have been so silly as to not recognize my own flesh and blood?" Vernon asked, enunciating every word. *She's gone crazy. Absolutely insane.*

Sera was sitting on her hind legs, rocking the infant with her front claw. "Isn't he adorable? Say Mama, Vur. Say Mama." The woman had told her the infant's name was Johann, but Sera hadn't thought it sounded very intimidating.

Grimmy let out a guttural laugh and slapped Vernon's back with his claw. "Congratulations on the healthy boy. He has your hair."

"But he doesn't have ha—. Oh," the red dragon said and nodded. "It's true. He most certainly has a mane as fine as yours, Vernon."

The surrounding dragons let out giggles. Vernon glared at them before turning to Sera. His brow creased as he asked, "Why does he look so ... human?"

Sera narrowed her eyes at him. "What part of him looks human? Why couldn't you recognize a human when they stole our egg?"

"Ah, that was, ahem. Never mind. I'm sure little Vur will grow up to be a fine dragon." Vernon let out a cough and looked towards the sky.

"Of course he will. I imprinted him," Sera said and nuzzled the baby's forehead with her snout.

"YOU WHAT?!" All the dragons turned to stare at Sera.

"Did you really?" the red dragon asked with wide eyes.

"Yes, he's one of us now. If any of you dare bully him," Sera said and narrowed her eyes, "then I'll kill you myself."

"She's really done it now. After all these years, she's finally gone insane," Vernon mumbled with his claws covering his face.

"Did you say something just now, dear?" Sera smiled at Vernon.

"No, I was only—"

"Volunteering to feed him? What a nice father you are," Sera interrupted. She held Vur out towards Vernon, and he had no choice but to accept. Vernon looked at Vur closely and frowned. The infant's eyes were golden with slit pupils exactly like Sera's. *She really did imprint him*, Vernon thought and sighed.

"Hello, Vur…," Vernon said. Vur looked into Vernon's red eyes and let out a roar.

"Holy sh—"

"No cursing in front of the child," Sera said as she smacked Vernon's snout with her claw. "I told you he was one of us."

"A blue mage," the silver dragon next to Grimmy whispered.

"Are we really taking in a blue mage?" Grimmy asked. He raised an eyebrow while turning over onto his belly to get a closer look at the infant.

"Mage? What mage? All I see is a blue dragon. Isn't that right, Sera?" Vernon asked.

"You really do learn well, honey." Sera smiled at him. "I'm tired after that little excursion. If you'll excuse me, I'll be taking a nap."

"Wait. How many towns did you destroy?" the red dragon asked.

"Only seventeen. Don't forget to feed the baby, Vernon," Sera said as she flew up into the air.

The golden dragon watched helplessly as Sera's figure shrank in the distance. "But. What does he eat?" Vernon sighed, peering at the infant sitting on his palm.

"I heard the meat of magical beasts is great for humans—increases their strength or something," Grimmy said. He poked the baby's belly with his front claw, causing him to cry out.

"But he doesn't even have teeth? Can he eat that?" the red dragon asked as she pinched Vur's cheeks to open his mouth.

Grimmy snorted and returned to the silver dragon's side. "Then make him drink their blood."

Vernon frowned at the crying baby who had just peed in his paw. His red eyes widened and glowed. A sphere of water formed in the air above Vur's head before falling on top of the infant, drenching him while washing away the pee. "Hold him for me?" Vernon asked the black and silver dragons while offering the spluttering baby towards them.

Grimmy raised an eyebrow as he plucked Vur off of Vernon's palm. He brought Vur to his nose and sniffed him with a nostril that was bigger than the baby's body. Vur let out a scream as he slipped out of Grimmy's claws and bounced against the floor. "Oops," Grimmy said and caught Vur before he could hit the floor again. The other dragons blinked as Grimmy dusted Vur off with the back of his scaled claw, smearing the crying baby's face with blood.

"Grimmy!" The silver dragon gasped and smacked her mate's snout. She snatched Vur out of Grimmy's palm and touched the baby's forehead with the tip of her claw. Her silver eyes shone white, and a halo of light enveloped Vur. Translucent tendrils squirmed around Vur's body, healing the gashes on the back of his head. Vernon sighed and shook his head before spreading his wings and leaping into the air.

The red dragon furrowed her brow as Vernon disappeared into the horizon before turning her head back to the now-squabbling couple. She cleared her throat. "No one's going to tell Sera we dropped him, right?" she asked. The dragons fell silent and exchanged glances before nodding. The red dragon exhaled and patted her chest before lying prone, curling her body around the top of the boulder. "Nice save by the way, Leila."

The silver dragon smiled at her before shooting a glare at Grimmy. He scratched his cheek and chuckled while smiling. Leila turned her head away and jostled Vur in her palm, attempting to stop his crying. "Give him here," Grimmy said and held out his palm. "I know how to make him stop."

"No."

The cries continued as the sun moved across the sky. The howling of wind interrupted Vur's voice as wings flapped. Vernon was returning with a dead bear dangling from his mouth. The ground trembled, causing Vur to cry even louder, as the golden dragon landed next to the couple and released the dead animal in his jaws. "How is he?" Vernon asked as he picked a scrap of flesh out of his teeth with his claw.

"Noisy," Grimmy said. Leila passed Vur back to Vernon before shaking her head and sighing.

"I wish you luck in raising him," she said. Vernon frowned as he placed Vur onto the ground and stripped a piece of flesh off the dead bear. As if noticing the change, Vur stopped crying and sat on his butt with his legs sticking straight out.

Leila curled up next to Grimmy's side. The sun shone on her silver scales, creating a rainbow pattern of light. She turned her head towards Grimmy and nuzzled his neck with her snout. She asked, "Is he really going to feed him that?" The duo watched Vernon wave a piece of bloody bear meat in front of the sitting baby.

"Doesn't it smell delicious? Go on; try it," Vernon said. He smiled at Vur, blood dripping from his jagged teeth.

Vur stared at the piece of meat before starting to cry. The red dragon snickered, causing Vernon to glare at her. "Quiet, Prika. I'm not in the mood."

Prika covered her snout with her paw, her eyes shining as muffled exhalations escaped from her lips.

Vernon sighed and turned his head back towards Vur. The dragon's eyes shone, and an invisible force knocked Vur over backwards, plastering him to the ground. Vernon held the meat over Vur's head and let the blood drip into the infant's open mouth. Vur's eyes opened wide as he spluttered, but Vernon wouldn't relent and manipulated the blood back into Vur's mouth with magic.

Vur drank mouthful after mouthful of the bear's blood until Prika called out, "Stop, stop! He's unconscious."

Vernon's eyes stopped glowing. He nodded at the infant who had bloody foam trickling out of his mouth before eating the chunk of meat in his claws.

***

A purple-eyed man with four curved horns, two sticking out of his forehead and two protruding out of his temples, stood by a bedside with his hand holding onto a smaller, whiter hand. His skin was pale, blue veins decorating his exposed skin like little snakes. He wore a purple robe with a golden, horn-shaped insignia embroidered on its chest. A large crown made of orange metal rested on his head, supported by the two horns on his forehead. His wife lay on the bed with a blanket covering her bulging belly but exposing her bare legs. She screamed and clutched her husband's hand, sweat rolling down her face onto the plush bed. Like the man, her skin was pale and she had four horns growing out of her head. A maid with a single horn sticking straight out of her forehead was by the foot of the bed, staring at the woman's private bits.

"How does it look?" the man asked, frowning as his fingers were crushed by his wife.

"It just started, Milord," the maid said. She clasped her hands together and closed her eyes. A white light enveloped the screaming lady, causing her to gasp. Her screams reduced to labored groans, and the light disappeared. The maid opened her

9

eyes and inhaled before speaking, "Talking to Milady may help distract her from the pain, Milord."

The man nodded and looked at his wife. He tucked a lock of black hair, damp with sweat and sticking against her cheek, behind her ear. "Did you hear?" he asked. "The humans provoked a dragon. They lost over fifteen settlements." He stroked his chin with his free hand. "It must be an auspicious sign. The future demon lord is born after hundreds of humans have died."

His wife gritted her teeth and glared at him with bloodshot eyes. "Does it look like I care about that right now?" she asked and hissed as her lower body spasmed.

The man scratched his head. "I was just trying to help," he said. He glanced at the maid who avoided his gaze. "How does it look, Prim?"

The maid resisted the urge to roll her eyes. "It just started, Milord," she said in the same tone as before. "Birthing can take up to eighteen hours, more if there are complications. You can't expect"—her eyes widened—"eh?"

"What's the matter?" the man asked. His wife's grip on his hand loosened, causing his heart to pound. "Is the baby alright?"

"Yes, Milord," Prim said, her eyes still wide. Her hands reached beneath the blanket into the area where the man couldn't see. Moments later, she raised her arms, revealing a silent baby. "I retract my previous statement."

The man released his wife and hurried next to the maid. He snatched the bloody baby out of her hands—seconds after she snipped the umbilical cord—and peered at it, occasionally flipping it around and upside-down. His face fell. "He has no horns," he said and looked at Prim with an accusing gaze.

Prim nodded. "That's to be expected, Milord. Only exceptionally gifted demons are born with horns," she said. A groan caused her to look back towards the wife lying on the bed.

Her body undulated, and a scream escaped from her lips. Prim's eyes widened as she stepped forward. "Twins, Milord."

The man's mouth fell open as he held the silent baby in one hand, using his palm to support its head while resting its back along his forearm. His wife gripped the edges of her bed with both hands and screamed again. The man's face paled, and he stepped back to his previous position, avoiding the sight of blood and liquid gushing out of his wife. He wasn't squeamish, but he saw no reason to develop a tainted image of something he admired. The baby in his arms opened its eyes and stared at him, but the man didn't even notice.

Cries were heard, and Prim lifted up another baby. The man stepped forward and swapped babies with Prim. He inspected it in a similar manner as before and sighed. "He's also hornless," he said. The baby cried, causing the man to wrinkle his nose. "I'll hold that one if—"

A guttural scream cut him off. The baby stopped crying as Prim and the man turned their heads towards the woman lying on the bed. Her stomach was still bulging. Her already white hands turned even paler as she clenched them and tore through the sheets covering the mattress. "Triplets," Prim said and handed the baby she was holding to the man. The man made a face as blood dripped from his elbows onto the ground. A dark color stained the rolled-up sleeves of his robe.

Within seconds, a third baby appeared, accompanied by a sloshing sound. Prim snipped the umbilical cord and inspected the woman before turning her attention towards her lord. The woman's belly had finally returned to normal, and short gasps escaped from her mouth. Something pricked Prim's chest. She looked down and opened her mouth. "Milord, this—"

"Horns!" the man said and tossed the two babies he was holding onto the bed, causing both of them to cry out. He snatched the baby out of Prim's arms and cradled it to his chest, not caring about the bloody stains it left on his robe. He laughed and extended his hands, holding the baby in front of his face. His face fell. "It's a girl."

"What's wrong with a girl?" the woman lying on the bed asked as she trembled and sat up. A white light enveloped her body thanks to Prim who was standing by the bed with her eyes closed and hands clasped. The woman picked up the two babies and frowned at the man.

The man chuckled and cradled the baby to his chest. "There's nothing wrong with a girl. How do you feel?" he asked. "It's amazing how you ... persisted through giving birth to triplets."

His wife's eyes narrowed. "I feel great," she said and ground her teeth together. "Just fine."

The man's eyes gleamed, and he focused his attention on the baby in his arms. "Your name will be Tafel," he said and smiled, revealing a row of white teeth.

"What about your sons?" his wife asked as she hugged the two infant boys to her chest.

The man shrugged. "How about Two and Three?" he asked. He wiggled his finger in front of Tafel's face, causing her to stretch her hands out.

"Gabriel and Lamach," his wife said and smiled at her children. Her smile didn't reach her eyes. "I'm sure they'll grow up to be as strong as their father." She glanced at the man who was still entranced by the baby in his arms. He hadn't heard her.

The man raised his head and laughed. "Tafel will be the greatest mage of this generation," he said. "Black, red, white, green. It doesn't matter what kind of mage she becomes!"

"Blue?" his wife asked as she handed the two babies to Prim.

The man snorted. "What are you thinking, woman?" he asked. "Use your head sometimes. What beasts are nearby for her to learn skills from?"

The woman frowned and crossed her arms. She lay back down on the bed, ignoring the warm fluids underneath her legs and muttered under her breath, "You said any." She eyed the smile on her husband's face. It looked more like a sneer. She snorted and turned over onto her side. "See if I'll let you get your way."

Prim turned her head away, pretending not to have heard anything.

2

Five Years Later

The human king stood on a platform in the back of a ballroom, a golden scepter in his right hand. Behind him, Gale stood with his hands clasped behind his back, wearing a white robe. To the left of the king, a youth stood with his chest puffed out. He wore a set of blue armor that was too big in the shoulders for his scrawny frame. The king cleared his throat and banged the end of his scepter onto the platform, causing the ballroom to fall into silence. Hundreds of eyes turned towards his direction, causing the youth to fidget.

"I'd like to thank you all for coming here today to celebrate my son's coming-of-age ceremony," the king said and gestured towards the youth with his free hand. The well-dressed guests applauded while a few of the armored guards in the back whistled. The king waited for the applause to die down before continuing. "As many of you know, he is an exceptional fighter with great aptitude in holy magic. Six years ago, I announced he would become the leader of the holy knights, but today, I am renouncing that declaration."

A few murmurs of confusion floated up as the nobles looked around at each other. The king waved his hand to silence them and paused, letting all the eyes fall on him.

"Today, he will become the first dragon knight!" the king said and slammed the end of his scepter against the platform. His voice boomed and echoed off the walls. "Elise!"

The metal doors swung open, and a woman with white hair holding an orange chain walked into the ballroom. She tugged on the chain that was as thick as her thigh, and a carriage-sized, sky-blue dragon lumbered through the entrance. Its eyes were wide, and its head was lowered like a dog that was caught chewing on a pillow.

"Nearly five years ago, the Red Blade Adventurers risked their lives to obtain a dragon egg. The result is in front of you," the king said. "Elise has done an excellent job as a beast tamer, raising the baby dragon all on her own. For her efforts, I will bestow her with the title of viscountess." A few nobles clapped but the majority remained silent in fear of drawing the dragon's attention to themselves. "With the addition of a dragon knight to our troops, we will be able to exterminate the demon menace at our borders and reclaim the lost city of Flusia." The king smiled as the nobles edged away from the walking dragon. The men trembled, and a few ladies fainted. "Even the demon lord is incapable of defeating a dragon. When we conquer the demons, we'll move on to the elves. We've been oppressed for far too long; our time is nigh!" The king paused and let the armored guards in the back howl and cheer to their hearts' content. He patted his son on the shoulder and said, "Rudolph, go and claim your prize."

"Thank you, Father," Rudolph said with a wide smile on his face. He strutted towards the dragon and held his hand out towards Elise. He made eye contact with the dragon and shivered before wetting his lips with the tip of his tongue. The dragon stared back at him with its wings and tail raised. Its lips were slightly parted, revealing a row of yellow teeth.

A twelve-year-old brat wishes to bond with a dragon. Ridiculous, Elise thought as she smiled at the prince. She put her hand on the dragon's snout, stroking it a few times before grabbing Rudolph's outstretched arm with her other hand. A pillar of white light emanated from Elise and illuminated the room. The dragon roared while Rudolph screamed as runes of light formed in the air and swirled around them. The dragon shook its head and slammed its feet against the floor while its tail thrashed around, knocking over tables filled with wine and food. Rudolph fell to his knees, held up only by Elise's grip.

After most of the tables were overturned, Elise released her hands, and the light faded away.

"It has been done," Elise said with her forehead covered in a sheen of sweat. Rudolph panted as he stared at his wrist and grinned at the green runes spiraling up his forearm. The nearby nobles had screamed when the dragon rampaged, and they were just beginning to calm down.

The king waited until everyone fell silent. "As expected of a master-class beast tamer, the bond was established on the first try," he said. Sparse applause rang out, and Elise took a bow. Her body trembled, and a hint of longing appeared in her eyes as she stared at the dragon. It mewled at her, as if knowing she would be leaving.

Elise turned her head away and curtsied at the king. Her lips quivered, but her voice was steady. "It was nothing," she said. "It was an honor to be of service. Now, if you'll excuse me, I must rest. Forming a bond is quite exhausting." She turned around and pursed her lips, ignoring the whimpers coming from the dragon as she walked outside of the ballroom.

The nobles began to chatter, softly at first. Rudolph stared at the dragon with his mouth slightly open. It had light-brown eyes with round pupils. *It's mine, I have a dragon*, Rudolph thought while almost squealing.

"What are you going to name it?" a voice called out, slurring the words. The voice belonged to a red-faced noble who had his arm around a scantily clad woman.

Rudolph met the dragon's watery eyes. "Johann. I'll name him Johann."

***

"Alright, Vur," Vernon said as he alighted to the forest's ground. The trees bent backwards due to the force of his wings slowing his massive body down. Vur was sitting on Vernon's snout with his legs straddled over a golden ridge of scales. He was completely naked with tangled, brown hair that hung down to his shoulders. Vernon lowered his head to the ground and

16

tilted his snout to the side, letting Vur jump off. "It's about time you learned how to hunt for yourself, you damned freeloader … err, beloved son. All dragons learn how to hunt when they turn five."

Vur blinked at Vernon, a blank expression on his face. "Hunt?"

"You'll figure it out, I think," Vernon said and furrowed his brow before shrugging his shoulders. "Just do what you feel is right." He spread his wings and jumped into the air, abandoning the naked five-year-old child in the forest. The dragons had never taken Vur hunting before, opting to bring him a dead bear once a month instead.

Vur scratched his head and looked up at the golden speck in the sky before wandering off into the forest. His feet and hands were calloused from five years of crawling around naked on the hard ground through many summers and winters. His body was tan and lean, and he crept through the forest on all fours like a cat. A rustling noise caught his attention, and his head turned towards the sound. He bounded ahead and brushed aside a bush blocking his view. There was a small, four-legged creature eating berries off of a bush. It had a squiggly tail and hooves on the end of its feet. The baby boar's eyes widened, and it let out a surprised squeal as Vur smiled and tackled the boar. He held the boar up. It was half his height with round, golden eyes and black stripes running down its sides, contrasting with its light-brown fur. Vur tilted his head as the boar squealed and squirmed in his grasp. He furrowed his brow because he wasn't quite sure what hunting entailed.

Up above, Vernon nodded to himself and began to descend after Vur caught the boar. It wasn't a bear or even an adult boar, but it was something. The child hadn't resorted to magic either. He furrowed his brow as Vur flipped the boar over onto its back. The child seemed to be forcing something into its mouth. As he approached the ground from the air, a flash of golden light, shooting out of Vur, blinded him, causing him to crash into a

17

tree. The tree groaned and snapped while the ground trembled. Vernon shook his head and blinked his eyes a few times. He stared at Vur and the boar in his hands. His mouth fell open as a golden rune flashed on both Vur's and the baby boar's forehead. *Shit. Sera's going to murder me.*

Vur turned around and beamed as he held the baby boar aloft. "Look, Papa," he said with a smile on his face. "I did it. I hunted."

"That's great," Vernon said with his voice trailing off. His face fell as the boar's irises and pupils glowed and changed shapes, becoming similar to Vur's. He bit his lower lip and sighed while shaking his head. "Excellent job. Let's go home, okay?"

"Un." Vur grunted and nodded while hopping onto Vernon's snout, using his nostril as a stepping stone. He cuddled the boar in his arms, and it licked his nose in reply.

Vernon's face cramped as he flew into the air and headed back to the valley where he lived. They passed over a sea of green and multiple mountain ranges. The boar in Vur's arms stared at the scenery with wide eyes. At last, the trio alighted in front of a cave with veins of golden ores decorating its exterior.

"Sera, dear. Are you home?" Vernon called out. He cleared his throat and sat on his haunches, praying she wasn't. His prayers were unanswered.

"You two are back already?" Sera's voice asked. A pair of golden eyes appeared in the depths of the cave before her sky-blue head came into view. "How was his first hunt? Did he kill a bear?"

"Uh." Vernon scratched his head, causing the baby boar to squeal. Vernon's left eye twitched. "He, uh"—his voice fell to a whisper—"imprinted a boar." He closed his eyes and covered his ears with his paws.

"He what?" Sera asked and rushed out of the cave, causing the ground to tremble and dust to fall from the ceiling. Her eyes widened at Vur tossing the baby boar up and down into the air like a ball.

"Mama, look," Vur said while dangling the boar out in front of him. The five-year-old smiled wide and hugged the boar to his chest. "I named her Snuffles."

Sera glared at Vernon, who was still isolating his senses, before directing her gaze to Vur. "Did you imprint it?"

"Imprint? No, I hunted her," Vur said while shaking his head. "Papa said I did a good job."

If looks could kill, Vernon would've died right then and there. Sera took in a deep breath and smiled at Vur before speaking, "Tell Mama how you found him."

"Snuffles is a girl; she has eyes like Mama. I was hunting, and I saw her, and I tried to feed her to hunt her, but she kept trying to run away, so I did what Papa does to me when I don't eat, but then she stopped moving, but I didn't want her to stop, so I hugged her and a bright light appeared, and then Papa came," Vur said in one breath and tilted his head to one side. "What is she, Mama?"

Sera looked at the trembling boar. *That is most definitely a male.* She sighed. "We're going to have a long talk, Vur."

Vernon opened one eye and uncovered his ears. "You're not mad?"

Sera smiled, showing her teeth while narrowing her eyes. "Come, *dear.* I think both of you can learn something new."

"Ah," Vernon said as he dropped Vur onto the ground and turned around to walk away. "I just remembered I had something to do. Prika needed me to—"

Prika's voice called out from below the cave. "Don't bring me into this!"

Vernon whimpered as Sera bit his tail and dragged him into the depths of the cave. Snuffles looked up at Vur who trotted after the two into the darkness. "Mama loves Papa," he said to the boar and stroked its forehead.

***

Elise sighed at her empty stables. There was so much space now that Johann had left. A month had already passed since she handed his reins to the prince, and she still hadn't replaced the partition he occupied. She was about to enter, but a fluctuation of magic caused her hair to stand on end. She whirled around just in time to see a half-naked old man appear out of thin air.

"Elise," the old man said as he ran a bony finger through his white beard.

"Exzenter," Elise said, unfazed by the man's appearance. "To what do I owe this pleasure?"

"The king sent me to bring you to him," Exzenter said. "Apparently the dragon's broken or something. He wouldn't let me take a look though. A shame really, I was hoping to study it a bit. Both you and that man are so stingy." He clicked his tongue.

Elise sighed and held out her hand. "Please teleport my clothing too."

"That's really not up to me," Exzenter said and smiled as he grabbed her hand. Elise's vision went dark. Moments later, the color reappeared, and she found herself standing in the center of a room with a red carpet on the ground. She glanced down and exhaled in relief when she saw all her clothes had remained with her. Exzenter released her hand and stepped to the side as she raised her head.

"Elise."

"Your Majesty," Elise said and knelt on the floor. A mewling sound caught her attention, but she resisted the urge to raise her head.

The king was sitting on his throne with the prince and the dragon by his side. Rudolph was sitting on Johann's back. "Why can't Johann use magic?" Rudolph asked. The dragon flinched when it heard its name.

"You may rise," the king said.

Elise stood up and observed the men in front of her. The prince was frowning, and the king wasn't smiling. Gale was like a statue of a bishop as he stood behind the king with his hands clasped and face expressionless.

"Johann has not been imprinted. All magical beasts can imprint their young to grant them their lineage which contains their innate magic," Elise said and lowered her head. "Without an imprint, a magical beast is just a beast."

"Then get him imprinted," Rudolph said and smacked his hand down on the side of Johann's neck. Elise resisted the urge to frown, but her eyes grew cold.

"Is that possible?" the king asked.

"Only if you can find a dragon willing to imprint him," Elise said.

"What about a different beast?" Exzenter asked. His eyes lit up as if a lightbulb appeared over his head.

Elise shook her head. "Johann is no longer a child. Finding a mother willing to take him in as her own would be quite difficult in and of itself," she said. "And even if you could find one, if you imprint Johann with, say, a magical boar, then his potential and abilities will be limited to the level of the boar."

Exzenter raised an eyebrow. "Then if a dragon imprinted a boar?"

Elise shot a glance at the old man who had managed to lose another piece of clothing through his teleportation. "Then that dragon's beyond stupid," she said. "What kind of question is that?"

"So there's a chance," Exzenter said and nodded, causing Elise to sigh.

"Can't you find me a dragon, Dad?" Rudolph asked the king.

"I'm afraid that's beyond our capabilities," the king said. "I'll put a request in to the guild, but you shouldn't get your hopes up."

Rudolph grumbled.

3

Three black-haired, purple-eyed kids, two boys and one girl, were eating at a rectangular table with a horned man and woman: The man sat at the head of the table while the boys sat on one side, and the mother and daughter sat on the other. The girl had two-inch-long red horns growing out of her temples, curving towards the back of her head. There were bumps on the boys' temples. Red curtains were draped across a massive window that let in a beam of sunlight. Outside, the tops of gray buildings with red-tiled roofs could be seen stretching off into the distance. The citizens down below were the size of ants.

The man placed his knife and fork down and dabbed a napkin to his lips. He pushed his chair back and stretched his feet out, letting the plush carpet brush against his heels. The children also placed their utensils down before wiping their mouths while the mother continued eating, furrowing her brow at her husband. He cleared his throat, and the children turned their heads. His gaze glanced over the two boys before lingering on the girl. His voice flowed like silk, "The three of you are now old enough to attend school."

His wife frowned. *Isn't it too soon?* she thought but didn't say anything, opting to stab the bottom of the dinner plate through her steak with her fork.

The man's lips twisted into a wry smile before he continued speaking, "You are the children of the demon lord—great things are expected of you. How can you achieve anything if you're stuck in school past adulthood? You will learn how to lead our people to victory against the humans."

The woman's frown extended and cracks formed on the dinner plate as her hand trembled. "Even Tafel?" she asked. Her four horns glowed with a red hue that was barely noticeable under the sunlight.

"Especially Tafel. She's only five years old, but her horns are longer than some demons' ever will be. Imagine how strong she'll be when she's an adult," the man answered. A smile crept onto his face as he stared at his daughter's blank expression. He picked up his fork and resumed his meal.

"I'm stronger than her, Dad," one of the boys said and snorted. "Older too."

"Shut up, Gabe. You're only older than us by a few seconds," his brother said.

Gabriel lifted his head and crossed his arms while smiling. "That still means I'm the oldest, Lame-o," he said. Tafel shook her head and resumed eating. Lamach made a face at Gabriel and picked up his own fork.

A plate shattered, causing the family to turn towards the sound. The woman's horns were pulsing with a bright-red light now. "How is Tafel going to get married if she's to spend her days learning about war? Will she find a husband who trained to be a wife?"

"It's fine, Mom," Tafel said, glancing at her father's face. His eyes were slightly narrowed. "I want to go to school." Her dad smiled at her.

"No. It isn't fine. You're going to be a proper young lady, not some warmongering tomboy," her mother said, causing the man to scowl. Tafel pouted at her father.

"Then how about homeschooling for Tafel? She doesn't need to learn any war methods, but she should at least learn how to defend herself," the man said. "We can hire"—the man's eyes narrowed for an instant—"Dustin to teach her magic, and Prim can watch over her. I trust this arrangement should be satisfactory?"

"That's not fair," Gabriel said. "How come she gets to learn from Dustin?"

"Hush, eat your food," his mother said, her horns dimming. She turned towards her husband and pursed her lips. "Fine. We'll have Dustin teach her. His rates will be extremely expensive though." Her face hardened.

The man shrugged and smiled. He placed his hand on his wife's before speaking, "We don't lack money. Hiring a top-tier mage to teach the future demon lord can be counted as money allocated for defense."

Tafel stuck her tongue out at Gabriel before picking up her fork.

***

Sera yawned and opened her eyes, smacking her lips together. "Vur?" she asked as she rolled her shoulders and sat on her haunches. She blinked and glanced around the cave which was illuminated by golden lines running along the walls. A snoring sound caught her attention, and she turned around. Vernon was lying on his back with his arms and feet sticking up into the air. The ground trembled as the golden dragon's mouth opened and inhaled with a rumbling sound. Sera's tail flashed and smacked Vernon's belly.

"Uahg!?" Vernon's eyes shot open as he was interrupted mid-snore. He wiped a strand of saliva away with the back of his paw and raised his head. His gaze followed the sky-blue tail on his belly until he ended up staring at his mate's scowling face. "Sera?"

"Where's Vur?" Sera asked and narrowed her eyes. "It was your turn to watch him."

"Eh?" Vernon asked as he rolled over onto his feet. "He's right ... not here...." He scratched his head and peered underneath himself. He frowned and muttered, "Did I squish him while sleeping again?"

"What the hell do you mean again!?" Sera roared and tackled Vernon, pinning him onto his back. "How many times have you done that?"

"Uh, twenty some…? I mean once! Once! I only did it one time!" Vernon shouted and covered his snout. Sera snorted and climbed off of her mate, her tail swishing and knocking piles of golden ingots over.

A red dragonhead peeked into the cave. "Hey-o, matriarch," Prika said and waved, the sunlight glinting off her red scales. "Did something happen?"

"Vur's missing," Sera said.

Prika blinked. Seconds passed. Prika blinked again as her head tilted. "So?"

"What do you mean so?"

"He always goes missing," Prika said. "Every time you go to sleep and Vernon's supposed to watch over him, Vur runs off with his adopted son."

Sera's eyes flashed as she whirled around to face her mate. She bared her teeth and growled. "Explain."

Vernon's eyes darted to the cave entrance, but Prika was already long gone. The red dragon snickered as she flew away from the cave towards the depths of the valley. Screams and whimpers reached her ears as she stretched her wings. She landed in front of a cave with red boulders by the entrance and smiled as she climbed inside, curling up into a ball. "That's what you get for stealing my dinner," she said and hummed to herself as the distant, strained voice of a pleading dragon reached her ears.

Meanwhile, in a location nearly fifty miles away from the dragons' valley, a naked boy and a baby boar were wandering through the forest—both of them on all fours. A golden rune was flashing on the boar's head, and every animal that saw the light quickly ran away. Some beasts made themselves scarce before the duo even came into view. Eventually, the duo reached a glade with an enormous tree.

"We finally made it!" Vur said and gazed at the tree. Ever since Vur had seen the tree from the top of the dragons' mountain, he wanted to see it in person. It was larger than he thought: The width of the trunk was as long as half a dragon, but the most remarkable part about the tree was its height. He couldn't even see the top while looking up at it from the ground. Golden sparkles in the branches caught his attention.

"Oink!"

"What? You want to eat that?" Vur asked while pointing. Snuffles nodded his head and wiggled his rump. Vur nodded at the golden fruit in the tree above him. "Alright." His eyes glowed with a golden light, and the branches near the top of the tree bent, but the fruit didn't fall. He frowned and furrowed his brow as his eyes narrowed. The golden light increased in intensity, and he reached upwards with his right hand.

The tree groaned as the branches dipped even further. A single horizontal line formed on its trunk.

"Stupid tree!" Vur shouted and stamped his foot. His eyes glowed as bright as the sun, and his hand trembled as sweat dripped from his forehead. The line on the tree trunk widened and splintered. Vur panted and let out a roar while stomping his foot against the ground again. The forest fell silent before a thunder-like noise echoed outwards with the tree as its epicenter. Leaves rustled and the top half of the tree leaned to one side.

"Oops," Vur said as he stared at the falling tree. His eyes stopped glowing as he tilted his head to the side and scratched his butt. The rumbling sound the tree produced while falling through the air was like thousands of waves crashing upon a rocky shore. The ground shook and a massive dust cloud flew into the air as the top of the tree landed on the forest below, shattering hundreds of trees and bushes. Vur and Snuffles braced themselves, digging their limbs into the ground as the shockwave from the impact washed over their bodies.

"Squee!" Snuffles squealed and ran over to the fallen branches, rummaging for the golden fruits with his snout. Vur dusted himself off before trotting over and picking up a fruit. The two indulged in the sweet fruit until their stomachs were

26

bloated and their bodies round. They couldn't count the number of fruit they had eaten even if they tried. Vur had learned from a young age to eat as much as possible because his next meal could be days or weeks later. Sadly, only the fruit on the lowest branches were gold and ripe—the ones near the top were black and solid like rocks.

"That was really good," Vur said as he groaned and curled up to take a nap. Snuffles waddled over and fell onto his side, exhaling as his perfectly round and bloated body wobbled back and forth.

"The Great Tree has fallen! Kill the trespassers!"

A group of seven women with pointed ears emerged from the direction opposite of where the tree fell. "Dragon! How dare you violate the treaty between … uh, dragon?"

"Do you see a dragon?" one of the women asked with her bow raised. She muttered, "Can we even fight a dragon?"

"No, but I can feel its aura," the one who spoke first said. She was wearing an outfit made of brown leather and had a wooden spear marked with golden etchings. She scanned the surroundings before her gaze stopped on the bloated duo. She glared at Vur and raised her spear. "Did you do this?" Her hands were white as she gripped her spear and pointed it at Vur. "Speak!"

Vur shook his head and hugged Snuffles. The woman with the bow said, "Don't be ridiculous, Celia. How can an elf … human? How did such a young human get here?"

"I'm not a filthy human," Vur said, copying Grimmy's language. "I'm a dragon!" He sucked in a deep breath, causing a golden rune to appear on his forehead. The elves stared at him with their brows furrowed and weapons raised. Vur roared. The ground trembled, and the surrounding forest fell silent. The group of elves jumped backwards and almost tripped over each other.

"What the Aeris was that!?" Celia asked. Her knees knocked together. The elves standing behind her weren't in better shape. They stared at the naked little boy who was glaring at them while holding a spherical boar. Celia bit her lower lip. *How can a child look so haughty while naked?*

"Was it his presence we felt earlier?" one of the elves asked in a whisper.

"It's possible. Could a dragon have imprinted him? What dragon would be crazy enough to imprint a human child?"

"I heard the dragon matriarch lost another egg a few years ago. Could it have been her?"

Celia raised her spear, cutting off further discussion between the elves. "Who's your bond-mother?" she asked, eyeing Vur with her brow furrowed.

"Mama," Vur said and nodded.

"Yes, who is your mama?"

"Mama is Mama. Are you stupid?" Vur asked while tilting his head. "Grimmy told me to stay away from stupid people or else I'll become stupid too."

"Grimmy? Grimmoldesser?" one of the elves whispered.

"Grimmy is Grimmy—not Grimmoldepants. You *are* stupid. Let's go Snuffles." Vur shook his head before turning around and walking away.

One of the elves stepped forward to stop him, but Celia blocked her. The elf she blocked raised an eyebrow. Celia waited until Vur's figure disappeared into the forest before saying, "We need to have a talk with the matriarch; let the elders know when we get back. Dragons are beyond our jurisdiction."

Vur lowered his head and petted the bloated Snuffles in his arms as he walked back towards the dragons' valley. "What do you think those things were?" he asked. "They looked like me but uglier and taller." Snuffles burped in reply and closed his eyes. Vur shrugged his shoulders. "I'll ask Mama when I get back."

The journey back to the valley took three days, but the duo encountered no troubles due to the golden mark on Snuffles' forehead. When Vur entered the valley—his body no longer

28

rotund—a silver dragonhead peered out of a cave and towards the entrance. Leila smiled and waved at him before opening her mouth to shout, "Vur's back!"

The ground rumbled as a sky-blue dragon holding a golden object flew towards the sky from the furthest mountain in the distance. Vur squinted his eyes. Sera approached him with Vernon in her claws. A red blur appeared from the west, and a black dragonhead appeared by Leila's side. The five dragons gathered around Vur, staring at him with their reptilian eyes. Vur took a step back and blinked while pouting. "Mama found out?"

"I told you she'd catch you sneaking out one day," Grimmy said, cupping his paw over his mouth while pretending to whisper. "This is why you should always leave an illusion behind. Want me to kidnap a fairy for you? They're good at trickery."

Leila tugged Grimmy's wing. "Stop corrupting the youth," she said. Sera glared at Grimmy, causing him to chuckle and wave his paw dismissively.

"Vur," Sera said and sat on her haunches, releasing Vernon. "Did you knock down the elves' Sacred Tree of Knowledge?"

Vur shook his head and hugged Snuffles. "Just a tree, no knowledge."

"…"

Sera cleared her throat. "Were there golden fruits?"

Vur nodded. "They were very delicious," he said. "Umm, not as juicy as bear meat though. They also gave me a bellyache."

"Did you eat them all…?"

"No, Snuffles ate half."

Snuffles raised his head and glanced around before going back to sleep. Sera sighed.

"What's wrong, Sera?" Grimmy asked while laughing. "The elves can just plant another one."

"That tree takes over 500 years to grow and one year to bear a single fruit. As the matriarch of this land, I can't just ignore their complaints. The elves want to take Vur and properly educate him," Sera said.

"No! I don't want to. I'll turn stupid," Vur said and shook his head back and forth. "You won't make me go, right, Uncle Grimmy?"

Sera glared at Grimmy. "It's your fault too for teaching Vur such nonsense."

Grimmy snorted. "You're the one who insisted Vur was a dragon. I just taught him our principles."

Vur pouted. "I am a dragon. Papa said I'll grow wings and scales when I grow up. Papa wouldn't lie to me because Mama said dragons don't lie."

All the dragons stared at Vernon who let out a soft cough. "Ah, Vur … didn't you lie about not knocking down the tree to the elves? That means you can't grow wings and scales anymore." Vernon smiled at the dragons who were looking at him and received a smack to his snout from Sera.

"What? I fixed it," Vernon said while rubbing his nose.

"I feel bad now; when are we going to tell him?" Leila mumbled to Grimmy.

"Tell me what?" Vur asked.

"You're adopted!" Prika said. All the dragons glared at the red dragon who clamped her claws over her mouth.

"What's adopted?" Vur asked and tilted his head.

"It means we love you no matter what," Sera said while still glaring at Prika.

"Oh, I'm adopted!" Vur said with a smile. "You're adopted too, Mama." Sera's head started to throb.

"Don't let Grandpa hear you say that or he'll get jealous," Vernon said.

"Grandpa's asleep though. How can he sleep for so long? I still haven't talked to him yet," Vur said.

"He used up a lot of energy a long time ago, and he still has to rest," Sera said.

Vur nodded and yawned. He walked over to Leila and curled up next to her elbow before falling asleep.

"Are we sending Vur to the elves?" Leila asked while watching the boy's tummy fall up and down.

"I think we should. It would be the best for him if he ever wants to leave this range," Vernon said. "He's only five, but he toppled a thousand-year-old tree with gravity magic. None of us are good at moderation; the elves should teach him."

Prika wrinkled her snout. "You just don't want to take care of him," she said. "I vote he stays. Unlike y'all, I don't have a mate. My life would be super boring without Vur."

Grimmy snorted. "You say that, but you do nothing to take care of him either. How many meals have you prepared for him?" he asked. Prika pouted. "Exactly. That boy eats so much food it's ridiculous. Sometimes you get tired of hunting, y'know? Let someone else take care of him for a while. I bet they'll send him back within a week."

Sera turned towards the silver dragon who was watching Vur sleep. "Leila?"

Leila frowned. "I'm awfully fond of him now that he doesn't cry at night, but for his future, I think it'd be best if he learned at least basic mana manipulation from the elves."

Sera sighed. "Very well then. That makes three votes to one. Tomorrow, he'll go learn with the elves," she said and smiled at Vur. Her face hardened. "But if something were to happen to him…"

Grimmy chuckled and licked his lips. "I was never on good terms with the elves anyway," he said as his eyes narrowed. "What's one or two missing villages?"

"Did you vote to send him just to create an excuse…?" Leila asked. Her snout wrinkled.

Grimmy chuckled. "Dear, there's some questions that shouldn't be asked because there are no good answers." He nudged Leila's cheek, causing her to sigh.

***

"Why do we have to learn history? Just give me a mace and I'll bash those humans' heads in," Gabriel said to Lamach. The two were sitting next to each other in a classroom with ten other demon children. At the head of the classroom, a three-horned demon was in front of a blackboard, reading aloud from a book. "I bet Tafel doesn't have to learn this."

"Gabriel! You may be a prince, but my word is law in this room. Do you understand me?" the teacher asked and glared at the two princes.

Gabriel looked down at his desk and mumbled, "Yes, ma'am."

"And you Lamach. I expected better from you. Do you two want to know why history is so important? How did the humans establish a foothold in our territory one hundred years ago? How did we take Flusia back from the humans? Who was the commanding general? Do you know?" the teacher asked and slammed the book down against a table. The children remained silent as their mentor's gaze passed over them. She exhaled and picked up the book, opening it back to the previous page. "Thousands of people have made mistakes so you don't have to. Knowledge is power. Never forget that."

Gabriel's cheeks burned. "I understand."

The teacher nodded. "Eight hundred years ago, demons and humans arrived on the north end of this continent we call Zuer. At first they worked together to clear the elves and their beasts to establish footholds suitable for growth, but then the demons found a mana source to the west in our now capital, Niffle, which greatly improved our capabilities as mages. The humans' greed overwhelmed them, and they declared war on us to take it. We forced them back to the east and were about to wipe them all out, but the elves couldn't let that chance go and tried to

32

eliminate us along with the humans. In the end, we were forced to retreat to the capital and the humans survived. The majority of both the demon and human forces were expended to stop the dragon patriarch at the time, forcing the elves to retreat."

"But how did the humans survive the attack if they were so weak?" Lamach asked.

"They had the pope who commanded the power of their god. Even if he couldn't use offensive magic, his barrier was strong enough to keep the demons out of their final city as the elves and beasts waged war against us," the teacher said.

"So they're cowards hiding in their shells," a voice called out.

"Sometimes, retreat is necessary. They're still alive after all," the teacher said. "I hope you future leaders never forget that. Do you see why history is so important now? We can learn from our mistakes, so next time, we won't lose."

***

Tafel sighed and took in a deep breath. *Using magic is so difficult.* She cupped her hands and an orange flame flickered into existence above her palms for two seconds before fading away.

"That's not bad."

Tafel raised her head. A six-horned demon, Dustin, stood over her. The horns were red and they grew out of his temples, three for each. A golden medallion hung from his neck over his black robe. Tafel pouted and said, "It's so weak though. I heard you could defeat a whole army with one spell."

Dustin laughed. "You can't believe everything you hear, you know? And don't forget, you're only five. You should feel proud. I bet there isn't anyone your age who can match you in magic: demon, human, or elf," he said and smiled. "But if you really want to be the best, you could ask your father to obtain a beast to imprint you to increase your mana and skill pool. Or you can eat a fruit of knowledge, although that may require hiring S-ranked adventurers."

Tafel's eyes lit up when she heard the word adventurer. "Can you tell me stories about your adventures?"

Dustin chuckled and patted Tafel's head. "Of course. This old SSS-ranked adventurer has many stories to tell," he said while grinning. "Speaking of fruits of knowledge, there was actually one time where my team accepted a request to bring one back. It's the request that ranked me up from S to SS. We traveled for many days through the wilderness—that's what adventurers call the beasts' mountain range—fighting off many creatures that you've probably read about in your stories: giant boars, bears, wyverns, phoenixes, cows. In the wilderness, everything will try to kill you if they think you're weak—that's why we go as a group. It's actually pretty easy to detect any danger because the things that can kill you have a unique aura which can be sensed from a mile away if you have a mage."

"Like what?" Tafel asked with her eyes wide open.

"Like dragons, demonic bats, behemoth bears, basilisks. There were a few snakes that gave off the aura too. It's an unsettling feeling—like someone is staring at you while you eat your food. You can't see them, but you know they're watching and judging you, ugh," Dustin said and rubbed his arms. "I felt a dragon's aura once." His face turned pale. "I seriously considered quitting my career as an adventurer right then and there.

"Anyways, to get a fruit of knowledge, we had to bypass the elves' village, which was actually pretty easy, but there was a patrol guarding the tree. Rumors in the adventurers' guild say the patrol is made of seven beautiful elves, each with the strength of an S-ranked adventurer with their leader at SSS-rank. We hid for days until the patrol went away. The tree itself was especially tough. It took ten of my windblades to knock one of the fruits down, and the branch wasn't even damaged."

"Is that even possible? You're not lying to me right?"

"Everything I say is true. There are some really amazing things that nature can accomplish, Tafel. When we use magic, we only borrow a tiny portion of nature's power," Dustin said. "People say dragons are the favored children of nature. The power they have is unfathomable to us, which is why there are so few of them. Never anger a dragon, Tafel. Now get back to casting fireballs; you want to be stronger than your brothers, right?"

4

"I want to cry," Celia said as she buried her face into her hands. Her golden-etched spear lay propped up against the wall behind her. Her blonde hair flowed around her arms like a curtain. "He's a devil. An absolute devil."

"Whatever do you mean?" her grandmother asked. She had silver hair and green eyes with crow's feet around the edges. The two were sitting in a circular room with a wooden table between them. "I doubt he can be as bad as you when you were growing up." Her grandmother chuckled and took a sip from her wooden cup.

"Did I destroy the Tree of Knowledge? Did I pin people down and force them to eat food? Did I ever make you *feel* like food!? Did I ever breathe fire!?" Celia sobbed. "He doesn't listen and does whatever he wants. He almost killed Mary for trying to put clothes on him, and he caused an earthquake when we tried to feed him vegetables. The children are too afraid to leave their houses because their bones break when he plays with them, and the animals defecate themselves when they see him to make themselves unappealing. We need your help, Grandma.

"You can't just request for the matriarch to send him over and not help us take care of him. That's just cruel. Do you know what Grimmoldesser said when he left that devil here? 'Have fun and try not to die.' Have fun and try not to die! Yvainne, Claudia, and Julie nearly had their faces ripped off when that boy woke up! He's only been here for two days, but it's like the village went through a succession of natural disasters. We're at the weakest we've ever been in years."

Her grandmother sighed and nodded. *So that's what caused the earthquake*, she thought. "Where is he now?" she asked and placed her cup down.

"After incinerating the vegetables, he said he was going to hunt some bears for proper food. I saw him eat once. He eats his meat raw and slurps on it," Celia said as she shivered. She grabbed her grandmother's hands. "Can't you send him back, Grandma? Please? Pretty please? I can't even punish him or the dragons will be mad at me."

Her grandmother laughed. "Imagine what all those adventurers you scared away would think if they saw you like this," she said with a wry smile.

"I'd rather fight a hundred adventurers with a toothpick than try to tame that devil," Celia said with tears in her eyes. "At least adventurers bleed. I—"

A high-pitched noise interrupted Celia's speech, causing her to wince and place her hands over her ears. She jumped up and wiped her tears with the back of her hand as the alarm continued to emit ear-piercing whistles. "That's the behemoth alarm. How did it get so close without us noticing its aura?" she asked as she snatched her spear off the wall.

Her grandmother stood up and grabbed a wooden staff which was lying next to her leg. "Let's find out," she said. The two exited the hollow tree trunk they were staying in and headed towards a cluster of elves in the distance. A few elves traveled alongside them.

"You shouldn't be here," Celia said to an elf with white-hair and frowned.

"Four of our guardians are recovering from their injuries," the white-haired elf said. "What if you aren't enough?"

"That's—," Celia started to say, but the alarm stopped. "Huh?"

"False alarm?" the old elf asked. He looked relieved. Celia turned to face her grandmother and nodded. The group hurried towards the entrance of the village. When they arrived at the entryway, they saw a towering bear in the distance inching towards the gate. The bear's head was as wide as four people, and if it stood on its hind legs, it would've been as tall as a fully grown tree. Its body had brown fur with black stripes circling it, forming strange patterns on its coat.

"Is he carrying that?" an elf whispered.

"Oh my Aeris, he is," another responded.

"Is that Vur?" Celia asked. She was behind the crowd and couldn't see the lower half of the bear.

"Yes. It is," the sentry at the gate said. The surrounding crowd gazed at Celia with looks of undisguised pity. *You don't have to look at me like that*, Celia thought but didn't say anything as she pursed her lips. She sighed and walked out the gate with her grandmother while the crowd parted to let them through.

Celia walked up to the bear and put her hands on her hips. "Vur, you can't bring that into the village," she said. "We don't kill for food here."

The bear stopped moving. A few seconds later, Vur crawled out from underneath the corpse. Grimmy had taught him how to hunt after the mishap with Snuffles. "Why not?" Vur asked and made a face. "It tastes much better than plants. You should try some."

"We bond with these animals. They give us strength through imprints, and we keep the humans out of the forest," Celia's grandmother replied. She pointed at the bear. "This is one less bear that can help our tribe now that you killed it."

"I didn't kill it," Vur said. "Snuffles did."

Snuffles oinked and wiggled his bloody rump.

Celia's grandmother frowned. "That doesn't matter. The point is, these beasts are to be respected."

"But Grimmy says these bears are just walking sacks of meat waiting to be plucked," Vur said. "And dragons don't lie."

"You're not a dragon," the elder said. "You're a human. Grimmoldesser's words don't apply to you."

38

"You've done it now, Grandma," Celia said as she covered her ears. The elves behind her copied her actions. An earth-shaking roar resounded through the forest, causing hundreds of birds to scatter into the air.

"I'm a dragon!" Vur yelled and stomped his foot. "Why does everyone keep calling me a filthy human?" His eyes glowed golden, and the ground buckled as an invisible force descended. A few elves fell to their knees while the stronger ones grunted and gritted their teeth, standing on shaky legs. Celia propped herself up with her spear while her grandmother barely stayed on her feet, using her staff for support.

"Silence."

With a single word, the pressure disappeared. A green figure walked out of the woods. It had the shape of a woman, but her body was covered with vines and leaves. Her hair was made of fine strands of wooden branches that flowed to the ground. Vur's eyes stopped glowing, and he glared at her while opening his mouth. No sounds came out. He dashed at her but fell over when she waved her arm and said, "Bind."

"Sleep," she said, and Vur's eyelids drooped before a snore escaped from his sleeping body.

"Many thanks, High Dryad Juliana," Celia's grandmother said as she cupped her hands together. A layer of sweat caused her forehead to shine in the sun.

The dryad shook her head, causing leaves to fall to the ground. "He's been keeping me up for days with his roaring. What is he?" she asked. She walked up to the sleeping boy, leaving behind a trail of growing pink flowers as she walked.

"He's a hu—"

"Dragon," Vur said in his sleep.

"It's best if you come inside so we can explain the situation," Celia said and sighed.

"What should we do about the behemoth?" the sentry asked.

Snuffles looked at Vur who was being carried into the village by the dryad and then looked at the bear. His eyes glowed, and a dome of ice encased the bear. He had seen Sera freeze the leftover bears multiple times and could use her magic since he had her lineage. Snuffles snorted then followed after Vur, ignoring the shocked looks of the elves.

***

"Do you think the elves are treating him well?" Sera asked Vernon and rolled over onto her belly. She stretched her wings out over the boulder she and Vernon were lying on top of. "He's so fragile. What if he gets hurt?"

"You worry too much. Vur's strong, and the elves wouldn't dare mistreat him," Vernon said with a yawn. He stroked Sera's wing and smiled.

"If anything, he'd be mistreating the elves," Grimmy said with a laugh. "I taught him a little something on the way there." He snorted. "Let's see them try to educate my nephew."

Leila blinked at him. "What did you teach him?"

"Oh, nothing. Just the principles of a dragon," Grimmy said with a grin. "Pride, arrogance, greed, gluttony, stubbornness, wrath, envy. You know, the usual."

Leila smacked his snout. "That's terrible," she said and giggled, "but that's why I love you."

Grimmy chuckled and kissed her neck.

Prika grumbled from her rocky ledge overlooking the four dragons sunbathing in the valley. She puffed her cheeks out. "I'm not jealous of them or anything. Totally not." Her tail slammed against the side of the cliff, causing a landslide on the other side of the mountain. She sighed. "I need to find a mate."

***

Vur's eyes opened. He was lying on the ground with a boulder on top of his stomach. He pushed on it with his hands, but contrary to his expectations, it didn't budge. Black bands of runes were encircling his wrists, forearms, and biceps. Similar bands of runes were wrapped around his neck, ankles, and torso.

"Oh, you're awake," a voice said. Vur turned his head to the side and narrowed his eyes. Juliana was sitting on a chair with a book in her hands. Her brown legs branched off into four strands like the roots of a flower.

"You're the bully!" Vur said and squirmed underneath the boulder. It didn't budge. He heard a snort. Snuffles was in a similar situation.

"I'm your new teacher," Juliana said. "The elves really don't like you, you know? I'm surprised they haven't killed you yet, especially since you're a human." Vur growled and tried to roar. A mewl came out of his mouth instead. "I placed a silencing curse on you. In the end, you're just a blue mage." She shut her book and stood up. She strolled over to Vur's side— black flowers sprouted out of the ground around her as she walked. She knelt by his side and stroked the golden rune on his forehead with her finger. Vur tried to bite her. "I really wonder why the matriarch imprinted you. You might've adopted her lineage, but that doesn't matter if your magic resistance is the same as a human's." She pinched his cheek and smiled while fending off his hand.

"Are you going to put some clothes on?" Juliana asked. "My student can't wander around naked, you know? That would reflect quite poorly on me."

"No," Vur said and glared at Juliana. She beamed at him.

"I'll remove the boulder if you put some clothes on," Juliana said and straightened the gnarls in Vur's hair.

"No," Vur said and wrinkled his nose. "Dragons don't wear clothes."

"Mm." Juliana hummed. She opened her mouth and asked, "Are you hungry? If you don't put some clothes on, I won't feed you."

"I won't," Vur said. If he could cross his arms over his chest, he would. "I'm a dragon."

Juliana chuckled as her green face darkened and turned purple. "You believe I won't kill you? The elves are completely fed up with you. If you don't listen to me…" Juliana's finger caressed the side of Vur's cheek.

"Then kill me. My parents will avenge me; it's a dragon's duty," Vur said and snapped his teeth at Juliana's finger. This time he managed to bite her.

"Who is teaching you this nonsense?" Juliana asked as she retrieved her hand. Her finger was gone, torn off at her knuckle. A green sap dripped onto Vur's face—it smelled like honey. Moments later, a flower bud appeared at the severed appendage, blooming into another finger.

"It's not nonsense. Dragons don't lie," Vur said and spat out Juliana's finger. It tasted like spinach.

Juliana stood up and made her way to the door. "Well, you're going to be stuck like that until you decide to put on clothes. Let's see how much of a dragon you really are," she said as she shut the door behind her.

Vur snorted and closed his eyes.

"How is he?" Celia asked. She had been sitting outside waiting for results.

"He's stubborn," Juliana said and nodded. "I wonder if positive reinforcement would've worked better." She shrugged. "I'll be back in a week. Make sure not to feed him anything unless he agrees to wear clothes."

"Is that really okay?" Celia asked and furrowed her brow. "He won't starve or dehydrate?"

"He's surprisingly resilient for a fleshly being," Juliana said and rubbed her new finger which was a different color from the others. "He should be fine. I'll take responsibility if he isn't. You can also teach him the basics of spellcasting while he's immobilized. That's what the dragons requested of your people, right?"

Celia nodded and lowered her head. "I guess I can convince the elders to hold the village lessons in this room," she said and rubbed her chin. "What do you think?" She raised her head and looked around. Juliana was gone.

***

A week had passed since Juliana left. The elves had held their public lessons in the room Vur was trapped in, but he didn't listen at all. The first day, he randomly yelled every time the elders tried to speak. When they talked over him anyway, he lay there mutely with his eyes closed. The days passed by, but Vur hadn't moved an inch or made any noise after the first day. Snuffles occasionally mewled, and a few elven children fed him snacks and water.

When the last lesson of the day ended, Juliana and Celia walked into the room. Although there was no more Tree of Knowledge to guard, Celia was busy helping clear out the destruction caused by the tree's collapse. There were dangerous beasts that didn't cooperate with the elves, and Celia had to defend the cleaners from them. The elf's lips pursed when she saw Vur lying on the ground, completely unresponsive. She hadn't checked up on him the whole time.

"Is he dead?" Celia asked, furrowing her brow.

Juliana snorted. She walked over and placed her hand on the crown of his head. "There's no flow of mana or blood in his body," she said. "That's odd. He should've been able to survive for a week without food with that body of his. Did I miscalculate?"

"You killed him? You killed the son of a dragon?! O Aeris, please have mercy on our poor souls," Celia said as she fell to her knees and prayed. Her heart pounded as her stomach lurched. A lump formed in her throat, and she swallowed nothing.

"Why is it my fault?" Juliana asked and rolled her eyes. "Your elders stayed with him the whole time. They should've informed me if he died." She flicked Celia's forehead. "Quit crying. I can fix this. Most likely. Probably. I hope." She rolled the boulder off of Vur's body and flipped him over. "He doesn't look emaciated at all—that's good. It should work better if his body is preserved." Juliana nodded. "I should remove these seals too."

"Are you going to resurrect him? What if he becomes a zombie?" Celia asked, staring wide-eyed at Juliana.

"If I was informed at his time of death, there would be no chance of him being a zombie," Juliana said and glared at Celia. "If he becomes a zombie, you'll just have to bind him, send him back to the matriarch, and pray for the best." Celia gulped as Juliana waved her hand and said, "Dispel."

The black runes decorating Vur's body disappeared, evaporating into black wisps of smoke.

"I'm going to start now," Juliana said. She placed both hands on Vur's chest and willed mana to them.

Celia waited with her back to the door as Juliana's hands glowed green. The intensity of the glow increased until the whole room was filled with a green hue. When Celia was about to shield her eyes from the light, it flashed and dispersed. She bit her lower lip and asked, "Did it work?"

Juliana gasped for breath and shook her head. "His soul must've dissipated already or something is preventing it from coming back."

Celia's heart sunk. "Now what?"

"There's one more thing I can try," Juliana said and narrowed her eyes. "Reanimate dead. He's definitely coming back as a zombie though."

Celia bit her lip and nodded. "We'll have to flee with the whole village after we reanimate him," she said. "We'll be gone by the time the dragons notice the decay. The Tree of Knowledge that our village grew around is already gone. Do it."

Juliana once again placed her hands on Vur's chest. This time, her hands glowed black instead of green, and a jagged pattern like the roots of a plant spread out on Vur's body. After the roots fully cocooned his body, a bright light flashed, dispelling the roots. Juliana coughed up bloodlike sap and covered her mouth with her hand. "It failed."

"That's … what do we do?" Celia asked with a pale face. Her chest compressed, and her breaths shortened.

44

"Let's consult with your grandmother," Juliana replied. The two left the room and closed the door behind themselves. Juliana waved her hand and said, "Seal."

A green circle with a rune inscribed in the center appeared on the closed door. Moments after the green light finished forming, Vur's eyes flashed open. *Fools. I knew they were stupid,* Vur thought. He canceled the play-dead spell he learned from a seven-foot-long mongoose and stood up to stretch. He kicked the black boulder off of Snuffles and smiled as he waved his arm and said, "Dispel." How angry would Juliana be if she knew he learned her spells?

The black runes on Snuffles' body disappeared, and the boar rolled over onto his legs. He shook out his limbs and wrinkled his nose before letting out a few low oinks. Snuffles yawned and mewled at Vur while standing on his hind-legs, indicating for Vur to carry him.

Vur laughed before picking Snuffles up. He pointed at the door and said, "Dispel." The green seal disappeared, and he opened it. A log slammed into him, launching him through the air until his back hit the wall behind him.

"Silence. Bind. Curse: weaken. Curse: fatigue. Curse: silence. Curse: immobility," Juliana said as she walked back into the room with a smile. Black runes spread along Vur's and Snuffles' bodies. "You're a thousand years too young to fool me, little one."

"Mommy, did Miss Celia just throw a log at that little boy?" a girl whispered.

"Hush, honey. Let's go," her mother replied as she dragged her child away.

"You little brat! I'll kill you!" Celia said as she stomped back into the room. "Do you know how worried I was?!" She picked Vur up by the back of his neck and placed him across her lap. She raised her arm and spanked him until his butt was swollen and red. "You're not even going to apologize?" Celia snorted as she continued to spank him. After a few dozen spanks, Juliana stopped her.

"Um, Celia? I silenced him. He can't apologize," Juliana said while scratching her cheek.

Celia froze and looked down at Vur. He stared at her with wide eyes and tears streaming down his cheeks. Celia's heart dropped as her anger was extinguished, and she rubbed his head. "I'm so sorry; don't cry," she said in a high-pitched voice. She hugged the crying boy to her chest and rubbed her hand on his back. "Do you want to eat meat? Let's go to that bear, okay?"

Vur nodded his head and sniffled as Celia picked him up.

Vur used puppy eyes on Celia—it was super effective, Juliana thought as she watched Celia comfort the child. "Stop," Juliana said to the duo who were about to leave. "You'll put some clothes on, right?" Vur made a face, but he still couldn't speak. "You don't want anyone to see handprints on your butt, right? Dragons don't get spanked. You can hide that if you wear this." Juliana smiled as she held up her hands. A robe made of green leaves cascaded out of her fingers.

Vur hesitated before he reached out and grabbed the robe. He looked at it and then looked at Celia. "You need help putting it on?" Celia asked as she took it from him and placed him on the ground. Vur nodded.

Juliana smiled as Celia dressed Vur. *Step one accomplished.*

***

Mary frowned. "Aren't you being too harsh on Vur?" she asked Celia.

Celia turned her head towards her patrol companion. The patrol, the elders, and Juliana were gathered in a hollowed-out tree trunk. The injuries the patrol had suffered from Vur had recovered long ago thanks to the elves' recovery spells. "I don't think so," Celia replied while shaking her head. Her chest still burned every time she recalled Vur's play-dead spell.

"He could've died," Mary said. "How is that not being too harsh?"

"He wouldn't have—not from that," Juliana said before Celia could reply. "I was keeping watch over him the whole time." She snorted. "He thought he could trick us with a simple spell. Play-dead lets him cease all metabolic movement. Essentially, it was a week-long time-out for him."

"But the curses—"

"Are there to keep his strength in check. If you haven't noticed he can carry a behemoth bear for who knows how many miles without getting tired," Juliana interrupted. "His diet's been the blood and meat of behemoth bears ever since he was born. Not only that, but he has the imprint of a dragon which practically makes him a dragon in a human shell."

"The spanking?" Mary asked, her brow furrowing.

Juliana coughed. "That was Celia's doing."

Celia looked down as her stomach churned. Vur had been healed, but he still avoided her like a scared animal. "W-well," she said and bit her lower lip, "I think it was a good thing. I was just showing him there are consequences to his actions."

"Couldn't there have been a better way to show him?" Mary asked. "Maybe sit down and explain. I still think—"

"Have you forgotten how he tried to rip your head off when you put a sock on him? We're not trying to be his friends, Mary," an elder said. "If it weren't for the matriarch, we would have executed him. A human living in the village of elves is unheard of, much less the human who destroyed our sacred tree. We're here to teach him how to control his magic—a favor for the matriarch. Nothing more, nothing less."

Another elder snorted. "I don't even understand why the matriarch would imprint a human. Humans forced her father to the brink of death and killed our clan leader"—he turned towards Celia—"your father. There's no need to feel bad for beating him. In fact, you should've done more. The dragons

47

have never imprinted an elf before, but the matriarch decides to imprint a human? That is just unforgivable."

Celia bit her lip. "Wasn't it the demons who did that?"

"They're the same," the elder replied with a wave of his hand. "The demons only started sprouting horns after the fairy incident."

"But—"

A sentry burst into the room. "Vur escaped!"

The patrol looked at each other and stood up.

"How? Wasn't he cursed?" an elder asked as he narrowed his eyes at Juliana.

Juliana stroked her chin. "It's possible to escape a curse if it's dispelled, but I cursed him with silence too. Did someone dispel him? Could he have learned mana manipulation? Now that I think about it, he did cast play-dead under silence." Her brow furrowed. "I seem to have seriously overlooked something."

"Didn't you say you were watching over him?" Mary asked with narrowed eyes.

"I was for the punishment, but I thought a guard would be enough this time since he was harmless," Juliana said while looking at the sentry.

The sentry rubbed his head and avoided the dryad's gaze. "One moment I was standing by the door, and the next moment I collapsed. I couldn't speak or move, and he just left."

"Aren't you glad you gave him more spells to play with?" Mary asked as she smiled at Juliana. The dryad's gaze darkened.

***

Tafel furrowed her brow as she stared at a boulder in the distance. She was standing in a courtyard with massive walls, purple patterns decorating their sides. Her tongue darted across her lips as she narrowed her eyes and focused her mana into her hands which were held up in front of her chest. "Firebolt!" she shouted as she mimed a pushing motion. An orange ball of fire

48

flew out of her hands and hit the boulder. Tafel sighed as she lowered her hands and inhaled deeply through her nose. She turned around and tilted her head, asking, "How did I do?" with her eyes.

"Well done," Dustin said as he nodded. "Want to learn something new? It might be difficult though if you don't have talent." He smiled. "But you clearly have that."

Tafel squinted at her mentor. "What is it?"

"Silent casting," Dustin said with a smile. "Another term is mana manipulation." He raised his hand and made a flicking motion. A fireball, similar to the one Tafel had conjured, formed in the air and hit the same boulder.

"How did you do that?" Tafel asked with wide eyes. She turned her head towards Dustin's hands before turning her head back to the boulder.

"When you cast a firebolt, the mana moves around your body in a special way unique to that spell," Dustin said. "I just copied the mana flow for firebolt. It's very useful for sneak attacks or when you're vocally silenced."

"Vocally silenced? Does that mean there's another type of silence?"

"Very astute. There's such thing as mana-flow silence. It's an interrupt that disrupts your mana making you unable to cast for a few seconds," Dustin said. "It's not something you can do. I've only seen dryads and fairies capable of casting it. You need a warrior and white mage combination to take care of dryads. Magic doesn't work too well on them."

Tafel nodded and closed her eyes as she raised her hands in front of her chest. She inhaled and felt her mana flow and build up in her hands. She opened her eyes and made a pushing motion, but nothing happened. Her hands tingled as the mana dissipated from her palms. "It didn't work," she said while pouting at Dustin.

Dustin laughed. "It takes practice and you have to be familiar with the spell. It takes me months to cast a new spell silently. You might be faster than me since your control over mana is better than mine," he said with a smile. "Keep practicing hard and you'll be strong enough to ignore your parents and become an adventurer. But don't tell them I said that."

***

"Daaad," Rudolph said. "I don't want Johann anymore. All he does is eat, poop, and sleep. And I don't think he likes me very much."

"You asked for him, and you said you would take care of him if I got him for you," the king said. "That was part of our conditions."

"But, Dad, the stories never say anything about how much they poop. I have to use a shovel to get it out of the backyard," Rudolph said. "And I have no allowance from all the meat I have to buy to feed him."

"Raising a pet builds character," the king said and shrugged as he cut a steak. "You'll thank me when you're older."

"Your dad is right, honey," the queen said. "I heard that Michelle, the pope's daughter"—she winked at Rudolph—"likes men with character and dragons."

Rudolph's face burned, and he lowered his gaze, staring at his plate. "Alright, I'll raise Johann. Then can I at least explore a dungeon with him?"

"No. Absolutely not. You're too young," his mother said. The playfulness on her face was gone, replaced by pursed lips and narrowed eyes.

Rudolph made a face. "But demons get to become adventurers when they're my age, sometimes even younger," he said. "Besides, I can make lots of money to feed Johann if we go."

"You're not a demon," his mother said. She turned towards her husband. "Talk some sense into him, Randel."

"Hmm, I don't see why not," the king replied.

"Randel!"

50

"What? He has Johann. We can send some royal guards to escort him too. Experience is a very good thing to have," the king said. "It'll be perfectly safe."

"Yeah, Mom. Johann's been getting fat recently. I think he needs some exercise too," Rudolph said, sending a glance and a smile at his dad.

His mother sighed. "An easy dungeon, okay?"

"Yes!"

5

"C'mon, Snuffles, let's go find someplace to sleep," Vur said. He was naked and dragging a behemoth bear's corpse with him. Faint, red handprints could be seen on his butt. Behind him, Snuffles was yawning while wobbling as he walked.

"We haven't really explored these parts of the mountains, have we?" Vur asked. Snuffles looked around before shaking his head and letting out an oink. Vur laughed and headed towards the base of a cliff in the distance. He pointed. "Let's dig out a shelter over there." When they arrived at the base and were about to start digging, they found a cave with an entrance lit up by green ores embedded in the walls.

"Doesn't this kinda look like home?" Vur asked as he tilted his head. Snuffles oinked and headed inside after sniffing the entrance. Vur shrugged and followed after the boar, squeezing the corpse through the entrance.

***

A young-looking boy wearing armor too big for his frame sat on top of a sky-blue dragon. Beside the dragon, there was a carriage which was pulled by two horses. Inside the carriage, there were a total of four people, including the driver. The boy sitting atop the dragon furrowed his brow and turned his head to the side.

"Aren't we going the wrong way?" Rudolph asked his entourage. Beneath him, the dragon inhaled and let out an audible sigh, causing the horses to jump. The young prince rolled his eyes and said, "The wilderness is to the south."

"Her Highness has asked us to escort you through an easy dungeon. The forest of bats in the northeast has a dungeon suitable for a beginner," the driver of the carriage said. He patted the rumps of the horses and whispered to them. A pair of runes on his arms lit up as the horses calmed down. The carriage driver was a beast tamer while his passengers consisted of two warriors and a white mage. That was simply the best conformation to carry a novice like Rudolph through a dungeon.

"But I was expecting adventure and excitement: magical beasts and demon adventurers competing against us," Rudolph said and frowned.

One of the warriors sighed. "We don't have a proper team composition and you want to go to the most dangerous region in the continent. All the dungeons there are purple and higher. The one we're going to is barely yellow. It's the perfect place for a greenhorn," he said. "As long as you're in my party, you have to follow my rules. Understood?" The warrior's gaze darkened. He was the leader of one of the most elite troops in the kingdom, yet he was relegated to babysitting duty.

Rudolph bit his lower lip and nodded. "Yes, sir," he said. His father told him to follow orders closely and not be disrespectful. A rancid smell wafted up to his nose, and he almost puked. "Wait, wait. I have to clear Johann's poop bag; I can't stand the smell."

The warrior snorted. "If we stopped every time your dragon took a dump we'd never make it to Shaldor before nightfall. Keep going. That smell is pleasant compared to carnage on a battlefield."

***

Tafel put down the book in her hands and raised her head. Dustin was sitting across from her on a couch, reading a thick book. She couldn't understand the letters written on its cover and promised herself she'd learn one day. Her gaze went back to her book, but her soul was weary. A sigh escaped from her childish lips, and she asked, "Dustin, how many dungeons have you cleared?"

"Twenty-seven and an eighth," Dustin replied without raising his head. He turned a page. "You should read that book—it's important."

Tafel frowned but resumed reading. After a few minutes passed, her legs fidgeted. She raised her head again and asked, "How do you clear an eighth of a dungeon?"

Dustin sighed and put down his book. "It was a white-ranked dungeon," he began. "I was with four other SSS-ranked adventurers. We thought it would be a breeze: the entrance to the valley was wide, and white ores lined the tops of the mountains. Lots of space makes kiting easier, but we were swarmed by summons: earth golems, water elementals, fire elementals, wind and ice spirits. It was terrible. We fought non-stop for two weeks before we reached a clearing. One of our companions, Doofus, died when he swallowed a water elemental hiding in his flask. He was our tank." Dustin paused as he stared at the pages of his book. A smile crept onto his lips before he continued. "At the clearing, a fairy was eating an apple and saw us. She came over and told us we did a good job and that there were only seven waves remaining before we got to see the dragons, but if we gave up and left, she would resurrect Doofus. When we heard that, we accepted the deal and retreated."

"Where's Doofus now? Are white-ranked dungeons really that hard?" Tafel asked with wide eyes.

"Doofus gave up on adventuring after that and became a teacher at the academy. Who knows, he might be teaching your brothers right now," Dustin said with a smile. "As for white-ranked dungeons; ah, if you see one, take a mental image and leave. It's not worth the risk."

"Why are dungeons ranked by color and not just levels?"

"Well, levels would be easier for people who've never been to a dungeon, but dungeon entranceways usually light up with a certain color depending on the strength of the mana source inside. So while a yellow dungeon is the equivalent of level one, it's easier to say 'that cave is glowing yellow; it's a yellow dungeon.' Right?"

Tafel nodded. "I guess that makes sense."

"Mm. Now you really should read that book. History is important even if it doesn't bring about tangible results."

Tafel sighed and buried her head into the pages.

***

A colony of bats hung upside-down, their toes clinging onto the ceiling of a cave. Beneath them, there was a stairwell leading up. Occasionally, a bat would fly to the top of the stairs and quickly fly back down. After one of the bats returned, it blinked at its companions.

"Is it sleeping?"

"I think it is."

"What the hell?"

"Is it not afraid?"

"Go … go poke it."

"Why don't you poke it? It smells like a dragon. I ain't touching that."

The space behind the bats distorted, and a pale woman wearing a red cloak appeared in midair. "What's the issue?" she asked with an expressionless face. Her gaze traveled towards the stairwell, and her eyes narrowed.

"Master! There's a thing sleeping in the mini-boss room," one of the bats chirped.

"There's two things!" another one said.

"Is it a dragon? It feels like a dragon, but how did it get in the cave?" the woman asked. Her face hardened as her mana churned, causing ripples to appear in the space around her. "I'll check it out."

"Be careful. It's scary, very scary. It dragged in a behemoth," a bat called out as the woman's figure disappeared.

"Think she'll be alright?"

"Of course. Master is always alright."

"Yes, Master's the best."

The woman arrived at the top of the stairs. The mana in her body stopped moving as her mouth fell open. Her brow furrowed as her head tilted to one side. What the hell was this? There was a naked boy and a pig sleeping on top of a frozen behemoth bear while the eight-legged basilisk mini-boss she owned was lying on its back, pretending to be dead. When it sensed the woman's presence, it scrambled to its feet and scurried behind her.

"Useless thing," she said and kicked it. "Can't you even kill a boy and his pig?"

The basilisk shook its head and ran down the stairs, making a racket on its way down.

"Why's it so noisy?"

The woman turned her attention towards the frozen bear. Vur sat up while holding a snoring Snuffles. He turned towards the woman and their eyes met. Her eyes widened when she saw his golden slit pupils, and she kneeled while lowering her head.

"I'm sorry for my lack of respect, dragon. May I know why you took residence here?" she asked.

Vur blinked and a wide smile appeared on his face. "That's right; I'm a dragon," he said and let out a roar. The cave shook, and dust rained down from the ceiling. The woman trembled, but she remained kneeling. Chirps and flapping sounds echoed throughout the lower levels as the bats fled deeper in. Vur placed Snuffles down and stretched. "I'm hiding from the mean elf ladies. Grimmy said I shouldn't kill things I wasn't going to eat, except for humans and demons, but he said I can't eat or kill elves. This is your home?" Vur's head swiveled as he looked around. "It looks nice—smaller than my mama's cave though."

The woman looked up and smiled, two fangs glinting in the torch light. "I'm glad you like it," she said. "Stay as long as you'd like. Could I offer you something to eat or drink?"

Vur tilted his head. "Why would you do that?"

"It's proper manners to offer guests food and drink, no?"

Vur made a face. "Those elves didn't have proper manners," he said. "They tried to feed me dirt and spanked me."

The woman blinked. "How old are you?"

"I'm a dragon," Vur said and crossed his arms over his chest. "Grimmy said dragons don't age." He looked at the woman before sighing and shaking his head.

The woman's eye twitched. "Why do you look like … that?" she asked gesturing at him.

"My papa said I'm not old enough to grow scales and wings yet."

"Then that means you can age, right?"

Vur's eyebrows bent towards each other, and he tilted his head. His lips curled into a pout. "I'm a dragon."

"Okay, okay. Forget I asked," the woman said with her hand pinching her forehead. "If you'll excuse me." The woman stood up, curtsied, and turned to leave.

"Wait," Vur said. The woman stopped and turned towards him. "I'm thirsty."

A vein bulged on the woman's forehead as she clenched her fist. She exhaled and said, "I'll bring you something to drink."

A few minutes later, she returned with a golden chalice that had a clear liquid in it. Vur took the chalice from her hand and was about to drink, but the woman grabbed his arm to stop him. "After someone gives you something, you say thank you," she said.

"Why? Isn't me not eating you thanks enough?" Vur asked. "Grimmy says that everyone who is not being eaten by dragons should thank dragons for not eating them."

The woman smiled. "Thank you for not eating me. Now you thank me for giving you that drink."

Vur frowned and tried to raise the chalice but found that he couldn't move his arm. His eyes glowed, but Juliana's face appeared in his head, and they stopped. He frowned and said, "Thank you for giving me this drink."

The woman released his arm and patted his head, ruffling his hair. "That's a good boy. You can call me Auntie Lindyss."

***

Rudolph's face was green as he sat down and gasped for breath. Behind him, Johann was lying on the ground while covering his nose with his paws.

"Not so easy compared to hitting wooden dolls in the academy, huh?" the warrior leader asked as he leaned against his sword stuck in the ground. Rudolph nodded. A few feet away, there was the corpse of a zombie with no head. The group of guards had let Rudolph lead the expedition, only helping him when he was about to die.

"I can feel myself getting stronger. It's amazing—although the smell could be improved," Rudolph said while scrunching his nose.

The white mage nodded. "When you kill things that have mana, you get a bit of that power to strengthen your body. Wait until we get back to an adventurers' guild where you can inspect your stats."

Rudolph nodded. He wanted to ask what their levels were, but he knew it would be rude. "Alright, Johann. Let's kill lots of zombies and level up!"

Johann puked out a corpse and shook his head while whimpering.

Rudolph sighed and asked, "Why don't you just bash them with a tree trunk?"

***

A group of demon children were in a cave, stabbing at slimes while working together in groups. Gabriel and Lamach were fighting against a green slime with three eyes.

"Isn't this too easy, Gabe?" asked Lamach as he pushed away the slime with his spear.

Gabriel shrugged and stabbed the slime's mana core. The core exploded, and the slime evaporated. "It's supposed to get harder," he said as he wiped slime juices off his face.

"Less talky talky, more stabby stabby," a voice called out. The voices of children soon turned into the sounds of squishing as slimes disappeared left and right.

"Mr. Doofus, when do we get to actually fight things?" Lamach asked. The surrounding kids stopped and turned towards the big man who was standing at the entrance to the cave illuminated by a yellow glow.

"When you reach level five. Then we'll move on to the next floor with bigger slimes," Doofus said.

"Ugh, more slimes," a boy with red hair said. "I don't think I can eat my mum's pudding ever again."

"Is this not good enough for you? Our ancestors fought a war over this mana source and you want to go somewhere else?" Doofus asked as he crossed his arms over his chest. His face darkened.

"N-no, no problem, sir. It's just a little … lame?" the red-headed child replied. A shiver ran down his spine. "Our ancestors fought over a slime spawner?"

Doofus glared at the boy before letting his arms drop and sighing. "Yeah, I know it's lame. That's what I thought too when I first started. But if you keep it up, you might become an SSS-ranked adventurer like me," Doofus said as he pointed to his face with his thumb and smiled. "And it's not only slimes. I'm only allowed to let you guys hunt slimes for now."

"But humans get to go to actual dungeons for their first time," Gabriel said. A slime approached him, and he kicked it away with his shoe.

"Yeah, but you're not a human," Lamach said and rolled his eyes.

Gabriel frowned and stabbed the slime.

***

Lindyss frowned at the naked boy eating a raw bear corpse in her mini-boss room as she sat on a chair made of bones. How did things end up like this? Her basilisk popped its head out from the stairwell and looked at Lindyss and then at Vur and then back at Lindyss again. His eyes asked, "Why is he still here? Where do I sleep?"

"Hey, Vur, do you know what this is?" Lindyss asked as she pointed at the basilisk.

Vur looked up and shook his head. He replied while chewing, "He tried to hurt me with his eyes, but then he ran away and played dead."

"You shouldn't talk with food in your mouth," Lindyss said with a frown. "It's not polite."

Vur tilted his head and continued to chew. "So why did you ask me a question?" he asked.

Lindyss stared and him before shaking her head. "Never mind," she said. "In the future, try not to talk with your mouth full. Dragons don't do that."

Vur thought back to all the times he ate with his family and nodded. After he swallowed he said, "Thirsty."

Lindyss didn't move, but she asked, "What's the magic word?"

Vur scrunched up his eyebrows and shook his head. "I don't know the word. I don't need words though," he said. His eyes glowed, and a massive amount of water materialized in the air and crashed to the floor, soaking Lindyss and the basilisk. He cupped the water in his hands and drank it before it flooded down the stairwell.

Lindyss spluttered. "Never do that again!" she said as she coughed out water.

"Master! What's going on? Is it storming?"

"I'm wet. I hate being wet."

"Stop touching me with your wet wings. No, I don't care if you're drowning!"

"I'm drowni—glub. M-master, h-help."

Snuffles oinked and climbed on top of Vur's head.

Lindyss glared at Vur. "Why'd you summon so much if you were only going to drink so little?" she asked as she placed her hand on the surface of the water. A vortex appeared, and after a short while, all the water had vanished into thin air.

"I don't know how else to do it," Vur said and shrugged, his hair still dripping.

Lindyss sighed and said, "I hope you didn't dilute my fountain. Who taught you magic?"

Vur tilted his head. "No one. I just do it," he said. "I asked Grimmy once, and he told me to do what I felt was nice."

Lindyss covered her face with her hands. "I'll kill Grimmoldesser. I'll kill him. Just do whatever you feel is nice? That's the kind of advice given to a child with a near infinite amount of mana?" she mumbled. She glared at Vur. "Right now, you are a disgrace to every magical being in existence. I'll show you what it really means to be a dragon. Dragons are intelligent, arrogant, greedy, and prideful pieces of shi—not. Pieces of snot. You, you are just a lizard with a really big stick!"

***

Tafel watched as Dustin chanted and summoned thirty earth golems in the field in front of them. "Phew. Alright, Tafel," Dustin said as he took a deep breath. "You're going to use these for target practice. They're fragile in the standard humanoid vital spots. You have half an hour to take out as many as you can."

Tafel nodded and began. Fireballs flew through the air and collided with the golems. Thirty minutes later, Tafel was lying on the ground and panting for breath. Six piles of rubble were in the field of golems. Dustin nodded his head and said, "Not too bad for your first try; you need to find the right balance of mana to take them out efficiently."

Tafel pursed her lips as Dustin pointed his finger to the sky and built up mana. He lowered his hand and pointed towards the golems. Twenty-four lightning bolts—one for each golem—struck them on the head, reducing them to rubble instantly.

"Wow," Tafel said with wide eyes. "That's amazing! When can I do that?"

Dustin shook his head. "Any competent mage should be able to do this. I suspect in a few years, you'll be just as good—if not better," he said. A wry smile appeared on his lips before he sighed. "I actually met someone whose mastery over magic was far greater than mine."

Tafel's eyebrows raised. "Who was it? How come I've never heard of him?"

Dustin smiled. "It's actually a her," he said. "She's the guardian of the Fountain of Youth." He raised his head towards the sky and squinted at the clouds. "She stomped our butts and made us cry. I'm lucky to be alive."

"How'd you get away if she was stronger than you?"

"Our beast tamer raised a basilisk, and we traded it for our lives. He's retired now; last I heard, he runs a stable in Fuselage," Dustin said.

Tafel blinked. "Fuselage? It really exists?" she asked. "How can a town like that not be a fairytale?"

"Oh, it exists alright. Maybe you'll see it one day," Dustin said while smiling. He ruffled Tafel's hair. "More golems?"

The demon princess smiled and nodded.

6

In a small room with two beds, a snoring woman lay with her arms and legs sprawled out, hanging off the sides of a bed. There was a choking sound, and the snoring stopped. The woman, Sophie, sat up and looked around while wiping the drool off of her mouth. *Why didn't Claire wake me?* she thought as she climbed out of bed and slipped on her red robe before entering the washroom. *There's a new wrinkle today,* she thought as she glared at her reflection and sighed. She shook her head and washed up before leaving her room, heading down the stairs of the inn.

"Look who's finally up," a voice greeted her when she entered the tavern on the first floor. The voice belonged to a man who was sitting at a table with three other men and a woman. He was wearing a blue chainmail, and his red sword was propped up against the seat beside him. If the king was here, he would recognize the man as the leader of the Red Blade Adventurers.

"Good morning, Aran," Sophie said as she sat next to the other woman. She pinched the woman's waist and asked, "Why didn't you wake me?"

Claire shrugged. "You sleep like a log," she said. "And you drooled on my arm when I shook you."

"Hey, hey. Don't ruin our image of her," one of the men said. He wore a blue bandana.

Another man wearing a black leather vest smacked his companion's head. "What image? We've already been traveling together for years now," he said and snorted. "We all know she's an ogre."

Sophie rolled her eyes. "If I'm an ogre, then you're a troll," she said and turned her head towards a counter. "Hey, chief! Can I get three drumsticks and a jug of ale over here?"

"Coming right up."

Sophie turned towards Aran. "What's the plan for today, boss?"

"We've accomplished 14 SSS-ranked missions since we ranked up four years ago. One more and we can finally go to Fuselage," Aran replied, his expression grim. "I already picked one."

"Without us? Ouch, boss, that hurts," the man with the blue bandana said as he clutched his own chest and smiled.

"Shut up, Zeke," the man with the black vest said. "Let him finish." He nodded at Aran.

"We're going to the Fountain of Youth," Aran said and raised his hand to stop his group from speaking. "It's the first triple-S that's appeared in the past three months."

"What's the rush?" Sophie asked with a frown. "We could've waited for a different one."

Zeke licked his lips and narrowed his eyes at Sophie. "Scared?" he asked with a smile on his face. "We stole a dragon's egg for heaven's sake. You're scared of the fountain?"

"As if," Sophie said and snorted. "I'm just wondering why we'd go to the riskiest place for our last mission before Fuselage."

Aran furrowed his brow before exhaling. "You know I'm almost 50," he said.

The group fell silent.

"Then we're all in agreement?"

***

Lindyss yawned as she leaned back in her skeletal rocking chair. She was in her mini-boss room with Vur floating in the air in front of her. His arms and legs were crossed while his eyes were closed. A constant flow of wind was keeping his body afloat, pushing up from below. Lindyss wiped away the tears

64

that formed from her yawn before nodding. "It's been two weeks and your control has gotten to a barely acceptable level," she said to the naked boy.

Vur smiled, showing his teeth. "This is fun," he said as he loosened his body and stretched. The instant he did, his body rocketed upwards and crashed through the ceiling, leaving a human-shaped hole. A few seconds later, he fell to the floor with a thud. A moan escaped from his lips as he sat up and clutched his head. "That wasn't so fun."

Lindyss facepalmed while Vur rocked back and forth on the floor. "You need to concentrate harder. Too much and aero will launch you, too little and you won't get off the ground," she said.

"I know," Vur said as he looked up and pouted. "It's just hard."

"Tough," Lindyss said and snorted. "Do it again."

Vur was about to protest, but Lindyss glared at him, stifling his words. He nodded and closed his eyes, letting streams of wind push his body into the air. A few more human-shaped holes were created that morning, but Vur was able to float without crashing by noon. When he managed to maintain his position for an hour, Lindyss stopped him.

"Are you ready to learn more spells?" she asked with a smile. Her voice was cloying when she spoke, and her eyes glinted. "I'm not too sure which of my spells a blue mage can learn, so I'll hit you with everything. Try not to die." She hummed as black orbs manifested in the air around her.

Vur trembled as he took a step backwards. "A-aren't you enjoying this too much?" he asked as his back came into contact with the room's wall.

"It's just your imagination, Chibi Grimmy," Lindyss said and laughed. The orbs flew through the air and whimpers rang throughout the cave.

When the moon began to rise, Lindyss exited the dungeon and stretched her arms towards the sky, arching her back. There was a smile plastered on her face, and she ran her fingers through her hair, brushing the light-brown locks behind her pointed ears. At the cave entrance, a flock of bats and a basilisk appeared. On top of the eight-legged beast, Vur was sleeping, using Snuffles' body as a pillow. Despite the nonstop screaming that occurred throughout the day, his body was completely uninjured. She smiled at the sleeping boy and placed her hand on his forehead. He mumbled something and turned over onto his side.

The basilisk turned its head to look at its owner, and Lindyss flicked its nose. "What?" she asked. The basilisk shook its head before facing forward. Lindyss hopped onto its scaly back, and it began to run through the forest. The cloud of bats dispersed through amongst the trees while a few decided to stick around, crawling into Lindyss' hair and clothes.

Lindyss wasn't sure when she fell asleep, but she woke up to Vur shaking her. "Where are we going?" he asked, looking around at the moving scenery. They were still atop the basilisk which hadn't stopped running through the night.

"On an adventure," Lindyss said as she rubbed the crud out of her eyes. She sat up and yawned. The moon was still shining overhead. She had probably gotten less than an hour of sleep. A sigh escaped from her lips as she smoothed out the tangles in her hair. "Since you're my student, I'm going to have you learn everything I can."

She patted the basilisk's back, and its pace slowed. "Make him fight the goblin chieftain, but don't let him die," she said. The basilisk bobbed its head as Lindyss hopped to the ground and created a shelter by manipulating the earth.

"Auntie?" Vur asked.

"I hate the sun," Lindyss said. "Come back after you learn all the goblin chieftain's skills. Try not to kill him if you can help it."

"But—"

Lindyss snapped her fingers, and the basilisk darted away. She let out a yawn as she lit a fire at the entrance of her makeshift shelter before curling up and falling asleep. The last thing she heard before she fell asleep was a distant goblin alarm call.

A few days later, Vur, Lindyss, and Snuffles were riding on the basilisk's back. They had traveled through twenty different monster habitats with Lindyss forcing Vur to learn their skills. There was only one mishap where he was swallowed by a miro, a giant tree-like monster with tentacles and fangs. Snuffles had to save him because the basilisk's gaze didn't do anything to the creature, and Lindyss didn't want to get her hands dirty. Miros stank.

"Are we there yet?" Vur asked. He squeezed Snuffles as he lifted his head to look up at Lindyss who was sitting behind him. She was braiding his hair while humming.

"Almost."

"You said that yesterday," Vur said and pouted.

"And I'll say it again tomorrow when you ask," Lindyss replied with a smile.

One of the bats hiding in Lindyss' hair spoke up and asked, "Is it fine to leave the fountain for so long, Master?"

"What if adventurers invade?" another bat chimed in.

"Shouldn't you have left some of us behind?"

"Hush, Master is all-knowing and wise."

"Master's the best."

"But she didn't help me when I was drowning."

"Second best?"

"It's fine," Lindyss said and rolled her eyes. "This brat drank it all. You guys couldn't stop adventurers if they came anyway. Who cares if a few drops are taken?"

"Master cares for us."

"As I thought, she's the best."

"But...."

"Quiet, it's your fault for not knowing how to swim."

The Red Blade Adventurers walked through the glowing, green cave entrance. Aran and Sophie were following a man dressed in a blue robe, while Zeke and the black-vested man stood behind Claire who was wearing a white robe.

"This is strange," Claire said and raised her staff to her chest. "It's too quiet."

"Are there any traps, Zul?" Aran asked. The blue-robed man shook his head.

"It's all clear. I detect traces of magic, but it's faint," he said as he trudged along, a web of runes floating in the air in front of his chest.

"I don't like it," Sophie said, clutching her short sword. She was dressed in a red robe with leather armor underneath. "Should we turn back?"

"We already came all this way and now you want to turn back? Where's that fearless ogre spirit?" Zeke asked with a smile, adjusting the bandana on his head.

The man with the black vest shook his head. "Stay vigilant," he said. "Too many adventurers have died here."

Zeke snorted. "Isn't that why you're here, Ross? To rez us when we die?" Zeke asked.

"Dying's painful; let's not do that please," Sophie said.

Zul raised his hand as his web of runes flickered with a bright light. The group halted and clutched their weapons. "The concentration of magic is a lot higher here. It's most likely the mini-boss or boss room," Zul said. He furrowed his brow as he double-checked his runes.

"Already? But we haven't even done anything yet," Claire said.

"Group buffs," Aran said. "And don't forget antipetrify. Rumors have it that a basilisk is the mini-boss." A white light encircled the group and faded as Claire raised her staff to cast shield: physical, shield: magical, and antipetrify. Aran pushed open the door with his foot while wielding his red greatsword.

The group inched in with their weapons raised and checked their surroundings.

"It's empty?" Zeke asked but didn't lower his daggers.

"It looks like it? Look. The stairs going down already appeared," Claire said and pointed with her staff.

"Uh, guys...? Look up," Sophie said while staring at the ceiling.

"Are those human-shaped ... holes?" Zul asked with wide eyes. The group stared at the ceiling without moving.

Ross adjusted his vest. "Should we keep going?" he asked, breaking the silence.

Aran nodded. "It seems like something happened; if we're lucky, we'll be able to get to the fountain without a hassle," he said. The group proceeded down the stairs and traveled with their weapons still raised.

"I think we reached the boss room," Zul said after the adventurers traveled through winding tunnels and encountered several dead ends. They had arrived at a room with a giant crater at the center. A few inches of liquid could be seen at the bottom.

"This is the Fountain of Youth?" Aran asked as he led the group down the crater. "Why is it so empty? Was it relocated?"

Claire raised her staff and pointed it at the puddle. "Scan," she said. A moment passed as she held her staff with her eyes closed. "It's definitely the fountain. That water is the water of life: restores age, boosts health recovery, and increases magic resistance when drunk."

"I think that'd be of most use to me," Zeke said with a grin as he reached into his bag and pulled out a cup, "because I'm always drunk."

Claire smacked his head. "Not that kind of drunk. Drank," she said. "There's enough for seven cups. Barely enough for all of us and the quest. I heard from someone who heard from a fairy that the fountain refills at a rate of one cup a day, so a week must've passed since it was last drained."

Aran nodded. "Let's clear it and leave," he said. "I don't want to stay here any longer than we have to."

"Guys, there's still a door over there in the corner," Zeke said and pointed at a conspicuously evil-looking door. Several non-human skulls decorated its exterior, and a black mist seemed to be leaking out of the bottom and sides.

"Ignore it," Aran said. "We got what we came for."

Zeke frowned, but he turned around and followed the group as they left.

***

Vur gulped as he craned his neck at the giant insect in front of him. Its red mandibles clacked together as four giant legs sprang out of the sandy ground. The ant-like creature dashed at him, lunging forward with the scythe-like protrusions on its face. "I don't like this," Vur yelled as he dodged a mandible that was as thick as a tree. "Make it stop!"

Lindyss smiled as she sat on the edge of a thirty-foot deep circular pit with Snuffles sitting in her lap. The moon was bright and shone on the antlion which was chasing a black speck, Vur, in the pit. Countless ant corpses littered the floor, but their bodies were gradually disappearing into the ground. Lindyss cupped her hands around her mouth and yelled down, "Watch out, there's another one behind you."

A pair of mandibles sprung out of the sand and moved towards the speck. Snuffles snuffled and looked up at Lindyss. "Don't worry, he'll be fine," she said as she rubbed the boar's head. A few seconds later, the ant pounced on the speck, and the speck disappeared.

"Oh. Or not," she said as a wrinkled formed on her forehead. "I guess I spoke too soon." She placed Snuffles down and cracked her neck before jumping into the pit.

A few minutes later, a naked boy covered from head to toe with slime was crying on top of the cliff. Lindyss wiped her hands on a towel as she stared down at Vur and asked, "Do you see why you need a weapon now?"

70

Vur shot her a dirty look and wiped the snot off his face with the back of his hand. Earlier that night, Lindyss had told Vur about weapons and Vur claimed he didn't need one saying, "I can blow up anything with magic." He was promptly covered with honey and thrown into the first antlion pit she found.

"That wasn't fair," Vur said as he shook his head like a dog trying to get water out of its coat. Slime flew everywhere, but all of the drops approaching Lindyss stopped an inch away from her before dropping to the ground. "There were too many of them. I ran out of mana."

Lindyss laughed. "Fair doesn't matter if you're dead," she replied.

Vur frowned but didn't say anything.

"Go take a bath. You smell like stomach juices," Lindyss said and pinched her nose.

Half an hour later, Vur smelled better and was lying down, chewing on an antlion's leg. "Where do I get a weapon?" Vur asked after he swallowed a mouthful of meat and carapace.

"Oh? The mighty dragon needs one now?" Lindyss asked with a smile that showed her fangs. "What changed your mind?"

Vur pouted. "You were right."

Lindyss patted his head. "Of course I was right. I'm always right," she said and took out a dagger. "You can have this."

Vur took the red dagger and ran his fingers over the runes etched on the side.

"Most blue mages use swords, but you're a bit minute," Lindyss said. "Its name is Lust. Take good care of it."

Vur caressed the dagger's edge before turning his gaze on Lindyss. He furrowed his brow and asked, "Where should I keep it?"

Lindyss snorted. "In your pants."

***

Prika yawned as she lifted her head off the boulder she was resting on. Her neck curved towards the silver dragon curled up

71

below her. Her wings spread out and flapped twice before resting by her sides. She picked a piece of bone out of her teeth using her claws before asking, "How many towns do you think they'll burn this time?"

Leila sighed. "At least eighty. You know how Grimmy gets when he's mad."

Prika nodded. The dragons had spent over a week searching for Vur or a sign of his aura, but none of them were able to find anything. Prika and Leila were guarding the hoard while Sera, Grimmy, and Vernon were taking out their anger on nearby human and demon villages. Sera had uprooted the remains of the sacred tree and set them on fire when she heard Vur went missing, but she didn't hurt any of the elves because of her promise to her father. Their village was left in ruins however, and they were forced to relocate several mountain ranges away.

"I hope he's alright," Prika said and rested her head on her paws, looking in the direction of the wilderness' border. She thought she saw a faint golden speck flying in the air. She shrugged and closed her eyes. It was probably Vernon.

The golden speck was indeed Vernon, and he was flying over a group of human soldiers. He roared and crashed to the ground like a golden meteor, scattering the fortunate soldiers and crushing the unfortunate ones. His knees bent on impact, and his tail thrashed into the midst of the small army, breaking through their defenses like a hot knife through screaming butter.

"Sera," he said as he swiped his tail again and knocked over a company of a dozen soldiers, "we should leave now." His mate was surrounded by burning buildings and charred corpses. Clouds of ash hung in the air, and the ground was blackened. Soldiers encircled the town, trembling as they watched the two dragons.

Sera snorted and flew into the air, spewing a frigid breath filled with icicles out of her mouth at the soldiers one last time. They screamed while Vernon spread his wings and leapt after Sera.

"They're starting to respond now. It'll be dangerous if we continue," Vernon said. "Grimmoldesser's already heading back."

Sera didn't respond, but she continued to fly south. Her eyes were narrowed and blood dripped from her body. A few of her scales were missing. Below the two dragons, the plain's previous green and brown appearance had transformed into a sea of ash and scorched earth.

***

Tafel and Dustin held their breaths, sitting behind a table with a crystal orb placed on it. Images of blackened earth and dying soldiers were playing on the orb's surface. Tafel's face paled as a company of human soldiers turn into a fine mist of blood as thousands of icicles rained down on them.

"Dustin," Tafel asked, her lips trembling. "Why don't they kill all the dragons?"

"That's impossible," Dustin said, his face expressionless. He sighed and touched the orb's surface. The images disappeared.

"But why? Couldn't we kill them if every adventurer went?"

"Dragons aren't stupid," Dustin replied. "They'd just fly over and burn our capitals to the ground before we reached them. There's not that many groups strong enough to fight against a dragon. Besides, everything in the wilderness is hostile towards us. It wouldn't be easy to get to the dragons' roost with a large group."

"What if we teleport?"

"Too much mana," Dustin said and shook his head. "Believe me, the adventurers' guild has thought about it many times."

"But—"

"No buts; besides, the dragons keep the scary things in check," Dustin said.

"Aren't the dragons the scary things?" Tafel asked while tilting her head.

"No. Dragons usually don't bother us. It's only in the past few years that they've been acting up." Dustin shook his head. "Something must've made them angry."

Tafel nodded. "Never make a dragon angry," she said. She paused. "What are the scary things then?"

"Maybe you'll find out when you're older," Dustin said as he ruffled her hair. She couldn't see it, but Dustin's expression turned grim as he stared at the orb on the table.

7

In the human's capital, on the opposite side of the city from the royal castle, there was a white building with steeples and a cross embedded on its two metal doors. The windows were made of colorful stained glass, and doves could be seen roosting on the roofs and windowsills. On the second floor of the church, a blonde-haired girl was sleeping on a white bed while cuddling a pink stuffed dragon.

"Michelle, get dressed and come downstairs. Rudolph returned to the city last night," a muffled voice called out. "If you get dressed fast enough, you might be able to eat breakfast with him."

The girl yawned, sat up in bed, and rubbed the crust out of her eyes. She washed her face with the bucket of water in the corner of her room and changed into a white robe. After clipping on a silver cross necklace, she skipped down the stairs while humming. "You forgot to comb your hair," her mother said when she saw the smiling girl. "Are you that excited to see him?"

Michelle giggled and ran her fingers through her hair, smoothing out the tangles. Her mother smiled at her. Ever since Rudolph had his coming-of-age ceremony, Michelle always wanted to see him. At least, if they got married, the church and state would be united. After the mother and daughter donned their shoes, they left the church and held hands as they made their way to the royal castle. They arrived just in time to see Rudolph riding Johann towards his parents.

Michelle ran towards the prince and said, "You were gone for three weeks; I missed you so much!" Rudolph smiled as his face turned red, and he was about to say something in reply, but

75

Michelle hugged Johann and kissed him on the snout, completely ignoring the prince. Michelle giggled as Johann snorted and licked her face.

"I don't get a hug?" Rudolph asked as he dismounted Johann. He opened his arms and waited.

"Of course not," Michelle said and pinched her nose. "You stink."

Rudolph frowned and dropped his arms to his side. "It's not my fault. I just emptied Johann's poop bag. Alistar wouldn't let me for the whole journey," he said and lowered his head.

Michelle stuck her tongue out at him. "C'mon, Johann. Let's go to the gardens," she said and tugged on Johann's reins.

"Wait for me," Rudolph said as he chased after them.

The queen smiled at the two kids. "It's good to see you again," the queen said to Michelle's mother. "Come inside; we're about to have breakfast."

Michelle's mother curtsied. "Don't mind if I do."

***

The moon shone overhead, bathing Johann and the two kids sitting by his side with a soft glow. Michelle let out a sigh as Johann curled his neck and rested his head against her leg. "You're going to another dungeon already?" Michelle asked as she rubbed the dragon's snout. "You just got back though."

"Why does it seem like you're talking to Johann and not me?" Rudolph asked as he stared at the back of her head. His body was even separated from hers by one of Johann's paws.

Michelle smiled. "Does it really?" she asked. "You must be imagining things."

Rudolph sighed. Every time he spent the day with Michelle, she'd always insist on Johann being there. One time, Johann didn't show up because he was napping and Michelle suddenly felt ill and went home. "I'll be going to an orange-ranked dungeon this time. Maybe I'll reach level ten," Rudolph said. He hesitated and stared at the ground. "So…"

Michelle waited, but Rudolph didn't continue. "So …
what?" she asked and tilted her head.

Rudolph's face turned red. "N-nothing," he said and looked
away.

"It's not nothing. Tell me what you were going to say," she
said and leaned forward. "I want to know."

Rudolph shook his head. "It really was nothing."

"Stop lying. Pleeeease?"

Rudolph looked at Michelle, her eyes glittering as she stared
at him. He took a deep breath and asked, "I-if I reach level ten
… will you, um, go out w-with me?" His cheeks were on fire,
and he stared at his hands as he waited for an answer.

"Oh. Um. I really don't know what to say to that," Michelle
said as she blushed and bit her lower lip. "D-do you hear that?
I think my mother is calling for me. I think I should go." She
stood up and dashed away before she had even finished
speaking.

Rudolph watched her back as it disappeared around a
corner. His chest tightened, and he gritted his teeth. "Let's go,
Johann," he said and exhaled.

The sky-blue dragon blinked a few times before standing up
and stretching out his wings. He followed after Rudolph but
occasionally glanced in the direction Michelle went. A small,
white figure waved at him, causing his tail to wag. The dragon
nodded at Michelle before leaving the gardens with Rudolph
tugging on his reins.

***

A naga stared down at the hooded figure in front of him as
he crossed his arms over his chest. His upper body was that of
a human's, but his lower half was similar to a snake's. Black
tattoos spiraled up his bare arms, ending at his sleeveless vest.
On his neck, there were dozens of golden chains with different
kinds of teeth hanging from them.

"I'll give you 50 red crystals for him," a naga said in
snaketongue. The language of the nagas sounded melodic like

a lark singing. His body swayed from side to side as he poked and prodded the half-naked humanoid creature by the cloaked figure's side.

Lindyss shook her head underneath her hood. "That's too low," she said back in snaketongue. Vur tilted his head at the hissing sounds and furrowed his brow. The duo had arrived at the central city of the nagas and lamias and a few had taken a special interest in Vur.

"What are you saying?" Vur asked as he tugged on Lindyss' cloak. He was wearing black pants made out of sandshark skin, and the outline of a dagger could be seen on his thigh.

Lindyss smiled at him and rubbed his head. "They're asking to play with you like mock fighting," she replied in elvish, the only language he understood.

"I want to play!" Vur said. He looked at the naga and then back at Lindyss.

Lindyss asked the naga, "He'll be set free if he wins one hundred matches, right?"

The naga nodded before frowning at the boy who was staring up at him. Vur really was small compared to the merchant. "How about 75 red crystals?"

"300," Lindyss said.

The naga snorted. "That's too much. People will be interested since it's exotic, but it looks like it can only last half a match. I'll be losing too much."

"I guarantee you, he'll make you a lot more than 300. He knows how to fight," she replied. "I'll pay the difference if he doesn't manage."

The naga narrowed his eyes at her without speaking. His arms uncrossed as he smiled. "Alright. 300 crystals. You have to bring him food though," he said with a nod.

Lindyss smiled back. "Good. 300 red crystals and he goes free after winning a hundred matches," she said. "I'll be watching." She removed her hood, and smiled at the naga, revealing her pointed fangs. The naga's eyes widened as his tail trembled, and he bowed until his head touched the ground.

"Corrupted One," he said, his voice quavering. "Forgive me. I was impudent."

Vur tugged on Lindyss' cloak again. "Can I play yet?"

"In a bit," Lindyss said and beamed at him as the naga got up and readied a pouch, adding an extra amount of crystals. "Go with the nice man. When you're done playing, I'll get you a nice present."

***

In a circular coliseum at the center of the snakemen capital, hundreds of nagas and lamias gathered, filling up the seats in the elevated edges. The center of the coliseum was filled with sand, and there were a few black clumps where blood had dried. The sun shone directly over the battleground, leaving no shadows in the arena. Two gates, underneath the seating area, faced each other from opposite sides: In one gate, there was the figure of a naga wielding two shortspears. In the other, Vur was sitting next to Lindyss with Snuffles sleeping on his lap.

A lamia with a young-looking face climbed onto a platform in the seating area which was specially made for announcers. She cleared her throat and used wind magic to amplify her voice as she said, "Ladies and gentlemen! Today, dear guests, we have a rare exotic species for our opening match—the servant of the Corrupted One. She brought this human here to test his mettle, and since today is his opening match, no one knows his ability, but a servant of the Corrupted One is bound to be strong. Don't underestimate him just because he's small. His opponent is, Nar'lith, seven-time winner and son of the Slhill tribe's chieftain. As many of you know, the Slhill tribe was conquered by the Svathi a few moon cycles ago. Nar'lith is their only hope at redemption if he can win one hundred matches. Will he go on to claim another victory today? Or will the servant shut him down? Place your bets!"

"What are they saying?" Vur asked Lindyss. He frowned at the metal gates holding him back. "Can I play yet?"

"Very soon. They're saying the rules for the game," Lindyss replied as she lifted Snuffles off of his lap. "You'll be fighting that snake over there. You're not allowed to use dragon magic or show your aura. Only unnoticeable self-buffs and weapons allowed."

Vur nodded. "Okay," he said. "No dragon magic."

"Also, you can't eat him," Lindyss said.

Vur pouted. "Just a taste?" he asked and stared up at her with puppy eyes.

Lindyss shook her head and said, "Not in front of all those people. I'll feed you one tonight if you win."

"Okay," Vur said, his lips widening into a smile. "Grimmy says dragons never lose."

"All bets have been placed, and the fighters are ready. Remember the rules: there are no rules and we want to see blood!" the announcer shouted. The seated snakemen let out roars and thumped their tails against the floor. "Open the gates!"

"It's starting," Lindyss said as the metal gate creaked and swung open. "Have fun."

Vur dashed out of the room and waited at the center of the arena for Nar'lith. Contrary to Grimmy's teachings of 'attack first, ask questions later,' Lindyss had taught him firsthand to observe his opponents before making a move.

Nar'lith circled around Vur, getting closer with each rotation. "I'll make this quick child," he hissed. "It's a shame killing someone so youn—. Wait. What are you doing?"

Vur pulled his pants down to his knees and retrieved his dagger after rummaging around. Lindyss facepalmed. She should've made him a belt sheath instead. Nar'lith stared as Vur put his dagger on the ground and grabbed the top of his pants to pull it back up.

Swish!

80

The naga dashed forward and stabbed his spear towards Vur's head.

"Wah!" Vur cried out and fell over onto his butt as the spear grazed his scalp. Nar'lith raised his other spear and stabbed down at Vur who quickly turned over and leapt forward. The spear stabbed through the top of his pants, but Vur's body continued forward, slipping out of them.

Lindyss sighed. "Why do I even try...?" she muttered to Snuffles as the naga impaled her handiwork.

"That's not nice!" Vur said as he scrambled to his feet and turned around. "Auntie made those for me."

The naked boy pounced towards Nar'lith with his hands outstretched. The naga twisted his body to the side until his back was parallel to the floor and stabbed at Vur with the spear in his left hand as the boy passed over him. Nar'lith's eyes widened as Vur contorted his body, dodging the spear before grabbing it with his right hand and using it as a pivot to redirect himself towards the naga. Nar'lith gritted his teeth and stabbed at Vur with the spear in his right hand, but Vur caught it with his left. The naga looked up at the boy whose body was suspended in the air above him and tried to pull his spears apart. The muscles on his arms bulged, and a bead of sweat rolled down his forehead.

The naga grunted and gritted his teeth. "Let go!" he roared as he tried to rip his spear out of Vur's grasp. Instead of releasing the naga's weapons, Vur opened his mouth and puked onto Nar'lith's face. The naga screamed and dropped both his spears as he clawed at the vomit which was corroding his skin. He gagged and dry heaved, but Vur punched him in the temple, causing Nar'lith to pass out.

Lindyss shook her head and sighed again. Snuffles raised his sleepy head and looked at her before letting out an oink.

"W-winner! The servant has triumphed over Nar'lith," the lamia said as she pinched her nose. "Someone hurry up and clean up that vomit—it smells terrible. I believe that was the miro skill, dissolving acid. It looks like the servant is the most versatile class out there—the blue mage!"

The audience glanced at each other, and a few half-hearted hisses sounded out from the seating area. Vur picked up the dagger that he didn't use and put on his torn pants before returning back to Lindyss. She glanced at Vur's dangling second dagger and pinched the bridge of her nose. *Is there a point in putting on pants if it doesn't cover anything?* Another sigh escaped from her lips as she stared at Vur with no expression on her face. "Good job."

***

The Red Blade Adventurers stood at the edge of the wilderness with their mouths agape. The once flourishing, green plains were scorched with layers of thick ash floating in the air. Everywhere they looked was a sea of black and gray, providing a stark contrast to the viridian forest they had just left.

"What happened here?" Sophie asked as she tightened her grip on her sword.

Zeke crinkled his nose as he undid his bandana and tied it around his nose and mouth. "It smells like burning hair. And death."

"Look," Claire said and pointed towards a cluster of shambling figures. "There are people."

"Let's ask them what happened," Aran said as he equipped his greatsword. The wrinkles on his face had disappeared, and his pepper-and-salt-colored hair lost the salt.

"Something's not right," Zul said as they got closer.

The figures ahead of them were stumbling with tattered clothes and disheveled hair. One of them turned around and stared at the group. Half of his face was covered with burn tissue, and flesh hung from his other cheek. He raised an arm and moaned.

"Zombies," Claire said and sucked in her breath. She raised her staff and chanted. A white light covered the group as she cast shield: physical and shield: magic.

82

Ross and Aran charged forwards and engaged the group of zombies. The adventurers made quick work of them. "Man, I didn't even get to do anything," Zeke said. "They were too weak."

Zul crouched next to the zombies and hovered his hand over their corpses. A web of runes formed in the air, and he furrowed his brow. "These were just villagers," he said. "Could the liches be on the move?"

"You think the graveyard is expanding?" Ross asked as he wiped brain matter off his leather gloves. "Why now?"

Zul shook his head. "I don't know, but we should hurry back and report this." The group murmured in agreement and disappeared into the clouds of ash with their weapons raised.

***

At the front of a classroom, a one-horned demon was blathering on about geography. Gabriel and Lamach were sitting next to each other, bored expressions on their faces. Gabriel's eyes were half-closed, and every so often, Lamach's head would dip down before bouncing back up again.

Gabriel yawned. "I never thought I'd say it, but I miss killing slimes," he whispered to Lamach.

"Me too," Lamach whispered back.

"Am I interrupting you two?" the teacher asked Gabriel and Lamach, snapping his book shut.

"No, sir," Lamach said. "Gabriel was just asking me a question."

"Oh? What question might that be?"

"Uh … what does, um, what is … to the"—Gabriel looked around and saw a map—"south? What is to the south of the wilderness?"

The teacher blinked. "A very good question," he said and nodded. "The simplest answer is, we don't know. We know of some regions and landmarks in the wilderness, but we have never been able to travel past the dragons' roost. Since you're so intellectually inclined today, how about you name the four key landmarks in the wilderness?"

Gabriel made a face. "There's the dragons' roost, uh, the Tree of Knowledge, um … the Fountain of Youth, and the graveyard? That's all of them, right?"

"Very good. I wasn't expecting someone like you to know that many," the demon said and nodded. He was about to say something else, but the door to the classroom swung open, and a burly demon, Doofus, stepped inside.

"The graveyard's expanding," the ex-adventurer shouted, ignoring the glare the one-horned teacher sent him. "C'mon, kids. It's time for you to get some real combat experience." He smiled at Lamach and Gabriel. "And I don't mean slimes. We're going to kill some zombies."

***

Tafel bit her lower lip as she glanced at her father who was eating his meal. She stabbed at her vegetables, shifting her gaze from her plate to her father's face.

"What is it?" the demon lord asked as he placed down his cutlery.

"Can I go fight the zombies too?" Tafel asked.

Her father raised an eyebrow. "Of course," he said. A smile crept onto his lips. "It would—"

"No," her mother said as she cut her steak without looking up.

"But, Mom," Tafel said, her purple lips pouting. "Gabriel and Lamach are going."

"And that's all the more reason you don't need to," her mother replied.

"But I want to get experience too," Tafel said. "Dustin thinks I'm strong enough. I'm even starting to grow more horns, see?" She pointed at her forehead. Two small bulges were protruding above her eyebrows.

"You can get more experience from Prim. She tells me you've been spending more time with Dustin than her," her mother said as she dipped her steak in a plate of sauce.

"You didn't even look," Tafel said with a frown. She wanted to stomp her feet, but she knew that'd work against her. "Dad?"

"Your mother said no," her father said and shrugged. "There's always other chances. Besides, there might be danger from the dragons. They've been causing trouble near the border."

"But if you say yes, that means I can go right? Doesn't Mom have to listen to you?"

"Oh, Tafel," her father said while shaking his head. "You're sadly mistaken. I signed away my rights when I married her. You'll understand when you get older." He sighed. If only his wife's family wasn't so influential, then maybe more things would go his way. He peeked at his wife. There was a smile on her face when she met his gaze, but her eyes were colder than ice.

***

Tafel took in a deep breath as she stood outside Dustin's room. She pinched her cheeks and smiled before pushing the door open and skipping inside.

"What did your parents say?" Dustin asked when he saw the intruder was the princess.

"They said I can go," Tafel said. Her smile widened.

"Really?"

"Yeah. Dad said I needed experience and Mom agreed."

"Huh, I guess that makes sense," Dustin said as he lowered his head. His voice lowered. "She was an adventurer after all."

"What?"

"Nothing," Dustin said as he shook his head and stood up. "Alright then. Since you have their permission, we'll head over there now. I'll call in a favor from a teleporter I know. We have to get there before your brothers kill everything—don't want them to get ahead of you."

"Right now? Let me leave a letter for my parents first. I didn't think we'd be going so soon."

Tafel took out a piece of scrap paper and grabbed a quill. She dipped it in ink and wrote in curvy script:
'Dear Mom,

I'm going to fight zombies to become strong enough to take away my husband's rights in the future.
Love,
Tafel'.

***

Lindyss walked into the room that Vur was occupying in the fighters' quarters. She threw a shiny gold object at the half-naked boy who was sleeping. It landed on his chest, waking him up. "Wear this," she said as Vur rubbed his eyes. The object was a ring—a golden band with three rubies embedded in it.

"It doesn't fit," Vur said as the ring fell off his finger.

Lindyss frowned. She tore a leather strip off the bottom of Vur's pants and threaded it through the ring. "Tie it around your neck," she said and held the makeshift necklace towards him.

"Okay," Vur said. He had learned how to tie knots from Lindyss when she made a belt to hold his dagger.

Lindyss nodded at the ring hanging from Vur's neck. "Time for lessons."

Vur's face brightened as he sat up and nudged Snuffles until the boar woke up. Lindyss had been teaching Vur and Snuffles how to read and write in between his arena matches by drawing letters on the ground. He had already won twenty-seven matches without receiving any injuries. The managers decided to pit Vur against desert beasts, hoping to create a more balanced match, but were horrified when he ate them. The crowd loved it though, and some lamia even went to the fighters' quarters to offer him food. After Vur learned to read and write the elvish language, which was spoken by the sentient
86

residents in the wilderness, Lindyss began teaching him to speak snaketongue and human.

There was a faint smile on Lindyss' lips as Vur read out the characters she wrote on the floor. He was squatting with his butt on his ankles and was using Lust to underline the characters. His dark-brown hair reached just below his neck and was braided at the ends. Snuffles was sprawled out on his head, peering at the characters as well. Vur's figure reminded her of the times she had spent learning with a certain dragon friend.

"Do you want to hear a story?" she asked Vur. He stopped reading and looked up. He nodded, and Snuffles oinked as he slid off of Vur's head.

"This is the story of how I met your mother," Lindyss said as she cleared her throat. She stared up at the ceiling and sighed. "It was over a thousand years ago when I had my coming-of-age ceremony with all the other elves who were born in the same decade as me. The ceremony's held once a decade, and the adults take the adolescents into the wild to find magical beasts to imprint them. The children would be accompanied by their parents to make sure they were safe, but they had to convince the beast by themselves. It's hard to convince a beast to imprint you because they usually only imprint when their young are born.

"My parents died a little after I was born, so I went by myself. I guess I wanted to prove that I was just as good as, if not better than, everyone else by finding an imprint on my own. I wandered for three months before finding a bat that had just given birth to its young. One of its newborns was sickly, and I healed it. I used to be a white mage before I became … this," Lindyss said as she gestured towards herself.

"Beasts with lineages are intelligent, and the bat appreciated what I did. She imprinted me, and I obtained her lineage. I stayed with her for a long time, providing her children with food and helping fend off other beasts. She gave me a home when I didn't have one." Lindyss smiled with her eyes shining. "But all things must end. A behemoth bear invaded the cave, and I couldn't stop it. She entrusted her children to me and fought the bear to give us time to escape. She could've flown away with her offspring, but she didn't want to abandon me," Lindyss said, her voice lowering. "Days passed. I was living with the bats in a separate cave we found. I was so weak and angry at myself. I kept going back to the place where she died, looking for a chance to kill the bear, but I never found one. One day, when I was watching the bear, the sky turned dark and I felt my hairs stand on end. Grimmy descended and did what I couldn't do with a single bite. I was outraged that my prey had been stolen, but at the same time, I was relieved that it was over.

"Grimmy turned and looked at me with the corpse still in his mouth as I yelled at him and cried. He listened to me rant as he ate the bear and fell asleep before I even finished talking—that asshole. When he woke up, I was curled up in a ball, sitting in front of the cave while crying. He flicked my forehead and asked me if I wanted power." Lindyss stared at her hands and fell silent.

Vur waited. When it was clear Lindyss wasn't going to say anything else, he asked, "What about my mother?"

Lindyss snorted and rolled her eyes. "Grimmy might as well be your mother with how much you take after him."

8

The sun shone overhead, causing the air above the sand to shimmer. The seating area of the arena was packed and filled to the brim. Outside of the arena, snakemen were clustered everywhere, trying to bribe their way inside.

"And now for the match that we've all been waiting for! On one side, we have the forty-nine-time winner, the hungry servant. On the other, we have the legendary rhimon! Countless numbers of contenders have participated in our arena, but less than a dozen have ever reached this stage, and none of them have ever gotten past it. That's because of the legendary beast you see in front of you. People say one look into its eye can instantly kill the faint of heart—if you're a coward, look away! It's the embodiment of death itself," the lamia from before announced. "Will the servant eat this beast too? Or will his streak finally end here?"

"Wow, he sounds scary," Vur said to Lindyss as he sat behind his metal gate. By now, he understood snaketongue and had accused Lindyss of lying about playing games. She had just smiled at him and said she wasn't a dragon before rubbing his head.

"Didn't you say the manticore sounded scary too?"

"He did sound scary! Just not as scary as he was tasty though."

"Then this should be the same."

"But that's a giant eyeball with wings. I don't like eating eyes. They're too squishy and slimy," Vur said with a frown.

"Just fry it with fire first then," Lindyss said. "I still think it's barbaric you don't cook your food first."

"It's not as tasty or chewy if you burn them," Vur said. "Grimmy told me that's why he never hunts with fire or magic."

Lindyss sighed. She was about to speak, but the gate swung open, and Vur and the rhimon dashed out at the same time. The rhimon looked like a giant, yellow ball with wings, a tail, and two clawed feet. It had one eye that took up 85% of its body and a mouth below it filled with rows of shark-like teeth. It was over eight feet tall and had a wingspan of 24 feet. It flew up into the air and let out a screech that made the audience tremble and wail. There was a layer of magic that prevented Vur and the rhimon from seeing the audience members, but it did nothing to stop the sound.

Vur fell to his knees and plugged his ears with his fingers. He gritted his teeth and circulated mana through his body, loosening his tense limbs. The rhimon's screech ended, and it dove towards Vur with its claws outstretched. Vur raised his hand and cast aero towards one of its wings. A torrent of wind engulfed it, causing the rhimon to spiral to the ground. It crashed onto its back, and Vur dashed forward while unsheathing his dagger. He wanted to stab it in its weakest spot—its eye—but he didn't want to be caught off guard in the air if he jumped. Instead, he stabbed its next most vulnerable spot.

Its butthole.

The rhimon let out a miserable shriek, and its legs thrashed as it felt pain in a place it never felt pain before.

Lindyss fell off the bench and landed on her face. Snuffles oinked at her. "I'm okay," she said as she sat up. "But I really have to rename that dagger."

The rhimon struggled to climb to its feet as it flapped its wings, but Vur was relentless in his pursuit. He repeatedly stabbed Lust into the rhimon's newfound weakness before it could take flight. Tears the size of basketballs sprang from the rhimon's eye as it shrieked while spreading its wings. Its eye glowed with a black light, and a roulette wheel appeared in the air above its body with images of Vur's and its faces on it. The wheel spun, and Vur stopped his assault to watch it with a furrowed brow. The wheel rattled before the arrow above it landed on the image of Vur's face.

Vur's hairs stood on end as a shadow descended behind him from above. It was a black-robed figure, without a face, holding a scythe over Vur's head. Vur's body collapsed onto the ground, but his view didn't change. He could see the back of his own head, and he saw an ethereal figure of himself standing over his material body. The scythe in the figure's hand swung down and rent his spirit in two. Vur's misty body dispersed as his vision went black.

The figure cackled as it rose into the air, turning into a wispy, undiscernible strand. The audience fell silent as they took in the scene. The rhimon panted as it glared at Vur's body. It flapped its wings as it leaped forward, ready to tear his corpse to pieces.

The lamia announcer broke the silence. "The rhimon used its riskiest skill, roulette, and it seems like the heavens were in its favor. It's a pity, but—. Wait! What's this!?"

A red light engulfed Vur's body before fading away. His body twitched as he groaned and propped himself up. The ring he wore as a necklace had one less ruby on it. Vur looked at it before turning his head towards Lindyss who gave him a smile and pointed at the rhimon.

The rhimon's yellow body turned as white as a sheet as its claw froze in midair. It let out a wail and flew back into the gate it came from, pulling the metal shut with its claws. It curled up into a ball and covered its eye with its wings.

"I-it seems like the rhimon has surrendered. The winner is the servant! History has been made today, folks—the first contender to reach fifty wins has been crowned!"

***

Tafel stared at her hands with tears in her eyes. Her mother and father were standing over her while Dustin looked in from the doorway. The demon princess' escapade lasted all of an afternoon before Prim discovered her note and reported it to the demon lord. Tafel's mother immediately sent a time mage to teleport her daughter back to the capital.

"Do you know how much trouble you're in, young lady?" Tafel's mother asked. Her arms were crossed over her chest, and her eyes were narrowed into tiny slits.

"I'm sorry," Tafel said and sniffled. She pursed her lips and clenched her hands, wrinkling her dress.

"You deliberately ignored us, and you lied to Dustin," her father said. "That wasn't a very nice thing to do. Your mother was worried sick about you."

Tafel remained as silent as a board.

"No more magic training for you," her mother said and glared at Dustin. "Ever."

"But—"

"No buts. You brought this upon yourself."

Dustin frowned. "Isn't that too much? It was my fault too for not verifying her words."

"There's no need for Tafel to learn magic," her mother said. "There are things more valuable for her, like politics and etiquette. As for you, Dustin, you should know me well enough to not have let her go."

"Mina...," Dustin said. Tafel's mother let out a hmph and brushed past Dustin as she left the room. Tafel's father sighed and walked after her with a crease in his brow.

"It's not fair," Tafel mumbled as her tears dropped to her hands. "Why does she always treat me like this?" She stamped her feet as she brushed her eyes with the back of her hands, trying to hold back her short breaths, but she couldn't. Her body shook as she hyperventilated, giving off sporadic sobbing sounds.

Dustin walked up to her and patted her head. "I taught you all the basics of magic. You can still practice even if I can't teach you. Work hard and you'll be strong enough to do what you want one day." He took off his necklace and clipped it over Tafel's neck. "This should help you when you practice. Return it to me when you become proud of your strength."

Tafel grasped the blue jeweled necklace and looked up at Dustin with tears in her eyes. He smiled at her and turned around to leave the room. He closed the door behind him, but he could still hear her sobs as he walked away. He arrived at the guestroom in the castle where the demon lord and his wife were shouting at each other. Dustin cleared his throat and knocked on the door, causing their argument to cease. "Tafel has so much talent in magic," Dustin said. "It'd be a shame if she stopped."

"See?" the demon lord asked and glared at Mina. "We have to make her as strong as possible. Cutting her magic lessons won't achieve anything."

Mina ignored her husband and said to Dustin, "How I raise my children is none of your concern."

Dustin's chest tightened. "Tafel became my concern when I was entrusted to teach her."

"And now she is no longer your pupil. You don't have to worry about her affairs any longer."

Dustin opened his mouth to speak but stopped when Mina raised her hand. "Thank you for teaching her, but you should leave now," she said. "Of course, the request will be counted as fulfilled and you can retrieve your reward at the guild."

Dustin gritted his teeth and nodded. "Then I bid you farewell," he said. He bowed before turning to leave.

The demon lord turned to his wife after Dustin left and asked, "Did Dustin do something?" There was a mischievous glint in his eyes, and his lips had a slight smirk on them.

"Have Prim take care of Tafel," Mina said as her expression darkened. "I need to lie down for a bit."

***

The Red Blade Adventurers stopped in front of a small wooden cabin on a cliff overlooking the ocean. The sun was setting, casting a red hue over the sky and sea. They had traveled for weeks after reporting the zombie outbreak and turning in their Fountain of Youth mission.

"This is the place," Aran said. He strode up the porch steps and knocked on the door. A crash resounded in the cabin and smoke billowed out of a window. Footsteps approached the door, and the hinges creaked as the door swung open. A human wearing a blue conical hat and striped, pink boxers opened the door. He had no hair anywhere on his body, and the outlines of his bones could be seen against his skin. There were dark bags underneath his eyes, and his face was smudged with ash. Aran stared at the man with his mouth open. The man stared back for a second before he closed the door.

"W-wait," Aran said. "We're adventurers seeking passage into Fuselage."

The door stopped just before it shut. The door opened, and the man smiled, revealing a mouth of missing and blackened teeth. "Why didn't you say so earlier?" the man asked. "How many of you this time? Six? Ah, there are even two women." He grinned at Sophie and Claire. "Not many of those where you're going."

Sophie shivered. "Are you Charon?"

"Indeed. Never liked that nickname. My old name was a lot better," the man said as he sighed. "Do you know the rules?"

"We completed the fifteen SSS-ranked missions," Aran said and nodded.

"Not those rules. If you didn't do that, you wouldn't be here," Charon said and shook his head while clicking his tongue. "Youngsters these days, not so bright. Once you go to Fuselage, you can't come back unless you do five missions there. And if you want to go back to Fuselage, then it's another 15 missions here."

The Red Blade Adventurers exchanged glances with each other before nodding.

"Is that all?" Aran asked.

"Just one more thing," Charon said and smiled as he stuck out his hand. His fingernails were an inch long and yellow. "Give me all the gold you have—you won't be needing it over there."

The Red Blade Adventurers frowned, but removed their leather pouches and handed them over. "So that's why you're called Charon," Claire muttered.

"Good, good. Now stand there in that circle of stones," Charon said, ignoring Claire's comment. The adventurers did as asked, and Charon clapped his hands together once. A ring of light emerged from the stones and engulfed the group. When it faded, the adventurers were gone.

Charon weighed the leather pouches in his hands and frowned. "So little," he muttered as he entered his cabin.

***

The light had blinded Sophie, causing her to close her eyes. When she opened them again, she discovered that the group was on a cliff. It was similar to the one they were just on, but the grass was purple, and the trees were gnarled and black with red nettles hanging off their branches. The sun couldn't be seen, but the land and sky was lit up with a purple light.

"It looks like we made it," Zeke said. He inhaled through his nose while stretching his arms towards the sky and coughed. "Ah, the sweet smell of sulfur. Just what I was looking forward to."

"There's a town over there. It must be Fuselage," Zul said as he pointed towards a small settlement with a semi-spherical, blue barrier covering it. There was a black road in the purple grass leading towards the town. The Red Blade Adventurers looked at each other and nodded before taking their first steps along the path.

***

Vur sat next to Lindyss while cuddling Snuffles. They were once again in the lower section of the arena, waiting behind the metal gate. Vur asked, "This is my last match, right?"

"Yes. Use your dragon magic and stop hiding your aura once you're out there," Lindyss said as she petted Snuffles. Over the weeks, she grew strangely attached to the fluffy boar. "Although they probably don't want to keep you here, it won't hurt to show off your strength once in a while." Lindyss showed her fangs as she smiled. Vur nodded.

"Today is a special day folks. The ninety-nine-time winner, the devourer, will be fighting his last match here today regardless of whether he wins or loses. His opponent will be a cerberus which was tamed by our very own tribe chieftain. The cerberus is a three-headed monstrosity with the ability to manipulate hell fire. Its speed is unmatched, and it took a raid of twenty-four of our strongest warriors to weaken it enough to be tamed. It has been starved for three days, and it will be out for blood!"

The crowd hissed and thumped their tails against the floor. The arena shook, and dust fell from the ceiling above Vur and Lindyss. "She's really firing them up today," Lindyss said. "They're expecting a long, drawn-out, bloody battle. Make sure to disappoint them."

The gates opened, and Vur dashed out. His eyes flashed with a golden light, and a sky-blue, web-like pattern of runes spread from his forehead down to his toes. The cerberus that had been charging at Vur stopped and growled as its hackles rose into the air, making it seem twice as large. Its body was pitch-black, and its three heads had round, red eyes. Its teeth were as long as Vur's hands and two tails pointed at the sky. The audience fell silent as an invisible pressure descended, their bodies tensing. The atmosphere was suffocating, and a few snakemen gasped as they tried to breathe.

The cerberus' eyes shone, and a halo made of black flames surrounded its body. It roared, causing the ring to expand and crash against the walls of the arena, setting them ablaze. The naga and lamia sitting in the first rows let out screams as the magic shielding them from the cerberus' sight was destroyed, and they scrambled away from the spreading flames. Vur had crossed his arms and disrupted the halo as it crashed into him. His eyes flashed golden, and the black flames on his arms crystallized, dropping to the ground.

Vur let out a roar that caused the audiences' ears to ring and charged towards the cerberus while unsheathing Lust. The cerberus' body tensed as it pounced towards Vur. Vur's eyes glowed once again, and a dome of purple surrounded the cerberus while it was in midair. Its eyes widened as it crashed to the floor, causing a shockwave to spread out in the sand. It raised its head and stiffened. Vur was standing over it with his dagger raised.

"Stop!" a voice called out, and Vur turned towards the voice with his eyes still shining. The naga that spoke was the chieftain of the tribe, and he shivered when he met Vur's gaze. His throat pulsed as he swallowed and said, "You win." Phoenix downs were expensive, and he didn't want to use one if he didn't have to. Besides, if the cerberus died and was resurrected by the item, its abilities would lower. Only a proper white mage could resurrect someone without consequences.

Vur's eyes stopped glowing, and the runes surrounding his body faded away. The dome above the cerberus was lifted, and it rolled over while whimpering, exposing its belly.

"The w-winner is the devourer!" the lamia announcer said. Her face was pale, and goosebumps decorated her skin. The audience let out a collective sigh as Vur returned to Lindyss' side.

Lindyss smiled at Vur who was yawning. "Good job," she said. "Are you ready to go home?"

9

"What is that?" A demon adventurer shielded his eyes from the sun with his hand and peered into the distance. The other adventurers finished decapitating the zombies they were fighting before turning to look. The plains were still scorched, the grass blackened, and corpses littered the ground. Vultures circled the sky, and their feasting figures could be seen all over the plains like strange crops growing out of bodies.

"It looks like a cloud of ash?" another adventurer asked.

A shiver ran down Doofus' spine, and he called for his students to retreat.

"What's going on?" Gabriel asked. His short body was a mess: his mace dripped with ichor, his clothes were spattered with dried blood, his black hair was matted and disheveled. There were tiny horns just beginning to sprout from his temples. The smile on his face vanished when he noticed his classmates' grim expressions.

"I don't know," Doofus said and frowned, "but it's not good. We're pulling back to Traurig." The students didn't complain as they headed back to the north—they were all tired from fighting and none of them were in the mood to speak after partaking in the slaughter. Although they were only fighting zombies, nothing they had done previously had mentally prepared them for killing something so human. They trudged past adventurers heading towards the plains, coming from Traurig, and soon the fortified city was in sight.

Back on the plains, adventurers were still killing zombies, ignoring the cloud of ash in the distance. "Is it getting bigger?" a white mage asked after causing a zombie to disintegrate with holy magic.

"Something doesn't seem right about that," a man said, wiping the ichor off his blade with a dirty rag. "I'm going back." A few voices murmured in agreement.

The cloud grew larger as time passed, and more adventurers chose to leave. "Do you feel that?" a woman with a rapier asked. A circle of rotting corpses lay around her. The grass trembled as the earth shook. Flecks of ash bounced off the ground like jumping fleas.

"It's cavalry!" an archer shouted as he ran north. The remaining adventurers turned towards the cloud and stiffened. Tiny figures—black horses with riders—were rapidly approaching. The sounds of hooves resounded as thousands of skeletal horses charged, their bones rattling as their skeletal riders urged them forward. The adventurers turned to run, throwing spells and traps into the distance, but the wave of riders didn't stop.

Screams sounded out in the air as the horsemen caught up to the slower adventurers. "I'm too pretty to die!" a man shouted as he was engulfed by the sea of bones. Everywhere the horsemen went, the living and zombies alike were turned into bloody paste. The flood or bones only came to a halt after it reached the edges of the charred plains.

The leader of the undead horsemen was a black skeleton wearing a mithril helmet and riding a six-legged skeletal beast. It pointed towards the east with its bloody spear, and the flood turned before resuming its charge. The bodies of the fallen adventurers twitched as a group of liches rode through the carnage and reanimated them, stitching the shattered bones back together.

***

A messenger stood in front of the king, reading from a scroll. The contents described the brutality of the undead: how they slaughtered everything with impunity, how they swept through villages bordering the wilderness, how they reanimated demons and humans alike to increase the size of their army.

When the messenger finished listing the towns destroyed, he was dismissed by the king who had a weary look on his face. Behind the king, wearing a white robe, Gale stood with his body trembling.

"Something must be done about this," Gale said as he clenched his fists. His brown hair reached just above his watering, blue eyes. His frame was thin, and his knuckles were white from grasping his metal staff. "The people are suffering. Let me lead the charge, Your Highness."

The king nodded and the fat underneath his neck jiggled. "Very well, I'll entrust you with the operation, Archbishop Gale. You may act with my authority."

"Thank you, Your Highness," Gale said and bowed his head before leaving the throne room, heading for the church. All members of the clergy were white mages, a class adept at dealing with undead through holy magic. The enforcers of the church also included paladins—warriors with the ability to use light magic. With these people, Gale didn't believe he'd lose to a mob of unruly undead.

***

Tafel sat beside her father as he stamped a piece of paper. She frowned at the word "approved" that appeared in bright-red ink. She could clearly see the title of the paper from where she was sitting. It read, "Armistice between our two nations."

"Won't the humans attack us?" Tafel asked her father. Her second pair of horns had already grown as long as her first pair. They curved over her head and pointed behind her. Red and blue lights lit the horns from the inside and traveled along their lengths.

The demon lord shook his head. "Although our hatred for each other runs deep, the undead is a greater threat to both of us. Of course, we won't send in our full strength; we'll send just enough to make it seem like we're helping. I'm sure the humans are doing the same."

Tafel frowned but thought it made sense. "But the humans never offered us a peace treaty like this before. A coalition army of this size, can it work?"

"Stop worrying about stuff like that and come eat your food before it gets cold," her mother said, appearing at the doorway to the study. "This is what happens when you fill her head with magic and warfare."

"Your mother's right. You shouldn't worry about these things," her father said in a monotonous voice. "You're just a child after all."

"I'm almost six," Tafel said and pouted.

"You're almost a child then," her mother said. "Now come along."

Tafel made a face as she left her father's side. *I'll show them,* she thought as she closed the door to the study. She didn't need Dustin to teach her. She was a genius. Losing Dustin's guidance was just a minor setback.

***

"Mama! Grimmy! I'm home!"

At the entrance to the valley, demarcated by white boulders with ore veins running through them, Vur waited with Lindyss behind him and Snuffles on his head and shoulders. His skin was tanned from the desert sun, but Lindyss' remained unchanged, her face as pale as the moon in the sky. The basilisk and the bats had returned to the Fountain of Youth to rest. Lindyss wanted to hide away as well, but Vur insisted she come with him, threatening to tell Sera bad things about her if she left. The grass within the valley glowed with a silver light, and shining herb patches of all colors speckled the silver landscape. The ground shook, causing the colors to shimmer within the moonlight. Voices echoed through the valley, startling some birds into flight.

"Vur's back?"

"He's really back!"

"I knew he'd be okay."

Five figures flew into the sky, coming from different mountain tops, and landed in the valley. The grass was pressed to the ground from the wind. Like the herbs, Lindyss lowered herself to the floor, kneeling and lowering her head.

The golden dragon with red eyes was the first to speak while the others examined Vur. "Don't think I didn't notice you called for Grimmy and not me," Vernon said as he blew a puff of smoke at Vur.

Vur giggled and batted away the smoke with his hands. "I missed you too, Papa," he said. His dark-brown hair with multiple braids at the ends swayed with the movement.

"Ah, does this mean I'm going to have to start hunting again?" Grimmy asked and sighed. His eyes closed as he shook his head and lay prone on the grass. "What a pain."

Leila nuzzled Grimmy's neck with her silver snout. "Don't act like you weren't the one who missed him the most," she said and turned towards Vur. "He burned down who knows how many towns and convinced the liches to invade the humans because he was upset, you know? I missed you, child. Welcome home."

"Are you wearing pants?" Prika asked and blinked. She poked the black leather with her talon, careful not to cut it.

Sera smacked away Prika's claw and picked Vur up before nuzzling her cheek against his body. "Don't ever disappear on me again. Do you know how worried I was about you?" she asked. "Have you been well?"

"Yeah! Auntie Lindyss took me to lots of places. She fed me to a miro, threw me into an antlion pit, and sold me to the nagas," Vur said with a smile. He stuck his tongue out at Lindyss as all the dragons turned to stare at her.

Lindyss' hands started to sweat. She cleared her throat as she raised her head, still kneeling. "H-hey, Grimmoldesser, long time no see," she said and did a small wave with her hand.

Grimmy blinked and raised his head off the ground to stare down at her face. "It's you! The little bat," he said. "I'm surprised you're still alive."

For now, Lindyss thought as sweat rolled down her back. "Thanks for the vote of confidence," she said. An awkward laugh escaped from her lips as she fixed her hair. "I see you're still well. You found yourself a mate?"

"Who's she?" Leila asked Grimmy, raising an eyebrow.

"She's an elf I used to roam with."

"Roam, eh?" Leila asked, her expression neutral.

Grimmy laughed and looked away.

"What's this about selling my baby to the nagas?" asked Sera as she glared at Lindyss. Smoke drifted out of the sky-blue dragon's nostrils.

"Ah, that must've been a misunderstanding," Lindyss said as she winked at Vur. "Right?"

"Nope. She made me her servant and then sold me to the rich man."

Lindyss fell onto her face. "Are you trying to get me killed!?" she asked, raising her head and grabbing the strands of grass in front of herself, tearing them out by their roots.

"No, no. It's just training," Vur said, echoing back the words he heard from her many times.

A vein popped up on Lindyss' forehead. *This brat.* She took in a deep breath and pursed her lips. How was she going to explain this to the angry dragon?

"How much did you sell him for?" Prika asked.

Aren't you asking the wrong kinds of questions? Lindyss thought but said, "Three hundred red crystals."

"She's lying. She bet on me every time and has close to a billion red crystals," Vur said. He counted with his fingers. "That's like ten thousand green crystals."

"You want to take not only my life, but my fortune too!?"

Prika nodded her head and scratched her chin. She hummed. "One billion red crystal's not too bad of a dowry I guess."

103

Everyone, including Snuffles, stared at Prika.

"What?" she asked, curling her tail. Her chest puffed out as she sat on her hind legs and folded her arms over her chest. "She has to take responsibility for her actions, right?"

"What's a dowry?" Vur asked, tilting his head.

"It's a gift that someone gives you when they've troubled you," Sera replied while glaring at Prika.

"Oh. She already gave me a dowry then. She gave me Lust and put a ring on me," Vur said.

Lindyss buried her face in her hands.

Prika's eyes twinkled. "Do you have anything to say about that?" she asked, her smile widening.

"Nothing. Nothing at all," Lindyss mumbled with her face still in her hands. "I've come to the conclusion that it's best if I stop talking."

Grimmy laughed and his tail thumped against the ground, causing the valley to shake. "You have a never-ending fountain of water, yet you're still this thirsty," he said with a grin on his face.

Leila smacked his snout. "Don't use that kind of language in front of Vur."

"It's fine, it's fine. He's too young to understand anyway," Grimmy said while rubbing his nose. The ground continued to rumble as he chuckled.

Sera coughed. "Well, I'd like to know how Vur ended up in your care," she said to Lindyss.

"He came into my home one day and fell asleep after scaring my basilisk to death. I found out his control over magic was just as horrendous as his manners"—Lindyss glared at Grimmy—"so I decided to teach him out of respect for Grimmoldesser."

"What exactly is your relationship with Grimmy?" Leila asked.

Lindyss pursed her lips and stared at the ground. The moonlight shone on her, causing her hair to cast shadows over half her face. Her lips trembled. "Grimmy...," she said and sighed. "Grimmy was my light when everything was dark. He was the moon that lit up my night. He brought warmth to my heart when it was cold. I—"

Grimmy flicked her forehead. "Stop messing around; she'll take you seriously."

Lindyss rubbed her eyes and clutched her chest while turning her head to the side. "Even now you reject me, my lo—. Okay, okay, I'll stop," she said while waving her arms in front of herself. "Don't shoot."

Grimmy closed his mouth and glared at her, black smoke billowing out of the corners of his mouth.

Lindyss sighed. "You were much more fun before you got hitched," she said and faced Leila. "Serious answer. He stole my prey and then performed unspeakable experiments on me that had lasting effects to this day. In the end, he became my best friend."

"Wow. Your taste in friends is terrible," Prika said. "Don't worry though. You'll become my best friend once you become my goddaughter."

Lindyss sighed.

"Stop sidetracking her," Sera said, poking Prika's ribs, "and let her finish her story."

"I taught him how to control his mana and helped teach him new skills since he's a blue mage," Lindyss said.

"She shot me with lightning bolts and fire balls and ice spears and dark orbs," Vur said while nodding.

"That's because he drank the whole fountain!" She rose to her feet and clutched the hem of her dress with both hands.

"Ah, such a petty reason," Grimmy said while clicking his tongue. "Oh, how the mighty have fallen."

Lindyss stamped her foot. "You!" she said and then sighed. "You're right. He reminded me too much of you; I couldn't help but tease him a bit."

"Oh? So she used to tease you, dear?" Leila asked as she rested her claw on Grimmy's shoulder.

Grimmy snorted and stroked Leila's cheek with his claw. "You're the only one for me."

Lindyss stared at the two dragons who were gazing into each other's eyes with faint smiles on their faces. "Oh, how the mighty have fallen," she echoed.

Prika sighed. "I wish I had a mate."

***

"They retreated? What do you mean they retreated?" Gale asked the demon standing in front of him. The archbishop was wearing a robe, threaded with blue lines of refined mithril. In his right hand, there was a blue metal staff, and in his left hand, there was a white book with golden inscriptions on the cover. His holy army had just arrived at the makeshift camp set up in the charred plains. Simple wooden stakes were hammered into the ground at an angle, specially made to trip up cavalry. On one side of the camp, dozens of tents with white coverings were arranged in a rectangular formation. On the other side, purple tents were arranged in a spiral pattern.

Dustin shrugged, his gaze roaming over Gale's attire. It was similar to his own, but the demon wasn't holding any weapons or books. "The cavalry stopped riding and pulled back into the forest," Dustin replied. The two leaders of the armies stared at each other before Gale stuck out his hand. Dustin raised an eyebrow and paused before grasping it.

Gale had ordered his men to leave first and coordinate with the demons. It was his first time meeting their leader. "I appreciate your help coming out here. I wasn't sure what to expect when I sent that letter."

"Please. Our lord isn't as unyielding as your king," Dustin said and snorted. *We're all allies in the end.*

Gale nodded. He did think His Majesty was a bit stubborn at times. "We should maintain vigilance for at least a month," Gale said, judging Dustin's reaction. The demon's expression

106

didn't change. "That's how long it'll take before our mages can finish purifying the land."

"Why wait and defend? Why not take the fight to them?" Dustin asked with a smile that didn't reach his eyes.

Gale frowned. "We only need to destroy their cavalry to prevent another invasion. There shouldn't be enough corpses for them to reanimate once they're gone."

"And if they refuse to come out until we leave?" Dustin asked. "Destroy their source and we never have to worry about being invaded again."

"The consequences are too large if we fail. Not only do we not wipe them out, we also increase their numbers," Gale said and shook his head. "All the top-ranked adventurers are in Fuselage. We can't guarantee a victory."

Dustin nodded. "You're right," he said and clapped his hand on Gale's shoulder. The demon's expression softened. "It would've been nice to have adventured with someone as level-headed as you. If you were going to make a rash decision, I might've eliminated you." He chuckled.

Gale nodded, glad to have passed the demon's test. "It would be nice if we could build a fortress here maintained by both our races."

"Maybe one day in the future our people could forget their differences, but there's too much hatred right now. You can see it in their eyes," Dustin said and gestured towards the humans and demons resting behind them. "It'll be a long time until then."

Gale rubbed his chin. The tension between the humans and the demons was palpable. His eyebrow raised as he faced Dustin and said, "But I don't see it in your eyes."

"Because I've been to Fuselage," the demon said, his expression empty.

***

Lindyss stood next to Grimmy on a cliff overlooking a horde of skeletons riding into a marsh. The trees within the marsh were oozing black sap, and their leaves—the few that existed—were blood-red and pointed. The ground was brackish, occasional bubbles rising to the surface and popping, releasing wisps of black smoke. The skeletons dismounted on top of the marsh, letting their bodies sink into the ground along with their steeds. They disappeared without a trace.

"Why'd you call them back?" Grimmy asked.

"Nothing good comes from bothering the humans," Lindyss said and rolled her eyes. "The undead are our buffer in case they ever invade. They shouldn't be sent out because someone got a little angry."

Grimmy snorted. "I made them. I can do what I want with them."

"Technically, I made them. You just gave me the power," Lindyss said with a smile.

"Same thing."

"Just let me get the little victories, alright? You're a dragon; stop being so petty."

Grimmy snorted again and nuzzled his snout against her, wrinkling her black dress. "I missed you."

"I missed you too," Lindyss said and sighed, "but there really was no other option."

"Are you better now?" Grimmy asked as he crawled onto his stomach.

Lindyss sat down and leaned her body into the crevice between his neck and shoulder. "In a decade or two, I should be fully healed. It's gotten to the point where I can stand in the sun without having my skin fall off, but I still lose my mana," she said as she stretched her right hand towards the moon.

Grimmy fell silent as Lindyss lowered her arm, placing it on the dragon's body.

"I'm sorry."

"Don't be. I wouldn't be here right now if it weren't for you," Lindyss said as she sighed and closed her eyes. The heat coming off the dragon coursed through her body and warmed her back. She had missed this feeling.

10

Needles clinked. Colors flashed. Wool stitched. Lindyss pursed her lips and raised the child-sized sweater in front of her face. It was blue with the image of a large-headed bat stitched into the center. She sighed and placed it into her lap, folding it before placing it on the pile of woolen clothes by her rocking chair. The chair tilted backwards as Lindyss sank into it. She wasn't sure why she bothered knitting sweaters for Vur when he never wore them or completely destroyed them after romping through the wilderness for a day.

Thumping sounds drew Lindyss' attention towards her closed door. A low-pitched whine droned through her ears, and seconds later, there was a clawing noise. Had Vur come to visit? She stood up and smoothed out the wrinkles in her blood-red dress before tucking her light-brown hair behind her pointed ears. Her heels clacked against the ground as she sauntered towards the door. As expected, her basilisk was outside, staring at her with puppy eyes and a frown on its face. A slight smile appeared on the corner of her lips but quickly disappeared. It seemed like Vur really was here. The basilisk ran into her room and curled up on her bed when she stepped outside, refusing to follow after its master.

The sounds of bats squealing rang through the air as Lindyss walked up the stairs. She bit the inside of her lower lip. How many times had she told Vur to not harass the bats? She reached the top of the stairs and crossed her arms over her chest. Vur was chasing after a bat, a gleam in his eyes. As the bat made a turn, he lunged and soared through the air, grabbing its body in a way that wouldn't hurt it. It squealed louder as it struggled and bit at his hand. Lindyss sighed and asked, "Can I help you?"

Vur hugged the squirming bat. "Hi, Auntie," he said, ignoring the tiny blood droplets oozing out of his fingers. "I want more books."

"I don't have anymore."

"What about those books you said I couldn't read?"

"You still can't read them. Ask the elves for theirs."

"But I read all the elves' books," Vur said and pouted. "They told me to ask you."

"Did you really?"

"Uh-huh. I even read the boring ones too," Vur said and crinkled his nose. "Why would they make a book on plants?"

Lindyss' brow furrowed as she tapped her feet against the floor. She rubbed her chin and stared at the ceiling. The human-shaped holes still hadn't been repaired. In fact, the bats had used them as new sleeping quarters. Lindyss exhaled and crossed her arms over her chest before meeting Vur's expectant gaze. "I know where we can get more books, but we'll have to ask your parents."

"You're the best, Auntie."

***

Tafel bit her lip as she pushed her peas to the side of the plate with her fork. Her mother didn't even look up from her food while saying, "Eat your peas."

Tafel made a face as she stabbed one with her fork, eliciting a clink from her plate. Gabriel and Lamach were away from the castle, living in their school. Maybe they were still fighting zombies. Since they weren't home, all her mother's complaints had fallen onto Tafel instead: her hair was too messy, her dress was too wrinkled, her walking pace was too fast, her hands were too fidgety, her walking pace was too slow. Tafel imagined the pea on her fork was her mother and chomped on it. It still tasted disgusting, but she felt a little better after eating it.

"Eat more elegantly," her mother said. "I know Prim taught you manners. Show them."

Tafel glanced at her father. He chewed on a piece of steak as he held his hands over his plate, a knife and fork in either hand. He hadn't spoken a word since the meal started. His motions were robotic: cut, chew, swallow, repeat. It didn't seem like he was willing to help her this time. Occasionally, he'd spoil her by smuggling books on spells and mana control into her room, but when it came to dealing with his wife, he was willing to let Tafel suffer instead of himself. Tafel sighed as she scooped the remaining peas onto her fork instead of stabbing them.

"Sighing's not ladylike," her mother said. Tafel's eye twitched.

Rapid footsteps sounded from the hallway. Tafel put down her fork as the door burst open. "M-Milord!" a sentry shouted and saluted. "Urgent news!"

Tafel's father frowned as he put down his knife and fork, wiping his lips with his napkin. "Didn't I say no one may interrupt my meals?" he asked. "This is the only time I have to talk to my family."

Tafel resisted the urge to roll her eyes. Her mother would've accused her of being barbaric.

The sentry bowed until his torso was parallel to the floor. "Forgive me, Milord, but there are five dragons in front of the city gates. They demand to speak with you or they'll raze the capital."

Tafel's eyes lit up while her mother's face paled. "Go to your room, Tafel," her mother said.

"Yes, Mother," Tafel said as she slid out of her seat and walked past the sentry, rounding a corner. She glanced behind herself before sneaking off in the opposite direction of her room. There was no way she was going to let a chance like this go.

***

Sweat rolled down the demon lord's neck as a giant golden pair of eyes stared at him, unblinking. A sky-blue dragon was resting her front claws on the city walls, propping up her chin. Her stomach leaned against the wall while her tail curled and uncurled, ruining the fields below. Two humanoid figures were on her head: one sitting, the other standing.

"How may I help you, mighty one?" the demon lord said and lowered his head, staring at his feet. He flinched as a high-pitched voice that sounded like it came from a child rang through the air.

"Books! I want all your books."

The demon lord's face twisted, and he opened his mouth to speak.

"You can't just ask for all their books," Prika said before he could say anything. The demon lord let out a sigh of relief. "I don't want to carry any duplicates," Prika finished. His right eye twitched.

"Come again?" the demon lord asked.

"Are you deaf? Auntie, how can he be the ruler if he's deaf?" Vur asked. "Let's ask her instead." Vur pointed at Tafel who was hiding on the steps leading up to the city walls.

Tafel froze.

"Tafel! What are you doing here!?"

"I wanted to see the dragons," she whispered, unwilling to meet her father's eyes.

Grimmy laughed and stretched his neck to get a better view of the girl. "Aren't you a brave child? Don't you know dragons eat children for breakfast?"

Tafel trembled and collapsed onto her knees before shaking her head back and forth. "Y-you can't eat me then. I-it's dinner time."

Grimmy laughed even harder and thumped his tail against the ground, causing the wall to shake. "Maybe I should kidnap you and save you for breakfast," he said with a grin. Tafel squeaked and curled up into a ball as the dragon's hot breath washed over her.

"Quit teasing the little ones," Leila said and nudged Grimmy's neck.

"Ahem. Sorry about that," Lindyss said and jumped off of Sera's head. She smiled at the demon lord. "We'd appreciate it if you gave us all the books in your royal library. Of course we'll provide fair compensation."

Sweat rolled down the demon lord's back. "I can't do that. The royal library is a collection of all our history and knowledge. If you take it away from us, what will we have left?"

Lindyss' smile widened. "Then it's fine if we use it like a library, right? We'll be sure to come back and return the books once we're done with them," she said as she took a step forward.

The demon lord took a step back. "There's no guarantee you'll return them," he said while shaking his head.

Lindyss continued towards him, her hips swaying. "I'm sure there's some kind of agreement we can come to, don't you think?" she asked while staring into his eyes with a slight pout. Her lips glistened red in the moonlight.

The demon lord swallowed as he maintained his distance by walking backwards and stumbled when his foot hit the edge of the wall. He almost fell over, but Lindyss caught his shoulder and brought her face in front of his. Their noses almost touched. She tiptoed, leaned forward, and whispered into his ear, "You should be careful."

She smiled at him and giggled before pulling away. The demon lord's face was flushed, and his heart threatened to jump out of his chest. He opened his mouth to speak, but nothing came out.

"I'm telling Mom," Tafel said.

Lindyss laughed and sauntered towards Tafel. "Such a cute child," she said while squatting. She ran her fingers through the demon's hair. "You should let the adults talk, okay? You can go play with Vur." Lindyss put her hands underneath Tafel's arms and lifted her up while standing.

114

Tafel screamed as Lindyss lobbed her into the air towards Sera's head. She closed her eyes and curled up into a ball, bracing herself for the pain. Instead, she was caught by a cushion of air and landed soundlessly next to Vur. Sera released the walls and took a few steps back.

"Tafel!" the demon lord yelled. "You witch! I'll have you burned!" He turned towards Lindyss and almost fell over when he saw her standing less than an inch away.

Lindyss beamed as she wrapped her arm around his. "Now, now. Let the children play while we discuss business, alright?"

The demon lord's mind blanked when he saw her smile and nodded with a dazed expression, letting himself be led away.

***

"Wow," Vur said and grabbed Tafel's horns. He moved his hand back and forth, running his fingers over the ridges before asking, "Are these real?"

Tafel nodded and lowered her head, biting her lower lip as her face flushed. "It's very rude to touch someone's horns," she whispered. Prim told her to never let anyone touch her horns unless it was her wedding night.

"Oh, sorry. I didn't know that," Vur said and released her horns. "Why do you have horns?"

Tafel clutched the hem of her dress. "I'm a demon," she said and met Vur's eyes. "Demons have horns. Didn't you know?"

"Eh? Mama said you were a human"—Vur looked down and caught Sera's eye—"and dragons don't lie. Right, Mama?"

Sera snorted which caused Tafel to squeak and fall over. "Humans and demons are the same thing."

Vur nodded. "See," he said and sat down next to Tafel. "I'm Vur. What's your name?"

"Tafel," she replied, staring at his golden, slit eyes. "Are you a human? I've never met one before."

"I'm a dragon," Vur said and stuck his chest out. "I just haven't grown my wings and scales yet."

"Oh. I didn't know dragons looked like this when they're little," Tafel said with her eyes wide.

Vur smiled. "A lot of people don't. Do you want to be my friend?"

Tafel's head bobbed up and down, her hair flying. "Yes. I don't have any friends," she said and looked down. "My mom never lets me out of the house."

"Oooo, what's this?" Prika asked and hung onto Sera's shoulders. "It looks like Lindyss has some competition?" She grinned at the two children on top of Sera's head.

In the guardroom closest to the dragons, Lindyss was sitting across from the demon lord. A piece of paper was laid out on the table separating the two. Lindyss smiled at the demon lord as he lifted the quill in his hand. "So it's agreed then?"

The demon lord nodded as his hand flourished, a gaudy signature appearing on the paper. Lindyss retrieved the paper, blew on the wet ink, and rolled it up while the demon lord spoke, "The boy may freely enter the library and borrow books—but no more than twenty at a time. The dragons will stop destroying our outskirt towns, and Tafel will be returned safely."

"Great," Lindyss said and leaned forward, running her fingers down the side of the demon lord's neck. She tapped his nose with her finger. "It was a pleasure doing business with you."

The demon lord nodded. He gulped as Lindyss sauntered out of the room, giggling as she disappeared around the doorway.

11

Screams echoed through a city as demons rushed into their homes or fell to their knees and clasped their hands. The sun shone overhead, but winged shadows blanketed the ground as a group of dragons roared and sailed through the skies. Plumes of fire filled the air, just inches above the tallest buildings, coming out of a black dragon's mouth. The sound of a dragon's laughter overrode the screams below as a child's voice shouted from atop the dragon's head, "Do it again!"

"Maybe on the way back, we're almost there."

***

Mina was eating lunch, sitting across from her husband and daughter. She brought her fork to her lips as she inspected Tafel's manners—they were impeccable. The child wasn't moping or pushing around her vegetables like she usually did. There were even the hints of a smile on her face as she bit into her peas. Mina's stomach sank as her brow wrinkled. How long had it been since her daughter last smiled? An almost inaudible sigh escaped from her nostrils as she bit the end of her fork.

Her husband raised his head. "What's the matter?"

"Nothing," Mina said after she finished chewing. Her gaze happened to pass over the window. The fork clattered against the table as she froze, eyes wide. "D-dragon."

A second later, a sentry burst into the room and shouted, "Milord! They're back! The dragons are back!"

The demon lord frowned as he said, "It's only been two days." He removed the napkin from his lap and folded it on the table as he stood up.

"Vur's back?" Tafel asked, standing up and pushing in her chair at the same time. "Can I go see him?"

"Absolutely not!" Mina shouted as she regained her composure. Tafel flinched and lowered her head. "He kidnapped you and held you hostage. If it weren't for your father's negotiation, who knows what would've happened. You could've died, young lady."

"It's not like you care," Tafel muttered to herself before raising her head. She pouted. "And all Dad did was flirt wi—"

A violent fit of coughing escaped from the demon lord's mouth. "I think it'd be fine if Tafel came along," he said. "My great-great-great-grandfather believes building a good reputation with the dragons will establish a good foundation for the future."

"Your great-great-great-grandfather's been dead for over a century," Mina said and crossed her arms.

"Well, I know if he were alive now, he'd agree with me," the demon lord said and gestured towards Tafel as he made his way out of the room. "Let's go greet the dragons."

She beamed at him. "Thanks, Dad. You're the best," she said and skipped to his side.

"I'm coming too," Mina said and placed her hands on her hips. "You don't mind, right?"

"Ah, of course not," her husband said with a furrowed brow, "but it's best if we hurry. Shouldn't keep a dragon waiting."

***

"Hi, Tafel," Vur said and waved his hand at the group exiting the building. He was standing next to a trembling guard with a bag filled with books by his side. Grimmy and Prika were nearby, sniffing the buildings and scaring the citizens.

Tafel waved back. "Good afternoon, Vur. You're back so soon" she said and looked around "Is Auntie not here?"

"No, she sleeps when the sun is out," Vur said. "But I brought Snuffles. Snuffles, come here and say hi." Vur waved at the boar who was biting the guard's polearm. Snuffles ran over and oinked at Tafel.

"This is Snuffles," Vur said as he lifted him up. "Mama says he's my son."

"He's so cute," Tafel said and rubbed the boar's head. Snuffles oinked and wiggled his rump.

"Scan," Mina said out of habit, using a standard detection spell on Snuffles. Her face paled as her mouth fell open. Her body tensed as Snuffles glared at her with his dragon-like eyes. He snorted at her, causing her to take a step back.

"What's wrong, dear?" the demon lord asked.

"The boar's stronger than you," she whispered.

The demon lord stiffened. "Tafel, honey. Come here for a second," he said with a strange smile on his face.

"What is it, Dad?"

He whispered, "That boar is very dangerous. You should stay awa—"

"Oink." Snuffles appeared behind Tafel and sniffed her foot. The demon lord jumped back while pulling Tafel towards himself.

"Oink?" Snuffles tilted his head and continued to walk towards the family of demons. They continued to retreat, Tafel struggling and being dragged along by her parents.

"I think they're scared of you, Snuffles," Grimmy said and laughed as his tail swished. It collided against a building, knocking it over with a crash. The black dragon blinked and looked behind himself before addressing the demon lord. "Oops. Accident."

Snuffles whimpered as his eyes glistened. Tears formed in the corner of his eyes as he lowered his head and looked up at Tafel like a puppy. There was a tug on her heart, and she broke out of her father's grasp to embrace the crying boar. "It's okay, Snuffles. I'm not scared of you," she said as she rocked him and patted his back.

Mina stumbled and grabbed her husband for support. "I think I need to lie down. If anything happens to Tafel...," she said and glared at him before staggering away.

The demon lord watched his wife leave before clearing his throat. Before he could say anything, Vur grabbed Tafel's hand and said, "C'mon, let's go to the library." Her face turned red as Vur pulled her along. "You have to show me the good books."

Tafel peeked at her father and noticed he wasn't saying anything. "Okay," she said and nodded while smiling at Vur.

"I know the stories say dragons kidnap princesses, Vur," Prika said with a grin, "but we don't actually do that."

Grimmy nodded at the two children. "We actually prefer to eat them," he said and licked his lips. He blew a puff of smoke out of his nostrils at Tafel.

"Eep!" Tafel squeaked and hid behind Vur.

"He's just kidding," Vur said. "We don't eat humans—Mama says they're bad for digestion, so we have to burn them instead."

"That doesn't make me feel any better," Tafel said with a pale face.

Vur frowned. "I won't let anyone burn you."

"Promise?"

"Promise. Dragons never lie," Vur said as he stuck his chest out. Tafel relaxed and they went to the library with Snuffles in tow.

"The elf isn't here to chaperone this time?" the demon lord asked after Vur and Tafel rounded a corner.

Grimmy snorted. "I don't think Vur would destroy your city if Tafel is close to him," he said. "You don't have to worry about that."

The demon lord broke out into a cold sweat. "I was more worried about his safety, but I see I was a bit foolish," he said. "What level is Vur anyway?"

Grimmy shrugged his shoulders, the motion shaking the ground. "We don't keep track of nonsense like that," he said. "But if I had to classify his strength.... He's probably stronger than your so-called SSS-ranked adventurers."

Vur and Tafel stood outside a massive wooden door inside the castle. Tafel whispered to Vur while fidgeting on the red carpet, causing wrinkles to appear in the silk, "Ask my mom if you can eat dinner with us. If I ask, she'll say no, but if you ask, she'll say yes."

"That's weird, but okay," Vur said and nodded.

Tafel knocked on the door before pushing it open three seconds later. Inside the room, Mina was reading a book, a lamp with a golden crystal acting as a light source on the table beside her. She raised her head and pursed her lips at Vur.

"Hi. Can I eat dinner with you?" Vur asked.

A shiver ran down Mina's spine. "Of course you may," she said. Sweat dripped down her forehead. *How can I refuse?*

"I knew it would work," Tafel said and grabbed Vur's hand. "Let's go wait at the table." They walked to a room with a circular table and five seats lined up against the wall. Tafel pulled out four chairs and placed them under the table. "This is where we usually eat. There's extra chairs because my brothers aren't home."

Vur tilted his head. "Don't the wooden thingies get in the way when you eat?" he asked and pinched a chair. "There's not enough room for the bear."

"Bear?" Tafel asked. "There's no bear? We sit on the chairs and eat the food off the table."

Vur's nose crinkled. "You're like the elf people," he said. "I hate eating like that."

"How do you eat then?"

"First, I break the neck because Grimmy says I shouldn't play with my food. And then I pull off the skin. After that, I eat the meat," Vur said and nodded. He added after a thought, "But I don't like the guts—I feed those to Snuffles."

Tafel's face blanched. "What do you count as ... food?"

"I eat the big bears—the little ones aren't as chewy. Sometimes I eat fruit. In the desert I ate a lot of cacti and

121

scorpions and antlions," Vur said and drooled. He swallowed and stared into Tafel's wide eyes. "Those were really tasty. Have you ever tried antlion?"

Tafel shook her head. "We usually eat a little meat with vegetables," she said in a small voice.

Vur frowned. "I'll take you home and feed you lots of delicious things," he said. "Grimmy says you can't grow big and strong if you don't eat enough."

"Oh," Tafel said and blinked. "I look forward to it." She scratched her head and wondered what an antlion was, but before she could ask, servants brought in plates of food. The two children stepped out of the way as Mina and her husband entered the room, following the butlers and maids. The demon lord was wearing a purple robe with golden embroidery while Mina wore an elegant white dress and heels.

"It's a pleasure to have you for dinner with us, Vur," Mina said with a slight curtsy.

"I know," Vur said and nodded. Mina's face cramped.

Tafel nudged Vur. "You're supposed to say 'the pleasure is all mine,'" she whispered. "My mom's a stickler for etiquette."

"Oh. Oops," Vur said and turned to Mina. "The pleasure is all yours."

Mina sighed and her husband placed his hand on her shoulder. "At least he tried right? Come, let's not worry too much about manners this evening. We're amongst friends," he said and proceeded to take his seat with Mina sitting beside him. Tafel pulled Vur over to the table and sat across from her mother while Vur sat beside her, across from the demon lord. The servants passed out the plates, some trembling as they handed Vur his.

Vur leaned forward, sniffed the steak in front of himself, and poked it with his finger. Mina stared at him, hands white from gripping her utensils too hard. Tafel saw her mother looking like she wanted to stab Vur, so she nudged her friend's shoulder. "You're supposed to use the fork and knife," she
122

whispered and made sawing motions with her knife, "like this. See?"

Vur observed Tafel as she cut the steak with her knife before he moved his hands to mimic her. He stabbed the fork into the meat, and a shattering sound resounded through the room. Cracks spread along the plate, causing it to break into dozens of pieces. Tafel's mouth fell open, and her father stopped moving. Mina paled as her hands and lips trembled. Vur tilted his head and shrugged before proceeding to cut the steak with his knife. There was a sawing noise, and a line of gouged-out wood could be seen after Vur lifted the steak.

"Honey, don't you think it'd be better if Vur sat on the floor?" Mina asked.

"Are you kidding me?" the demon lord whispered back. "It's easy to replace this table, but you can't say the same about the floor."

"You can't make Vur sit on the floor; he's a guest," Tafel said. "Prim says we have to treat our guests with courtesy and respect."

Mina smiled. "Yes, of course. Silly me for suggesting such a thing," she said as her teeth ground together. "Please forget I even mentioned it, Vur."

"Mentioned what?" Vur asked. He grabbed the rest of the uncut steak, folded it, and ate it in one bite.

Mina just stared and shook her head. "Never mind," she said with an exhale. Her temples throbbed.

The demon lord coughed. "So," he said. "What did you two do today, Tafel?"

"We went to the library, and Vur read me stories," Tafel said. "Did you know that Vur can read elvish? All the scribes and librarians sat down to listen too."

Mina raised an eyebrow at Vur who was still chewing with his cheeks bulging like a chipmunk. "Really? I wouldn't have expected that."

Vur swallowed and a huge bulge traveled down his throat. "Auntie says I'm very smart because I ate lots of fruits of knowledge," he said while nodding.

"Really!?" Tafel asked, her eyes lighting up. "Is the tree really as big as the stories say it is? What did they taste like? Can you get me some?"

Vur shook his head, causing Tafel's expression to dim. "The tree was very big. The fruit tasted sweet, but not as good as bear meat," he said. "I can't get you any because I knocked the tree down, so there's no more fruit."

"That was your fault?" the demon lord asked. He had received a report saying the Tree of Knowledge no longer existed when he inquired earlier to obtain a fruit for Tafel. His face paled when he recalled what Grimmy had told him: He's stronger than your so-called SSS-ranked adventurers.

"It wasn't my fault. It was the tree's fault for being too weak," Vur said and pouted, "but I got blamed anyway."

"I see," the demon lord said while nodding. "Yes, it was the tree's fault. You're not to blame. I completely agree with you."

"Vur also told me stories about his home. Can I go visit?" Tafel asked.

"No!" Mina yelled, causing everyone to stare at her. She cleared her throat. "I mean, no, sweetie, you wouldn't want to impose on the dragons. I'm sure they're busy doing dragon things."

"Not really. We usually just sleep all day after hunting," Vur said. "Although I started reading a lot recently. I think it'll be a lot of fun if Tafel came to play."

"I think it should be fine as long as I go with her," the demon lord said and stroked his chin. Tafel smiled, dimples appearing on her cheeks.

Mina's expression softened as she turned her head away from her daughter. She glared at her husband and asked, "Does this have anything to do with that pretty elf lady?"

124

His face reddened. "Of course not. It would be rude to refuse an invitation from a dragon," he said. "I'm just making sure Tafel stays safe."

"Nonsense. What if something happens to you two? Who will lead the country?" Mina asked.

"Oh, don't worry about that. Nothing will happen to them," Vur said and patted his chest, leaving a greasy stain on his skin. "Dragon's honor."

12

Tafel peered over the edge of Grimmy's head, balancing on all fours. She was wearing brown leather pants and a woolen blue sweater. Her lips pursed as she turned her head to face Vur. "Will my father be okay?" she asked and looked over the edge again. Grimmy was stationary, but he yawned, causing Tafel to squeal and crawl over to Vur's side at the center of the black dragon's head. Beside them, Prika was laughing with Snuffles sleeping on her head.

"He should be fine," Vur said with a nod. "Grimmy's only dropped his prey once or twice before."

"Please don't refer to me as prey," a voice called out from one of Grimmy's claws. "I'm frightened enough as is."

The demon lord had thought he would be standing on the dragon's head or back, but Grimmy had snorted and refused. "Not just anyone can ride a dragon," he had said and picked the demon lord up with his claws.

"Be careful," Mina said from the city walls. Her face was pale as the dragons spread their wings and leapt into the sky. A scream resounded through the air, but it faded away as Grimmy got further and further away from the city. Mina sighed as she turned around to face the capital. She wanted to stop Tafel from going to the dragons' roost, but she knew her husband wasn't going to yield. He was always adamant when it came to Tafel's future as a demon lord. *Stay safe*, Mina thought and closed her eyes as her hands clenched the hem of her purple dress.

***

Tafel hugged Vur's right arm, admiring the scenery below. "This is amazing, but a little scary," she said with her eyes wide open. "Everything looks so small. Is that a roc? It's so tiny."

126

Vur nodded. "Do you want to eat it?"

Tafel's mouth fell open, and she shook her head. Eat a roc? Rocs were kings of the sky on the same level as wyverns and phoenixes—which were all second to dragons. The roc noticed the two dragons flying overhead and dove towards the ground, fleeing under the cover of nearby trees.

"It's a little chilly," Tafel said and shivered.

"Sit behind me so the wind doesn't blow on you," Vur said.

Tafel shook her head and hugged Vur's arm tighter. "I'm afraid to move," she whispered. "I don't like heights."

Vur blinked and turned his body while lifting Tafel into the air. She closed her eyes and screamed, but she stopped when something solid pressed against her back. Her eyes opened, giving her a view of Grimmy's wings and tail with the sky and ground visible behind them. She was sitting on Vur's lap leaning against his body as he sheltered her from the wind. Tafel's face reddened as she squirmed.

"I told your mom I wouldn't let anything happen to you," Vur said. "I can't let you get cold." Tafel let out a small sound as she lowered her head and hugged Vur's arm tighter, ceasing her struggles.

The demon lord sneezed. Tears streamed from his eyes as the wind buffeted his face. *I hope Tafel's not too scared,* he thought as he tried to readjust his body. His arms were pressed to his sides, and one of Grimmy's claws was uncomfortably close to his neck.

"Quit squirming around or I might drop you," Grimmy said and snorted. "Not that I'd mind."

Tafel watched as city after city, town after town, trees and mountain ranges, vast oceans of green and gold passed before her eyes. Water pooled in her eyes and she smiled, sniffling as a tear ran down her cheek.

"Are you crying?" Vur asked. "Is it still too cold?"

Tafel shook her head and leaned her head on his shoulder as she turned to face him. "I'm happy," she said with a choked voice. "Thanks for being my friend."

Vur's heart jumped as he stared into her purple eyes. "You're welcome," he said and turned his head away with red cheeks. Tafel blinked and then giggled.

Prika turned her head and grinned at the two children. "Doesn't that just make your heart warm, Snuffles?" she asked her sleeping flying companion. Snuffles continued to snore.

***

"Don't worry, dear," Vernon said to the sky-blue dragon who was pacing around inside the cave. "I'm sure they'll be back soon."

"I'm going with them next time," Sera said with her teeth bared. "It shouldn't take more than a few hours to borrow books."

"Maybe Vur's exploring. Grimmy and Prika are with him—they wouldn't let him get hurt," Vernon said.

Sera stopped pacing as her tail perked up. Her head whipped around towards the cave entrance. "They're back," she said and exhaled while spreading her wings. She flew out of the cave and into the green valley. Two specks in the sky grew larger while Sera waited, sitting on her haunches. Leila and Vernon appeared next to Sera, watching the incoming dragons with her.

The first thing Prika said when she landed was, "Vur kidnapped the princess." The red dragon lowered her head and let Snuffles climb down. "He stole her heart too."

Grimmy slowed his descent before landing heavily on his hind legs. "And father," he added as he opened his claw, dropping the demon lord to the ground.

"O ground. I never realized how much I loved you," the demon said as he collapsed onto his knees, tears falling from his eyes. "Please, don't leave me again."

"You two love birds can get off now," Prika said.

Vur and Tafel were still holding each other. Tafel squirmed. "You should let go now," she whispered with a red face.

"I like sitting like this," Vur said and yawned. Tafel lowered her head and stopped squirming, leaning against him instead.

"What exactly happened?" Leila asked Grimmy as the black dragon crawled onto his stomach.

"Vur wanted to play with Tafel and the demon didn't want her going alone, so he came too," Grimmy replied as he yawned.

"Isn't it bad if we remove the demon lord from the capital?" Leila asked and frowned at the disheveled man kissing the earth. "Won't that be taken as a sign of aggression?"

"It's fine, it's fine. I didn't drop him," Grimmy said and closed his eyes.

Leila sighed.

***

Lindyss was sleeping when a basilisk jumped onto her bed and hid underneath her blanket, shoving her onto the floor with its bulky body. Seconds later, a voice called out while she was rubbing her bleary eyes.

"Auntie, the deaf man came to see you."

Lindyss cursed at the shivering basilisk as she stood up and opened her closet. She took off her pajamas and slipped on a red robe before fixing her hair in the mirror hanging on the closet's door. She put on one of the many pairs of high heels laying around and walked up the stairs.

"Why are they here?" she asked when she reached the top. Vur was holding Tafel's hand and the demon lord was standing behind the two with flowers in his hands.

"He said he wanted to tell you something, so I brought him here," Vur said and tugged Tafel's arm, bringing her towards the entrance. "Let's go play with the bats."

"Did you miss me that much?" Lindyss asked the demon lord while raising an eyebrow. Back at the capital, she had used a simple seduction skill. She thought it would've worn off by now.

"Ah, n-no. It's just that I never got to properly introduce myself to you the last time we met," the demon replied and bowed his head. "My name is Zollstock the Fifth—demon lord with a subclass of warrior."

"Surely you didn't come all this way just to introduce yourself to me," Lindyss said. "Did you want to drink from the fountain? I'm afraid it's running quite dry these days, so the price will be a lot higher than usual."

"No, I wouldn't dare to drink from your precious fountain," Zollstock said as he offered her the flowers he was holding. "Please accept this."

Lindyss raised an eyebrow. "This is a pitiful dowry if you're trying to marry your daughter off to Vur," she said as she received the flowers.

"That's not what this is!" Zollstock said, his body stiffening. He cleared his throat. "This—"

"I'm just messing with you," Lindyss whispered as she stepped closer and put a finger on his lips. The demon lord's eyes widened and rolled up, revealing their whites. He fell to the floor, unconscious.

Lindyss channeled mana to her finger and placed it against his forehead. She stripped off his outer garments and dragged his body into a corner of the mini-boss room.

"What are you doing to my dad?" Tafel asked as she watched from the entrance, hugging an exhausted bat to her chest.

"He was tired, so I decided to give him a nice dream," Lindyss said with a smile.

"Why'd you take his clothes off?"

"He said he was hot," Lindyss said. "You two should go out and play."

"But—"

Vur pulled on Tafel's hand and shook his head. "He'll be fine," Vur whispered and pulled her away. "We shouldn't bother Auntie right now. She's mad because we woke her up."

Lindyss smiled at the leaving children. Her expression darkened at the sight of the demon lord who giggled in his sleep. *I'm going back to bed,* she thought and walked away while shaking her head.

"Oh, you're so naughty," Zollstock said in his sleep as he hugged a rock.

***

Tafel's face paled as she hunched over while hugging her stomach. Her lips trembled as she resisted the urge to vomit. Vur was standing in front of the corpse of a behemoth bear, blood dripping from his hands. He turned around with a smile on his face, but his expression stiffened when he saw Tafel's condition. "Are you okay?" he asked while reaching towards her, a furrow in his brow.

Tafel fell over and scrambled backwards, dragging her clothes against the grass. She stared at Vur with wide eyes as her body shook.

Vur took a step forward.

"D-don't touch me!" Tafel yelled as tears sprang to her eyes. She curled up into a ball and clutched her shoulders.

Vur lowered his arm and tilted his head. He looked at his hands and remembered being scolded by Lindyss for spreading blood everywhere. His eyes glowed with a golden light and a stream of water materialized in front of him. He rinsed the blood off and crouched next to Tafel.

"The blood's gone now," Vur said while raising his hands. "See?"

Tafel raised her head and bit her lip as she maintained eye contact. She didn't say anything.

"What's wrong?" Vur asked.

Tafel's lips trembled. "Y-you're scary," she whispered and lowered her eyes.

Vur's eyebrows knit together. He sat down next to her, leaving more space than usual. "I don't understand," he said. "The elves said that too."

Tafel shook her head and closed her eyes. The two sat unmoving. A rabbit hopped out of a bush and scampered past the bear's corpse.

"Do you ever get scared?" Tafel asked with her eyes still closed.

"Sometimes," Vur said. "Auntie's very scary if you wake her up."

A moment of silence passed. Tafel raised her head and looked at Vur. "Is that it?"

Vur nodded. "Why are you scared of me?"

"When your eyes glowed and you killed the bear and smiled…. You didn't seem like a person anymore," Tafel said, looking away. "I thought you were going to eat me next." Her body shivered as she balled up her hands inside her sleeves. She heard Vur stand up and flinched when his hand touched her head.

"I would never hurt you," Vur said.

Tafel craned her neck and stared him in the eyes. "Promise?"

Vur nodded. "Promise."

***

Zollstock groaned as his eyes fluttered open. Gray stalactites hung tens of meters above him. A breeze rolled over his body, causing him to shiver. He inspected his surroundings and found his discarded clothes hanging from nearby stalagmites. *It wasn't a dream?* he thought as he stood up.

Lindyss was sitting on a rocking chair in a corner, knitting a sweater. "You should put some clothes on before the children get back," she said without looking up. She was wearing a purple robe, her light-brown hair tied in a bun behind her head.

Zollstock stared for a second before nodding. He stumbled as he got dressed. "That was amazing," he said. Lindyss smiled

132

but didn't say anything. "Was that a one-time thing or…?" Zollstock's voice trailed off.

Lindyss laughed and placed her knitting needles down onto her lap. "You want to do it again already?" she asked with a smile as her eyes twinkled. "The children will be back with food soon, you know?"

Zollstock laughed and scratched his nose. He stretched and winced after taking a few steps. Sweat beaded on his forehead as he clutched his groin and fell to the floor while panting.

"Was I too rough?" Lindyss asked with a chuckle.

Zollstock shook his head and took in a deep breath. "It's nothing," he said and grimaced.

"Then you should look forward to tonight," Lindyss said with a wink. "I hope it won't be too hard on you."

"Auntie!" Vur's voice rang out from the entrance. "We're back."

Zollstock stood up and took controlled breaths before adjusting his posture. Vur walked in, holding Tafel's hand with his left and the behemoth bear's hind leg with his right. Zollstock's mouth dropped open. "How is that going to fit on a table?"

Vur looked at him, sighed, and shook his head. "Dragons don't use tables." He moved the bear into the center of the mini-boss room and sat down with Tafel taking a seat next to him. Zollstock waddled over and winced as he sat down.

"Are you okay?" Tafel asked her father. Zollstock nodded while breathing in.

Vur stabbed Lust into the bear's side and sliced off a strip of meat and fur. He grabbed the blade of the dagger and offered the hilt to Tafel. Her hands trembled as she accepted it before looking at her father. His eyes were closed, and labored breaths escaped from his pale face. Tafel shrugged and tried to copy Vur's previous actions, but she couldn't break the bear's skin.

Vur placed his hand over hers and guided her actions. Soon, Tafel also held a strip of bloody bear meat in her hands. *It's so*

133

squishy, she thought. Her face paled while her mouth opened slightly.

"Don't let the blood drip," Vur said as he lifted one end of the strip and stuck it into Tafel's mouth before she could react. Her eyes widened, and she was about to spit it out, but she stopped when she realized it tasted sweet. Warmth flowed from her throat into her belly, causing her body to relax.

"Tastes good, right?" Vur asked with a grin.

Tafel nodded and bit off a tiny piece of the meat. "It tastes really good," she said while chewing, not caring about manners, and swallowed the piece.

Vur smiled and cut off another strip of meat. Zollstock fell over and twitched as his hands clenched into fists. "I don't think your dad is okay," Vur said and poked the demon lord with the dagger, trying to bring about a reaction. "Should I heal him?"

Zollstock whimpered. "Plea—"

"No," Lindyss said as she stepped over the demon lord's body. "He said it was nothing. You shouldn't heal him or else it'll hurt his pride as a man." Lindyss smiled as she tore off one of the bear's legs and brought it to the basilisk in the other room. Vur shrugged and continued to eat.

"Sorry, Dad," Tafel said as she brought the rest of her food to her mouth. "I don't know any healing spells."

Tears rolled down the demon lord's face.

***

Mina sat across from her mother, a table with a tea set separating the two. Her mother looked identical to her, but wrinkles framed the older woman's face and hands.

"It's been such a long time, Mina."

Mina smiled. "I'm sorry I haven't come to visit often, Mother," she said. "I've been busy recently."

Her mother grunted. "The lord left with the dragons?" she asked. "Everyone's been talking about it. Rumors say he angered one of them and was kidnapped. A few people say they saw him dangling from its claws."

134

Mina's lips twisted into a smile. "Well, he was taken by the dragons of his own volition," she said as she picked up a steaming tea cup. "Just not in the manner he wished to travel."

"Aren't you worried something will happen to him?" her mother asked and sipped her tea.

Mina shook her head. "I'm more concerned about what I found in his room."

Her mother placed the tea cup down and furrowed her brow. "Some things are better left unsaid," she said, staring at her daughter. "He's the demon lord, Mina."

Mina fidgeted in her seat. Her fingers turned white as she gripped her cup and took a sip. "I know. I'm just worried for Tafel."

13

Sera and Prika lay in the valley, facing each other on their bellies. Between them, a rectangular platform with a chessboard pattern had multiple golems standing on top of it. Prika nudged one of the golems with her claw, urging it forwards. "Eh?" Sera tilted her head. "That's allowed?"

"I just did it, didn't I?" Prika asked in return.

"I'm going to have to ask that little cursed elf for a rulebook," Sera said as she swatted the golem closest to the advancing golem. Her head turned when Vur and Tafel came out of a nearby cave, their faces smudged with dirt.

"Mama, can I imprint Tafel?" Vur asked.

"What? Ew. No. That's gross," Prika said. "She'd be like your daughter then. Let me do it."

Sera glared at Prika. "I thought we agreed it was best not to imprint non-dragons."

"Yeah, but I want kids too. I don't even have a mate," Prika said while frowning.

"Why does Tafel want to be imprinted?" Sera asked.

"I want to be strong like Vur," Tafel said with her head lowered. She still couldn't stare any of the dragons in the eyes. "So he doesn't have to always protect me when we play. And if I get stronger, then I won't have to listen to my parents."

"Good enough for me!" Prika said and approached Tafel, abandoning the game of golem chess.

Sera put her claw on Prika's snout and pulled the red dragon back. "What will the elves think if we imprint a demon?" Sera asked. "What will the humans think? There's a very delicate balance that has to be maintained."

Prika pushed Sera's claw away. "You imprinted Vur," she said. "Who cares what anyone else thinks?"

"Vur's not an heir to a throne. Tafel can be," Sera said. "Don't forget what my father said about angering the humans."

Vernon and Grimmy coughed from within their caves.

Prika rolled her eyes. "Fine, I get what you're saying," she said and turned to Tafel. "Sorry, squirt."

Tafel shook her head and waved her hands in front of herself. "That's okay," she said. "I can get stronger on my own."

"Just because you can't get a dragon to imprint you doesn't mean other beasts won't," Prika said. "Why not a behemoth bear?" She licked her lips. "I can convince one for you."

"My teacher told me that you can only get imprinted once," Tafel said and lowered her head. "I wanted to be like Vur." Her face turned beet red as she clutched the edge of her woolen sweater.

"Oh?" Grimmy said, popping his head out of his cave with a grin. "You know he can still make normal babies, right? There's no need for a dragon imprint."

Leila nudged him. "Hush, they're not even six yet."

"Eh? Don't tell me you two don't know how babies are made," Grimmy said towards the children.

The two shook their heads.

Vernon coughed and emerged from his cave. "Well, you see," the golden dragon said as he scratched his chin, "when a boy and a girl love each other very much, they form a connection. When they eat together, talk to each other, live in the same cave together, hold hands with each other, that connection grows stronger. When the connection reaches a certain level—"

Sera smacked him. "You'll make the children stupid."

Vernon sighed and rubbed his snout.

"So I can't imprint Tafel?" Vur asked.

Sera shook her head. "It's best if you didn't."

137

Vur frowned, but Tafel tugged his hand. "It's okay," she said. "I'm happy enough that you asked for me. Let's go play in the forest, okay?"

"Okay." Vur nodded. The two turned and left the valley.

Prika stared at their backs and sighed.

***

The two children stood next to a bananerry bush. It was a green bush shaped like a ball with large fern-like leaves. Banana-shaped berries hung from the branches of the bush, hence its name. "I told you I could find some," Vur said and pointed.

"They're so tiny," Tafel said with her eyes wide. But she wasn't referring to the fruit.

"Hey! Just because we're tiny, it doesn't mean we don't have ears!"

A trio of fairies were hovering around the bush, picking bananerries. The fairies had purple horns similar to Tafel's: they sprouted from their temples and curved around their heads. They were all one foot tall and wore leaves as gowns. Four dragonfly-like wings grew from their backs. The only difference between the three were their eye and hair colors, which were red, blue, and yellow.

"Isn't that a demon?" the one with red eyes asked.

"It looks like a demon," the blue-eyed one said.

The one with yellow eyes nodded.

"Hello, my name is Tafel, daughter of the demon lord," Tafel said while curtsying with her shirt. "What are your names?"

"Daughter of the demon lord? Maybe we shouldn't talk—"

"I'm Bella," the blue-eyed fairy said, interrupting the red-eyed one. She pointed at her peeved sister. "She's Rella."

"And I'm Yella," the yellow-eyed one finished. Rella crossed her arms and puffed her cheeks out.

"Don't be like that," Bella said to Rella.

138

Rella stuck her tongue out. "Why would the demon lord's daughter be here in our land?" she asked. "I think she's lying." Rella flew up to Tafel's nose and sneezed on her.

Tafel flinched and rubbed her eyes. "Did she just sneeze on me?" Tafel asked Vur in a high-pitched voice.

Vur nodded. "I think that means she likes you."

Yella sighed. "It's the naïve dragon boy too," she said and clicked her tongue while shaking her head.

"She cursed you," Bella said and giggled. "Now you can only tell the truth and only the truth for one month. No more and no less."

"What? You shouldn't curse someone when you first meet them," Tafel said and pouted. "That's not very nice."

"Fairies aren't nice people," Rella said and nodded. "Now tell us who you really are."

"I'm Tafel, daughter of the demon lord," Tafel said. Her eyes widened, and she put her hands over her mouth.

"Is she really cursed?" Vur asked.

"Yes," Tafel said in a muffled voice. The trio of fairies nodded.

Vur frowned. "Dispel," he said while waving his arm in front of Tafel's body. "Did it work?"

"No," Tafel said with her hands still over her mouth.

Rella giggled. "You can't dispel a fairy's curse that easily," she said and stuck her chest out.

"Yup, we can't dispel it either," Bella said while nodding. "I guess she really was the demon lord's daughter. Sorry about that. We'll be going now." Bella waved.

"Wait! You can't just curse me and leav—actually you can. You shouldn't curse me and leave!" Tafel said while interrupting herself.

Rella stuck her tongue out at Tafel. "You can blame yourself for being a demon. I'm glad I could make at least one of you honest," she said and turned to leave.

Tafel faced Vur with an aggrieved expression. His eyes glowed and the fairy trio, who were about to fly away, found themselves pinned to the bananerry bush.

"Hey! Gravity magic's not fair," Bella said and pouted as she flapped her wings to no avail.

"That's cheating!" Rella said.

"Why don't you like demons?" Tafel asked Rella.

"You're all liars," Rella said and crossed her arms while looking away.

"Demons tricked us out of our cave and imprisoned our queen," Yella said. "We had to give up our home and our stuff." The yellow-haired fairy pouted.

"I miss my slime bath," Bella said and sighed.

"I miss my kitchen!"

"I miss my bathroom…"

The three fairies sat down and cried.

"Huh? Don't cry," Tafel said. "I'm sorry. Please stop." Tafel bit her lower lip and tugged Vur's hand. His eyes stopped glowing and the fairies stopped sobbing, exchanging glances with each other. Tafel opened her mouth to speak.

"Itwasnicemeetingyoubutwehopetoneverseeyouagainbye!" The fairies flew away before she could say anything. Vur and Tafel stood there for a moment, Tafel's mouth still partially open.

"Fairies are weird," Vur said as he shrugged and picked a handful of bananerries. He held one out to Tafel. "Want one?"

"Yes, I do, and I want you to feed it to me," Tafel said. Her face turned red as she covered her mouth while turning away. *Stupid, stupid curse!*

Vur appeared in front of her with a berry and smiled. "Say, 'Ah.'"

Tafel's cheeks burned as she ate the berry. "No more questions, please. Okay?"

"Do you—"

Tafel covered Vur's mouth with her hands. "Okay?" she asked again while smiling.

An image of Lindyss' smile appeared in Vur's head. He nodded.

***

"We finally reached level 15," Lamach said as he sat down. A slime, which he just stabbed, bubbled and dissolved into a layer of white powder.

"Let's ask Doofus if we can go deeper," Gabriel said. The two were killing slimes in the mana source located in Niffle. After the undead cavalry began their purge, the students had returned to grinding away in the slime dungeon. The two went up to their teacher and asked if they could go deeper. Doofus nodded.

"Be careful. The next types of monsters are dangerous metal elementals. Don't go past the second room," he said. "I'll be keeping watch on you two."

Gabriel and Lamach smiled at each other. The two puffed their chests out and tilted their chins up as they passed their classmates who were still killing slimes. Gabriel equipped his morning star mace while Lamach readied his lance. They walked through a corridor and arrived at a cave with a few other adventurers in it. Ringing sounds rang out as metal clashed against metal.

Gabriel stopped walking as his mace fell out of his hand. His mouth fell open as he turned his head towards his brother.

"Is that a floating … spoon?" Lamach asked.

"There's a floating fork over there too…" Gabriel said.

"Instructor Doofus did warn us about dangerous metal elementals…" Lamach said. "But utensils? What's next? Chamber pots?"

Gabriel picked up his morning star. "Don't jinx it," he said and sighed. He raised his arm and thwacked the spoon.

***

"You were cursed by fairies?" Zollstock asked his daughter. He was sitting in front of a bear corpse with Vur and Tafel.

"Yes, Father," Tafel said, unwilling to make eye contact.

Zollstock sighed. "What's your mother going to think? I can't have you go back to her like this."

"She'd probably blame you for not watching over me," Tafel said as Vur cut out a piece of bear.

"It's not my fault the fairies cursed you," Zollstock said while adjusting his pants.

"No, it's not your fault," Tafel said and covered her mouth. "You just stayed in the cave all day with Auntie."

Vur blinked at Zollstock. "Your pants are on backwards."

The demon lord looked down. "No they're not," he said. "This is how I always wear them. You're imagining things."

"He's lying," Tafel said with her voice muffled by her hands.

I really can't take her home like this, Zollstock thought. "We should go back soon or your mother will be worried sick," he said. "Do you want to go back?"

"No. I don't want to go back. Mom and Prim are too strict," Tafel said and lowered her head. "I hate learning how to act like a lady, and I have no friends there. I want to stay here with Vur." Her eyes glistened as tears leaked from the corners of her eyes.

Zollstock rubbed his chin. "Alright then," he said and nodded. "You can stay for now."

Tafel looked up with wide eyes. "Really!?"

He nodded again. "Your mother's going to be furious at me," he said and smiled, "but I think it'll be worth it to let you gain experience and grow."

"Thank you!" Tafel squealed and tackled her dad with a bear hug. "I won't tell her about the adult things you do with Auntie."

Zollstock winced and groaned as his face blanched. "You're welcome," he whispered back.

142

"You did what!?" Mina screeched. Zollstock hung his head with his eyes closed. Some fights weren't meant to be won. This was one of them. "It was your idea to let her go! Now you don't even bring her back!? Does she mean nothing to you? Do my words mean nothing to you!?"

Mina's horns pulsed red as her hair rippled in the air. She glared at her husband who refused to say a single word while she yelled at him. She had received reports that her husband returned without Tafel and went to the clinic before coming to see her.

"Please. Calm down," Zollstock said with his head still lowered. "I can explain."

"I'm waiting," Mina said with her arms crossed over her chest. Her hair stopped rippling, but her horns still glowed red.

Zollstock looked up. "The resources in the wilderness are a lot greater than they are here. She can eat magical beast meat for breakfast and drink from the Fountain of Youth when she's thirsty. She can even find a beast to imprint her. Given enough time, she'll be one of the strongest leaders we've ever had."

"I don't care about that," Mina said. "You could have brought her back and explained it. Did you even see how Vur acted? What if Tafel becomes as wild as him? Did you even think about that when you abandoned her in the forest?"

"But—"

"Tafel doesn't even need to be strong," Mina said. "I don't know why you insist on molding her into a combat freak. If you brought Gabriel or Lamach there, then I wouldn't mind as much, but Tafel?"

"She has so much potential," Zollstock said. "We shouldn't stifle that just because she's a girl."

"Potential to do what? Run off and get herself killed?" Mina asked. "Aren't we in the process of making peace with the humans? There was no need for her to become strong before, and there's even less of a reason now."

"But weren't you an adventurer before?" Zollstock asked. "Shouldn't you know why she needs to become stronger?"

Mina's horns stopped glowing as she glowered at him. "It's because I was an adventurer that I know she shouldn't live that kind of life," she said. "Tafel is not going to be an adventurer." Mina slammed the door to the bedroom, leaving Zollstock in the hall.

The demon lord stared at the door and sighed. *I knew I should've brought her flowers and chocolate. Well, that wasn't so bad. That could've gone a lot wor—.*

The door flew open.

"I forgot to ask," Mina said with her horns glowing. "When is she coming back?"

"Um. I don't … know?" Zollstock said in a questioning tone. "Wait! Wait!" He waved his hands in front of his body as Mina stepped closer to him, her fist glowing red.

***

Mina's mother was pouring tea when her house shook. She stood up and walked to the window, opening the shutters. There was a hole with smoke pouring out of it on the top floor of the demon lord's castle. She shook her head and went back to her seat. *Oh dear,* she thought and sipped her tea. *I did warn him about her temper when he proposed.*

14

"The dragons are back, Milord."

Zollstock raised his head and placed his quill down. He was doing paper work in one of the unoccupied storage rooms. For the past month, he had avoided Mina for the sake of the castle's integrity. It would've been a problem if the populace knew, but they didn't. A smile appeared on the demon lord's face. How strong would Tafel be after spending a month with dragons? He straightened his clothes and clapped the sentry on the shoulders and said, "Take me to them."

Tafel and Vur were sitting on Prika's head. Vur wore black leather pants with Lust sheathed on his belt while Tafel wore brown leather pants and boots. She was also wearing a white woolen sweater with the image of a bat knit on the center, courtesy of Lindyss. In the past month, a third pair of horns had sprouted from her temples. They grew towards the back of her head, but curved downwards once they passed her ears unlike the other pairs.

Tafel and Vur held each other's hands and chatted as Zollstock and Mina came towards the capital's gate from opposite directions.

"Tafel," Mina said. "I'm glad you're okay. Come here and give your mother a hug." Her arms opened, waiting for her child to climb off the towering red dragon.

Tafel shook her head and hugged Vur's arm. "I don't want to go home," she said.

Mina's face cramped as Zollstock panicked. *Is the curse still not gone?* "Don't say that, dear," he said with a smile. "Your mother missed you very much. Come and give us a hug. Then you can tell us about everything that happened."

"You won't listen to me," Tafel said and hugged Vur tighter. "You never do. It's always Tafel do this, or Tafel do that. I never get to do what I want." Tears leaked from her eyes as she sniffled.

Mina glared at Zollstock, her horns pulsing with a bright-red glow. The demon lord avoided her gaze and cleared his throat. He pointed at the ground and said, "Tafel. Come here. Right now."

Tafel shook her head and buried her face into Vur's shoulder. Her body shook as she sobbed. Vur patted Tafel's back and turned his head towards Sera.

"Mama, Tafel doesn't really have to leave, right?" Vur asked.

Smoke rose out of Sera's nostrils as she sighed. "She has to. We can't keep the princess of a nation."

Grimmy grinned. "You know, she won't be the princess of a nation if the nation's gone," he said. His eyes flickered to the two demons by the gate. They paled and retreated backwards.

"Grimmy!" Leila said and tugged her mate's wing. "Don't even joke about things like that in front of them."

Grimmy laughed at the two rulers. "I'm only playing around," he said while swishing his tail. "You have such a nice looking city; it'd be a real shame if something were to happen to it." He yawned and smiled, showing off his teeth.

"Is that really necessary?" Vernon asked Grimmy.

"Of course. I'm just reminding them of their place in the food chain lest they get any stupid ideas," Grimmy said. Smoke puffed out of his nostrils, jetting towards the demons. "Uniting with the humans and building a garrison on the borders of our forest? If it weren't for the patriarch's orders..." His expression darkened. "Just give me a reason to go to war."

Zollstock and Mina fell to their knees and lowered their heads. "We would never think to do something that audacious. The garrison is only there to protect our lands from the undead,"

Zollstock said. A bead of sweat rolled down his back. "Thank you for taking care of our daughter for the past month."

Grimmy's gaze lingered on the two. When they thought they couldn't stand it anymore, Grimmy snorted and turned away. Prika lowered her head until Vur and Tafel were level with the city wall. Vur and Tafel didn't move.

"Go on," Prika said and tilted her head towards the wall. Vur hugged Tafel and turned towards Sera. She nodded once.

Vur lifted Tafel and walked onto the city wall. "Let's go to the library, okay?" he asked. Tafel clutched his shoulders tighter. He jumped off the wall, causing a nearby civilian to scream, and headed towards the center of the city.

Mina took in a deep breath and raised her head. "As a reward for taking care of our daughter, feel free to take as many books from the royal library as you want," Mina said.

Zollstock's brow furrowed. He hadn't agreed to this.

"But once you're done, please, never come back," she said. "The citizens are scared every time they see a dragon outside the city and our productivity drops. Further visits after this one will be treated as an act of aggression." Her body was trembling, but she maintained eye contact with Sera without flinching. Zollstock held his breath as Sera raised an eyebrow.

"From one mother to another," Mina said and lowered her head. "Please." She closed her eyes and waited.

Sera stared at her for a moment before nodding. "I understand," she said as her tail swished. "And will Vur be allowed inside the city?"

"Currently, only nobility or highly ranked human adventurers on a mission are allowed in the border towns of our lands," Mina said, keeping her head lowered. "And these are just tentative steps towards peace. It is highly unlikely for any low status human to step foot in our capital in the foreseeable future."

Prika sighed. "Poor Vur," she said. She added after a thought, "And Tafel."

Sera turned her head towards Prika. "We're not going to spill blood for the sake of a rebellious demon child."

Prika nodded and sighed again. "I know," she said and shrugged, breaking off a piece of the capital's wall by accident. "It's still sad though."

***

The sun was setting, the sky bathed in red. Five dragons lazed about in the field outside the capital—a decent distance away from the walls—with Vur standing on Sera's head. Each dragon had a large leather bag filled with books. Zollstock and Mina stood at the top of the capital's walls, their hands on either of Tafel's shoulders.

"Vur...," Leila said as she sat up. "We're not going to come back for a long time."

Vur blinked. "What? Why not?"

"We're not welcome here anymore," Leila said. "Dragons shouldn't mix with demons."

"But what about Tafel?" Vur asked. "She's my friend."

Leila shook her head.

"I'm sorry," Sera said as she spread her wings.

Vur jumped off of Sera's head, but Prika caught him with her claws.

"Let me go," he said and squirmed. His eyes glowed with a golden light. The air around him fluctuated for an instant, but in the next second, his eyes closed and the ripples died down.

"Sorry, Vur," Grimmy said after casting a sleep spell, "can't let you wreck the town, even if I want to also."

Sera nodded at Mina. The demon said something to Tafel. Tafel stared up at Mina and then looked at Vur with wide eyes. She tried to run forwards, but the hands on her shoulders prevented her from going very far. She opened her mouth and shouted, but the dragons were too far away to hear what she said. Tafel fell to her knees and cried. Zollstock tried to rub her back, but she knocked his arm away with her elbow and continued to sob. The figures of the dragons became smaller

148

and smaller until only five black specks could be seen in the sky.

***

"Why can't I play with Tafel anymore?" Vur asked Sera. The five dragons were grouped up in their valley: Vernon and Sera were sunbathing next to each other. Leila and Prika were playing golem chess. Grimmy was chatting with Lindyss who was knitting and using his wing as shade.

"The demons don't like us," Sera said as she scratched Snuffles' exposed belly. "They're scared of what we can do. It makes them jumpy when we visit them."

"But they should be scared, right?" Vur asked. "We're dragons. Does it matter what they want?"

Sera sighed. "Dragon's aren't invincible, Vur. If the demons really had to, they would be able to kill some of us, but they'd lose too much. We'd win the fight and wipe them all out, but none of us"—Sera lifted her head and gestured towards the dragons—"want to see each other die. The demons don't bother us, so we don't bother them."

Vur pouted. "Are they really that strong?"

Grimmy nodded. "I remember when the humans first invaded. They were pretty strong. They could kill behemoth bears and force elves back. They even managed to take over the fairy queen's cave, but honestly, no one really cared about that since fairies are annoying. The demons might seem weak now, but that's only because the strongest ones go somewhere else after a few adventures in the wilderness."

"Grimmy's right. I've seen many adventurers come for my Fountain of Youth," Lindyss said. "Sometimes, the same adventurers come back after many years stronger than before. They tell me stories in exchange for drinks. There's a man named Charon who's visited me eight times already. The world's a lot bigger than you think."

Vur lowered his head. "I want to see Tafel."

"Tafel's a princess," Lindyss said. "Princesses rarely associate with nobles, much less commoners. She's the future of the country even if she doesn't become the demon lord. Political marriages to unite factions are pretty common amongst the demons and humans. If I'm not mistaken, the current demon lord is in a political marriage with his wife."

"Wouldn't marrying Tafel to Vur be good for them then?" Prika asked, turning away from her game. "Peace with the dragons would—actually, never mind. We don't bother them too much anyway."

Lindyss nodded. "The humans wouldn't approve of the demons allying with us. They'd declare war. You"—she gestured towards the dragons—"probably wouldn't fly out to help fight against them, no offense," Lindyss said. "So it's actually a loss to marry Tafel to Vur instead of using her to keep the nobles in check. And can you imagine the outrage of their people if they marry her to a human?"

"But Tafel's going to marry me," Vur said with a frown. "We promised."

"Oh?" Prika said. "You sure work fast. Feeling jealous over there?" Prika smirked at Lindyss.

"Shut up," Lindyss said and threw a lightning bolt at Prika.

The red dragon swatted it away with her paw and laughed. "When did you get so brave?" she asked and sighed. "I miss the days when you would tremble in your boots when you saw me."

Lindyss shrugged.

"Well, I guess it's okay. You're more like Vur's older sister than his wife," Prika said. "It's a shame. A real shame. You two would've made some cute babies."

Lindyss threw another lightning bolt at Prika.

"If you want to marry Tafel," Lindyss said, turning towards Vur, "you'll have to become a noble."

"How do I do that?"

"It's simple. Get the human king's attention and have him bestow you a title," she said and paused. "Good attention, not
150

the 'I burned down your city' kind of attention. Becoming an SSS-ranked adventurer will probably do it."

"That sounds easy," Vur said.

"That's because that's the easy part," Lindyss said. "The hard part is learning the etiquette of the nobles. And you might have to unite the humans and the demons, but the former is definitely harder for you."

Vur frowned and tilted his head.

"Don't worry; it'll be easy to find you a teacher."

***

"The undead are approaching!"

Gale dropped his book and stiffened before retrieving his equipment from the corner of his Spartan room. He donned his mithril robe and equipped his staff, stepping outside while putting on his hat. Outside of his lodgings, human paladins and white mages, demon knights and black mages were rushing into the courtyard in front of the wooden gate.

"Let them approach the walls and have the white mages rain purification down on them when they're close enough," Dustin said. "And have archers with silver and mithril-tipped arrows at the ready."

The stone buildings in the small garrison shook as the ground trembled. "They're almost here," an archer in one of the two watchtowers said.

Gale climbed up the steps of the wall, heading towards Dustin's position. "What do you think?" Gale asked, looking over the edge of the wall.

"It's going to be a long battle. The undead don't get tired or hungry. They can wait us out for weeks and strike when we're exhausted if we don't receive reinforcements," Dustin said with a grimace. Thousands of skeletons and undead horses appeared over the horizon. "We only have so much mana that can be used a day."

The ground stopped trembling as the undead cavalry halted and formed a neat 200-by-100 rectangle just outside of the shooting range of the archers and mages in the garrison. The sole undead rider leading the formation stepped forward and pointed at Dustin and Gale with his sword.

"A duel!" the undead leader shouted. Its voice sounded like rocks grinding against each other. "Send your most noble human. If he wins, we'll leave."

"You expect us to believe that?" Dustin asked. A demon mage amplified his voice with magic.

The undead leader nodded. "You have no choice," it said and waved at the army of 20,000 knights behind it.

Gale's face paled at the sea of black knights. He couldn't even see the ground beneath their feet.

"I'll go!" A knight wearing full mithril platemail stepped to the front of the courtyard. "Open the gates!"

Gale exchanged glances with Dustin. The demon adventurer nodded. "There's no other way," Dustin said and gestured to the men near the gates. They opened the gates a tiny bit. The undead cavalry didn't move. After they confirmed the undead weren't going to attack, the gates swung wide open. The blue knight stepped into the field with a morning star mace and kite shield. He advanced towards the formation as the gates closed behind him.

The undead leader dismounted and waited for the knight to approach, sword lowered.

"State your name and title!"

"My name is Opfern. I am the Baron of Blod," the knight said as he raised his morning star towards the sky.

The undead leader rubbed his chin and nodded. "Alright, a baron will do. I surrender! You win," it said. "Get him, boys!"

"Huh?" Opfern's mouth fell open.

The undead cavalry charged forward, swallowing the blue knight inside the mass.

"As per our agreement, we'll be leaving now!" the undead knight said while cackling.

"Those cowards!" Gale shouted. "Fire the arrows!"

A wave of arrows flew towards the mass, but the undead cavalry turned around and retreated before the arrows reached them. A cloud of dust flew into the air as they galloped away. The men in the garrison stood in silence as the undead knights disappeared over the horizon.

A voice broke the silence.

"Did that really just happen?"

15

"T-Tafel's missing, Milord!"

Zollstock raised his head and furrowed his brow at the sentry holding a salute at the entrance to the storage room. He placed down the quill in his hand and stood up, pushing in his chair. There were bags underneath his eyes, and his hair was disheveled.

"Where's Prim?" he asked.

"She was tied up and gagged in Tafel's room," the sentry said.

"Does Mina know?"

"Yes, she sent me to come find you, Milord," the sentry said, keeping his gaze glued to the floor.

Zollstock sighed and placed his forehead into his hand. "Just kill me now."

"Don't worry, Milord—Prim wasn't tied up long. We have all the guards searching for the princess. She couldn't have gone very far," the sentry said. "Would you like me to tell the lady that we were unable to find you? I can notify you after the princess is found."

"Please do. What's your name?"

"My name is Retter, Milord."

Zollstock nodded. "When she's found, expect a promotion."

"Thank you, Milord," Retter said, meeting the demon lord's eyes. "As a fellow husband, I understand your plight."

***

"He couldn't be found?" Mina asked. Retter couldn't help but shudder under her gaze. "Is that so?"

"Y-yes, Milady."

"So he's hiding from me too?" Mina's purple dress and hair fluttered. "Very well. You're dismissed."

Retter saluted and left the room with a pounding chest. Mina turned towards Prim. The maid was wearing a black dress with a white apron over it. Her usually pristine hair was disheveled while her dress had wrinkles where the ropes had left their marks.

"I'm sorry, Mina," Prim said. "She overpowered me and gagged me before I could do anything. I didn't realize she had become so strong."

Mina shook her head. "It's not your fault. It's Zollstock's," she said and ground her teeth. "That useless husband of mine. Abandoning her in the wild with a family of dragons. Why couldn't I have been married to a better man?"

Prim didn't say anything.

Mina sighed. "I didn't mean to get angry," she said and shook her head. "It's just ... whenever I look at Tafel, I see myself in her. I don't want her to make the same mistakes I made. I don't want to see her cry when her heart breaks. But she's always fighting against me." Mina bit her lip. "I just don't know what to do."

Prim put her arm around Mina's shoulder and pulled her close. "Sometimes children fall when they learn how to walk," she said. "That doesn't mean you should stop them from learning."

Mina leaned into Prim. "There's no happiness to be found if she becomes an adventurer," she said and sniffled.

"Do you regret becoming an adventurer?"

Mina nodded. "I do. I miss the nights spent sleeping under the moon. I miss the thrill of winning against a stronger opponent. I miss the satisfaction of raising my level. I miss my companions who I traveled with. Most of all, I miss him. My heart hurts every time I see him, knowing I can't be with him, knowing I have to be cold to him, pretending to hate him. It would have been better if I never adventured at all; at least, I wouldn't know what I was missing."

Prim sighed and stroked Mina's hair. "You poor, poor child," she said. "Maybe you should've gone with Tafel to see the dragons instead of Zollstock."

***

How'd they find out so quickly? Tafel was crouched behind a house across the street from the demon lord's castle. She was wearing a black cloak on top of her woolen white sweater. The hood cast shadows over her face, only revealing her mouth. Sentries bustled through the streets calling for Tafel. Bystanders whispered to each other, discussing the behavior of the princess. Her mother was going to throw a fit once the rumors spread.

"Oh? Isn't that Tafel?" a voice called out from above her.

Tafel jumped and fell over. Above her, her grandmother's face was peering over the edge of a window. Tafel shook her head and scrambled to her feet.

"Wrong person."

Her grandmother smiled. "I can recognize your aura from anywhere, child. Would you like some tea? You won't get anywhere with all those sentries around anyway. Come, keep your lonely old grandmother company."

Tafel paused. Her grandmother was right. She was a mage, not a rogue—there was no way she could sneak past all the patrols. She sighed and entered the house, head hanging. Her grandmother was wearing pink pajamas. Wrinkles adorned her face, and her white hair was wrapped around two horns sprouting from her temples. Tafel took a seat on the chair opposite her grandmother. The old demon had prepared a second cup of tea.

Tafel picked up the steaming tea cup and pursed her lips before meeting her grandmother's eyes. "You won't tell?"

Her grandmother shook her head. "I'm too old to care about these things anymore," she said. "Just drink some tea with me."

Tafel sipped the tea, and her belly warmed up as if she swallowed fire. Her mana flared up, rampaging through her body like a lion. Her eyes widened as her hand trembled.

Her grandmother smiled. "Good tea, eh?" she asked. "It's made from the leaves of the Tree of Knowledge. A rare commodity now, I hear. Why don't you tell me what's wrong?"

Tafel nodded and fiddled around with her cup before speaking. "Mom never lets me do what I want. She makes me practice the harp for two hours every day. Then I have to read books about politics and history and geography.

"She makes me wear stuffy dresses that takes hours to put on and take off. She makes Prim teach me how to act like a lady, and I get punished when I do something un-lady like. I'm not allowed to read the books I want to read. I don't get to play with other children. I finally made my first friend and now Mom won't let me see him." Tears pooled in Tafel's eyes as her breaths shortened. "I hate being a princess! I hate it! Why can't I just be normal!? I want to have adventures and see the world like the people in the stories." Tafel sniffed and wiped her eyes with the backs of her hands, staring at her lap.

Her grandmother sighed. *Oh, Mina. What have you done?* "Tafel. Look at me. Do you want me to help you?" she asked. "I used to be a pretty strong black mage you know? It runs in the family."

Tafel raised her head and asked through sobs, "R-really?"

Her grandmother nodded. "Your mother shouldn't have any problems if I teach you," she said. "I did raise her after all."

Tafel fell silent as she clutched the edges of her sweater's sleeves. She wiped her nose with the napkin on the table. "Why does Mom hate me?" she asked and lowered her head, wrapping her hands around the tea cup.

"Oh, Tafel. She doesn't hate you," her grandmother said. "She just doesn't know how to raise you. Your mother used to be an adventurer too, you know? Although she had to stop because your father took a fancy to her when she was seventeen

157

and passing through the capital. Of course our family—including me—was ecstatic that the prince liked her, so they arranged a marriage with the royal family. Mina wasn't so happy about that." Her grandmother sighed. "I think she's afraid something similar will happen to you."

Tafel frowned. "She's still mean to me," she said and drank her tea. "And I don't like that."

"You're right. You shouldn't like that," her grandmother said. "More tea?"

Tafel nodded.

***

"The undead are back!"

Gale stopped writing and rubbed his temples. He still hadn't figured out a way to explain Opfern's incident with the noble's family, yet the undead were already back. He sighed and picked up his staff before exiting his quarters.

"You think it's going to be the same as yesterday?"

"I hope so. If they seriously fought us, we'd lose."

"Would you volunteer to duel them?"

"Heck no. You crazy? I have a wife and kid waiting for me at home."

The knights and paladins ambled to the courtyard as the ground trembled. A few demons yawned and stretched as they made their way to the gate. Gale shook his head but didn't say anything. He walked up to Dustin who was standing on top of the city wall.

"It's about the same size as last time," Dustin said.

"Same plan as before," Gale shouted towards the soldiers. "Don't let your guards down."

The ground stopped trembling as the undead cavalry took the same formation as yesterday, once again outside of attacking range.

"Return him," the undead leader at the front said.

A few cavalry rode forward and threw a naked Opfern onto the ground before returning to the formation. His legs were tied together with rope, and his mouth was gagged.

"What's the meaning of this?" Dustin asked.

"We need a real noble. Not a fake one who poops his pants in the presence of a child," the undead leader said. Opfern shivered and covered his head with his hands as tears leaked from his eyes.

"Aren't there any—. Wait. Give me a second," the undead leader said and froze in place.

A few moments later, he turned around and faced the undead army. "I just got a message from the mistress. We're going back."

The cavalry rode away, leaving the bound Opfern behind. Dustin and Gale stared at each other without saying anything.

Two knights opened the gate and went outside to retrieve Opfern. They reached him and were just about to pick him up when forty skeletal hands sprang out of the ground and grabbed them. Twenty skeletons rose up from the earth along with twenty undead horses. Ten skeletons lifted each knight, and they rode off into the distance, chasing the undead cavalry.

The men in the garrison were silent as the screams of the two knights trailed away into the distance. They looked at Opfern.

"Think we should just leave him there?"

***

"I'm terribly sorry," the undead leader said while lowering its head. "I just assumed the knights would be humans, not demons."

Lindyss shrugged. "It doesn't matter. We were going to need some demons later on."

The two knights were in their undergarments, and two skeletons wore shiny new platearmor. The knights were seated on one end of a wooden table while Vur and Lindyss sat on the other. A dozen undead knights formed a ring around the table.

159

Outside, hundreds of undead stood at attention. They were at the marsh where the skeletons usually slept.

"W-what do you want with us?" the knight on the left asked. He had three blue horns while the knight on the right had a single red horn.

"Oh, just a few answers to our questions," Lindyss said as she clasped her hands in front of herself on the table. "And some tutoring. Don't worry, you'll be set free when it's over."

The two knights gulped. Lindyss was wearing a red robe that hugged her body and accentuated her curves. She flashed them a smile.

"Alright," the red-horned knight said.

"Great. Let's get on with it then," Lindyss said. "What qualifications do you need to marry into the royal family?"

The two knights glanced at Vur before facing each other with eyebrows raised. "Well, for starters, you'd have to be a demon noble…," the blue-horned knight said.

"What else?"

The knight shrugged. "You'd have to bring more benefits than every other potential suitor. Usually that means owning a lot of land and money."

"Can't Tafel pick who she marries?" Vur asked.

The two knights' mouths fell open. "You're talking about the princess?" the blue-horned knight asked. "I thought you were asking about a side branch of the royal family. You'd need to be richer, smarter, and stronger than the rest of the suitors. You'd also need the approval of the majority of the family. It's easier for a woman to marry a prince, but the criteria to marry the princess is a lot higher."

Lindyss leaned forward, resting her chin on her hand. "Wow, this is going to be a lot easier than I thought," she said. The two knights stared at her but didn't say anything. She smiled and pointed at Vur. "Teach him etiquette befitting a demon prince."

The demons glanced at each other, doubt in their eyes.

160

"Don't worry. He's a quick learner," Lindyss said. "Let me know if there's anything you need to teach him but can't."

"The royal family places heavy emphasis on music. And a prince must know how to dance," the red-horned knight said while rubbing his chin. "He also has to be a competent strategist and commander."

Lindyss turned towards the undead leader. "You heard the man," she said. "We'll need a commander, a dancer, and a musician. Remember. No killing."

"As you command." The undead leader saluted, and the skeletons left the cave. Lindyss stood up and turned to leave.

The blue-horned knight scrunched his eyebrows together. "Aren't you afraid we'll escape?"

Lindyss laughed. "Be careful," she said as she walked away. "He bites."

The two knights judged the half-naked human boy in front of them.

Vur frowned. "I don't bite demons," he said. "Grimmy says they'll give me a stomachache."

***

"The undead are back!"

A groan escaped from Gale's lips as he dropped his quill. The letter to Opfern's family explaining his disappearance had turned into a letter about the noble's mental instability. It was even harder to write than before. Once again, he retrieved his staff and stepped outside. Everyone was trudging towards the courtyard. Dustin was already waiting at the top of the garrison's gate.

"Why do you think they're doing this?" Gale asked Dustin.

Dustin shook his head. "It feels like they're stealing our equipment or gathering information. Why else would they return Opfern alive?" he asked. "Has he said anything?"

Gale sighed. "He's been curled up in the fetal position ever since he came back," he said and shook his head. "He refuses to talk to any of us. He was a good man." Gale faced the approaching cloud of dust. "There seems to be more of them than last time? I requested reinforcements from the capital. They should arrive here in two weeks. If they come back within that time we can wipe them out."

Dustin nodded. "I requested some reinforcements also. To your stations everyone," he said, and the soldiers scrambled to attention.

The undead stopped just outside of the garrison archers' range. They formed two rectangles of 200-by-100 undead cavalry. The undead leader dismounted and stepped forward. He was wearing Opfern's old mithril armor.

"What do you want from us?" one of the knights shouted.

"We want a commander, a dancer, and a musician," the leader said. "I'll give you everything I have in my right pocket for them."

"… You don't even have pockets!" one of the archers shouted.

The leader tilted his head.

"I'll give you everything in his right pocket," he said as he pointed at Gale.

"He doesn't have pockets either! He's wearing a robe," the archer said.

"What?" the leader said and shook his head while looking down. "What kind of unfortunate fellows are you to not have pockets?" The undead cavalry behind him all shook their heads and clicked their jaws together.

"Are you trying to make us mad?" Gale asked. "What are your real intentions?"

"I already told you: I want a commander, a dancer, and a musician to accompany us home."

"What if we refuse?" Dustin asked.

"Then I hope you're prepared to face the consequences," the leader said. "Isn't it better to sacrifice a few for the sake of many?"

162

"We would never sacrifice our own to rotting liars like you," Gale said.

"Then you will voluntarily come," the leader said. "Men! Just like we practiced!"

All the skeletons drew their swords and equipped their sheaths in their other hand.

"Get ready, archers," Gale said as he flourished his staff. "Mages prepare your purification magic."

"Start!" the leader shouted and waved his sword. "A one, a two, a one two three four!"

The skeletons banged their swords against their sheathes and sang,

There's a song I heard that goes on and on and on~
It never stops, no~
It never stops, no!~
There's a song I heard that goes on and on and on~
And that was the first veeeeeerse~

There's a song I heard that goes on and on and on~
It never stops, no~
It never stops, no!~
There's a song I heard that goes on and on and on~
And that was the second veeeeeerse~...

The sound caused the ground to tremble and the walls to shake. The glass windows in the garrison vibrated, and all the animals within ran around. The voices of the forty thousand skeletons sounded like rocks grinding against each other. A lich in the back of the formation used wind magic to amplify the sound.

The knights and soldiers in the garrison tried to speak to each other, but they had to shout to be heard over the constant drone of the skeletons. After ten minutes passed, a few knights were on the ground, sobbing and covering their ears. They wanted to charge out and fight the skeletons, but Gale and Dustin refused to open the gate. After half an hour, Dustin and

Gale looked at each other and sighed. An hour passed of non-stop singing. The knights were sitting in the courtyard, covering their ears while gritting their teeth. Two hours passed, then three hours passed.

"I can't take it anymore!" one of the knights shouted and ran to his quarters. "They're tone deaf too!" He came back a few minutes later with a lute and harp. He unlatched the gates and went outside. Nobody stopped him. "I'm a musician," he shouted in front of the undead leader, waving his instruments.

The leader nodded. "Go behind the formation. There's no noise over there."

"Thank you, thank you," the knight said with tears in his eyes. He went behind the formation where ten skeletons grabbed him and rode away.

Another two hours passed. The knights weren't allowed to eat lunch in case the undead attacked while they were off guard, and dinner was approaching. A demon stood up and left the garrison. He was whisked away by skeletons also. The lich amplified the undead leader's voice. "Now we just need a commander."

The people in the courtyard looked at Gale. Gale shook his head and shouted, "We just need to hold out for two weeks until our reinforcements arrive."

Four days later, two demons rode out of the garrison with a tied up Gale wearing pajamas in tow. Every person in the garrison had black circles underneath their eyes. A cheer resounded in the air after the singing stopped.

The two demons came back with a few silver coins.

"What's this?" Dustin asked.

"It was in Gale's right pocket."

16

There was a hint of concern on Lindyss' face when the undead leader brought back a commander. The man was bound with ropes, and there were black bags underneath his eyes. He was wearing pajamas and had a sock stuffed in his mouth. She was in the same cave as before, but there were now three additional people sitting across from her and Vur. The undead leader grinned at her before dumping Gale onto a chair.

"What did you do to him?" Lindyss asked.

"The same thing as the other two," the leader said with a cackle. "I wooed him with a song."

Gale shook his head and tried to speak, but only gargling sounds were heard through the sock. Lindyss smiled at him. "Thanks for your cooperation," she said and gestured at the other four sitting next to him. "These men will fill you in."

"Can we ungag him?" the red-horned knight asked.

Lindyss nodded.

"What's going on?" Gale asked as he rubbed the lint off his tongue with his fingers.

"Simply put, we're here to teach this boy how to be a noble," the blue-horned knight said.

"So why am I here?" Gale asked.

"You're here to show him how to be a leader."

"I don't think I'm qualified," Gale said and sighed. "My own people mutinied against me and threw me to the pack of undead."

"So he's useless?" Vur asked while tilting his head.

"No, no," the human with the harp said while waving his hands. "He's an archbishop who understands the plight of the people. Understanding your citizens is a very important quality for a leader to have."

"I don't care about the people," Vur said. "I just want to play with Tafel."

Gale turned his head towards the four men sitting next to him. They were trembling and none of them dared to look Vur in the eyes. He frowned and waved his hands at Vur. "Sca—"

Before he could finish casting his spell, the blue-horned knight slapped the back of his head and glared at him.

Gale glared back. "What are you doing?"

"Don't anger the boy," the knight said with a growl, "or we'll die. He can kill a behemoth bear with his bare hands."

Vur nodded. "Now teach me," he said while smiling.

"I can teach you, but that doesn't mean you can become a noble," Gale said. "I'm a close friend of the king. He won't bestow a title or plot of land on someone who kidnaps others even if they are as strong as an SSS-ranked adventurer. You need the blood of a noble flowing through your veins to be a noble. I personally don't agree with it, but that's just how it is."

"Is that so?" Lindyss asked with a smile on her face. "You don't have to worry about that. Just teach the boy." She turned to the undead leader. "Gather all the undead. We're making a trip."

The leader saluted and turned to leave with Lindyss, followed by the rest of the skeletons.

The five men exchanged glances. The man with the harp sighed. "I guess I'll start first this time."

***

The ground trembled and bugle horns resounded in the distance. Dustin opened his eyes and was greeted by the sight of dust raining down from the ceiling. "The undead are approaching!" a voice yelled. Dustin sighed and rubbed his eyes while sitting up. Humans and demons stumbled out of their barracks. Some moaned once they saw the moon shining overhead.

166

"Why can't they just let us sleep?" a man complained as he equipped his armor.

Others cursed and nodded their heads in agreement. The soldiers gathered in the courtyard, and the ground shook even harder, causing some of them to fall over. A few tiles on the roof of the barracks slipped and cracked against the ground.

Dustin's face paled at the approaching dust cloud that filled up half the horizon. "There's easily a hundred times more undead than last time," he said to himself. He waved a soldier down. "This needs to be reported to the demon lord and the human king. If we don't receive the help of the adventurers in Fuselage, the undead could wipe out both nations. Go to the teleporter and pass the message on." The soldier's eyes widened before he nodded and ran off.

Dustin held his breath as twenty 500-by-200 rectangles of skeletons lined up in a 10-by-2 rectangular formation. There wasn't a single patch of land visible from the garrison to the horizon. At the head of the undead army was the undead leader and Lindyss, who was riding her basilisk. Dustin's eyes widened when his gaze fell on her. *What's she doing here?*

"Ahem, ahem," the undead leader said while bowing his head to Lindyss. "Our mistress is going to speak. Listen well, mortals."

"Hello. Can you hear me? Great. As of today, I'm establishing the kingdom of Konigreich. We'll be claiming all the land that the dragons burned down," Lindyss said. "You have two days to get out of our territory. Inform your leaders for me, thanks. Have a nice day."

Dustin frowned. Even if the reinforcements arrived, they wouldn't be able to do anything against an army of this size. "If we refuse?" Dustin asked.

"Then we'll sing!" all the skeletons shouted at once.

Dustin winced. The soldiers in the courtyard let out a collective groan. "Alright," Dustin said and faced his soldiers. "Men. We're going home first thing in the morning. Get a good night's rest and pack your things." A few men cheered, and they all went back to their quarters to sleep.

Lindyss turned to the undead leader. "You'll threaten them with song?" she asked with one eyebrow raised.

The undead leader cackled and grinned.

***

"Your Highness! We've just received an urgent report from the garrison in the south," a sentry said outside of Randel's door.

Randel groaned and climbed out of bed. He put on a robe and sat on his couch. "Come in," he said. He yawned as the door swung open. "What's so urgent?"

"Gale requests the help of the adventurers in Fuselage to stem the tide of the undead. There are too many of them, even the reinforcements sent before won't be enough to stop them if they attack," the sentry said while kneeling.

The king frowned. "The adventurers are needed in Fuselage. It isn't so easy for anyone, even me, to call them back," he said. "Tell Gale to figure out a solution. The adventurers must be saved as a last resort."

Another sentry ran down the hallway to the king's room. "An update, Your Highness," the sentry said while dropping to one knee. "The undead have declared they are founding a new kingdom that encompasses all of the burnt lands. Our soldiers have been forced to retreat in fear for their lives."

"A kingdom? Composed of what?"

"Reports say there's a total of two million undead, Your Highness."

"Two million? That doesn't seem like too much," the king said. "What could they possibly want to found a kingdom for? They don't need food or money. Their population can't grow. They're dead."

***

A farmer was sleeping in his bed with his wife when he was awoken by a knock on the door. His wife groaned. "You should

168

answer that," she mumbled while still half-asleep. The farmer stirred and climbed to his feet, shielding his eyes from the moonlight pouring in through the window. He stumbled to the door and opened it. He screamed.

"What's wrong?" his wife asked and bolted up in bed.

"Sk-skeleton!" the farmer shouted as his knees knocked together. He fell over backwards. "G-get away!"

The skeleton was wearing tattered leather armor that was dyed gray with mud. It cleared its throat, but it sounded like rocks clattering to the floor.

"Hello. I mean you no harm. Have you heard of our lord and resurrector, Lindyss the Corrupted One who accompanies us after death?" it asked as it scratched its head with a rusty axe. The farmer sat in a pool of expanding yellow liquid. He shook his head with his eyes wide. His mouth opened, but no words came out.

"Oh good, do you mind if I enlighten you?" the skeleton asked.

The man stared without saying a word, and his wife covered her head with the blanket.

"I'll take your silence as a sign of agreement," the skeleton said and walked in. "We're founding a holy kingdom to the south and we're looking for some fresh me—, err, population to help our holy kingdom grow. Skeletons will provide all the labor for the farms and construction. You just have to help increase the population of our kingdom. The demon lord and human king have already acknowledged our sovereignty. Come, accompany us and I'll tell you all about it on the way."

The farmer was silent. "Um, will yo—"

"How about this? I'll flip a coin. If I win you come with me, agreed?"

"N—"

"Great, it's agreed then. Heads I win, tails you lose," the skeleton said as it pulled a coin out of its femur and flipped it. The coin bounced off the floor. "It's tails. You lose."

The farmer sat in a daze as a group of skeletons came into the room, lifted him and his wife, and carried the screaming couple out the door.

***

Dustin and the soldiers gathered outside of the tents they had set up after being forced out of the garrison. They received orders to keep watch on the undead kingdom and wait for the reinforcements to arrive to assess the situation. Two lines of soldiers could be seen coming from different directions: the northwest and the northeast. One line consisted of demons wearing platearmor and wielding spears. The other consisted of humans wearing chainmail with swords and shields.

Dustin took the position at the front of his men who were arranged in a rectangular formation. Behind him, to the south, the undead capital's buildings could be seen, tiny figures moving on the walls.

"Where's Gale?" a knight asked as he lifted his visor and stepped to the front of the human line.

Dustin shook his head. "He volunteered to investigate the actions of the undead," he said as he sighed. "He's a brave man. I pray he comes back unharmed." The human soldiers behind Dustin turned and glanced at each other but didn't say anything. A few nodded.

The knight frowned. "Those damned undead," he said. "That's their city over there?"

Dustin nodded as the line of demon soldiers arrived. The demon at the front halfheartedly saluted and asked, "What's the situation like, Dusty?"

"Hound, it's good to see you again," Dustin said with a smile. He sighed and shook his head. "The undead are shameless. Absolutely shameless. But they don't seem to have any bloodthirst. They've been gathering the nearby villagers, humans and demons alike, for the past week or so."

"And you didn't do anything to stop them?" the human leader asked as he spat on the floor. "You worthless demons."

Dustin narrowed his eyes at the man. "We confronted them, but the villagers stopped us. They're voluntarily going with them. Every single one of them are enamored with the undead."

"Could it be a curse?" asked Hound.

Dustin nodded. "It could be, but the undead escorting them are just normal skeletons. None of them can cast magic. Look, there's a group passing through here now." Dustin pointed at a group of figures in the distance—three skeletons followed by a family of three demon children and their parents.

The human leader unsheathed his sword and equipped his shield. He marched towards the group and pulled his visor down.

"Halt!" he shouted towards the skeletons.

The skeletons exchanged glances before stepping in front of the demon family while unsheathing their axes. The knight dashed forward while raising his sword into the air. One skeleton bent its knees and raised its axe horizontally to block the blow. The knight snorted and bashed the axe away with his shield before cutting the skeleton's head off with his sword. He pivoted and swung his sword at the skeleton to his right.

"Stop!" the demon father shouted. The skeleton parried the knight's blow and stepped back. The knight pursued and swung his sword once again.

"Fire!" the demon father said and threw a fireball at the knight.

The knight blocked it with his shield. "So you want to die too?" He kicked the skeleton's sternum and knocked it away before pointing his sword at the demon.

Before either the father or the knight could react, a spearhead appeared next to the knight's throat. "I can't let you do that," Hound said. He held his spear with both hands, ready to stab through the man's neck at a moment's notice.

The knight snorted and sheathed his sword. He knocked away the spear with his hand and glared at Hound through his visor.

Hound retracted his spear and turned to the demon family. The skeleton that had its head cut off was sitting and holding its head over its neck while tying it back on with a rag. "That was rude," the skeleton said as its head drooped forward and fell off again.

Hound ignored the skeleton. "Why are you going with them?" he asked the demons.

The father stepped in front of the sitting skeleton. "They're offering us a better life."

"And you trust them?" Hound asked as he removed his helmet.

The man nodded.

"Why?"

"They have no reason to lie. They could've killed us a long time ago if they wanted to," the man said. "They're promising us food and shelter. In return, we give them mana."

"How's that a better life?" Hound asked. "You have a home and shelter here. The nobles protect you in return for taxes."

The demon stared at Hound. "Are you a noble?"

Hound shook his head. "I'm just an ex-adventurer turned royal knight."

"Then you wouldn't understand. You have power," the demon said. "What about the common farmers who can't make a living as an adventurer? What do we have? The nobles barely leave us with enough food to live as we work on their farms. They say they'll protect us, but they run away when the dragons and undead come."

Dustin frowned. "You really believe everything the undead are telling you?"

The man nodded. "I have to," he said, clenching his hands. "For the sake of my family."

The three children were hiding behind their mother. The two uninjured skeletons stood in front of her, observing the soldiers with their axes in front of them.

"Let them through," Dustin said.

172

"You can come with us and become a citizen," the skeleton with the rag around its neck said as it stood up. "We have cookies and songs."

Dustin shook his head. "Thanks for the offer, but I think I've heard enough singing for a lifetime."

***

"How's the city looking?" Lindyss asked the undead leader while yawning. She was sitting up on a bed with bleary eyes. Her hair was disheveled, and she was wearing pink pajamas.

"Good evening," the leader said and nodded. "It's coming along quite well. We've received a lot more incoming citizens than expected, so we reallocated the wall builders to shelter building instead."

"That many?" Lindyss asked.

The leader nodded. "We're very persuasive," he said and grinned. "Although there seems to be a gathering of soldiers near our borders. They're composed of the people we scared away and some reinforcements."

Lindyss frowned. "Make them leave," she said. "Don't kill any of them. We don't want to start a war just yet. Make sure they're far enough away to not interfere with our recruitment."

The undead leader cackled. "We can do that."

Lindyss nodded. "What's the food situation?"

"The farms are tilled and crops have been planted. We've been feeding the newcomers fruit and meat found in the forests, but we ran out of grain so we can't make any more cookies," the leader said and sighed. "The newcomers also gave us all their gold which we can use to trade for some foodstuffs. We sent word to the dryads and requested their help to speed our crop growth, but there's been no reply so far."

Lindyss smiled. "I know a dryad that I can convince to help us with a little persuasion from Grimmoldesser and the matriarch," she said. "Keep up the good work."

The undead leader saluted.

***

Two knights sat outside a cluster of tents, wrapped in heavy furs.

"Do you think the undead will come tonight?" one of them asked.

"I doubt it. They haven't bothered us for over a week," his partner said. "Man, I wish I didn't have guard duty today. I still feel as if I haven't slept enough ever since that dreadful singing." He shivered.

"Was it that bad? I've heard a few things about it, but I wasn't here for it."

His partner shook his head. "You don't understand," he said and sighed while tilting his head towards the sky. A twig snapped, and a bush rustled. The two knights turned their heads towards the sound and drew their swords while holding their breaths. A few moments of silence passed.

"It's probably just a fox," the knight said and sheathed his sword. He turned to look at his partner and came face to face with a grinning skeleton. He opened his mouth, and the skeleton stuffed a sock in it before he could make a sound. The knight's partner was on the ground with four skeletons on top of him, stripping him of his furs and armor. The knight groped for his sword, but he grabbed air instead. Bony hands appeared behind him and knocked him over. He struggled as he was stripped and bound, but he couldn't do anything to stop the skeletons.

***

Dustin opened his eyes and was greeted by the stars and moon shining above him. *That's odd,* he thought, *the moon seems a lot brighter than usual.* He rolled over and closed his eyes. Ten seconds passed. His eyes shot open. He sat up and looked around. All the soldiers were sleeping on their blankets in the field.

"Where'd the tents go!?" Dustin shouted.

Groans and curses rang throughout the field as demons and humans stirred.

"My armor's missing!"

174

"Where's my pillow?"

"My spear!"

"Why am I naked?!"

"It smells like … horse manure?"

Dustin looked down and froze. Brown smiling faces were drawn on his blanket. He lifted his blanket to his nose and sniffed. He threw up. The person closest to him also threw up. A few men cried fat tears.

"I'll kill them!" the human leader shouted. "I'll kill every last one of those damned skeletons!"

After a chain of vomiting, sobbing, and squirming, the soldiers gathered in the field north of their ransacked campsite. Many of them were naked; none of them had weapons. A wind blew past their shivering bodies, carrying the grating voices of the skeletons.

> *Good day, good day!*
> *We'll steal your clothes and run away.*
> *We'll take your food!~*
> *And strip ye nude!~*
> *We'll set your horses free.*
> *Leave this place,*
> *To keep your grace,*
> *And give us liberty.~*

The skeletons cackled in the distance, causing the ground to shake from the noise.

"Thanks for the donations," the undead leader shouted. "We'll be back tomorrow!"

Tears appeared in Dustin's eyes, and he buried his face in his hands.

17

"Milord, there's a messenger from Konigreich seeking an audience," Retter said while saluting. He was wearing a purple steel chestplate with three horns engraved on it. Zollstock and Mina were talking to a few well-dressed demons in a ballroom. It was Tafel's sixth birthday, and her parents were hosting a party with all the influential noble families as guests.

"Pardon me," Zollstock said to the nobles he was conversing with. He turned to Retter. "Take me to him."

"I'll accompany you," Mina said and curtsied to the nobles. The trio left the ballroom.

Tafel was at the center of the ballroom, wearing a purple dress. Her cheeks were sore from holding her smile for the past few hours. A few boys were talking to her when she saw her parents leave.

"And that's how I—"

"Oh, wow, that's really interesting. Sorry, but it seems like something came up," Tafel said, interrupting the boy who was talking to her. She sprinted after her parents, ignoring the boys who called after her. Her parents rounded the corner, and she slowed her pace, making sure to stay silent. She followed them until they arrived at the city gate, where an armored figure was waiting. She snuck up behind her parents and waved at Retter who had noticed her. She put her finger to her lips and smiled. Retter tilted his head down a tiny fraction and turned his gaze back onto the armored figure.

"Greetings, demon lord," the armored figure said and removed its helmet, revealing a yellow skull. "I have a message to you from our mistress."

Zollstock frowned. "Is your mistress the one you worship?"

176

"That's right. She's our lord and resurrector, Lindyss the Corrupted One," the skeleton said while smiling. "I take it you've heard of her?"

Zollstock coughed. "I, ah, know a bit about her," he said while angling his body away from Mina. "Just from the rumors though."

"That's excellent," the skeleton said. "Would you like a pamphlet?"

"No," Zollstock said. "I just want to hear the message."

The skeleton nodded. "I understand. Can I ask why you don't want a pamphlet though? Do you already have a figure you worship?"

"Get on with it," Mina said as she glared at the skeleton. "Please."

The skeleton cleared his non-existent throat and reached into his eye socket. He pulled out a piece of paper and handed it to Zollstock. The demon lord held the paper in front of himself and raised an eyebrow.

"Five ways to achieve immortality through daily prayers?" Zollstock asked as he read out the first line.

The skeleton snatched the paper away. "I'm sorry. That was the pamphlet," the skeleton said. "We store them in our heads to spread the word just in case an adventurer bashes our skulls open." He reached into his pelvic girdle and pulled out a brown piece of paper. "Here's the message."

Zollstock took the paper and read it. His face cramped. He folded it and was about to put it in his pocket when Mina snatched it out of his hands. Zollstock tried to grab it, but Mina dodged and turned her back to him while reading it. It said, "Dear Zollstock,

I miss you. Pay me a visit to improve the relationship between our two kingdoms. We can stay up the whole night talking about politics and biology. I'm sure our kingdoms will get along just fine with an arranged marriage between the royal families. I'm sorry about the whole incident where your soldiers lost their clothing. Forgive me? I look forward to seeing you and your precious jewels again.

P.S. Sorry about Tafel.

From,

Lindyss"

"Oh?" Mina asked as she turned back around. "And just what precious jewels might she be talking about?"

The skeleton knight coughed and sidestepped away from the two. "Well, I passed on the message to the demon lord and didn't let his wife see it. The demon lord let his wife see it; it wasn't me, nope," it said while nodding. "I'll be going now."

"Wait!" Tafel said.

Zollstock and Mina jumped and took a step back. "Tafel!" Zollstock said as he stepped towards her. "What are you doing here? Come, I'll take you back to your party. Let's hurry along now."

"No you don't," Mina said as she grabbed his shoulder. "Explain. Now."

Zollstock sweated bullets and turned around. "We should take Tafel back to the party first. I'll explain everything in detail once we're back."

Mina glared at him.

"Um, I don't mean to interrupt," Retter said, "but shouldn't you stop her?" He pointed at Tafel who climbed onto the messenger's skeletal horse. The skeletal horse dashed forward, kicking up dust.

"Wait!" Zollstock shouted as his horns glowed red. "Bring Tafel back here!"

"What was that? You'll have to speak up," the skeleton shouted back as it got further and further away. "I can't hear you. I don't have ears, you know?"

***

Lindyss walked into the cave, accompanied by a group of fifty undead. Vur was eating a chunk of bear meat in his hands, and the five men were on the ground sobbing. They raised their heads when Lindyss stood over them.

"We've done all we can," the blue-horned knight said through tears. "Please, just let us go or kill us now."

Lindyss raised an eyebrow. "What happened while I was gone?"

"He's hopeless. Absolutely hopeless," the human musician said. "He's more tone-deaf than the skeletons."

"He breaks the cutlery when he tries to eat properly," the red-horned demon said.

"He refuses to dance with any of us because we're men," the demon who volunteered to teach him how to dance said.

"He has no morals. He feels no empathy for humans," Gale said. "He'd make a terrible leader."

One of the skeletons spoke up. "Sounds like someone I'd follow," it said and grinned. A few skeletons cheered.

Lindyss frowned. "I guess that was to be expected," she said and sighed. "I shouldn't expect the mice to teach the dragon how to behave." She turned to Vur. "And why aren't you saying anything?"

A lump moved down Vur's throat as he swallowed. "You said not to talk with my mouth full," he said. The five men glanced at each other, their faces cramped.

"Ah, I guess that'll have to do," Lindyss said and sighed again. "Tafel's probably going to arrive here soon. I set up a new playground for you guys to play in."

She pointed at the five men and spoke to the skeletons, "Take them to the nearest demon city."

The skeletons stepped forward and stripped the men of their clothes before lifting them up.

"Did you really have to take their clothes?" Lindyss asked.

"We get shy when we walk through the kingdom naked," one skeleton said. The other skeletons nodded.

***

"Your Highness," Gale said keeping his eyes on the floor. "I have returned. Forgive me for my failures." He was kneeling in front of the king who sat on the throne. The silver cross necklace he usually wore was missing. The skeletons had taken it along with his dignity.

"Rise, Gale," the king said and motioned with his hand. "Some losses can't be prevented. I'm just glad you're unharmed."

Gale stood up. "I've made a few important discoveries in the time of my captivity," he said as he pulled out a book from his robe's newly sewn on pocket and cleared his throat. "The leader of the new undead kingdom is the Corrupted One who guards the Fountain of Youth. The reasons for founding the kingdom are unknown, but she intends on maintaining a close relationship with the demons. In my time as a captive, I was forced to teach a human boy manners. I suspect she's raising the boy as her child."

"Hmm." The king rubbed his chin. "Was there anything unusual about the boy?"

Gale nodded. "His eyes were golden and his pupils were slit. He was most likely imprinted by a snake or a lizard. He also regularly ate raw meat, and he didn't behave like a human child. It seemed like the Corrupted One wanted to establish a relationship between the demon princess and the boy."

"Are the reports about the undead true?" the king asked. "They really don't kill?"

"From what I've seen, it's true. The Corrupted One doesn't want to establish hostilities with any of the nations," Gale said. "I've also seen many human and demon villagers migrating to the undead kingdom. The border villages that I passed through are devoid of people and livestock."

The king frowned. "That is unacceptable. Simply unacceptable."

Gale lowered his head. "Forgive me for my impudence, but I think a few policies need to be changed in order to keep our
180

people from leaving. The undead are offering food and shelter to the people at the cost of mana. The people no longer need to work for gold or food. A few low ranking adventurers have defected because of this."

The king's eyebrows knit together. "Our policy has worked for hundreds of years. Even when the villagers and serfs rose up in rebellion, we were able to continue without changing anything. We'll just have to post guards at the borders and prevent the undead from coming in and the people from leaving."

Gale continued to stare at the floor. "Times are changing, Your Highness," he said. "The undead are a new faction that have the power to support a rebellion. Posting guards won't work against an enemy that doesn't need to sleep or eat."

The king glared at Gale. "Are you questioning my judgment?"

"No, Your Highness," Gale said as a bead of sweat rolled down the side of his head. "I am only speaking from my experience. Forgive me."

The king nodded. "Very well. I'll stay my hand," he said. "Tomorrow, the court will convene and we will discuss the best method to deal with this problem."

***

"We should crush them, Your Highness," a man said. "Overwhelm them with military force." He was the leader of the reinforcements that was stripped by the undead army. He sat at a round table with a dozen other men, including the king and Gale. His head was bald, but he had a black goatee.

"I disagree," Gale said. "Recklessly attacking them won't benefit us in anyway."

"What do you know?" the man asked as he slammed his fist against the table and stood up. "You're just a turncoat who lived with those damned skeletons."

"Geralt," the king said. "Calm down."

Geralt glared at Gale and sat back in his chair. A thin man with a white beard and blue wizard robes cleared his throat. "Gale's right, you know?" he asked. "If we attack the undead, what's stopping the demons from attacking us? We're in the same situation as before, but this time, the undead and demons will be colluding against us."

"Oh? Then what do you suggest?" Geralt asked and snorted.

The man smiled as he stroked his beard. "It's simple. We also become allies with the undead. Not only do we remove the threat of invasion, we will benefit from trade. A three-way trade can definitely be prosperous for our nation. Think of all the items that we had to send adventurers into the wilderness for that we could obtain through trade: magical beasts, rare herbs, water from the Fountain of Youth, maybe even phoenix downs." The man's eyes twinkled. He sighed. "It's a shame the Tree of Knowledge no longer exists."

"But what can we offer them?" the king asked. "I imagine they don't need any of our resources."

The wizard laughed. "Knowledge," he said. "Everybody loves knowledge."

Geralt rolled his eyes. "You think they need your stinking knowledge, old man?" he asked. "They're over hundreds of years old."

The wizard's mouth dropped open. "You're right!" he said and turned to the king. "Quickly, establish an alliance with them. Think of everything we could learn! Just throw gold and silver at them. Money's useless anyway."

"If you think it's going to be that easy, then go do it yourself," Geralt said and crossed his arms. "I still say we annihilate every last one of them."

The wizard asked the king, "Can I?"

The king's eyebrows knit together. "I mean if you think you can—"

"Thank you, Your Highness," the wizard said. "Leave it to me!" He stood up and spread his arms to the side. Wind rushed

182

through the windows and circled around him, causing his robes to flutter. A second later, a white light flashed and he disappeared, leaving behind a blue robe.

The remaining men stared at the space he had occupied and shook their heads.

***

A skeleton stood over a naked man lying prone on the ground. It was patrolling the fields outside of the undead kingdom when the naked man had fallen out of the sky and landed in front of it. The skeleton took a few steps forward and prodded the man with its axe handle. There was no response. It shrugged and stepped around the body.

"Wait!" the naked wizard said as he crawled onto his knees. "Take me to your leader!"

The skeleton paused. "You are seeking the meaning of life?" it asked. "Come with me. I'll enlighten you."

The wizard's mouth fell open, and he jumped to his feet while grabbing the skeleton's skull. "You can really speak?! Just what level of necromancy has your master achieved? What's one plus one?" he asked as he peered at its throat and body.

The skeleton coughed. "It's rude to grab my head, you know?" it asked. "And one plus one is two. Hey! What are you doing?"

The wizard poked his fingers through the skeleton's eye sockets and pulled out a piece of paper. "What's this? Is this the source?" he asked as he opened it.

"No, that's—"

"Five ways to achieve immortality through daily prayers?" the wizard mumbled to himself. "I've never heard of these methods before. Coming here was definitely the right choice." He nodded at the skeleton. "Tell your master that the human kingdom sent an envoy to discuss our future alliance."

"Oh? Will the envoy be arriving soon?"

"I'm the envoy. Me!" the wizard said and stuck his chest out.

"Okay, I'll let her know," the skeleton said and nodded. "Definitely. How about you come with me for a walk first as I tell you about our lord and resurrector?"

***

Lindyss stood by her window, searching for any signs of Tafel's arrival.

"Rest assured," the undead leader said. "That was one of our best men sent to retrieve Tafel. He wouldn't fail."

Lindyss sighed and nodded. "Alright, let me know when she arrives. I'll accompany Vur until then," she said as her eyes passed over the wizard and skeleton in the distance. Her brow furrowed. "And stop stripping people. You'll scare away potential inhabitants."

18

Celia sat next to a green sprout that had two leaves poking out of the top. It was eight inches tall, and the stem pulsed with a golden glow. She was reading a book out loud with her wooden spear on the grass beside her. She wore leather breeches with a green cotton halter top. Her gold hair cascaded down to her lower back.

A shadow fell over the glade, causing Celia to stiffen. She snapped her book shut and grabbed her spear as she rose to her feet. Two dragons, one black and one red, were circling above her.

"This should be the spot, right?" Prika asked while squinting at the ground.

"Yeah, look," Grimmy said and pointed. "You can see the crybaby down there."

"Who's a crybaby!?" Celia shouted as her right eye twitched. She shook her spear at the two dragons. A second later, she knelt on the grass as her face paled. "I mean, greetings, Grimmoldesser, Pyrrhicandra."

Prika and Grimmy landed in front of Celia who lowered her head even further and gulped. Grimmy snorted. "This is the new Tree of Knowledge?" he asked. "Isn't it too tiny?"

It's your faults! Celia thought but said, "Yes, it has only sprouted recently."

Prika nodded and grinned. "And you elves are bound to protect this, right?"

Sweat formed on Celia's brow. "That's correct," she said. "Is there anything I can help you with?"

"You've probably heard of the new kingdom that Lindyss founded, right?" Grimmy asked as he flapped his wings before pressing them against his sides.

Celia's face contorted. "The Corrupted One? We've received reports about it but decided it would be best not to interfere with her actions."

Grimmy slammed his paw in front of Celia, causing her to fall over backwards. "Don't call her that," he said with his teeth bared. He snorted and raked back his claws, leaving fissures in the earth.

"U-understood," Celia said as her eyes grew hot. Her vision blurred. "I-it won't happen again."

Prika cleared her throat. "Anyways, about that new kingdom. The skeletons are numerous, but they really can't stop a wave of high-ranked adventurers without abandoning the city in a siege," she said. "We'd like the elves to help out." She stepped forward and sniffed the new Tree of Knowledge.

Celia frowned. "I'd have to ask the elders. I don't control our policies," she said as she sat up and wiped her eyes with the backs of her hands.

"Oh, don't worry. The elders will agree," Prika said and smiled.

Celia tilted her head. "Why do the dragons care about the undead kingdom?"

"It's going to be Vur's playground," Prika said. "And quite frankly, I'm bored. It's been a while since I've done anything entertaining. Wouldn't it be fun to rule over a kingdom in the shadows?"

Celia stared at Prika. "I-I guess?" she asked. Her eyes widened at Grimmy. "Hey! What are you doing!?"

Grimmy was using his claws to dig away the dirt surrounding the Tree of Knowledge. "Digging," he said and lifted the chunk of soil carrying the sprout's roots.

"You can't do that!" Celia said. "This is the holy land!" She reached for the sprout in Grimmy's claw.

186

Grimmy laughed. "No, no. That's where you're wrong," he said as he lifted his paw above Celia's head, keeping the sprout out of reach. "The tree wasn't planted here because the land is holy. The land is holy because the tree was planted here, you see?" He grinned before flapping his wings and leaping into the air.

Prika winked at Celia. "I told you the elders would agree," she said and flew after Grimmy.

Celia's shoulders hunched forward as the two dragons got smaller and smaller. She turned her head towards the hole in the ground and sighed. She picked up her book and trudged out of the glade. What would the elders think?

***

"Is that a dragon?" the naked wizard asked, his mouth open and eyes on the sky. "Is that two dragons!?" He was standing in the middle of the street with a skeleton. The people in the streets glanced up at the sky before continuing what they were doing.

"Quick, let's go after them," the wizard said as he grabbed the skeleton's arm and pulled it with him.

"Isn't that Exzenter?" a man on the street asked the woman beside him. They stared at the naked man pulling the skeleton while running through the streets of the undead kingdom. The woman's face turned red as she turned her head away.

"What's the number one time mage doing here?" the man asked out loud and scratched his head. He shrugged and turned back to face the woman as Exzenter got further and further away.

Exzenter stopped running and smacked his forehead. "Why am I running?" he asked and spread his arms open. Wind swirled around him, and he disappeared along with the skeleton in a flash of light.

***

Lindyss sat underneath a tree on a hill, reading while waiting for Prika and Grimmy. She was wearing a green robe, and her hair was wrapped in a bun behind her head. The ground shook, and Lindyss stood up. She frowned as cracks spread beneath her. She stepped to the side, and a moment later, a hand broke through the earth. Lindyss tilted her head as another hand shot out of the ground and proceeded to dig a hole into the surrounding dirt. A face with a white beard popped out of the earth and looked up at her. Lindyss stared back.

"Help?" Exzenter asked as his hands flailed above him.

Lindyss took a step back and coughed. She turned her head away, admiring the approaching dragons in the distance.

"Please don't act like you didn't see me," Exzenter said as he spat out a clump of dirt. He wrinkled his nose and muttered, "Stupid elevation teleporting nonsense."

Lindyss' brow furrowed at the man. She knelt to the ground, scooped up a handful of dirt, and placed it on Exzenter's forehead. "I'll be sure to bury you properly," she said and nodded. "May your soul rest in peace."

"No, no, no, no," Exzenter said as he shook off the dirt from his head. "Wrong kind of help. Dig me out?"

A skeletal hand popped out of the ground next to Exzenter. Another hand popped out, and a skeleton slid out of the earth. "Oh. Greetings to the lord," the skeleton said and nodded at Lindyss.

Lindyss pointed at Exzenter. "What is this thing? And why can it speak?"

The skeleton clawed away the dirt in its eye sockets. "Oh, that's just a crazy man. He fell from the sky. I think he was seeking salvation."

"How rude. My name is Exzenter," Exzenter said and pouted. "I'm the envoy sent to establish a relationship with the kingdom of Konigreich. The human kingdom sends its regards."

Lindyss raised an eyebrow. "Is he serious?"

"I think everything he says can be taken with a grain of salt," the skeleton said and nodded.

"No, no. I'm really—oh, they're here!" Exzenter said with wide eyes as he twisted his neck to look behind himself like an owl. Lindyss turned away and shielded her eyes as Prika and Grimmy landed, causing a gust of wind to blow outwards.

"We got it," Grimmy said and grinned as he held out the sprout towards Lindyss.

"What's this?" Prika asked, blinking at Exzenter's face. She poked his forehead with the tip of her claw, causing him to yelp. Prika turned towards Lindyss and clicked her tongue. "You should really stop planting such strange things. This is why you haven't gotten married yet."

Lindyss' right eye twitched, and she threw a thunderbolt at the cheeky dragon.

Prika swatted it towards Exzenter with her claw. "Violent tendencies too," Prika said as she shook her head. "Tsk, tsk."

Exzenter coughed out smoke through his frizzled beard.

"Should we plant it here?" Grimmy asked as he sniffed Exzenter's head.

"No," Lindyss said and dusted off her hands. "The nutrients in this soil will make the tree stupid. We should go somewhere else."

Grimmy nodded and lifted Lindyss onto his head. His wings flapped, and he jumped into the air. Prika shrugged at Exzenter before taking off.

"Wait!" Exzenter shouted. "Let me study you!" The figures of the dragons got smaller and smaller as they flew away. Exzenter's eyes shifted towards the skeleton. "Help?"

"Have you tried praying?" the skeleton asked. "When everything seems to be going wrong in life and you just can't seem to get free, a prayer can heal your soul."

***

"We're actually fighting chamber pots...," Lamach said as a bronze cauldron floated in front of him. He was with Gabriel in the third room of Niffle's mana source. The walls pulsed with a white glow, illuminating floating cauldrons and bath towels.

Gabriel lowered his morning star mace as a bath towel folded itself into a crane.

"From slimes, to utensils, to outhouse supplies," Gabriel said. He shook his head. "Well, it doesn't matter. Experience is experience." Gabriel wore steel chainmail and gauntlets. His two horns grew an inch past his ears, their silver color standing out against the black of his hair.

Lamach nodded. He tightened his grip on his spear and stepped forward. He wore black leather armor, and his horns curled forward like a ram's. He jabbed the bottom of the floating bronze chamber pot, causing sparks to fly. The chamber pot tilted towards Lamach, and a pair of eyes opened on the side of the rim furthest from him. The eyes squinted and a rumbling sound rang out. The chamber pot flew towards Lamach.

Gabriel stepped forward and bashed it with his shield before it reached his brother. He swung his mace down and knocked the chamber pot to the ground. Tears sprang from the chamber pot's eyes, and a high-pitched ringing noise assaulted Lamach's and Gabriel's ears. Gabriel gritted his teeth and stomped on the rim with his heel as Lamach stabbed one of its eyes.

The chamber pot rolled onto its side, its opening facing the two brothers. It shut its one good eye and made squelching noises. Lamach lunged forward with his spear. Gabriel opened his mouth. "Wai—"

A fountain of brown liquid shot out of the chamber pot and covered the brothers. Lamach's eyes watered as he pierced through the center of the pot with his spear. He fell onto his knees and clutched his stomach as he threw up on the floor. Tears streamed out of Gabriel's eyes as he vomited in rapid succession.

After they finished hurling and crying, they stripped off their armor and wiped away the brown stains with their undergarments. They looked each other in the eye. "This never

190

happened," Gabriel said. The two were dressed in only their boxers.

Lamach nodded as he frowned at the pile of clothes and armor on the floor. They headed back towards the second room with the utensils. They killed their way through and made it back to the slimes.

"Lamach! Gabriel!" Doofus said. "Your sister's been kidnapped and—. Why are you almost naked?" He sniffed the air and winced. "Did you guys go to the third room?"

"What happened to Tafel?" Lamach asked, ignoring Doofus' question.

Doofus frowned. "I don't know the exact details, but I know your father mobilized the army," he said. "I'll tell you everything as we head back to the castle. The royal family requested me to escort you two back in case you're also targeted." The trio walked through the first room, gathering the rest of the students. Doofus ordered them to return to the academy and brought Gabriel and Lamach to the nearest street to hail a carriage.

"It happened during your sister's birthday party," Doofus said as he sighed and boarded the carriage. "A messenger from Konigreich came. He delivered a message to your father and kidnapped Tafel right in front of your parents' eyes."

"Good thing we didn't go, huh?" Gabriel asked.

"Don't say things like that," Doofus said as his eyebrows knit together. "She's your sister."

Gabriel snorted. "Better her than us," he said as he puffed his chest out. "There's no way Tafel's going to be the next demon lord. It doesn't matter what happens to her."

Lamach narrowed his eyes at Gabriel before asking Doofus, "How strong is Konigreich?"

Doofus shook his head. "I've only heard rumors about it. Their skeleton soldiers induced nightmares in our most hardened spear corps," he said. "Your father rates them as at least an SSS-class threat. He mobilized the heavy cavalry and

191

the black mage corps. Your mother, Dustin, and a few other SSS-ranked adventurers are going as support."

"All that for a bunch of skeletons?" Gabriel asked with a snort. "I could kill them in my sleep."

Doofus sighed. "Confidence is fine, Gabriel," he said. His eyes narrowed. "But arrogance is not."

Gabriel rolled his eyes and muttered, "Whatever."

Doofus shook his head and leaned against his seat.

***

"Is this really okay?" Tafel asked the skeleton messenger. She was sitting on the skeletal horse, using the skeleton knight as a backrest. The front of her purple birthday dress was speckled with dried blood, and the edges of her mouth were stained black.

"Of course. Do you want another piece of meat?"

Tafel shook her head and adjusted the cushion underneath her. She leaned back against the metal armor and closed her eyes. The pair had been riding for a week straight, only stopping when Tafel needed to use the bathroom. The outline of Konigreich could be seen on the horizon as the two rode through a green plain bordered by a forest.

"Halt!"

The skeleton turned its head towards the forest with its body still facing forward. Four demons, riding giant yellow chickens, emerged from the brush and pursued the skeletal horse. The pursuers wore leather armor with swords strapped to their backs.

Tafel opened her eyes and twisted her body to look at them, peering through the gap made by the skeleton's armpit. "That's the Four Yellow Riders," she squinted and said. "They're an A-ranked scouting party."

The skeleton laughed. "It seems like they're gaining on us too. Maybe I should leave them a present."

"Don't worry, Princess Tafel!" one of the riders shouted. "We'll save you soon."

192

Tafel frowned and stood up while holding onto the skeleton's pauldrons for support. Her gray horns pulsed with a green light, and she pointed at the riders. A wall of wind formed behind the skeleton and rushed towards the demons, knocking them off their mounts.

"What are you doing!?" one of the riders shouted.

Tafel stuck her tongue out and sat back down.

"Oh," the skeleton messenger said. "That was pretty good. I was just going to fling poop at them."

"Eww," Tafel said as her eyebrows knit together. "Is that what smelled so bad this whole time?"

The skeleton's body shook. "They're leftovers from a previous operation," it said while cackling.

"That's so gross," Tafel said as her face paled.

The skeleton grinned. "Only if you have a nose."

***

"You failed?" Zollstock asked the four adventurers who had their heads lowered. Their yellow chickens were sitting behind them outside the tent with their heads curled under their wings. Zollstock and Mina were in their tent within the camp the army had set up.

"Yes, Milord," the leader of the riders said. "The princess knocked us off our mounts with aero before we could catch up."

Zollstock frowned. "Very well," he said and nodded. "You're dismissed."

The four riders stood up and left, not willing to stay behind for another second.

Mina sighed. Zollstock put his hand on her shoulder. "Don't worry," he said. "We'll get her back. We'll reach their borders tomorrow and make them pay."

Mina's eyes remained closed. "Is it my fault?" she asked as she opened her eyes. "Was my mom right?" Light illuminated her wet eyes, causing them to glitter. "You saw just as well as I did. She left with him; she wasn't taken."

Zollstock hugged her while rubbing her back. "It's not your fault," he said. "The skeletons must have some charm magic on them that convinces people."

Mina put her hands on his chest and pushed him away. "There was no magic," she said as tears fell from her eyes. "You know there wasn't. Don't lie to me." She wiped her eyes with the backs of her hands and stood up. Zollstock started to stand.

"Don't," Mina said. Zollstock stopped and sighed before sitting back down.

"I'm going to take a walk," Mina said and curtsied before leaving.

Zollstock pinched his forehead with his hand. "Seth," he said. A demon wearing a black cloak and mask appeared next to him. "Keep an eye on her."

Seth nodded and disappeared.

Zollstock's eyes narrowed as he stroked his chin.

19

The moon shone overhead as Mina meandered through the camp. After walking for a while, she reached the camp's makeshift barrier leading outside.

"Halt," a voice called out above her. "Who goes there?"

Mina raised her head and saw a familiar figure sitting on a watchtower. Her chest tightened. "Dustin," she said with a neutral face.

"Mina...," Dustin said and let out a breath. "You shouldn't be wandering around at night; it's dangerous."

"I appreciate the concern, but I can take care of myself. Why are you on guard duty?"

"You're underestimating the undead," Dustin said and shook his head. "I'd like to not get robbed this time. I figured the best way to do that is take up guard duty myself."

Mina nodded. "I'll keep that in mind," she said as she took a step outside the camp.

"Stop," Dustin said. "I can't let you leave. No one's allowed to go out during the night in case of ambushes."

"You think I can't handle myself?" Mina asked. Her horns pulsed with a faint red color.

"That's beside the point," Dustin said and sighed. "I know you're worried about Tafel, but she's strong, Mina. She inherited your personality, you know? We'll get her back tomorrow. I'm sure the you from back then would've loved to explore the undead kingdom, wouldn't Tafel too?"

Mina clenched her hands and glared at Dustin for five seconds before turning back towards the camp. "Thank you...," she muttered towards the ground. Dustin watched her disappear into the shadows before turning around to face the fields again. He sighed.

***

"Auntie!"

Lindyss was in her room, sitting on the edge of her bed with mana crystals laying around her. She opened her eyes and was greeted by the sight of a dirty child running towards her. Tafel spread her arms open for a hug and leapt at Lindyss. Lindyss stuck her finger out and poked Tafel in the forehead before she could reach her. The demon princess fell to the floor and looked up with tears in her eyes.

"You smell gross," Lindyss said as she got off the bed. "Take a bath first." She bent down and ruffled Tafel's already disheveled hair. "It's good to see you again, Tafel." Lindyss grabbed Tafel's hand and pulled her to her feet.

Tafel pouted. "I couldn't take a bath for a week," she said and frowned at her dress.

Lindyss smiled and rummaged through her closet. She pulled out a Tafel-sized sweater and a pair of pants. "Vogel, take Tafel to the baths and bring her to Vur when she's done," Lindyss said as she passed the clothes to Tafel. A vampire bat dropped down from the ceiling and perched on Tafel's head.

"Yes, Master!" it said and grabbed Tafel's upper horns like reins. "This way." It tugged on her right horn. Tafel nodded and made her way to the baths.

Lindyss waited until Tafel left before storing the mana crystals in a chest underneath her bed. She stretched her arms out in front of her chest and motioned for the skeleton messenger to come in. "Report," she said.

The messenger nodded. "The demon lord saw me take Tafel away. They sent men to stop us, but they couldn't do anything," the skeleton said and scratched its head. "I suspect I may have angered him as I left."

"So we should be expecting company?" Lindyss asked and rubbed her chin.

196

The skeleton nodded.

Lindyss smiled. "Good," she said. "Let's ready a welcoming party for them."

***

Clanging sounds rang throughout the field as metal collided against metal. Bones snapped and crunched as blunt weapons smashed against them. Cackling filled the sky as skeletons laughed and swung their weapons. The knights on the final line of defense were wearing full mithril platearmor, guarding a tent. The skeletons surrounded the knights and swarmed them, bringing them to their knees with sheer numbers.

The undead leader cackled. It was standing in a tent behind its army. "You lose again," it said. The skeletons tore down the tent in front of them and knocked over Vur's table. He pouted.

"That wasn't fair," Vur said. The undead leader and Vur were separated by a field filled with fallen skeletons who were collecting their bones and climbing to their feet. The two were standing over their own tables that let them command the skeletons on the field.

"All is fair in war," the leader said and grinned. "Dead men can't complain about a loss."

Vur tilted his head. "But aren't you—"

"Hush, it's just a saying," the undead leader said. "Want to play again?"

"Oka—"

"Vur!"

Vur turned his head and got tackled to the ground by Tafel.

"Tafel," Vur said with a smile as he put his arms around her. "You're finally here."

"Never leave me again, okay?" Tafel asked as she buried her head into his chest and clutched his back.

Vur ran his fingers through her hair. "I won't," he said and closed his eyes. "I promise."

The nearby skeletons inched away from the two and tiptoed back to the leader across the field. The leader approached the two children on the floor. "So this is Tafel, eh?" the undead leader asked as it sat down next to them. "Isn't it a little too early in the morning to be doing this?"

Tafel climbed off of Vur and sat up with her face red. Vur got up and held her hand.

"You're the princess of the demons?" the leader asked.

Tafel nodded.

"I have to thank you," the skeleton said. "I haven't had this much fun messing with people since I died."

Tafel tilted her head. "Err, you're welcome… I guess?"

The leader's teeth clacked together as it chuckled. "I look forward to serving you in the future."

"Me?" Tafel asked. "Why me?"

The leader stared at her. "Because you're going to be our empress, no?" it asked and pointed at Vur. "If he's the emperor, then you're the empress."

"Wait. What about Auntie Lindyss?" Tafel asked with wide eyes. "Isn't she the ruler?"

"No," the leader said. "She's our lord and resurrector. Our god, if you want to call her that."

"God…," Tafel mumbled. "What does she get from creating this empire if she doesn't want to rule it?"

"Mana," the skeleton said. "Everyone here pumps their mana into crystals to exchange for food and shelter. Our lord takes the crystals and uses the mana to purify the illness in her body."

"She's sick?" Tafel asked. She thought back to all the times Lindyss cast magic and shook her head.

"A long time ago—"

Lindyss appeared behind the skeleton leader and punted its head off with her foot. "Stop spreading rumors about me."

The undead leader saluted with its headless body and walked over to retrieve its cranium. It twisted its head back on. "Maybe some other time," it said to Tafel and went back to the army of skeletons on the other side of the field.

Lindyss smiled at the two children. "We're throwing a party," she said and turned to Tafel. "I think I interrupted yours. Sorry about that."

Tafel shook her head. "It's okay," she said. "I didn't like it."

"What kind of party?" Vur asked. "Will there be cake and cookies?"

Lindyss paled. "Only two slices of cake at most for you, okay?" she asked. The first time Vur discovered cake, he ate three of them and wrecked a portion of the forest in the following sugar rush.

Vur pouted. "Okay."

"Wear nice clothes too. Tafel's parents are going to be there."

"Yes, Auntie," Vur said.

"Really?" Tafel asked. "My parents will be here?" Her body trembled.

Vur tightened his grip on her hand.

"Don't worry," Lindyss said and smiled. "You won't be in trouble. Come, the party's starting in a few hours." She turned around and walked back towards the city. The two children exchanged glances before following her.

"When did you start wearing nice clothes?" Tafel asked Vur who was shirtless.

Vur shrugged. "Grimmy said that even dragons have to look nice sometimes to impress the ladies," he said. "And since I don't have my scales or wings yet, I have to wear clothes to look better."

Lindyss laughed. "Didn't you also want to wear a bow tie like the one I made for Grimmy?" she asked and turned to wink at Tafel. "He's dressing up just for you."

Tafel's and Vur's faces turned red as they looked away from each other, but their hands held the other's tighter.

***

The sun shone over the main plaza of Konigreich. Thousands of people—humans and demons alike—chatted with one another as they browsed the stalls and sat in chairs. The majority of the buildings had been relocated by Exzenter through his time magic. Massive boars, bears, livestock, fruits, and pastries were spread throughout the plaza in piles. Barrels of wine encircled the people, and floating bubbles of water hung overhead within arm's reach, suspended by magic. The air was fresh, and no traces of undead could be seen or smelled. A group of musicians had set up their instruments at the center of the plaza, and people stumbled as they drank and danced with each other. Laughter filled the streets, and children chased each other through the crowds.

Tafel and Vur were sitting at the perimeter of the party near a pile of sweets and meat. Tafel wore a white woolen sweater with black cotton pants. Her hair was tied in a ponytail with a ribbon that was the same shade of purple as her eyes. Vur wore black leather pants along with a sky-blue scaled vest. He wore a gold bow tie, and his hair fell just above the base of his neck.

"You're not going to play with the other children?" Tafel asked as she leaned her head against Vur's shoulder.

Vur shook his head and held Tafel's hand. "They're scared of me," Vur said. "Also, they're too soft and run too slow. The skeletons are much more fun to play with. They don't cry when their bones break."

Tafel shuddered and tightened her grip on his hand. The two were silent, watching the people drink and dance in the plaza.

Vur cleared his throat. "Did I say something wrong? Auntie found some people to show me how to be noble, but Gale said I still say inappropriate things."

Tafel shook her head. "It wasn't wrong. Just a little scary. Who's Gale?"

"He was one of the people Auntie found," Vur said. "I learned to dance and play instruments too."

"Really?" Tafel asked as she lifted her head off his shoulder. "Do you want to dance with me?"

Vur nodded. The two stood up, and Vur placed his left hand on Tafel's shoulder and held up his right arm.

Tafel tilted her head. "Um, isn't my left hand supposed to go on your shoulder and your right hand under mine?"

"That matters? I've only watched two men dance together."

"Yeah," Tafel said and nodded. "Boys do the leading and girls follow." She giggled. "If you only know the girl part, I can lead this time."

Vur scratched his head. His cheeks were tinged with red. "Okay. You can lead."

Tafel led and the two waltzed in time with the music.

"Am I doing it right?" Vur asked with his gaze glued to his feet.

Tafel giggled. "You make a pretty good girl," she said. "You're supposed to look at me though, not your feet." She smiled when Vur raised his head. "That's better."

Vur smiled back.

***

An army of 30,000 demons formed up in ten 60-by-50 rectangles of people. The vast majority wore chainmail and had clubs and shields. A thousand or so cavalry were wearing plate armor and rode atop horses, spears in hand. The remaining demons wore cloth armor, wielding metal staves. Across the plains, facing the army, there was an elf with a red robe standing on top of a basilisk. A skeleton with mithril armor and a human male wearing a toga stood on either side of her. The sun shone overhead, causing sweat to roll down the demons' backs. At the head of the demon army stood Zollstock and Mina. Sounds of laughter and music permeated the air behind Lindyss.

"Waaah," Exzenter said as he straightened his toga. "That's a lot of them. They have their heavy cavalry and the mage corps it seems."

The undead leader laughed. "They're just fodder to puff up their numbers."

Exzenter glanced around. The trio were alone. "That's a lot more fodder than we have," he said. "Are you sure this is going to work?"

The undead leader grinned. "Of course it'll work. They're all nobles who're afraid to step on poop with their shoes."

"Return Tafel to us!" Zollstock shouted from across the field.

"Return? You make it sound like we stole her," Lindyss said with her voice amplified by wind magic. "From what I heard, she willingly came here with my messenger."

"Shut your mouth!" Zollstock roared.

Lindyss laughed. "Or what? You'll use your puny army to fight against ours?" she asked. "Didn't you receive any reports on the size of our army? You should've recruited some more villagers." She tilted her head and smiled. "Oh right. I forgot. All of them came over and joined our kingdom."

Zollstock's body shook as his face turned red.

Lindyss giggled. "Well, it's to be expected," she said and shrugged. "You can't even get your children to listen to you, why would a nation?"

"All troops forward!" Zollstock yelled as spittle flew from his mouth. Metal clanked as the infantry shouted and charged ahead of Zollstock.

Lindyss turned to Exzenter. "Do it," she said. "Drop it right on top of them."

Exzenter's eyebrows knit together. "Isn't this a bit ... excessive?"

"You want to set up an alliance between our kingdoms, right?" Lindyss smiled. "Just do this one little thing and I'm sure negotiations will go smoothly."

Exzenter sighed and nodded. He spread his arms open, and wind rushed towards the approaching army, encircling them. Streams of blue light flowed into the time mage's body from a pile of mana crystals behind him.

Dustin gaped as he walked up to Zollstock and Mina. "That's Exzenter," he said. "The strongest human time mage. And that's a tremendous amount of mana he's manipulating. The scale of that spell must be huge. We can only hope our soldiers reach him before he finishes."

Zollstock frowned. "Time mages aren't offensive. Is he trying to warp all our soldiers away? Is that even possible?"

Dustin's eyebrows knit together. "It seems larger than that, he—. Watch out!" Dustin tackled Zollstock and Mina forward. Hundreds of little portals appeared above the army and blotted out the sun. Dozens of large portals appeared above the little ones.

Exzenter released his breath and wiped his brow. "I know I'm not religious, but may god have mercy on my soul," he said and clasped his hands together.

The army screamed and cursed as thousands of brown objects fell from the sky, splattering their bodies. They raised their shields above their heads and wept as sulfurous fumes invaded their nostrils. Some of the objects were dry and brittle, others were wet and stuck to their armor and hair.

Mina screamed as she covered her head. "This is disgusting!" she shrieked as Dustin vomited next to her.

"Forward! Forward!" the soldiers yelled, pushing and shoving each other to escape the torrential downpour. The brown storm started to let up as fewer clumps fell.

Then it happened.

The large ones came.

Boulder-sized turds fell from the sky and splattered on impact. Skeletons cackled as they crawled out of the fallen comets and pulled soldiers down to the ground while embracing them. A symphony of wails and shrieks filled the air, peppered with the sounds of retching and splashing.

A tear leaked from the undead leader's eye. "It's beautiful," it said and sniffed. "Truly the epitome of strategic warfare." It turned to Exzenter. "Thank you for making this happen. I can die happy now."

Exzenter sighed and shook his head. "All those wonderful dragon stool samples," he said and sniffed, "wasted on this."

The storm passed, and the sun illuminated the brown battleground as the portals vanished. Wails and sobs rang out as the skeletons systematically stripped the army of their armor and weapons while tying the soldiers together. A few spells flew through the battlefield, but a retaliation of brown goop put an end to that.

Lindyss coughed after the skeletons finished. "Everyone who wants a bath has to join Konigreich as a citizen of our kingdom. You'll be given fresh undergarments and food along with drink," she said and glanced at Zollstock. "The rest of you will have to wait here until our party is over."

Zollstock opened his mouth. "That's—"

"Or … we can come to an agreement between our two nations," Lindyss said, interrupting him with a smile. "What do you say? But say it from far away. You stink."

***

The moon shone overhead as Mina walked out of the plaza towards the forest. Tafel and Vur were sitting against a tree, leaning on each other with bloated bellies. Mina opened her mouth to speak but closed it when she saw Tafel's face. Her daughter was smiling with her eyes closed. Mina's eyes grew wet, and she loosened her grip on her cup. She sighed, took a swig, and walked back towards the plaza.

Interlude

Snuffles sniffed the cluster of mushrooms in front of him. The ground shook, and the leaves on the trees rustled. Snuffles turned away from the mushrooms and peered into a gap between a pair of trees in the forest.

The shaking stopped, and Snuffles stared into the distance for a few more seconds before turning back to the mushrooms. He dug them up with his snout and ate them. He let out a squeal and arched his back while extending his front hooves forward like a cat. He walked under a tree and yawned while curling up into a ball.

The shaking resumed, and a howl rang out, followed by a bird's shrill cry. Snuffles lifted his head and squinted in the direction of the shaking. A few seconds later, the shaking stopped. He tilted his head to the side and lowered it again, closing his eyes. His breathing slowed, and his mouth fell open a tiny bit every time his stomach rose. Drool pooled in his lower mouth and leaked onto the grass.

Ear-splitting howls echoed through the forest as a bird shrieked. White flames sprang up in the distance and smoke rose into the air. Snuffles' eyes shot open, and he climbed to his feet. He stared in the direction of the sound with his eyes glowing. A sky-blue light spread out from his forehead and wrapped around his body like a web as he let out a squeal that drowned out the howls. The tree trunks in front of him cracked, and the trees toppled over with a crash. The forest fell silent as the flames disappeared, only leaving behind a trace of smoke in the air.

Snuffles snorted and trotted in the direction of the sounds. He arrived at a clearing with charred craters and deep gouges in the earth. On the left side of the clearing was a pack of wolves with silver fur and red eyes. Patches of burnt fur and skin peppered their coats. Across from them, on the right side, was a phoenix, roughly the same size as Snuffles. It was dark blue with white flames dancing around its feather tips. Dark-red gouges dripped blood onto the ground beneath the bird. The two sides remained motionless as Snuffles meandered into the clearing, eyes still glowing. He turned his gaze on the wolves. They flinched, and their hackles rose as they bared their teeth at him.

Snuffles snorted. He turned his head towards the phoenix. One of its wings were torn and hung limp at its side. The phoenix met Snuffles' eyes and didn't move. White flames flickered around its body. Snuffles tilted his head and approached the phoenix. The wolves growled and stamped the ground, but Snuffles ignored them. The phoenix took a step back and then another step as Snuffles got closer.

A wolf howled and dashed towards Snuffles, its eyes glowing red. Snuffles stomped the ground with his front left hoof. A web of cracks spread throughout the clearing. The lunging wolf leapt backwards and stared at the ground before looking at the boar in front of it, growling. Snuffles snorted and roared at the pack of wolves. He glared at them with golden glowing eyes, and a faint image of a dragon's head materialized above Snuffles' body. The wolves' ears flattened against their heads, and their hackles lowered as they crawled onto their bellies. The biggest wolf let out a bark, turned around, and sprinted into the forest. The other wolves scrambled to their feet and followed.

The image of the dragon faded away, and Snuffles directed his attention towards the phoenix. It shivered and tried to flap its wings, but only its good wing moved. It let out a soft cry as Snuffles walked closer to it and stopped in front of its body. Its silver eyes stared at Snuffles, unblinking, as the boar bent his knees and motioned towards his back with his head. The
206

phoenix tilted its head and took a tiny step forward. Snuffles nodded and leaned towards the phoenix. It hesitated before grabbing onto Snuffles bristles with its talons and climbed onto his back.

Snuffles trotted out of the clearing towards the direction he came from. Other beasts looked at the pair but didn't approach. Instead, they knelt on the ground as Snuffles walked past. The two arrived at a cave that Snuffles liberated from a behemoth bear a few days prior. Its corpse was still frozen at the entrance, and the phoenix gaped at it as they passed by.

Snuffles stopped at a bed made from moss and grass. He crawled onto his belly and tilted the phoenix towards the bed. It slid off and turned around, blinking at Snuffles. He snuffled and nudged the phoenix with his snout before nodding and moving to the entrance of the cave. The phoenix sat down, tucked its head under its wing, and fell asleep. Snuffles watched the phoenix's chest rise and fall a few times before he curled up into a ball and lowered his head. His eyes stopped glowing, and he yawned before falling asleep.

***

Sounds of slurping and munching permeated the cave. The phoenix opened its eyes and saw Snuffles chewing on a bear paw at the entrance. It stood up and winced as it looked down at the gouges in its chest. The majority of the wounds were clotted, but a few areas still leaked blood.

Snuffles' ears twitched, and he turned his head towards the phoenix with a piece of meat in his mouth. He walked forward and placed the chunk of flesh in front of the phoenix. The phoenix stared at him without moving, and he nudged the meat with his snout before snuffling. The phoenix pecked it and tore off strips of meat.

Snuffles dug a hole in the ground. A chunk of ice materialized in it as his eyes glowed. He pointed at the chunk of ice with his hoof and then pointed at the phoenix. The phoenix tilted its head before its eyes glittered. It spewed white flames at the chunk of ice, melting it into a pool of water. Snuffles took a few sips before motioning towards the phoenix with his head. It finished eating the chunk of meat and waddled over to drink the water. Snuffles sat down and observed the phoenix's wounds as it drank. It waddled back to the bed and blinked at Snuffles before tucking its head under its wing.

Snuffles waited a few moments before leaving the cave, freezing the entrance with a block of ice before he left. He wandered around the forest, looking for herbs that cured injuries. Vur had pointed out all kinds of plants and their functions as they wandered the forest together during Vur's reading craze. Snuffles wandered and gathered as many plants as he could, careful to not crush them in his mouth as he carried them back to the cave. The ice blocking the entrance vanished, and the phoenix raised its head. It stared as Snuffles walked past it towards the pool and dropped the herbs into the water.

Snuffles approached the phoenix. It flapped its good wing and screeched as Snuffles nudged it towards the pool and pushed it inside.

It struggled and flailed, flinging water everywhere, but Snuffles wouldn't let it climb out. After a few moments, the phoenix stopped struggling. The gouges on its chest had stopped bleeding, and there were traces of new feathers on its torn wing. The phoenix deflated as it looked at Snuffles, lowering its head. The phoenix chirped and floated in the water. Snuffles grunted and trudged back to the entrance of the cave to eat some more meat.

The phoenix climbed out of the pool as Snuffles was finishing up a portion of the bear. It shook its body, flinging water droplets out of its feathers. It preened itself before approaching Snuffles who had curled up into a ball. It tugged on his tail with its talons and gestured in the direction of the bed. Snuffles raised his head before tilting it to the side. The phoenix tugged on his tail again and hopped towards the bed. It stood next to the moss and stared at Snuffles. Snuffles climbed to his feet and trotted over before curling up on the bed. The phoenix sat in between his front and back hooves and snuggled against his belly before tucking its head under its wing. Snuffles closed his eyes and fell asleep.

***

Snuffles dreamed he was a blue, female, baby bird. He was sitting in a nest which was on the peak of an average-sized tree in the forest. There were five red chicks huddled together on the opposite side of the nest. In between him and the red chicks was a grown red phoenix with its head under its wings. Snuffles recognized the phoenix as his father. His mother hunted for food as his father watched over the nest, defending it from would-be predators. His brothers and sisters ignored him and stole food from him whenever possible.

He dreamed that days, then months, passed as he got bigger. Feathers started to poke through his downy fluff. One day, while his mother was hunting, a wyvern flew towards the nest and his father flew up to confront it. The five red phoenixes waited until his father was engaged in battle before lifting Snuffles and tossing him over the edge of the nest.

He flapped his wings, slowing his descent, but he was unable to takeoff into the air. His wing crashed against a branch, and he tumbled to the ground. He tried to chirp, but no noise came out. Only tears.

He crawled to his feet and scratched the tree trunk, but his father was still engaged in battle and couldn't hear him. A badger passed by as he tried to climb up the tree to no avail. It charged him, and he flapped his wings while clawing at the badger. It ignored his strikes and pinned him to the ground as its mouth lunged for his throat. He struggled and a burst of white flames erupted from his body, launching the badger. It screeched as it was blasted two meters away, and it turned to run.

He watched the badger flee before tilting his head up to look at the nest. He couldn't see the treetops from the bottom. He lowered his head and chirped as tears fell from his eyes. He tried to fly, but his flight feathers hadn't fully developed yet and he could only get a foot off the ground. Rustling sounds came from the bushes nearby. Snuffles took one last look at his birth tree before turning to flee.

Days passed as he lived in foxholes and hunted rabbits to survive. Some days, he wouldn't eat anything at all. Days turned to weeks and weeks turned to months. He didn't know where he was. He couldn't remember where his birth tree was. He learned to fly, but couldn't find any traces of his home or his family.

One day, as he was sleeping in a foxhole, a pack of dire wolves found him. The wolves outnumbered him, and the alpha tore his wing before he could take off. They attacked him, ignoring the white flames dancing around his body. His body got heavier and heavier as the wolves harassed him. His eyes glowed silver, and a ball of white flames expanded outwards with him at the center. His vision went black.

Snuffles opened his eyes and saw the phoenix staring at him, tears in her eyes. She blinked and wiped away the tears with her good wing. Snuffles blinked back and nudged her chest with his snout. She tucked her legs under her body and leaned her head against his belly with closed eyes. He snuffled and closed his eyes.

20

Tafel and Vur were sitting on a blanket underneath a tree with a basket of food beside them. Lindyss was busy negotiating with Zollstock and Randel inside of Konigreich's castle. Exzenter had teleported the human king to the kingdom, much to the misfortune of the king and his privacy.

"Where's Snuffles?" Tafel asked.

Vur shrugged. "He disappeared a while ago, but Mom said not to worry about him since he's strong," he said and sighed.

Tafel thought back to the time she heard a father tell his son that his favorite duck had run away after coming back from the butcher. Tafel patted Vur's shoulders. "I'm sure he's doing fine," she said and nodded. "Maybe he found a girlfriend."

"But he only has the dragon class; what if he gets attacked?" Vur asked. "I hope he's okay."

Only..., Tafel thought as she grabbed Vur's hand. "We can go look for him together if you want."

Vur shook his head. "If he's alive, he'll come back. If he doesn't come back, then he got eaten."

"That's kind of bleak."

Vur shrugged. "That's what Leila says. The strong eat the weak. But don't bully the weak just because you're strong."

The undead leader's skull popped out of the ground by their feet. "That's a good policy," the leader said. "This Leila sounds pretty smart."

Tafel blinked at the skull. "Were you here this whole time?"

The leader nodded and laughed. "We're everywhere," it said. "How else are we supposed to stop crimes?"

"Everywhere?"

"Except inside the outhouses. We stay outside the outhouses."

"What about the baths...?" Tafel asked, her cheeks turning pink.

"Don't worry," the leader said and grinned. "There are female skeletons too."

Tafel shuddered. "That's a bit unsettling."

"It's fine," the leader said and waved his hand. "We don't have eyes."

"But you can still se—"

"Oops, gotta go." The leader's head vanished back underneath the ground. A voice floated out of the hole it left behind. "Mistress is calling."

Tafel stared at the hole and sighed. She turned to the basket of food and bit her lower lip. "Suddenly, I'm not hungry anymore," she said. She tugged on Vur's hand. "Do you want to go to the adventurers' guild?"

"Sure."

***

The adventurers' guild was located in a small building by the entrance to Konigreich. It had two floors and a wooden exterior. Vur pushed open the door and the two walked inside. A few men were drinking alcohol and sitting by the tables in the corner. Food, water, and shelter were provided to the citizens for mana crystals, but alcohol had to be bought with gold. A couple of the men raised their eyebrows when they saw the two's short statures, but they paled and looked away after seeing Vur's eyes.

"What's wrong, Jack? You look like you saw a ghost," a man said. He turned around in his seat. "Oh." He turned back, hunching his shoulders as he drank.

"H-hello," the receptionist said as he wiped his brow. He wore a white dress shirt and had thick rectangular glasses.

"What did you do?" Tafel asked Vur. "Everyone's afraid."

212

Vur tilted his head. "I didn't do anything," he said and looked around. No one made eye contact. "Everyone's just always afraid. Grimmy says that's the natural state for humans."

"What can I help you with?" the receptionist asked as he tried to smile. His lips twitched instead.

"We'd like to sign up as adventurers," Tafel said as the two walked up to the counter which was taller than both of them.

"Just the two of you?" the man asked as he leaned over the counter. "Are you registering for an already established party?"

Tafel shook her head and smiled. "We're starting our own."

The receptionist's eyes landed on the adventurers in the corner. They coughed and looked the other way. "Alright. Just fill these papers out," the receptionist said and passed the two three forms. They took the papers and sat at an empty table in the middle of the adventurers. Only the sloshing of liquid could be heard and even those sounds stopped once Vur cleared his throat.

Minutes passed in silence except for the sounds of quills scratching against paper.

When the duo finished filling out the papers, Tafel skipped over to the receptionist and handed them over. "All done."

The receptionist nodded and pulled out two metal cards. "Let's see," he muttered as he placed his hand over one card. "First name, Tafel. Last name, Besteck. Class, Black Mage. Hometown, Niffle. Age, 6. Gender, female. Eye color, purple." His hand glowed blue as the information engraved itself into the card. He double-checked the card and nodded before offering it to Tafel. She took it, and her face broke out into a huge smile.

"Alright. Next," the receptionist said as he held Vur's paper in his left hand with his right hand on the remaining metal card. "First name, Vur. Last name..." The receptionist raised an eyebrow, peering at Vur over his eyeglasses. "Last name?"

Vur shook his head.

Sweat formed on the receptionist's brow. "Okay," he said and turned his attention back on the paper. "Class, Dragon..."

He glanced at Vur again but didn't say anything. "Hometown … blank again. Okay. Age…" The receptionist sighed. "Gender, male. Eye color, gold." His eye twitched when he passed Vur the half-empty card. "Here you go." The receptionist lifted the last sheet of paper. "Party name, Tafel x Vur. Members, Tafel Besteck, Vur, Snuffles…?" He squinted at the paper before addressing Tafel. "Well, you're both registered as adventurers now, and your party has been recorded. Would you like to take a test to determine your starting rank? If you don't take it, you'll start as an E-ranked adventurer."

Tafel nodded while grinning.

The receptionist made a strange face. "Alright, let me get the guild master," he said and walked up the stairs.

The adventurers sitting in the corner exchanged glances with each other. One of them whispered, "Alright, why are we being so quiet? I'm new here. Who's the kid?"

"You know that giant crater in the forest?" another one whispered back. "He's the one who made it. Apparently, he ate too much cake and got excited. A bunch of people tried to stop him, including the guild master and the elves, but they all got thrashed."

The man sucked in his breath. "You serious? That crater's huge."

The other one nodded and lowered his voice even further. "Yeah, don't mess with him. He's a monster."

Tafel frowned. "They're saying weird things about you."

The men fell silent, faces pale.

Vur nodded and smiled. "I like compliments."

A thud rang out from above. "Alright," said a man as he walked down the stairs with a giant silver claymore on his back, "where are the newbies who want to die toda—" The man's eyes locked onto Vur and Tafel. His expression was blank as he made eye contact with the fidgeting receptionist behind him. "Don't tell me it's him."

The receptionist nodded. "It's him."

The guild master's face contorted. He pursed his lips and narrowed his eyes at Vur. He took the giant sword off of his back and pointed it at the two children. His chest expanded as he took in a deep breath. Then he fell to the ground and clutched his chest. "Urgh," he said. "I'm defeated. You pass." He scrambled back up the stairs. "Make them SSS rank and don't bother me until I finish recovering."

"But the girl—"

"I said don't bother me until I finish recovering!" A door slammed shut.

The receptionist sighed. "Congratulations on reaching SSS rank," he said as he took Tafel's and Vur's cards and channeled mana into them.

Tafel hugged Vur's arm. "Thank you," she said and pecked his cheek. "I'm so happy."

Vur blinked at Tafel, his face flushing.

"Let's go on an adventure!" Tafel said while tugging his arm, dragging him to the nearby bulletin board. "Let's pick a fun one. Collect ten corpses? That's too morbid. Steal books from neighboring kingdoms? ... Stealing is bad. Collect dragon stool samples? That's gross, who would even—oh. Exzenter."

"How about collect a bottle of fairy tears?" Vur asked. "We get a chocolate cake as part of the reward."

"Let's do it," Tafel said as she ripped the paper off the bulletin board. "Dustin told me about this one once. He said his party couldn't complete it. I want to beat him." She smiled.

The receptionist looked at the paper. "Are you sure you want to do this one?" he asked. "Fairies are tricky to find, and they're supposed to be pretty deep in the wilderness."

Tafel nodded. "It's fine," she said and giggled. "We're SSSers."

A skull popped out of the floorboards beside Vur and Tafel. "The mistress is looking for you two," it said. "She's at the mansion."

"Okay," Tafel said and turned to the receptionist. "Thanks, mister."

The receptionist nodded at her. "Good luck, you two." He added in a whisper as they left, "Please don't rip requests off the board next time."

***

"Dustin!" Tafel said. "I'm an SSS-ranked adventurer!"

"What?" Dustin asked. Tafel and Vur were at the entrance to the living room of the castle. Lindyss, Exzenter, Randel, Gale, Zollstock, Mina, and Dustin were sitting on couches with a round wooden table separating them.

Tafel nodded. "Vur and I went to the adventurers' guild today and signed up. We passed the test and became SSSers," she said as she pulled out her card. "See?"

Zollstock and Mina glanced at each other. The demon lord cleared his throat. "That's great, Tafel," he said. Mina stayed silent. Zollstock turned towards her and raised an eyebrow.

"We picked a mission too! We're going to get a bottle of fairy tears," Tafel said and stuck her chest out. Vur yawned and stretched while walking over to Lindyss. Mina's chest tightened, and Dustin coughed while looking away with a cramped face.

"Why that mission?" Mina asked with her voice trembling.

"Dustin told me his party couldn't complete it. If I do it, then that means you'll have to accept that I'm strong enough to be an adventurer," Tafel said and pouted.

Mina frowned at Dustin. "I wonder what else you've told her," she said with her eyes narrowed.

"Don't blame Dustin, Mom," Tafel said, biting her lower lip. "Please."

Mina sighed and turned her head away, hiding the wetness in her eyes.

Dustin scratched his head. "It's not that I wasn't strong enough to complete it," he said. "There were just ... circumstances." He gazed at Zollstock for a brief moment.

The room fell silent.

Lindyss let out a cough. "Anyways," she said and clapped her hands, "I'm sure many of you have met or heard about him." She gestured towards Vur.

"What is he?" Randel asked.

Exzenter's eyes twinkled. "A specimen!"

Lindyss ignored the time mage. "He's the adopted child of the dragons," she said and smiled at Randel. "Since *someone* stole their egg."

The human king gulped as his face paled.

"Don't worry; we're not asking you to return the dragon," Lindyss said. "It's just a beast without an imprint after all."

Randel raised an eyebrow. "Really? Aren't its parents furious?"

"They were, but Vur filled the void in their hearts," Lindyss said. "Personally, I think Vur is much more lovable than any dragon child could ever be."

Randel scratched his head. "That just seems too easy…"

Lindyss narrowed her eyes. "Why are you complaining? If you feel guilty, then just return it."

Randel's face cramped as he smiled. "Ah, if that's how it is, then that's just the way it was meant to be."

"He's the reason you want us to unite our kingdoms?" Zollstock asked.

Lindyss nodded. "I want Vur and Tafel to be happy together when they get married," she said, ignoring Mina's frown. "I'd rather not have either of them be discriminated against because of their race."

Randel frowned. "It's not that easy to forget eight hundred years of enmity."

"And yet here we are. Elves, demons, and humans talking with each other peacefully," Lindyss said and leaned back. "Make it happen."

"What do you gain from this?" Gale asked, a furrow in his brow.

"Obviously, I just want Vur to be happy," Lindyss said and narrowed her eyes at Gale. "Nosey people should take care or they might get bit."

Gale shuddered and nodded.

"Great. Now, who wants lunch?" Lindyss asked with a smile.

21

"I think I should subclass as a time mage," Tafel said as she brushed dirt off her sweater. Brown roots and green grass were tangled in her hair. Vur's head popped out of the ground, and he coughed out a clump of mud. Exzenter had teleported the pair to the wilderness.

Vur frowned. "I don't like teleporting. Too much dirt."

Tafel shrugged. "It's only wonky when the distance is really far," she said as she helped dig Vur out of the ground. Her cheeks flushed pink. "At least we kept our clothes."

Vur shook the dirt off his body and looked around. The two were in a jungle with a canopy of leaves blotting out the sun.

"Do you know where we are?" Tafel asked.

Vur shook his head. "I think we're near the graveyard," he said and sniffed the air. "But there could be other places that look like this."

"That's okay," Tafel said and hugged his arm. She smiled. "I'm glad I met you. I didn't think I would become an adventurer this quickly. It's all thanks to you."

Vur's face flushed as he smiled back. The two walked through the forest while holding hands. Tafel kept turning her head to look at the animals and the trees, an expression of awe constantly on her face.

"Why wouldn't your mom let you be an adventurer?" Vur asked after they'd been traveling for a while.

Tafel pouted. "I don't know," she said. "I've asked her, but she always avoided the question. Always saying, 'you'll thank me when you're older,' or 'because I said so.'" Tafel rolled her eyes. "Don't your parents ever tell you things like that?"

Vur shook his head. "Mom lets me do whatever I want and Dad's too afraid of Mom to contradict her. Grimmy sometimes tells me I can't do things. Like that one time he said not to wake Auntie up and I did it anyway." Vur shuddered and nodded. "Always listen to Grimmy."

Tafel laughed. "You're lucky," she said. "I wish I could live like you."

Vur squeezed her hand. "You can now."

Tafel sighed and leaned against him.

A green bush speckled with yellow dots caught Vur's eye. "It's a bananerry bush," he said. Tafel raised her head.

A few figures were flitting over the bush. The two waved at the bush and walked over. "Ah! It's the demon and the bully!" a blue-eyed figure said.

"The dragon boy?" a red-eyed figure asked. "Quick. Hide me!"

The yellow-eyed figure rolled her eyes. "If he wanted to hurt you, he wouldn't just walk over here like that."

Vur peered at the fairies. He held out an empty bottle. "Cry for me."

The red-eyed fairy snorted at the yellow-eyed one. "You were saying?"

The yellow-eyed fairy stared at Vur with her mouth gaping.

"Vur ... you can't just ask them like that," Tafel said. The red-eyed figure nodded and stuck her chest out. Tafel smiled. "You have to say please."

"You!" the red-eyed figure said and pointed at Tafel. "I'll curse you again!"

Tafel hid behind Vur and peeked over his shoulder. "Don't do that, Ral... Rei... Reila?"

"It's Rella!" Rella said and stuck her hands on her hips as she flitted above the bananerry bush.

The blue-eyed figure flew in front of Vur. "What's my name?" she asked as she circled the children's heads.

"Berry," Vur said and pointed at the yellow-eyed figure. "And she's Yellow."

Yella facepalmed and crouched while turning around.

"Your memory sucks for someone who practically ate the Tree of Knowledge," Bella said as she tapped his forehead.

Vur shrugged. "You weren't important enough to remember."

Rella gasped.

"Ouch," Bella said and clutched her chest. "You'll make me cry."

Vur nodded and held the bottle out towards her.

Bella puffed her cheeks out and smacked the bottle. "That's like half my height! I can't cry that much."

Vur frowned, and his eyes glowed. The three fairies plummeted to the bananerry bush.

"Rude!" Rella said as she squirmed, trying to get up.

"What are you going to do to us?" Yella asked with wide eyes.

Tafel smiled and pulled out a feather.

"Oh god," Bella said. "Please, no."

"You three shouldn't have cursed me," Tafel said and ran the feather over Bella's body.

Vur sat down and munched on bananerries as Tafel extracted the fairy tears.

"I'll die! I'll really die!" Rella said as she gasped and shrieked, tears streaming down her cheeks.

"I'll," Yella said and gasped as her eyes glowed, "curse you… and… Stop! Stop! I'll pee!" Her eyes stopped glowing as she writhed under the feather. The fairies shrieked and wailed for an hour while laughing before Tafel relented. She smiled at Vur.

"We got a whole bottle," she said. The fairy trio glared at Tafel with tears and snot running down their faces. Their eyes glowed.

"May you stub your toe every night before you go to bed!" Bella yelled.

"You'll always have to sneeze but never get to!" Rella cried out.

"I curse you with the inability to hear any spoken words! You'll hear the speaker's true thoughts instead," Yella said and pouted. The other two fairies turned towards her with eyebrows raised.

"How's that a curse?"

"Yeah, you should've made her step in a puddle of water every time she put on socks."

Yella frowned. "I thought it was pretty good," she said and lowered her head.

Tafel glared at the three fairies. She turned the bottle upside down. "Oh, it looks like we need more tears," she said as she raised her feather.

The fairies wailed.

***

"Where's Tafel?" Mina asked Zollstock. She stood at the entrance to the dining room wearing a blue dress.

"She should be playing with Vur," the demon lord said as he lifted his fork to his mouth, not bothering to turn his head away from his plate.

Mina frowned and sighed. "I haven't talked to her at all since we came here."

Zollstock stripped a piece of meat off the chicken leg on his plate. "We've been busy. She's been busy. It's understandable."

Mina narrowed her eyes at her husband. "Did you really agree to marry her to Vur? Won't the royal family object to her marrying a human?"

"Becoming allies with Konigreich is much more important than what the royal family thinks," Zollstock said as he put down his utensils.

"They'll disown her," Mina said as she studied Zollstock's face.

222

Zollstock shrugged. "Then aren't we lucky we had triplets?" he asked, dabbing at the corners of his mouth with his napkin. "I'm sure Tafel will be happier with Vur. Don't you agree?" Zollstock smiled, his eyes slightly narrowed.

Mina's horns flashed red. "When have you ever cared about someone else's happiness?" she asked. Her arms crackled with electricity as her dress fluttered around her. "Everything you do is for yourself. You never think of others!" Mina screamed as her face flushed. "I absolutely loathe you, you monster."

"Monster?" Zollstock asked as he raised an eyebrow and folded his napkin. "Isn't that too hurtful? I think it's best if you calm down and think about what you're doing, Mina."

"Oh, I know exactly what I'm doing," Mina said as she stepped towards Zollstock, hands glowing blue. "Don't think I don't know when you lie, when you cheat, when you murder." She narrowed her eyes. "Don't think I don't know what goes on in that basement of yours, harvesting horns for mana. You make me sick."

Zollstock stopped smiling. "Why now?" he asked. Before Mina could respond, he raised his left index finger up. "It's because of Tafel, isn't it? I was wondering why you were so insistent on keeping her so weak." He tilted his head as his hand moved towards the sword propped against the seat next to him.

Mina struck his chest with a thunderbolt. His body slumped over as he crashed against the wall behind him. He raised his head, his horns glowing blue. Flames flickered along his fingertips as he wrinkled his nose and spat out blood. He grinned at Mina. "This is the woman I chased after," he said and licked his lips.

A crashing sound resounded through the room. The walls and floor trembled as a circle of stone fell from the ceiling. Lindyss stood on top of the stone disk wearing pajamas, her hair disheveled and frizzy. Her eyes were bloodshot as she glared at Zollstock and Mina. "Make one more sound," she said, practically growling. "Just one more. I dare you."

223

Zollstock turned pale, and his horns stopped glowing. He glanced at Mina. She threw a thunderbolt at his face. He yelped.

Lindyss' eyes glowed. The building collapsed.

***

"How long does this curse last?" Tafel asked and poked Yella's belly with her feather.

Yella stuck her tongue out. "Not telling," she said as she crossed her arms. Rella and Bella turned their heads away.

"Three months?" Tafel asked. "I'm going to have a headache." She sighed.

"Serves you right!" Bella said while pouting. She turned to Yella. "Your curse is terrible. You made her a mind reader."

Yella laughed. "Don't worry," she said. "She's a princess, right? Everyone's probably spouting nonsense praise for things she doesn't deserve. Just wait until she hears what they really think." Yella nodded. "I bet she'll break down and cry."

"Oh. That's evil," Rella said while covering her mouth with her hand. She grinned. "I like it. Too bad I can't redo my curse. I should've made something better." She sighed.

Tafel tickled her with the feather.

"No more, no more. Please," Rella said as she wriggled on the bananerry bush. "I'm sorry!"

"Yeah, it's too bad you can only curse me once," Tafel said as she moved the feather faster.

"You and your stupid curse!" Rella shouted at Yella with tears streaming down her cheeks.

Vur yawned and stretched. "I'm running out of mana," he said to Tafel.

The fairies cheered. "Even freaks run out of mana, huh?" Bella asked.

Tafel rummaged through her sweater and pulled out a bottle with a blue liquid in it.

"Mana potion?" she asked and offered it to Vur. The fairies wailed.

Vur shook his head. "Tastes bad."

224

"Yeah! It's disgusting," Bella said and clasped her hands together. "Don't drink it."

"Maybe we should trap them in a cage…," Tafel muttered.

The fairies' eyes grew wide. "You can't do that!" Rella said as she tried to squirm away from the feather.

"We're bad luck; you wouldn't want us," Bella said. Tears sprang to her eyes.

"Yeah," Yella said and nodded. "We've met you twice now! That's worse than getting struck by lightning seven times. Think of what'll happen if you take us with you."

Tafel frowned as her body shuddered. She stopped tickling Rella. "I'm sorry," she said and shifted her eyes away from the fairies. She faced Vur. "You should let them go."

Vur nodded and his eyes stopped glowing. The fairies raised their eyebrows and exchanged glances with each other. They shrugged and flew into the branches of a nearby tree.

"Why'd she let us go?" Bella asked as the trio huddled around, taking glances at Tafel and Vur. Rella shrugged.

"It was probably my curse," Yella said and nodded. Bella nudged her off the branch. "Rude!" Yella said as she flitted back up. "Don't be jealous you couldn't think of a better one."

"Ssshh," Rella said and put her finger to her lips. "They're talking."

Tafel took a seat beside Vur and looped her arm around his. "Are demons evil?" she asked. She bit her lower lip. "Am I evil?"

Vur tilted his head. "You're not a bad person."

Tafel squeezed his hand and leaned her head against his shoulder. She sniffled. "But demons imprisoned the fairy queen and took the fairies' home away from them," she said. "When I said 'cage,' they became so scared. I, I feel so bad for them." Tafel's eyes grew wet.

Vur frowned. Tafel shook her head. "They were terrified of me," she said. "Their thoughts felt like mine after you left for a year. A lot worse than mine." She buried her face into Vur's shoulder, sobs escaping from her shaking body.

"Wow," Rella said to Yella. "Your curse really does work."

Bella nodded. "I almost feel bad for her. You made a little girl cry."

"Don't look at me like that!" Yella said as she glared at her two sisters. "You cursed her too!"

"Yeah, but our curses only annoy her."

"Uh-huh, your curse is going to destroy her emotionally and mentally."

Yella pouted. "Serves her right. You two seem to have forgotten she made us cry for two hours."

"Monster," Rella said. "She's just a kid."

"Heartless," Bella said and nodded while crossing her arms.

Yella sighed and lowered her head. "Fine," she said. "I'll go apologize." She flew down from the tree and hovered in front of Tafel's face. She reached forward and flicked Tafel's forehead. "Stop moping. It's not your fault the demons took our home and trapped our mother. I definitely don't blame you or anything."

Tafel blinked her eyes and furrowed her brow.

"What?" Yella asked. "If you really feel bad, then go and free our mother."

"It's just … really weird. Your mouth opens, but the wrong words come out and they're out of sync."

Yella puffed her chest out. "Of course," she said. "I'm good at cursing."

Tafel smiled and wiped her tears with her sleeves. She placed her hand on top of Vur's.

"Want to make a trip to Niffle?"

***

"Imprisoning your allies. Is this really the approach you want to take?" Zollstock asked. He was locked in a cell with blue shackles binding his arms and legs. Black markings encircled his neck. There was a bed in the corner, and a tray of

226

food left untouched on the floor. Mina was sitting in the cell opposite of Zollstock, eating her food, her hands and legs unfettered.

"Orders are orders," a voice said. "Personally, I don't care what happens to you two, but the Corrupted One told me to watch over you until she woke up." Juliana was sitting at the entrance to the corridor of cells with her legs crossed and a book in her lap. Her green, leaf-like skin was paler than the last time Vur saw her. Her hair was made up of thorny brown vines with hints of green offshoots.

"And why does a dryad follow the orders of the undead?" Zollstock asked. "Aren't your people diametrically opposed to them?

"That's none of your business," Juliana said and turned to the next page.

"So there's no chance to convince you to let us go, huh?" Juliana ignored him.

Zollstock sighed. "Mina," he said, frowning at his wife.

She also ignored him and bit into her sandwich.

"You know there's no turning back from what you've done," Zollstock said. "Free us and I can overlook this incident. What would your family think if they found out you assaulted the demon lord?" He smiled.

Mina paused for a moment before continuing to eat her food.

"Hmm, no reaction, huh?" Zollstock asked. "Ah, I wonder what Dustin would think." He shook his head and sighed. Mina glared at Zollstock, and her horns glowed with a faint red light.

"That's right," he said. "Do your worst."

Mina raised her hand. Electricity crackled and buzzed through her cell. Juliana raised an eyebrow and turned her attention away from her book. A burnt sandwich flew between the cells and hit Zollstock's face. It slid off, leaving a streak of ash. Zollstock glared at Mina who snorted and turned away.

"Why doesn't she need to be bound?" Zollstock asked Juliana.

"She behaved," Juliana said and shrugged.

"You call that behav—"

"Curse: silence," Juliana said and pointed a finger at Zollstock. A second ring of black runes encircled his neck. "You're too noisy. It's no wonder why you woke her up." She clicked her tongue before resuming where she left off in her book.

Three hours later, Lindyss walked down the stairs and nodded at Juliana. The dryad nodded back and left the cellar. Lindyss pulled the chair that Juliana was sitting on to the space in front of Mina's and Zollstock's cells. Her expression didn't change when she saw Zollstock's ash covered face; instead, she turned around to face Mina.

"Explain."

"I threw a sandwich at him," Mina said.

"You destroyed one of my buildings by throwing a sandwich at him?" Lindyss asked and blinked.

Mina frowned. "I don't think we're talking about the same thing," she said. "And you were the one who destroyed your own building."

"No, I would never do something like that," Lindyss said. "I do expect to be compensated for the repair costs." She waved her hand at Zollstock, dispelling the curse on his neck. "I invited you inside my kingdom to discuss peace. I let your men bathe, gave them food, and sheltered them. You repaid me by casting destructive magic inside closed quarters and destroyed my favorite dining room. What do you have to say for yourself?"

"She started it," Zollstock said.

"What are you?" Lindyss asked. "A child?"

Zollstock frowned.

"He's a freak," Mina said and wrinkled her nose.

"Explain," Lindyss said.

"You don't get to be the demon lord by being stupid and nice," Mina said. "He acts like an idiot, but he's ruthless and coldblooded. He'll sacrifice anything for strength."

"But why bring your domestic disputes to my kingdom?" Lindyss asked.

"You're the only person left who can help," Mina said and lowered her eyes. "I admit I came here to take Tafel back, but you can take much better care of her than I ever could."

"You could've let her come with us a long time ago," Lindyss said and raised an eyebrow. "What changed?"

Mina smiled and turned her head away. "I saw her with Vur the other day and I realized it then. Do you know how many years it's been since I've seen her look so happy?"

Lindyss snorted. "That's really not my problem."

Mina's chest tightened.

"But I'll take care of her," Lindyss said and folded her hands, "if only for Vur."

"Thank you," Mina whispered and wiped her face with her blanket.

"As for you," Lindyss said to Zollstock. "Pay up." She stuck her hand out and motioned towards herself.

"You already stripped our entire army of its equipment," Zollstock said, his face cramping. "Isn't that enough?"

"No, no," Lindyss said and smiled. "That was just compensation for using our baths. You still have to pay for your army's room and board. And, of course, the cost of repairing damaged buildings."

Zollstock groaned.

22

"Presenting His Royal Highness, Randel the Second," a man wearing a suit said as he lowered his head and lifted one arm into the air. He was standing on a stage in front of an audience composed of children and teenagers who were dressed in pristine clothes. The boys wore bow ties and the girls wore dresses. They stood in rows and columns, each child the same distance away from the others.

Thumps were heard as the king walked onto the stage from an entrance hidden behind the curtain. The children lowered their heads while kneeling and saluted with their right hands across their chests.

"We greet His Majesty."

Randel nodded. "You may rise," he said. The children stood up, a few fidgeting. Rudolph was standing in the back corner. Randel cleared his throat. "You're all here today as the promising hopes for our future, the students at our most prestigious school with the noblest of backgrounds. Today, I'm offering you a chance to become even greater: Prestige, power, benefits. Everyone wants them."

The king swept his gaze across the room of children. "As some of you may already know, we have officially signed a peace treaty with the demons and undead." A few children frowned and others clenched their fists. "I understand many of you have lost parents, siblings, friends," the king said as he stared into the eyes of the children, "to the demons during our conflicts.

"This treaty does not mean we're disregarding their lives or disgracing our ancestors and their sacrifices, but rather, we're biding our time. Wars can't be won with pure offense. There are times when you need to pull back to cut your losses or rebuild your strength.

"As part of the peace treaty, the demons have offered to open their mana source to us. Of course, not everyone can go to the mana source. They're allowing us to send three parties of six for the time being. Not only that, but as part of our treaty, we will be establishing a school in Flusia that will be attended by both humans and demons alike. Those of you who'd like to grow stronger at their mana source will be required to attend this new school. After a year of attendance, the top seventeen students will be selected as candidates.

"Times are changing, and those who are able to understand demons will definitely be more valuable in the royal court than those who can't," the king said. "Discuss this with your parents. You have two weeks to let your principal know your decision." The king walked off the stage, and the children started to murmur. They split into groups and discussed amongst themselves.

Michelle and four other teens, two boys and two girls, approached Rudolph. The boys wore similar white clothes and black pants: one had red hair and the other had black hair. The girls wore dresses of different colors.

"I'm guessing the eighteenth spot is reserved for you?" Michelle asked Rudolph. Rudolph nodded. His skin was tan, and he had a scar that cut diagonally across his eyebrow. His hands were calloused, and he was taller than Michelle by a few inches. Michelle opened her mouth.

"I should go back with my dad," Rudolph said and brushed past her.

Michelle bit her lip but didn't say anything as he left. The girl with blonde hair turned to her. "Aren't you supposed to be childhood friends with him?" she asked. "You didn't even introduce us and he already left."

The black-haired boy laughed. "Seems like he doesn't like you. You break his heart?"

Michelle shrugged. "He's probably really busy," she said. "Doing prince stuff."

The boy snorted. "Right," he said and nodded. "Prince stuff."

The girls giggled. "Are you guys planning on going to the new school?" the blonde-haired girl asked.

The other girl, who had black hair, shook her head. "No way," she said. "I'm just going to find a rich and handsome guy." She turned towards Michelle. "The prince was pretty cute."

"Hey, rich and handsome guy right here," the black-haired boy said as he pointed towards his face with both hands.

The girl rolled her eyes. "Which part of that is handsome?"

The blonde-haired girl turned to Michelle. "What about you?" she asked and smiled. "Pope's daughter and all that, you should convert some demons right?"

"Hmm. I don't know," Michelle said. "I do want to get away from home though. Ugh."

The red-haired boy snickered. "I would too with a father like yours," he said. "How many prayers do you say a day? Ten? Twenty?"

Michelle sighed and shook her head. "Too many," she said. "It's like he wants me to get possessed by a sacred spirit."

"Yeah, right," the boy said and rolled his eyes, "like anyone'd want to possess you. They'd be too freaked out by your … preferences." Michelle glared at him. He smiled and patted her on the shoulder while winking. "Don't worry, it's our secret."

Michelle knocked his hand off her shoulder. "You disgust me," she said and walked away.

"C'mon, Roy," the blonde-haired girl said. "You shouldn't tease her like that."

Roy shrugged. "Whatever." He grinned at Michelle's back as she mingled with another group of people.

***

"We're going with them?" Bella tilted her head and asked Yella. "Why would we do that?"

"They're going to free our queen," Yella said as she tugged on Bella's and Rella's arms.

"Why would they do that?" Rella asked. "I certainly wouldn't help her save anybody."

The trio arrived in front of Tafel and Vur. Yella sat on Vur's head while Bella and Rella clung onto Tafel's horns.

"You're really going to save our queen?" Bella asked as she leaned over Tafel's forehead to look her in the eyes.

"I said I would, so I will," Tafel said. "And if I can't, then Vur can do it. Vur can do anything."

"Maybe you're not too bad of a person," Bella said. "I still hate you though."

Tafel smiled. "You're welcome," she said. "And no, I don't want anything out of it. I just feel bad."

"Stop reading my mind." Bella pouted. "It's annoying."

"That's not my fault, now is it?" Tafel asked. "And I still have to sneeze, but I can't and it's really annoying me."

Bella shrugged. "The queen can dispel our curses," she said. "The faster you save her, the sooner it'll go away."

Tafel turned to Vur. "How long would it take us to get back?"

Vur tilted his head, and Yella yelped as she slid off. "About three weeks," he said.

"Hey, I'm not that slow," Tafel said and pouted. "You're just too fast."

Vur shrugged. "Same thing. Ready to go?"

Tafel nodded, and the party of five set off.

"How old are you?" Vur asked the fairies after they had been traveling for a while.

"You can't just ask a woman for her age," Bella said and gasped. "That's just rude."

Vur blinked at Bella. "So how old are you?"

"Can I smack him?" Bella asked Tafel. "I'm going to smack him."

Tafel's eyebrows knit together. "I'm a little curious too."

"I'm twenty-eight," Bella said and puffed her chest out. "Don't I look good for my age?"

"Wow," Tafel said. "You're older than Auntie."

"Cheater!" Bella said. She pointed at Yella. "This is your fault."

"They're nine hundred and twenty-seven," Tafel said to Vur.

"Then why are they so weak?" Vur asked.

Yella plucked a hair off of Vur's head and harrumphed. "We're not weak," she said and threw the hair away. "We're just not good against gravity magic."

Vur nodded. "That's why you're weak."

Rella tugged on Tafel's ear. "Just what do you see in him?" she asked. "He's mean and not cute at all."

Tafel pouted. "That's just how he was raised," she said. "He's my friend." Tafel looked down and mumbled, "I don't have a lot of them."

"Eh?" Bella asked. "How does the princess not have friends? Shouldn't people be flocking to you for favors?"

Tafel shook her head. "Those people aren't friends," she said. "My mom wouldn't let me make any friends. When I complained to Dustin, he just looked sad but didn't help."

"That's the problem with inheritance," Yella said and nodded. "Too many issues. Demons should just be like us. They'll be much happier that way."

"What do you mean?" Tafel asked.

"Only one person can be the demon lord, right?" Yella asked. "So what happens to the people who want to be demon lord but can't?"

Tafel frowned. "That can't be true," she said and knit her eyebrows together. "Then why wouldn't Mom let me get stronger?"

234

Yella shrugged. "Maybe she likes your brothers more," she said and yawned.

Tafel fell silent and squeezed Vur's hand as they walked through the forest.

"Wow, you don't even need to curse her to make her feel bad," Rella said towards Yella. "That's amazing."

"What?" Yella asked as she sat up. "Is she crying again? Please don't cry; it makes you look ugly."

"I'm not crying," Tafel said with red cheeks and swatted her hand at Yella.

"Joking!" Yella shouted as she dove into Vur's hair to dodge Tafel's palm.

Tafel smiled. "Thanks."

***

Tafel and Vur were sitting in a corner booth in the adventurers' guild. A chocolate cake the size of Vur was on the table in between the two. The fairies stared up at the towering confectionery with their mouths gaping.

"You traded our tears for this?" Rella asked, still staring at the cake with wide eyes.

"And some gold," Tafel said as she patted the cloth sack beside her. "We also finished our first mission." She smiled.

"I guess that's okay then…," Bella said and scooped out a piece of chocolate with her hands. "It looks like lizard poop. This thing is edible?"

Vur nodded. "Try it," he said and smushed a piece of cake into Yella's mouth.

Yella struggled at first, but then her eyes widened and sparkled. "It's amazing!" she said. "I never knew my tears could taste so good!"

Bella licked some frosting off her hand and had a similar reaction. She pushed the piece of cake into Rella's mouth. Rella's wings flapped, and she was lifted off the table.

"You have to make us cry more often," Rella said to Tafel and flew next to the cake with drool leaking from her mouth.

The adventurers in the guild looked at the cake next to Vur, then exchanged glances with each other. One of them whispered, "Didn't he make that huge crater because of a sugar rush from too much cake?" Their faces paled, and a few men scrambled out of their seats as they hurried to pay and leave. The receptionist's face paled at the growing pile of money on the counter that the adventurers left behind while fleeing. The guild soon emptied, and he was the only one left with Tafel and Vur in the building—excluding the fairies. A whimper escaped from his lips as he sorted the change and ducked under the counter when he finished.

The sound of a door opening came from upstairs, and footsteps resounded through the almost empty building. The guild master frowned at the receptionist hiding under the counter before sweeping his gaze over the guild. His eyes narrowed as they locked onto Vur and the cake. He inhaled and held his breath as he walked over to the receptionist. He tapped him on the shoulder and motioned towards the door with his head. Tears sprang into the corners of the receptionist's eyes, and he nodded as he took the guild master's hand. The two tiptoed out the building as the fairies chattered with Vur and Tafel.

"Let's go find Exzenter," Tafel said after the five devoured the cake. The fairies looked like bloated spheres with arms and legs. Drool leaked from Rella's mouth as she lay on her back.

"I feel sick," Yella said with a green face. Bella moaned and tried to stand on her feet, but she couldn't move.

"No parents?" Vur asked as he wiped his mouth with a napkin.

Tafel shook her head. "They probably went back to Niffle already," she said. "And if they didn't, I wouldn't want them to know what we're going to do."

Vur nodded. "Let's go then," he said. "I want to do something fun." He stretched his arms above himself, his fingertips crackling with electricity.

236

"Wait for us," Bella said as she halfheartedly raised her arm.

"I'm going to puk—urk!" Rella covered her mouth. She tilted her head to the side, and a rainbow fountain of liquid jetted out of her mouth. Her body diminished in size until it was back to normal, and her projectile vomiting ceased. "Phew. Much better."

"That was so gross," Yella said, her face even greener. Rella rolled her yellow sister next to Bella and shook the table by jumping up and down. The two fairies repeated Rella's performance and slimmed down.

Outside, the guild master and receptionist stood across the street from the adventurers' guild. "Do you hear that?" the guild master asked. "It sounds like water magic."

The receptionist nodded. "Well, the building hasn't collapsed yet," he said. "That's a good sign, right?"

The guild master nodded.

A few minutes later, Tafel and Vur walked out of the building with three fairies collapsed on their heads. The guild master and receptionist glanced at each other and approached the door. The receptionist opened the door a tiny fraction and peeked inside before opening it the whole way.

"Woah," the receptionist said. "It's a rainbow paintjob. I kind of like it." The corner that was reserved for adventurers was filled with color. Rainbow streaks lined the ceiling and floor along with the seats and tables.

"It smells like flowers," the guild master said as he sniffed the air. He nodded. "Let's keep it like this."

***

Mina sighed as she pressed her hand and face against the window by her bed. Zollstock had returned to Niffle with the army and left her behind. Lindyss had accepted Mina as a citizen of Konigreich, and the skeletons had inundated her with knowledge about their lord and resurrector along with the rules and requirements for living there.

A knock sounded on her door. "It's open," she said and removed her face from the glass. A skeleton opened the door and walked inside. It turned its head to the corner and picked up a basket of glowing blue crystals.

"Any word about Tafel or Vur?" Mina asked as the skeleton turned to leave.

The skeleton tilted its head. "Vur was seen eating a four-foot-tall cake in the adventurers' guild," it said. "You might want to stay away from there for the time being."

"Was Tafel with him?" Mina asked as she lifted the blanket off her legs.

The skeleton shrugged. A crack appeared in the floor, and a skull popped out. "Yes, Tafel was with Vur," the skull said and disappeared back into the crevice. Mina stared at the hole left behind with her mouth open.

"Does that—"

"Is that all?" the skeleton asked, interrupting Mina.

Mina closed her mouth and nodded. "Thank you," she said. The skeleton carried the basket away, and Mina covered up the hole with her dresser before changing clothes. She left the residential area and proceeded towards the mansion where Lindyss lived. A few demons in the streets murmured as she passed by, but she ignored their stares and continued forward.

The mansion was unguarded, and Mina arrived at Lindyss' room unimpeded. She was about to knock on the door when a skeletal hand popped out of the ground and stopped her.

"She's sleeping."

Mina paled and backed away from the door. "Do you know where Tafel and Vur are?" she whispered.

"They went to find Exzenter," the skeleton replied. "If you hurry, you might catch them."

Mina nodded as her horns glowed green. "Thank you," she said and sprinted through the halls. Her feet left no noise, and a wall of wind pushed her forward as she ran. Exzenter had been given a room in the guard tower closest to the wilderness. When he wasn't exploring the wilderness for materials, he was experimenting with potions and spells. She had passed by his place a few times.

Mina ran through the streets. As she approached the back corner of the kingdom, she saw Tafel and Vur with three figures on their heads standing in front of Exzenter in the field below the guard tower. Exzenter had his arms spread open and wind was encircling the group of five. Blue light streamed into his body from a few mana crystals on the ground.

"Wait!" Mina shouted, still running towards them.

Tafel turned her head towards the sound, and her eyes widened. She opened her mouth and said something to Exzenter that Mina couldn't hear. Exzenter remained motionless, but the wind swirled faster.

Mina was only a few meters away when a ring of light glowed beneath the group. She gritted her teeth as her horns glowed red. The pillar of light rose and shone brighter. An explosion sounded out from behind Mina, and her body was tossed forward into the pillar. The light faded and only Exzenter remained. He looked at the pile of clothes at his feet and scratched his head.

23

Dustin sighed as he took a swig from his mug, staring into his fireplace. He was sitting on a couch in a bathrobe with his legs propped up on a wooden table. There was a half-empty bottle of whiskey beside his foot. His face was red, and there were tears in the corners of his eyes.

Screams sounded out from his kitchen. His eyes widened as he stumbled to his feet and wobbled to the entryway. More screams pierced his ears. He winced and pinched his forehead with his hands. Mina, Tafel, Vur, and three fairies were in his kitchen—naked.

"Stop staring!" Tafel shouted and covered Vur's eyes with her hands. The fairies giggled and hid in Tafel's hair.

"Dustin!" Mina screamed. "Clothes!"

Dustin's face flushed with a deeper shade of red, and he undid the belt of his robe. A lightning bolt struck his chest, and he flew backwards, landing on his back.

"Why are you taking yours off!?" Mina screeched with her horns pulsing yellow. Her body curled up to shield herself from his view, her cheeks flushed.

Dustin coughed out a cloud of smoke. "Right," he said. "Clothes." He staggered to his feet and went upstairs.

"Why did you do that?" Tafel asked her mom with tears in her eyes. "Now Vur's seen me naked. Prim's going to kill me. It's all your fault; you messed up Exzenter's portal."

Mina pointed at Vur. Tafel glanced at him and her face flushed crimson. She turned her head away, but her eyes creeped downwards.

"She's peeking," Rella said as she propped herself up on Tafel's horn.

"Definitely peeking," Bella said and nodded.

"I'm not!" Tafel shouted and closed her eyes with her hands still covering Vur's. Dustin came back downstairs with a bundle of clothes in his arms. He tossed it into the kitchen and turned away.

A few minutes later, the six people sat on the couches in Dustin's living room. Tafel was sitting next to Vur, staring at her own hands with a red face. Vur was sniffing the cup of whiskey the fairies had poured for him. Dustin was rubbing his temples while drinking from a cup of water, and Mina was sitting across from him, holding a cup of tea.

"This never happened," Mina said, staring at the tea leaves in her cup. "Right?"

Dustin nodded. "I definitely did not see you naked or anything," he said. "Nope, never happened."

Mina's face turned pink as she sipped her tea. "Good," she said. She turned towards the two children. "As for you, young lady, why didn't you stop when I told you to?"

Tafel's mouth dropped open as she raised her head. She grabbed Vur's arm and stared at her mother while whispering to Vur, "That's my mom, right?"

Vur nodded as he drank a mouthful of the cup in front of him. His eyes widened, and he downed the whole thing in one go.

Mina frowned and crinkled her brow. "Why aren't you answering?"

Rella opened her mouth. "That's our—"

"Your water tastes like fire," Vur said to Dustin. "I like it."

Dustin raised his head. His gaze flickered from the bottle of whiskey in the fairies' hands to the empty cup in front of Vur. His face paled as he stood up and walked towards the stairs. "I can't deal with this," he said and disappeared from view.

Vur shrugged and held the cup out towards the fairies. They giggled as they poured him more.

Mina's face cramped, and she let out a cough, but the fairies didn't stop. She turned back to Tafel. "Well?"

"Do you hate me?" Tafel asked. Her hands were white from clutching Vur's arm.

Mina frowned. "No," she said. "Why—"

Tafel let out a breath and loosened her grip. "Then why do you never listen to me?" she asked, interrupting her mom.

"What's going on, Tafel?"

"I always say things, but you never agree. I ask for things, but you never listen," Tafel said as a tear rolled down her cheek. "Why?"

Mina bit her lip. "I'm sorry," she whispered and lowered her head. Her lips trembled as she smiled. "You must hate me, huh?"

Tafel's lips quivered, and she looked down, trying to blink back her tears. Mina sighed and shook her head.

The fairies placed the empty whiskey bottle on the table and flitted in front of Mina. They were wearing shredded strips of cloth wrapped around their bodies like bath towels. "So you're the little devil's mother," Rella said and tilted her head.

"She's very rude you know," Bella said. "She tickled us until we peed."

Yella nodded. "You have to take responsibility as her parent."

Mina crinkled her brow. "Are these fairies?" she asked turning her head towards Tafel and Vur. Vur's face was flushed, and his head was drooping.

"We can hear you, you know?" Rella asked and puffed her cheeks. "Of course we're fairies. You should at least recognize the people you rendered homeless."

"Like mother, like daughter," Bella said and crossed her arms.

"It must run in the family," Yella said and nodded.

Mina blinked at the fairies and asked Tafel, "Why did you bring fairies to Niffle?"

242

"She's doing it again," Rella said and pouted. She tugged on Mina's ear.

Mina glared at the red-eyed fairy. "What are you doing in Niffle?"

"We're here to save our queen," Bella said and stuck her chest out.

Mina's brow wrinkled. "Why would your queen be here?"

"Hello?" Yella asked as she rapped her fist against Mina's skull. "You demons kicked us out of our house and imprisoned her."

"The mana source," Tafel said. "Their queen's trapped in our mana source."

Mina frowned. "I've never heard of this."

"Well, it's true," Bella said and sat on Mina's horn. "You demons are bad people." She turned towards Tafel and Vur. "C'mon, we're finally here. Let's go sa"—Vur fell over onto Tafel's lap—"ve our mother…"

"I think you gave him too much," Yella said and flew over to poke Vur. He didn't move.

"Me? It was you," Bella said and pouted.

Rella let out a sigh. "Guess we'll have to wait."

"Tafel," Mina said. "There's something I need to tell you."

Tafel frowned and knit her eyebrows together.

* * *

Zollstock closed the wooden door behind himself. A metallic click sounded as a latch fell into place. He wiped his hands on a brown towel, leaving a black streak. The hallway was lit by a row of torches with stairs leading up on one end of the hall. Locked doors lined the corridor. A rat scampered into a hole in the wall, carrying a piece of dripping meat.

"Milord," Seth said as he appeared with his head lowered in front of Zollstock. He wore a black outfit that covered everything except for his eyes. "We've received a report. Mina has returned to Niffle and is currently residing in Dustin's lodgings. Tafel and the dragon boy are with her."

Zollstock rubbed his chin. "Very well," he said and nodded. "Maintain a close watch and report their movements to me. Don't let the royal family find out."

Seth saluted and vanished, leaving behind a black mist.

Zollstock straightened the creases in his clothes. He chuckled as he ascended the spiral stone staircase. The torches' flames were extinguished, and the clang of a metal door closing echoed through the corridor. A few sobs permeated the silence.

***

Aran grimaced as he downed the purple liquid in his flask. He was in a tavern with the other members of the Red Blade Adventurers. They were sitting around a circular stone table with a steaming crab on a metal plate at the center.

"I'm sick of crab," Zeke muttered as he hacked off a leg with his dagger. "What did we have for breakfast? Crab. What did we have for lunch? Crab. What—"

"We get it, Zeke," Sophie said as she drank the purple liquid in her glass. "We're all sick of it."

"I'm never eating seafood again once we go back," Claire said as she sighed. Her brown bangs covered her eyes as she lowered her head.

"*If* we ever get back," Zeke said as he stabbed the crab leg and peeled the shell off. "Two years. We've been here for almost two years and we only finished two missions. And that was with the demons' help." Bits and pieces of crab shell flew across the table as Zeke wielded his dagger.

"Calm down," Ross said. His hair had turned gray, and his black vest was tattered. Burn scars decorated his arms and fingers. He grabbed the steaming crab with his bare hands and snapped two legs off. "We've grown a lot despite the low number of missions."

Zul nodded. His blue robe was frayed at the edges, and the color had faded into a light blue. "We've upgraded Aran's armor and Ross obtained a new shield. Claire's proficiency in white magic nearly doubled, and we've all leveled more than

244

we would've if we stayed in Zuer. The longer we stay here, the stronger we'll get."

"He's just bitter the demons showed him up," Sophie said.

"Showed all of us up," Zeke said and rolled his eyes. "You weren't exactly that great compared to them either."

Aran nodded. "We shouldn't need to rely on them as much now that I have better equipment. I've also heard rumors that they're getting recalled to Zuer. Both Tina's and Chad's parties have already left. Something seems to have come up."

Sophie raised an eyebrow and asked, "Something that the adventurers over there can't handle? What? Did the dragons invade?"

Zul shook his head. "If that happened, then we would've been called back too."

"Lucky dogs," Zeke grumbled.

"It gives us a chance to pass them," Aran said as he refilled his flask. "You do want to surpass them, right?"

"I still feel cheated," Zeke said. "The adventurers' guild made Fuselage seem like a paradise. What part of this is paradise?"

"I mean," Sophie said as she broke the shell on her plate, "if you liked crab…"

"Well, I don't," Zeke said and made a face.

"Cheer up," Claire said. "Three more years and we can go back. I can't wait to see my family again." She sighed. "I wonder how they're doing."

"I'm sure they're doing fine," Zul said and patted her shoulder. "Our families get special treatment even if we die here."

Claire frowned. "Don't say that. I'm rather addicted to living," she said and poked her crab leg with a fork. She sighed. "But these things will probably be the death of me."

***

Lindyss was meditating on her bed, surrounded by a ring of blue mana crystals. A breeze whipped her hair behind her ears, and she opened her eyes. A man with a blue conical hat and pink robes stood in the middle of her room.

"Charon," Lindyss said and nodded her head. "I don't have any water from the Fountain of Youth with me—if you were wondering."

The man smiled, revealing yellow and black teeth. "I didn't come here for that," he said. "Can't a lonely old man drop by just to say hi to his favorite elf?"

"No," Lindyss said as she swept the mana crystals up into a box. "What are you here for?"

"I thought I'd come here to give you a warning," he said and tapped his chin. "Since one of my descendants has taken a liking to this place."

"Exzenter?"

Charon nodded.

"You two are similar," Lindyss said and tied her hair up into a bun.

Charon smiled. "It's good to hear that my greatness runs through the family."

Lindyss chuckled. "So what's the warning?"

Charon stopped smiling. "The demon lord recalled the two strongest demon parties from Fuselage."

Lindyss' forehead wrinkled as her brow creased together.

"This was shortly after he returned from your kingdom," Charon continued. "I'm not sure what he's planning on doing with them, but it's definitely not to attack the humans. The sacred spirits won't allow it. Your kingdom however..." He stopped speaking.

"Thank you," Lindyss said and lowered her head.

Charon nodded. "Take care of yourself."

Lindyss raised her head. The room was empty.

***

Mina and Tafel were standing outside of Dustin's room. They had decided to move somewhere else lest they disturb Vur's sleep. It was fine to let the fairies watch over him.

246

"What's going on, Mina?" Dustin asked as he rubbed his eyes. "First you assault Zollstock in Konigreich, then you appear naked in my house a month later."

"It's Zollstock. He's dangerous," Mina said and bit her lower lip.

Dustin nodded. "Of course. He's the demon lord. He has to be dangerous."

Mina shook her head. "You don't understand," she said. "He's dangerous to *us*."

Dustin's forehead wrinkled. "Elaborate."

Mina took in a deep breath. "I think he killed the previous demon lord."

Tafel stared at her mother with wide eyes. Dustin frowned.

Mina continued, "He seemed normal when we first met him that day. He even seemed normal after we had been married for a year. He was nice to me, gave me gifts, said sweet things to me, and supported my family with wealth. He tried to make me like him."

"Are you going somewhere with this?" Dustin asked. He stared into Mina's eyes with his hands clenching his blanket.

Mina exhaled. "He changed after he became the demon lord. He stopped paying attention to me and spent more time alone. He would disappear for hours at a time, leaving me to watch over the children. I looked through his room one day while he was gone." She hesitated. "And I found a golden horn. A demon horn."

Tafel's face paled.

Dustin's eyes widened. "Are you sure? It was a demon's horn?"

Mina nodded.

"You didn't tell anyone?"

Mina shook her head. "Would you? Who could I have told? I tried telling my mother, but she wasn't having any of it."

Dustin turned his head towards Tafel who was trembling. "Should she be here for this?"

"She deserves to hear it," Mina said and sighed.

Tafel yanked her hand out of her mother's grip and hugged her elbows while looking down.

"Tafel...," Mina said and moved her hands towards her daughter.

"Stop it," Tafel said, her voice shaking. "Why...?" She looked up at Mina with glistening eyes.

"I—"

The house shook and Dustin fell out of bed. Mina and Tafel dropped to their knees. Dust sprinkled down from the ceiling, and a low rumble echoed through the building. The house continued to shake for ten seconds before the trembling stopped. Dustin and Mina glanced at each other. Dustin rifled through his closet and pulled out three staves, two of which he gave to Mina and Tafel. Tafel admired the staff in her hands but remained sitting on the floor.

"C'mon," Dustin said and held out his hand towards Tafel.

Tafel reached for his outstretched hand but stopped midway and lowered her arm. She shook her head as tears dripped down her face.

Mina frowned. "Watch over her," she said and proceeded to walk towards the stairs. Her horns were glowing red, and the staff pulsed with a blue light.

Dustin squatted next to Tafel and ruffled her hair as Mina disappeared from view. Tafel's hands were white from gripping the staff.

Mina reappeared a few seconds later with a pale face. "Vur's gone."

24

A male and female demon dressed in black robes with golden embroidery meandered down the streets of Niffle. Both of them wore mithril medallions engraved with two interlocking horns. The male demon had three red horns protruding from his forehead in a straight line like a rhinoceros. The female demon had two silver horns sprouting from her temples that curved down then forward like hooks.

"Isn't that Chad from The Black Hounds?"

"That's Swirling Wind's leader, Tina."

Bystanders whispered and stepped back while lowering their heads as the two passed through. Children peered out their windows with their mouths gaping. A few shouted in excitement for their parents to come look.

The red-horned demon grinned and stuck his chest out. The female demon rolled her eyes and turned her head away. She furrowed her brow and frowned as she stopped midstride and peered down a dark alleyway. A pair of golden eyes glowed and glared back at her.

"Hmm?" The red-horned demon raised an eyebrow. "Why'd you stop?" he asked and followed her gaze. "Is that a human? Times are really changing if humans are allowed to wander around Niffle." He frowned and stepped forward.

"Leave it," the woman said. "He's just a child. His horns probably haven't grown out yet."

Chad snorted and brushed past her, stopping in front of the alley's entrance. "Hey, you a human or a demon?" he asked while hunching over and staring down at Vur, resting one arm against the brick wall. Demons tended to have darker shades of hair. This child's was on the lighter side of brown. "Why're you naked? Che, damn street urchins." He straightened his back and snorted while turning around.

"I'm no filthy human," Vur said as he stumbled forward and slurred his words. "You take that back right now." He tipped over to the side and leaned his body against the wall.

Chad turned his head back around and burst out laughing. "Check it out," he said while clutching his stomach and tugging on Tina's arm. "He's drunk."

Tina frowned. "I fail to see how that's amusing," she said. She knelt next to Vur, meeting him face to face. "Where are your parents?"

Vur blinked at her and frowned. He tilted his head up and squinted at the sun.

"Can you unders—"

"That way," Vur said and pointed towards the south.

Tina followed his finger and raised an eyebrow. "There's only a few shops that way," she said and pointed east towards the residential area. "Are you sure they aren't that way?"

Vur nodded and fell over onto his face. "I said they're that way. So they're that way," he said with a muffled voice.

"Just give up, Tina," Chad said and laughed. "He's too out of it."

"I see him! He's over there, next to the old hag and ugly-looking fellow."

"Ssshhh, you're too loud! They can hear you."

Chad frowned and narrowed his eyes in the direction of the voices. A yellow orb of liquid splattered against his face, the surface of the liquid releasing thick steam. Chad screamed and clawed at his face.

"Stay away from him, you toad!" Yella shouted and threw another orb. The three fairies hovered twenty feet in the air diagonally above Vur.

Tina's horns glowed green, and the yellow orb splattered against a wall of air, the liquid dropping to the ground. "You know him?" she asked, ignoring Chad's cursing.

250

"That's right!" Rella said and crossed her arms. "You better stay away from him."

"I'll kill you!" Chad yelled, tears streaming from his eyes. He clenched his teeth as a pillar of black fire erupted from his mouth towards the fairies.

"Eep!" The fairies cried out and flew back ten feet.

"Never mind!" Bella said. "You can have him. We'll be going now!"

The fairies turned around and darted away.

"Don't think you can get away that easily," Chad said. He crouched and leapt into the air, launching himself towards the fairies. He flew three feet past Vur before his eyes widened, and he accelerated face first towards the ground. He crossed his arms, bracing for the impact, and slammed against the stone surface, causing a small cloud of dust to rise. "Don't get in my way, Tina!" Chad glared at the woman. His face was flushed, and his horns glowed black as he struggled to stand with wide and unfocused eyes.

Tina shook her head. "That wasn't me."

Vur pushed his hand against the ground and raised his body off the floor. "Killing fairies is bad," he said as his head lolled over to one side. "You'll get bad luck." His eyes shone as they focused on Chad. The demon shivered as cold sweat broke out on his back. Tina leapt backwards and raised her hands in front of her face. Her legs trembled as she clenched her teeth.

"Whoa, there," Chad said and lowered his voice. "Take it easy. I was just joking around." He struggled to straighten his back under the increased gravity. His gaze shifted to Tina, and he mouthed out a word. Tina shook her head and kept her hands raised. The three fairies' heads appeared from around the corner.

"He's lying!"

"Kick his patootie!"

"Make him cry!"

Vur staggered to his feet and stumbled two steps towards Chad. A spear of ice flew through the air and pierced through Vur's left shoulder, knocking him off balance. He took a step forward and steadied himself before turning around, glaring at the woman who fired the projectile.

Vur roared.

The ground trembled and shingles fell off the roofs as the walls around him shook. Tina paled and fell to her hands and knees. Cracks spread outwards from her palms, forming a circle in the ground around her. The cracks grew wider and snapping sounds rang out from Tina's body as she screamed, her body plastering itself to the floor.

Vur snorted and ripped the ice spear out of his shoulder while facing Chad who had also collapsed. He raised his foot and stomped forward. A cracking sound exploded outwards, and the ground next to Chad's head splintered into fine slivers. Chad's lower body trembled, and a yellow fluid spread out from around his crotch. Sweat dripped from his pale face.

Vur swayed and placed his right arm against the wall. "Don't feel good," he mumbled. His eyes stopped glowing and drool dripped out of the corner of his mouth.

Chad gulped as his eyes widened at the figure standing over him. A stream of brown slime flew out of Vur's mouth and covered the demon's face. Chad's vision went black as he screamed.

Vur fell over backwards with his eyes closed. He grumbled and rolled over before starting to snore. The fairies glanced at each other and shrugged.

***

"You lost to a child?"

Tina was sitting up on a bed surrounded by five other women, her companions—members of Swirling Wind. She nodded. They were in one of the best inns in the capital. Luckily, she had been found by a patrol after her encounter with Vur, and her companions had picked her up. The room had a red carpet, and the bed was king-sized. A chandelier with glowing white crystals hung from the ceiling.

"I'm not sure if it was really a kid," Tina said, biting her lower lip. "He used gravity magic."

One of the women frowned. "Isn't gravity magic limited to raid-classed monsters and above? Are you sure it wasn't an advanced type of wind magic?"

"I'm sure," Tina said with her head lowered. "You can ask Chad. If we wore our equipment instead of those fancy clothes, this wouldn't have happened." She raised her head and gazed into each of the women's eyes. "No one is allowed to travel alone, and everyone has to wear their gear at all times."

The members of Swirling Wind nodded.

"How strong would you say he was?" a blue-haired girl asked.

Tina narrowed her eyes. "About as strong as a reaper in the tombs."

"That's not too bad. We could beat him easily if we used potions and buffs."

The women nodded, but Tina frowned. "He was drunk."

***

Zollstock was sitting on his throne, looking down on the two demons before him. Chad and Tina were standing a foot away from each other, below the steps leading to the throne. The two wore their hunting equipment, and there was no sign of the mithril medallions they had the day before. The trinkets had disappeared after the scuffle with Vur, presumably taken by the fairies.

Chad's armor was an amalgamation of various creatures' exoskeletons and hides. His torso was encased in a gray crab shell with symmetric black runes spreading out from his chest. Scaled black leather with claws at the ends covered his arms and legs. Bone-plated guards covered his shins and forearms. He wore a giant, red bird's skull as a helmet, his horns threading through holes at the top. The haft of his lance was made of orichalcum, the toughest metal known to humans and demons, and a glistening, black scorpion tail acted as the lance head.

Tina wore an orange robe with blue embroidered flowers decorating the front and back. The robe's threads were made of orichalcum and mithril. On her head, there was a blue tiara with shining rubies embedded along the edge. A silver metal staff was strapped to her back. Mounted on top of the staff was an eyeball with green irises that moved as if it was inspecting its surroundings.

"I heard you two were gravely injured yesterday while you were preparing to see me," Zollstock said and frowned, folding his hands in his lap.

Chad clenched his lance, but didn't say a word as he glared at Zollstock. Tina tilted her head downwards. "We were unprepared and let our guards down," she said. "We didn't expect a human child to be so strong."

Zollstock nodded. "That is understandable. That boy is one of the reasons why I called your parties back."

Chad ground his teeth together. "I'll kill him," he said and spat on the floor. "Then I'll revive him and kill everyone he's ever loved as he watches in despair."

Zollstock gazed at the stained carpet and crinkled his nose. "No. The boy must not be harmed for now," he said. "The dragons favor him, and they'll invade us if misfortune befalls him."

Tina wrinkled her brow and crossed her arms. "Then why are we here? And why would the dragons favor a human child?"

"There was a plan for your parties," Zollstock said and stroked his chin, "but I'm not so sure about your effectiveness after yesterday's ... mishap."

Chad's nostrils flared. "Are you doubting our strength?" he asked, a low rumbling sound coming from his throat.

"Quite frankly, yes," Zollstock said and nodded. "I am. The strongest warrior and mage lost to a child who didn't even have a subclass."

254

Chad snorted. "I'll show you weak," he said and stepped forward with his left leg while raising his lance over his head with his right hand. He launched his weapon towards Zollstock. Tina raised an eyebrow and took two steps away from Chad.

A black mist materialized in front of Zollstock, and Seth stepped forward with two swords crossed in front of his chest. The lance's tip collided with the swords and metal screeched as the scorpion tail pierced through the blades. Seth's eyes widened as the lance passed through his body and continued towards the demon lord.

The scorpion stinger lodged itself into Zollstock's chest, and the lance throbbed as it injected venom into his heart. Seth coughed out a mouthful of blood through his mask and collapsed onto the floor. He turned his head and raised his arm towards his lord. His vision faded to gray, and his hand fell to the floor. Zollstock's eyes were wide, and his head was thrown back. His limbs spasmed as white foam frothed in the corners of his mouth.

Tina frowned. "You probably shouldn't have done that," she said as Zollstock's body twitched.

Chad sneered. "He probably shouldn't have been so ineffective." He walked forward and stepped on Seth's corpse as he grabbed his lance. He twisted it in deeper, pressing it through Zollstock's body.

***

Retter's eyes widened at the scene before him. A body clad in black lay on top of a pool of blood at the demon lord's feet. Zollstock's skin was ashen, and his appendages were shriveled up, revealing an outline of the bones beneath. His chest was torn open, and his blackened heart lay in multiple pieces on his lap.

"Milord!" Retter shouted and ran towards the throne, his face pale. His spear clattered to the floor beside him. "White mage! I need a white mage! Hur—"

A blue light flashed, and a translucent image of Zollstock appeared in front of the sitting corpse. Retter fell over backwards with his lips opening and closing, his hand pointing at the ghastly image. The ghost frowned as it looked down on Retter. It flew in front of him. "Not even four horns," it muttered and circled the sentry's body.

"W-what's going on?" Retter asked as he followed the ghost with his head.

A chuckled echoed through the room. "You don't need to know," the ghost said and flew into Retter's body. Retter screamed as his eyes rolled back into his head, revealing their whites. He fell to the floor, his body wriggling and twitching.

Footsteps echoed from outside the throne room. A demon wearing white robes and a silver cross ran into the room with a metal staff. His eyes widened as his gaze fell on the spasming sentry and Zollstock's corpse.

"It's a nightmare ghoul!" the white mage shouted and raised his staff in front of himself. His staff glowed with a white light, and he smacked it against Retter's head. "I exorcise thee, foul creature!"

Retter's body stopped twitching, and a wisp of smoke rose out of his forehead. A translucent mouth appeared. "You fool! Stop at onc—"

"Aaaaiee!" The white mage shrieked and slammed the staff against Retter's head.

Thunk. "Exorse!"

"Sto—"

Thunk. "Exorse!"

"You—"

Thunk. "I exorcise thee!"

A miserable cry slipped out of Retter's lips and faded away into nothing. The white mage wiped his mouth and panted as he glared at Retter's head. He reached into his robe and pulled out a flask. He put it to Retter's lips and forced the liquid down the sentry's throat.

"Good," the white mage said and nodded while putting the empty flask away. "The ghoul's gone." He gazed at Zollstock's body and sighed. "I pray it didn't eat Milord's soul."

25

Vur sat up and groaned. His head throbbed, and he raised his hands to his temples, rubbing them in a circular motion. He was naked, and a star-shaped scar decorated his left shoulder and back.

"Hey, look who's finally up," Rella said as she flitted near his face. She pinched his cheeks apart and rocked his head from side to side. "Do you know how heavy you are? You weigh at least fifty pounds. Be glad we could carry you with magic."

Vur knocked her aside with the back of his hand. "Where am I?" he asked and glanced around. He and the three fairies were surrounded by a dome of gray mist. The interior was dim, but a few rays of sunshine poked through.

"Rude!" Rella said and flew next to Yella while pouting.

"We're outside our home!" Bella said and poked his left shoulder. "Does that hurt?"

Vur winced and shook his head. "Just sore," he said. "Everything feels sore. What happened?"

"Well...," Yella said and tilted her head. "What's the last thing you remember?"

Vur frowned and rubbed his hands against his face. "I drank Dustin's fire water. Then one of you tugged my ear and made me break the wall. Then ... was there fire? I remember lots of fire. Maybe screaming too."

The fairies all looked away and whistled.

"You're a very fun drunk," Bella said, not meeting his eyes.

"A real hotshot."

"Really warmed up the night."

"Anyways," Yella said and coughed. "We can save our queen now!"

Vur stretched his arms above his head. "Where's Tafel?"

Bella shrugged. "Probably with her mom," she said and flew up to the mist's edge. She popped her head outside and glanced around. To anyone outside of the hemisphere, it would've looked like her head materialized out of thin air. She flew back inside.

"It looks all clear," she said. "Seems like it's a holiday or something?"

"Or it's a trap," Yella said and nodded. The entrance to the mana source was devoid of the usual adventurers and students. Everyone had left because they wanted to see The Black Hounds and Swirling Wind. Or the destruction in the city.

Rella shrugged. "Let's hurry up before people get here," she said. "I can feel her aura calling to me." She trembled and flew in an upwards spiral.

Vur groaned and rose to his feet. He wobbled, and Yella helped stabilize him by grabbing his arm.

"We tried healing you with wind magic, but it doesn't remove poison or status ailments," Yella said. "It just closed your wound."

Bella perched on Vur's head. "Let's goooooo," she said and tugged his hair.

Vur walked out of the mist and approached the entrance to the mana source. A few slimes hopped around and squelched as the fairies flew towards them.

"I missed these slimes so much," Rella said and sighed. She hugged one and patted its head before flying in front of Vur again. The group continued onwards towards the next room as the slimes inched along behind them.

The next room was filled with flying spoons and forks. They screeched and swarmed the fairies, shoving each other out of the way. The trio petted and rubbed the utensils with tears in their eyes. Yella sniffled a few times, and Bella blew her nose with Vur's ear. The utensils attached themselves to the slimes and followed along as makeshift weapons.

Vur stopped at the entrance to the third room with the fairies and the army of slimes armed with utensils behind him. The fairies looked over his shoulder. Rella's mouth fell open as Yella gasped. Tears streamed from Bella's eyes as she buried her face in Vur's hair. "Oh, no."

"It stinks in here!" Rella said and pinched her nose. "You know the floor used to be white before? It's all brown and gross now."

Vur made a face.

Yella raised her head and frowned. "The ceiling's brown too. How did that even ... you know, never mind." She shook her head and flew to the center of the room. Chamber pots and brown towels hovered above the ground, gathering around the yellow-haired fairy.

Bella picked up a slime and tossed it on top of a towel. The brown sediments dissolved in the slime's body. "My favorite towel," Bella said and sniffled. "I'll never look at it the same way again."

The slimes marched forward and traversed through the room. Everywhere they went, the floor turned white as slurping noises permeated the air. The slimes increased in size as they consumed more nutrients. A few sprout wings instead of growing and flew up towards the ceiling. Less than fifteen minutes later, the room was sparkling, and the group could see their reflections in the floor.

The chamber pots flipped themselves over and mounted the tops of the slimes while the towels attached themselves as well, acting as togas and capes. Bella held a fluffy, blue towel at arm's length. She frowned at it, and a pair of eyes appeared in the center of the towel. Tears leaked out of them as the brown irises expanded. Bella sighed.

"Even if you've been soiled," the blue-haired fairy said while hugging the towel close to her body, "you'll still be the only one for me." The towel purred and enveloped the fairy.

260

Rella and Yella glanced at each other and shrugged. "Onwards!"

Vur followed the two fairies as Bella snuggled up into a ball on top of his head. The army of slimes made glopping sounds as they trudged behind them. The corridor after the third room branched off into three passageways. Above the left entrance was a sign with the words 'water elementals' written on it. The middle passage's sign said, "Plant Creatures – Bring antidotes." The rightmost corridor had a sign that said, "Lightning Elementals – Bring para-resist gear." The fairy trio burst out into laughter when they read the third sign.

"That way," Yella said with twinkling eyes. She pointed towards the right and landed on Vur's shoulder as she doubled over with laughter. Vur tilted his head but followed her directions. The crystals in the fourth room glowed pink, faintly illuminating the surroundings. Numerous egg-shaped objects flew towards the group and buzzed around them like bees.

"Don't touch them," Yella said and giggled. "They might be too intense for you."

"What are they?" Vur asked as he reached out to touch one. A blue lightning bolt shot out of the surface and zapped his finger.

The trio of fairies smiled. "Lightning elementals. Let's stop wasting time here and go," Rella said while tugging on Vur's arm. Yella snatched a tiny egg and slipped it into her makeshift pocket. The remaining eggs flew towards the slimes and attached themselves below the chamber pots, two to each slime.

"Our queen should be in the room after this one," Rella said. The group was surrounded by a multitude of fairy-sized beds and wardrobes. The fairies changed into dresses similar to the ones they wore when they first met Vur and Tafel. The group proceeded through the room unhindered. The slimes and the rest of the objects stopped at the center of the room, refusing to continue.

The corridor to the master bedroom glowed with a dark-purple light. It smelled like iron and blood. Two metal doors sealed with orichalcum chains were at the end of the passage. Circular blue runes glowed on the metal surface. Yella frowned and flitted in front of the door. A round indent with two crossed horns was engraved on the lock connecting the chains.

"That looks like this!" Rella said and pulled out the mithril medallion she borrowed from Chad with her sticky fingers.

"How convenient," Bella said with a raised eyebrow as Rella stuck her tongue out to the side and fitted the medallion into the slot. The blue runes emitted a light that forced the group to shield their eyes. A few seconds passed, and the light died down.

"Did it work?" Rella asked as she lowered her arm.

The medallion exploded, covering their faces with soot.

"Guess not," Yella said and coughed out a black cloud.

Rella wiped her face. "Let's try this one," she said and pulled out the medallion that belonged to Tina. She slid it into place, and the door shone with a red light. The group squinted their eyes and turned their heads away. A few seconds later, a click resounded through the passage, and the light died down. The group took a step back and shielded their faces while watching the medallion. Nothing happened.

"I think it worked!" Rella said and placed her hands on her hips while sticking her chest out. She flew towards the lock.

The medallion exploded.

Rella crashed into the floor.

"Well, poo," Yella said and poked Rella's body. "You alive?"

Rella coughed out smoke and nodded.

"Third time's the charm, right?" Bella asked and pulled out a golden medallion that had the crossed-horns imprint.

"Where'd you even get that?" Yella asked.

"I saw it hanging on Dustin's wall, and it flew into my hands," Bella said with a grin. She flew up to the lock and popped the medallion into place. The group ran behind a corner and squinted into the golden light that the door emitted. The light faded away, and the orange chains fell down.

"Hah!" Bella cheered and flew towards the door. She paused mid-flight and bit her lower lip. She glanced at Rella and turned back to the door.

"Nope," Rella said and shook her head. "I'm not going near that." She crossed her arms. The lock disappeared and reappeared in front of the floating fairy. The golden medallion exploded, and a second set of chains materialized in front of the door. Rella whimpered and peeled herself off the wall. "I hate locks."

"Try kicking the door down," Yella said and tugged Vur's hair. Vur swatted her away with the back of his hand. His forehead glowed blue, and a web of light spread throughout his body. His eyes lit up with a golden light, and he dashed towards the door. His fist connected with the chains.

Hong!

The sound reverberated all the way back to the previous room, and the slimes' bodies jiggled. The fairies were blown back as the earth cracked beneath Vur's feet. The door vibrated but remained standing.

"So weak," Yella said and shook her head. "You call yourself a dragon?"

Vur snorted and kicked the wall next to the door. It cracked and disintegrated, revealing a pitch-black room.

The fairy trio gaped. "I didn't say anything," Yella said and tilted her head towards the ceiling.

"Yella...?" A barely audible whisper leaked out from the darkness.

The fairies paled and looked at each other. "Mom!"

The three fairies flew into the newly made entrance.

"Quick, breathe fire into the room!" Rella said and tugged Vur's hand. "It's too dark to see. We're coming, Mom!"

The inside lit up with an orange light as fire streamed out of Vur's nostrils. The room was Spartan, a stone bed resting in one corner. A fairy sat on the bed with a chain attached to her right leg, leading into the wall. Her silver hair grew down to the top of her neck. A pair of golden horns, shaped like a stag's antlers, sprouted from her temples. She wore a gray dress that reached halfway down her shins.

The fairy trio tackled their mother, hugging her with tears streaming from their eyes. Their bodies trembled as they wailed, incoherent cries blubbering out of their mouths. The fairies clung onto each other for ten minutes before they separated with red eyes and snot dripping from their noses. Vur waited at the entrance, exhaling fire the whole time. The fairy queen clapped her hands, and the room was illuminated with a pale white glow.

"We should hurry and leave before someone finds us," Yella said and wiped her face with her sleeve.

Bella and Rella nodded while the fairy queen bit her lip. "This chain...," she said and motioned towards her leg.

The fairy trio turned to Vur, their eyes wide like puppies. "Pleaseee," they said at the same time and clasped their hands together with quivering lips.

Vur sighed and grabbed the chain. Cracking sounds echoed through the room as he pulled on it. A chunk of stone popped off the wall, and the fairies cheered.

"We need to take the lodestone before we leave," the fairy queen said. "I'll lead the way; please carry that rock for me, child." The group traversed through the dungeon and arrived at a room with a glowing blue orb the size of a human fist. It was hidden in the corridor between the lightning elementals and the bedroom. The fairy queen had to use a spell to reveal the entrance. The army of slimes waited outside, and the queen flew up towards the orb. She hugged it, her horns glowing with a myriad of different colors that illuminated the room in a

264

rainbow light. When the light dimmed, the orb was gone and the queen had a sheen of sweat on her brow.

Rumbling sounds rang throughout the dungeon as dust fell from the ceiling. The ground shook and cracks spread along the walls.

"We have to leave now!"

The group dashed through the remaining rooms unimpeded while the objects and slimes inside faded and dispersed into blue orbs of light. The group stood outside the entrance to the mana source, gasping for breath. A massive crashing sound echoed through the capital, causing all the windows to rattle. The fairy trio cheered and tackled their mother again. A hemisphere of mist rose up around them, and Vur sat on the floor while clutching his head.

"Is he alright?" the queen asked and patted the fairies' heads as she shook them off.

"He's just hungover; you can ignore him," Rella said and held her mom's hand. "We missed you so much!"

The fairy queen hesitated and furrowed her brow before turning away from Vur. "Is it just you three?"

The fairy trio looked at each other and lowered their heads with trembling lips. "Yes…," Yella said and wiped at her eyes. "Everyone else was h-hunted down by the humans. We t-tried asking for h-help, but no one w-would." Yella choked and sniffled as she spoke.

The fairy queen brought her hand to her mouth as her eyes grew moist. "I'm so sorry," she said and flew forward to embrace Yella. "If it wasn't for my decision that day…"

The three fairies raised their heads and glanced at each other. Their faces split with massive grins. "Just kidding!" Yella said and tackled her mother with her arms wide open. "Everyone's fine. We were just too excited and couldn't wait to come save you."

"You rascal!" the queen said as a tear leaked from her eye. "I believed you!" She head-locked Yella and ruffled her hair with her knuckles. All the fairies burst out into a high-pitched laughter that caused Vur to groan and clutch his head tighter.

"This is Vur, Mom," Bella said as she hovered above his head. "He's the dragon boy who helped us save you."

"Dragon?" the queen tilted her head to the side and released her hold on Yella. "I thought I sensed something, but I wasn't quite sure…"

Bella nodded. "The matriarch imprinted him."

The queen's eyes widened, and she flew down to Vur's face level. She bowed her head. "Thank you for saving me," she said. "My name is Stella Arger, queen of the fairies. It's a shame I have no valuables to give you as a reward. Would you like some clothes instead…?" She gazed at her naked savior.

Vur shook his head. "Rella, Bella, and Yella are my friends. I don't need a reward for helping them."

"Awww." The fairy trio let out a cry and encircled Vur with a hug.

"Then think of it as a gift for a friend," Stella said. "Wasn't there anything that you thought was interesting in our home? A slime? A plant?"

Vur tilted his head. "The lightning elementals seem pretty strong," he said. "Could I have one?"

"Lightning elemental…?" Stella asked and furrowed her brow.

Yella flew next to her mother and whispered into her ear.

Stella's face flushed red. She coughed a few times and nodded. "Alright, a lightning elemental it is," she said while the fairy trio giggled. Her body glowed with a blue light, and a buzzing pink egg materialized in front of Vur. "Infuse your mana into it to contract with it. Take good care of it." She seemed as if she wanted to say something else, but she bit her lip and kept silent.

Vur grabbed the elemental with his hands and infused his mana into it. "It makes my hand feel funny," he said. The egg buzzed harder in response. "Thank you."

266

"You should give it to Tafel when you're older to protect her," Rella said with twinkling eyes. The fairies giggled.

***

Chad knocked on the door in front of him. He wore a black cloak made of shadows. It hid the contours of his body and changed shapes constantly like a fire in the wind.

Dustin opened the door, and he narrowed his eyes at the visitor. "Chad," he said. "I heard you came back. What brings you here?"

"I'm looking for information on a boy," Chad said. "Human child with golden eyes. I thought you might know something."

Dustin furrowed his brows. "He's an SSS-ranked adventurer named Vur from Konigreich, the new kingdom. Child of the dragons. That's all I know about him."

Chad nodded. "Thanks. Oh, and have fun being the new demon lord."

"What?" Dustin asked and blinked.

Chad chuckled. "You'll find out real soon. It's a shame I couldn't stay longer. Take care of yourself, Dustin." A black light enveloped Chad's body, and he vanished.

26

Lindyss gasped as frigid air rushed past her face. She plummeted towards the sea of white fluffy clouds and gritted her teeth as a translucent blue membrane enveloped her body. Her hair fluttered behind her as she fell through the clouds. She frowned at the terrain beneath her—fractured, broken. A trail of destruction split the city into two jagged parts. A few charred and collapsed piles of wood were all that remained of the buildings on the fracture.

Did Exzenter send me to the wrong place? No.... What did Vur do this time?

A fang-shaped rune appeared on Lindyss' forehead, and it, along with her eyes, glowed with a purple light. A pair of translucent, violet batwings materialized in the air behind her back, spanning the length of two grown adults. Her wings flapped as she hovered in the air, observing the capital that had a massive crater on its edge. Lindyss sighed and flew towards the crater while rubbing her temples. Vur was definitely there. Craters and Vur went together like apples and pies.

***

"This aura...," Stella muttered and frowned while floating in the air. She had been watching Vur experiment with the lightning elemental when a chill ran down her back. She raised her head, squinting her eyes at the sky. "It's her." She clenched her hands as her eyes turned blood-red. Her horns turned black as her clothes rippled around her.

"It's Aun—," Vur said as he raised his head and instantly lowered it again with a groan. The hemisphere of mist around Vur and the fairies trembled before dispersing. Lindyss descended in front of Vur, separating him from Stella.

"What did you do to him?" Lindyss asked while baring her teeth. Purple lightning crackled down her arm, forming a protective barrier around Vur.

Stella snorted and waved her hand. A tendril of black smoke drifted towards Lindyss. "You should worry about yourself, witch."

Lindyss pointed her arm towards the smoke, and lightning flowed to her palm.

"Silence."

The lightning in Lindyss' hand dispersed, and her vision went white as a piercing pain drilled into her head. The black smoke enveloped her, causing her to cough and hack before she fell to the ground.

"Did you forget my specialty after four hundred years of lazing around?" Stella asked as she descended to the ground and sauntered towards Lindyss. "I didn't forget. I will never forget." A black mist billowed out of Stella's body as she loomed over Lindyss. "That day you took everything from me, I told you'd I pay you back a hundred times over. Every day, I cursed you in my head even as the demons tortured me."

Lindyss clutched at her throat, trying to grasp the smoke around her neck to no avail. Her face turned red and veins bulged around her neck. She looked up at Stella with wide eyes, her mouth opening and closing like a fish out of water.

"Stop! You can't hurt Auntie," Vur said. His eyes glowed with a golden light, and a faint image of a blue dragon head materialized in the air above him.

Stella pointed at Vur and said one word, "Sleep."

Vur's eyes widened as his body grew heavy. His head drooped, and his shoulders twitched as he struggled to stay standing. He took three steps forward before falling down, landing on his face.

Stella turned her attention back on Lindyss. "I'm not going to kill you," she said as she smiled. The black smoke receded. "That'd be too merciful."

Lindyss shivered as she gasped for breath and propped her upper body up with her elbow. Stella placed her palm on Lindyss' forehead, causing her to convulse as a red glow flowed into her body. Lindyss' eyes rolled up until only the whites were showing, and she let out a low moan. Her eyes turned pink, then red, as saliva dripped from her mouth.

Stella smiled as she took a step back and turned towards the fairy trio. She extended her hand towards them. "Come, let's enjoy the show." Her eyes were no longer red, but her horns still shone with a black light, casting shadows on the ground.

The trio glanced at each other and trembled before nodding. They floated behind their mother as she flew into the sky. Yella glanced back at Vur and sighed. She waved her hand, and a hemisphere of smoke enveloped his sleeping body.

Lindyss howled as translucent, red batwings flared up behind her. Her palms touched the ground as she crouched before springing into the air, chasing after the fairies. When they arrived in the center of the capital, Stella grinned and summoned a sphere of mist that engulfed her and her children. Lindyss' red eyes blanked for a second as her body came to a halt in the sky. Noises coming from the city below reached her ears. Her gaze lowered, focusing on the demons milling about. A drop of saliva fell from her mouth as she growled, lightning circling around her body.

***

"Father died?" Lamach asked. His eyebrows were furrowed as he frowned at the man in front of him. Lamach and Gabriel were sitting on a couch in a carpeted room. A man and woman, both wearing black clothes with purple crossed horns embroidered on their front pockets, were sitting across from the princes. The man nodded as he placed his elbows on the table between them and propped his chin up with his knuckles.

"He was killed by Chad of The Black Hounds," the man said and sighed. "And neither of you are strong enough to lead the nation."

270

"Bring him back," Gabriel said and glared at the man. "How am I supposed to prove my strength if he's already dead?"

The woman frowned and narrowed her eyes at Gabriel. She opened her mouth to speak, but the man raised his hand in front of her face.

"We tried. His soul was thoroughly dispersed. Even a phoenix down couldn't revive him," the man said, ignoring the woman's glare. "For now, the general populace doesn't know, but we can't hide it from them forever. We—"

"Then who's going to be the demon lord?" Gabriel asked.

The man's knuckles cracked. "Not you," he said and smiled. "It's—"

Boom!

The floor shook, and screams pierced the air. Thunderous reverberations echoed through the room as the windows shattered. Lightning flashed, flooding the room with a red light. The walls cracked and dust cascaded from the ceiling.

"What's going on?" The man stood up and stepped towards the shattered window. Black clouds with coils of red lightning snaking through them blotted out the sky. The city was ablaze, and an elf with red wings hovered in the air above the royal library. Lindyss turned her head towards the castle, and the man gulped as he met her gaze. His chest tightened as the hairs on the back of his neck stood up straight. A blood-red lightning bolt flashed, and he dove to the side without thinking. The bolt struck the table, setting it and the carpet on fire.

Gabriel cursed as he scrambled to his feet and fled through the door, followed by the rest of the occupants. Demons bustled through the hallways, shouting at each other.

The man seized a guard's shoulder. "Tell me the situation."

The guard wrinkled his eyebrows and reached for his sword, but relaxed when he saw the horned emblem on the man's clothes. "The Corrupted One is attacking the capital. We've been ordered to put out the fires and try to direct citizens out of harm's way as the demon lord prepares himself to combat the threat."

The man's expression didn't change. "Take the princes to a safe area," he said and nodded at the woman by his side. The two of them left as the guard blocked Gabriel and Lamach from following.

"Step aside!" Gabriel said. "Don't you know who I am?"

The guard gulped but didn't move. "Their orders precede yours, First Prince. Forgive me."

Gabriel ground his teeth together but didn't say anything.

***

Eight robed demons were standing in a circle, surrounding a glowing orange orb. The surface of the orb wriggled and bulged as worms swam around inside of it, pressing against the thin membrane. A circular rune inscribed on the floor shone with a red light, illuminating the demons as their mana was sucked out of their bodies.

"Is this really the only way?" a man asked. He was the demon who had been talking with Lamach and Gabriel earlier.

"No, but this is how we're doing it, Troy," one of the demons replied. "Chad and Tina disappeared after killing Zollstock. We can't rely on them."

Troy frowned at the worms wriggling inside the gelatinous orb. Their pulsating movements made him nauseous. The metal doors behind him swung open with a clang, and a demon clad in black dragged a hornless demon by his right leg into the room. The hornless demon remained silent and expressionless as his bare skin scraped against the rocky floor. The black-clad man tossed the demon into the red circle of runes underneath the orange orb.

The hornless demon grunted as his body collided with the surface. His eyes widened, and his body shook when he saw the worms. "Please, no," he said. His lips were cracked, and the outline of his bones were visible underneath his skin. "Not the worms. Please." Red tendrils rose out of the rune beneath the

272

hornless demon and wrapped around his body, pinning him to the floor. "No. No!"

One of the robed demons chuckled. "Don't worry, this'll be the last time," he said and smiled. He turned towards the black-clad man. "Bring all of them."

The man nodded and stepped outside of the room. Doors slammed open and shuffling sounds echoed through the chamber. A few moments later, a line of hornless demons stood at the entrance to the room. Their mouths were slightly parted, and their stares were unfocused as if they were looking through the walls past the men. Each of them shook as they approached the wriggling orb, a few wetting themselves. More red tendrils erupted from the runes and wrapped around the twenty or so hornless demons, positioning them around the orb.

"How do we stop them afterwards?" Troy asked.

"They'll die on their own ... given enough time."

"Too many lives will be lost," Troy said and frowned.

"Can you stop the Corrupted One?"

Troy's brow wrinkled. "No, but—"

"Then join hands with us," a bearded demon said. He motioned towards the pile of demons on the ground with his head. "Or join hands with them. The choice is yours."

Troy gritted his teeth, pausing for a second before extending his arms out to the side. "Well?" he asked. "Let's hurry up and do this."

The bearded demon smiled and extended his arms out to the side as well. The other robed demons followed suit. Pillars of red light blossomed and engulfed their bodies as the bearded demon chanted. Orange streams of light extended from the orb and made contact with the foreheads of the demons lying on the floor. The threads of light wriggled as worms squirmed out of the orb, following the paths into the bodies of the demons. The demons screamed with wide eyes as the worms dug into their skulls and disappeared from view. After a few moments, the screams stopped and were replaced by groans.

The hornless demons thrashed against the ground and grabbed the red tendrils trapping their bodies. The tendrils dimmed as they dissolved into particles of light which flowed into the demons through their hands. A breeze blew through the chamber and whipped into a cyclone around the struggling demons. A few managed to climb to their feet and lunged at the robed demons, but before they could reach, a white light flashed and they disappeared from the chamber.

The bearded demon let out a shaky breath before he nodded. The image of the hornless demon's outstretched hand reaching for his throat was still fresh in his mind. "Let's board the airship and get out of here."

***

"Disgusting."

Chad and Tina were sitting on the edge of a building with their respective groups standing behind them. Tina frowned as her eyebrows knit together. The two adventurer groups didn't say a word as Lindyss—wings and eyes still red—rained lightning down on twenty naked, hornless figures throwing rocks at her from the ground. Each time a lightning bolt struck their bodies, they grew a little bigger. Their flesh wriggled, and the head of a worm burst through their skin every so often.

"What are those doing here?" Tina asked as she gripped her staff. "How'd they even store those leeches?"

Chad snorted. "You're too trusting of the royal family. Of course they'd weaponize those freaks." He stood up and said to The Black Hounds, "Let's go."

"Wait," Tina said, looking up at him. "You're not going to stop them?"

Chad shook his head. "I was going to wait. Let the royalty sweat a bit before stopping the Corrupted One," he said. He motioned in the direction of the hornless demons. "But those things—they brought it on themselves."

"Dustin's still in the city, you know?" Tina asked and raised an eyebrow. Chad narrowed his eyes at her. He smiled, showing his teeth before leaving.

***

Bzz! Bzz!

The lightning elemental vibrated on top of Vur's sleeping head, emitting trails of blue electricity. Vur snorted and rolled over onto his side, causing the elemental to fall onto the ground. It rattled and bounced in place three times before jumping back onto Vur's head.

Bzz!

Red lightning trails snaked outwards from the elemental and enveloped Vur's body. A few wisps of smoke rose into the air as the lightning came in contact with his hair. Vur let out another snort and swatted the lightning elemental with the back of his hand before rolling over onto his stomach. The lightning elemental tumbled along the ground and stopped after crashing into a rock. It let out a low buzz before shaking itself off and hopping back towards Vur. It tilted its body to the side and remained motionless while facing the naked boy. After a moment, it straightened its body and wind swirled around it. A miniature black cloud appeared above the elemental and grew larger as the wind circulated faster. Tiny purple sparks coursed through the cloud, emitting low rumbles.

The wind stopped. A purple lightning bolt shot out of the cloud and struck Vur's left butt cheek. He twitched and yelped as his eyes shot open. His head swiveled around and his gaze focused on the dissipating cloud. The pink elemental froze as Vur glared at it with pink-tinged eyes. Vur rubbed his eye-boogers away with the back of his hand, and the elemental shuddered before hopping away.

"Wait!" Vur said.

The elemental didn't stop.

"Where am I?" Vur muttered as he clambered to his feet and trotted after the pink elemental. The ground was cracked and patches of burnt grass littered the path. Black clouds filled the sky, rotating around a single red orb hovering above a smoldering building. Vur squinted at the orb and sucked in his breath. Images of Lindyss choking on a black mist flooded his mind, and his eyes turned red. He shone with a golden light as a web of runes spread throughout his body, starting from his forehead. His feet left miniature craters in the ground as he dashed past the elemental towards the direction of the orb.

***

Troy sighed, his face pressed against the window of the airship. The hornless demons were still fighting Lindyss, who had decided to cancel her wings and fight on the ground. The demons' bodies had swollen to the point where it would've been appropriate to call them worm-filled water balloons. Black tendrils sprouted from Lindyss' shadow, fending the demons off as a torrent of spells flowed from her hands. The hornless demons were unharmed by Lindyss' spells, but at the same time, the black tendrils swatted them away before they could reach her.

A red moonlike object floated in the sky above Lindyss' head, glowing with a dim light. The demon corpses littering Niffle stirred and released a red mist as the light shone on them. The massive reanimation spell sent shivers down Troy's spine.

"Enjoying the show?" a voice asked from behind Troy. A cold spearhead rested against the back of his neck. He froze as the other demons turned around. Their expressions were dumbstruck when they realized who the man with the spear was.

"Chad!" the white-bearded demon said. "How'd you—"

Chad smiled. "I'm a dragoon, remember? Jumping's easy."

The demons' faces turned ugly as they channeled their mana and drew their staves.

Chad raised an eyebrow. "You really want to use largescale magic in such a confined area?"

"What do you want?" the bearded man asked as he gritted his teeth.

"I just wanted to ask a few questions," Chad said as he lowered his spear. "What I do next depends on your answers."

"Don't you know who you're threatening right now?" another robed figure asked with narrowed eyes and glowing blue horns.

"Yes, I do," Chad said and smiled as he sat down next to Troy, "and I honestly don't care. I've always despised the royal family, hated them even more ever since Zollstock stole Mina from us. It was quite satisfying to watch him die."

The demon hissed. "Die!" he shouted and waved his staff forwards. A black icicle materialized and flew towards Chad. Chad snorted and swatted the projectile with the back of his hand. The icicle slid along his glove and pierced through the ship's stern. The ship shook as air gushed out of the hole before another demon raised his staff, stopping the airflow.

"My armor's made out of crocodile hide from Fuselage. Anything less than a tier four spell won't even tickle," Chad said as he dusted off the back of his hand. "Now can we discuss this like civilized men? Or should I kill all but one of you?"

The demon with blue horns snarled. "Insolent—"

Clunk.

The bearded demon smacked the blue-horned demon on the back of the head with his staff and shook his head.

"Great," Chad said as he leaned back and crossed his legs. "Those parasites. You send SSS-ranked adventurers to Fuselage to cull the creatures and harvest their bodies for materials. What were you thinking when you brought live ones back here?"

The demons glanced at each other, but none of them spoke. Troy cleared his throat. "Biological warfare or, like in this case, last resort defenses. Zollstock was conducting experiments on prisoners to weaponize the worms in the most effective manner."

277

"So you do have a plan to stop them."

All the demons remained silent as they lowered their gazes.

"You," Chad said and put his hand on Troy's shoulder. "Speak."

"Err…. Like I said, we've been conducting experiments to—" Troy gasped as cracking noises resounded from his shoulder. Sweat flowed from his forehead as he gritted his teeth and clenched his hands. "We don't. No plans except to wait it out."

"Disgusting," Chad said as a white mist leaked from his mouth. It formed a layer of ice on Troy's neck when it made contact with his skin. Chad's eyes reddened and blood gushed out of Troy's shoulder as Chad's grip tightened. "You pampered dogs send us to die in Fuselage with the promise of treasure and glory. You think you can control everything from your cushioned seats—never once experiencing danger for yourselves. It seems the current generation of the royal family has forgotten why our ancestors fled to Zuer in the first place."

"Once we are able to control them—"

"Nonsense!" Chad growled. "I've seen the ruins of Verderb with my own eyes. They tried to control the parasites; look at them now." Chad's eyes narrowed and Troy screamed as his arm was torn off. "None of you are fit to rule."

27

Tina was standing on the edge of a building, overlooking the action in the streets. She shivered as a breeze blew past her, threatening to push her over the edge. But it wasn't the temperature or the height that made her blood run cold. It was the corrupted elf down below. A trembling voice spoke behind her, "Too scary."

Hundreds of demons with various injuries and gaunt bodies shuffled through the streets, converging towards the center of the city. Red mist continuously leaked out of their wounds and floated towards the spinning crimson orb in the sky. The twenty hornless demons were underneath the orb, tearing apart the horde of zombies approaching them. Lindyss was in their midst, entangling them with spells, aiding her zombie minions.

Tina nodded. "I'm glad we never had to truly fight her. I never thought a mage could kill infected ones by herself." The demons behind her murmured in agreement.

One of the hornless demons screeched as its limbs were torn apart by the zombies. A meter-long worm burst out of its chest and burrowed into one of the nearby zombies, disappearing from sight. A few moments later, the zombie disintegrated into a black smoke which was absorbed by the orb in the sky. The worm thrashed against the ground before attempting to burrow into the earth.

Tina frowned and waved her staff. A giant hammer made of ice materialized above her head and flew towards the worm. It smashed into the street and obliterated the worm along with the zombies surrounding it.

The red light in Lindyss' eyes gradually dimmed as more and more hornless demons were torn apart. Her eyes reverted to their original color when there were four infected demons remaining. She shot a glance at Tina as another ice hammer smashed into a worm by her feet. Tina nodded in Lindyss' direction and signaled her group to advance from the roof. A flash of light in the distance caught her attention. Dustin and Mina were leading a group of armed demons, fighting through the zombies to the red orb in the sky.

A worm burst out of one of the remaining infected demons and lunged towards Lindyss, but it was caught in midair by a black tendril. A fireball formed in Lindyss' hands and incinerated the worm. The last infected demon let out a cry and charged towards her. Its movements were stopped by the tendrils, but the worm flew out of its body, avoiding them completely. Lindyss leapt back while forming a wall of fire in front of herself. Her eyes opened wide as a winged figure materialized behind the lunging worm. *Stella!* "Sto—"

"Silence." Stella pointed at Lindyss and said one word before her body disappeared again, leaving behind a tinkling laughter.

The flames on the floor fizzled out, and Lindyss swung her left arm to stop the worm. She let out a cry as it pierced into her flesh instead of being knocked away. Her skin bulged as the worm wriggled in her arm, climbing towards her shoulder.

"Cut it off!" Tina yelled. A member of Swirling Wind released a blade of ice that flew towards Lindyss and severed her arm mid bicep. Her arm thrashed around on the floor, but wriggling could still be seen as the head of the worm continued to crawl up her shoulder and towards her heart.

"Too slow," Tina said as she gritted her teeth and materialized an ice spear above her head. It flew towards Lindyss and pierced through her shoulder blade, striking the wriggling bump and emerging from the other side with the worm's head attached to it. The Swirling Wind members released their breaths at the same time.

A roar resounded throughout the city. "AUNTIE!"

Tina's face paled at the winged figure with bloodshot eyes charging towards their group. "Heal her," she said towards the white-robed demon in her group. "The rest of us, hold him off!"

The robed figure nodded and the rest of the party dashed forward to intercept Vur. Their knees buckled as Vur approached, and one of them gasped from the sudden increase in gravity. Tina narrowed her eyes, and her robe released a white light that illuminated the whole city for a brief moment, causing the pressure to disappear. A giant ice hammer swung from behind Tina's back and smashed into Vur who had been blinded, knocking him off into the distance. Tina grinned. "That felt really satisfying."

A few moments later, the area she knocked Vur into exploded. Tina's party squinted their eyes and braced themselves as a shockwave passed through them. A translucent, golden dragon appeared with its head towering above the highest building. It opened its mouth and let out a roar that decimated everything in the path towards Tina. Half a dome of earth erupted from the ground and sheltered the group from the blast.

"I think you made him mad," the woman who summoned the bulwark said.

Lindyss' eyes flickered as a white light enveloped her body. She whispered, "Vur…. He awoke?" She shivered as the hole in her collarbone squirmed shut. She frowned at the white-robed demon who was chanting with her eyes closed. "Why are you helping me?"

The demon's eyes opened. She stopped chanting and said, "Tina's orders." Her gaze roamed along the ground. "Where's your arm?"

Lindyss grimaced as she sat up. She turned towards the area where her arm had fallen. "It must've been blown away by one of the aftershocks," she said as her head turned towards the five demons fighting Vur. They launched spells against the translucent, golden dragon and raised earthen shields to hamper its movements. Every time the dragon was hit by a spell, the region of impact distorted and the dragon shrank by a tiny amount. Vur was floating in the heart of the dragon with his eyes closed. Lindyss cupped her good hand around her mouth and yelled, "Vur! Stop! I'm alright."

The dragon's movements stopped for an instant before continuing to assault the demons. Its tail swept through the air and crashed against a wall of earth, shattering it. Lindyss bit her lower lip and tried to stand, but the demon next to her put a hand on her shoulder. She smiled and shook her head. "Let them handle it," she said. "We need to find your arm."

"Vur's more important than my arm," Lindyss said with a hiss as she knocked the demon's hand away. "I need to stop him before the imprint consumes him. You don't understand how dangerous it is to awaken a bloodline without guidance."

"You're right," the white mage said. "I don't understand the danger. However, I do know you're out of mana after fighting against twenty infected by yourself. I also know that one of the parasites is still alive in your arm and we have no idea where it is."

"Its head was cut off and impaled by an ice spear."

"The only way to kill one of those parasites is to pulverize its whole body or disintegrate it," the demon replied. "Cutting off its head will only create two new parasites. You're in no shape to fight right now. Trust me, my team can stop a child; although, we will expect some payment for this." The demon smiled as she cocked her head to the side. "Shouldn't be a problem for a dungeon owner, right?"

"Delphina!" a voice shouted from behind the two women.

The white-robed demon turned around and blinked. "Dustin!" Delphina said. "You always show up at the right times."

Dustin and Mina approached the two with an assortment of armored demons behind them. Their bodies tensed upon seeing Lindyss. "What's the situation?" Dustin asked as he tightened his grip on his staff, his gaze drawn towards Lindyss' arm stump.

"A parasite from Fuselage is missing along with her arm," Delphina said, indicating towards Lindyss. "Have the guards search for it and let me know when they find it. Under no circumstances are they to approach the arm by themselves."

Dustin nodded and faced the armed demons behind him. "You heard the woman."

The guards glanced at the golden dragon before nodding. A few let out sighs of relief as they dispersed. A small figure appeared next to Lindyss and tugged her good arm.

"Auntie, what's happening to Vur?"

"Tafel!" Mina shouted. "Why are you here? I told you to stay at the shelter!"

Tafel hid behind Lindyss and peered at Mina. "I followed you," she mumbled.

"You—I—What?" Mina inhaled deeply and held out her hand. "Come with me, we'll go somewhere safe."

Tafel flinched and held onto Lindyss' leg. Her lips quivered, and her eyes grew wet as she shook her head.

Lindyss placed her hand on Tafel's head, running her fingers through the child's hair. "Vur's awakening right now."

"That means?" Dustin asked.

"The bloodline in his imprint is activating. Bloodlines usually awaken at a certain age. It takes longer depending on the strength of the beast behind the imprint—at least for elves," Lindyss said with a frown. "I thought he had more time."

"Isn't awakening normal then?"

"Yes, but elves are guided by their elders. A little bit of power is released at a time," Lindyss said as she gestured towards Vur, "not all at once. His mind could break if we don't suppress the dragon aura in time. He's already unconscious. We have to weaken it to get close enough to wake him."

"I can wake him up," Tafel said with a trembling voice. "He'll listen to me."

"Absolutely not," Mina said as she approached Tafel.

Tafel stepped backwards as tears leaked from her eyes. "Why? Why do you pretend to care!?" she screamed. "You never cared before! Never listened to me! I hate you so much!" Her horns flashed green as she swung her arm outwards. A wall of wind roared into life and knocked the four adults over before they could react. She dashed towards Vur, leaving behind a blurred trail of green as she ran.

A black tendril flew towards Tafel from Lindyss' shadow but fell short before reaching her. "Not enough mana," Lindyss said as she ground her teeth together.

"Tafel!" Mina yelled as she scrambled to her feet. "Tina! Stop her!"

A thick sheet of ice smashed against the golden claw swiping towards Tina. She looked behind herself and frowned at the green blur running in her direction. Another crash resounded and flecks of ice sprinkled down from the sheet.

"Catch her; I'll stall him," one of the demons behind her said. Her face was pale, and sweat soaked through her blue robe. A wall of light appeared behind the sheet of ice, and Tina nodded as she dashed to intercept Tafel.

Tafel tried to maneuver around Tina, but Tina stuck out her arm and knocked her to the ground with a tackle. "Vur!" Tafel yelled as she squirmed in Tina's grasp. The translucent dragon shuddered and stopped. Tina opened her mouth in surprise and blinked at Tafel while relaxing her grip.

Another crash resounded, and the wall of light shattered as a golden tail slammed against it. The blue-robed demon shuddered and fell to her knees while vomiting. A golden shadow covered her figure as Vur's claw descended from above. Before it could smash her into pieces, a white fireball flew towards it and exploded, causing the claw to disperse. The golden aura around Vur's body shrank as a new claw formed in the air above the demon.

Tafel slipped out of Tina's grasp and ran in front of the kneeling demon. She spread her arms out to the side and glared at the dragon. "You promised you wouldn't hurt me," Tafel said, her voice shaking as her body trembled.

Tina dashed towards Tafel.

Mina screamed.

The claw descended.

A yellow blur charged out of thin air and pushed Tafel away. Her eyes widened as she flew to the side, watching the claw slash downwards at the fairy.

Yella smiled as she gazed into Tafel's eyes.

"Sorry."

Blood splattered.

Tafel crashed onto her side, her eyes wide open. Her already pale face was whiter than a sheet, and her mouth hung open. She tried to speak, but nothing came out. Her gaze was locked onto Yella's figure underneath the translucent, golden claw. Her stomach churned and a lump formed in her throat as Tina lifted her and retreated.

Blood radiated outwards from Yella's body and dispersed into the claw, tinging the golden aura black. The blood coalesced into a miniature fairy which streamed through the dragon and swirled around Vur's floating body before disappearing inside him. The dragon trembled as Vur's eyes flickered open. He furrowed his eyebrows and took in the scene in front of himself. His feet dangled in the air, and he lowered his head. A frown appeared on his lips before his body plummeted to the ground as the dragon aura fell onto its belly. The aura shrank as its claws dug into the ground. It roared and strained its neck away from Vur's body as if it wanted to escape. A constant flow of information overwhelmed Vur's senses as the aura condensed, leaving a trail of claw marks on the ground before vanishing. Vur gasped and turned his head towards Yella's desiccated corpse.

"Y-Yella," Vur said. His body trembled as he attempted to push himself off the ground. He managed to sit up before his body convulsed. His hands flew to his head, grabbing his hair as blood poured from his nose. Inside his pupils, an image of a golden dragon thrashed against his irises.

The Swirling Wind members glanced at each other and retreated backwards one step at a time, keeping their gazes fixed on Vur. Tina approached Mina and placed Tafel into her arms. Tears streamed down Mina's cheeks as she hugged Tafel to her chest.

"What's happening to him?" Tina asked Lindyss.

Lindyss frowned as she approached Vur. "The fairy sacrificed her soul to save Vur's," she said, crouching over Yella's body, staring into her empty eyes. She lowered her hand and closed Yella's eyelids with her fingers. "He isn't mature enough to handle the instincts of a dragon." A sigh escaped from Lindyss' lips as she approached Vur's convulsing body. She lifted his chin with her hand and frowned. The dragon in his eyes seemed to notice her and stopped thrashing as it glared back.

"Auntie...," Vur whispered. "I'm scared."

Lindyss stroked his hair and leaned forward. "Don't worry," she said as she tilted his head back. Her lips touched against Vur's, and his body shone with a golden light, which dimmed as time passed. The spectating demons let out little coughs and turned their heads away. Lindyss pulled herself back, and Vur's chin drooped to his chest as Lindyss' hand released his chin. His eyes closed as Lindyss lowered him to the floor. Her body spasmed as she coughed out a mouthful of black blood and grimaced. She crossed her legs and sat beside Vur. Two auras leaked from her body: one gold, one purple. They clashed and swirled against each other, neither side gaining an advantage.

Dustin approached Tina and asked, "What do we do? Take them prisoner? Where's Zollstock when you need him?"

"Zollstock's dead," Tina said, voice flat. "Chad killed him."

286

Dustin froze. "What!?" he asked, his voice cracking. "You can't be serious."

Tina sighed. "Chad lost a fight against that dragon boy. You know his ego." She rolled her eyes. "Zollstock questioned his strength, so he decided to show him how strong he actually was."

Dustin's eye twitched. "The royal family's going to execute him," he said, glancing towards the airship in the sky. Purple crossed horns were painted on both sides.

Tina followed Dustin's gaze. "I think it's going to be the other way around," she said and shook her head. Her eyes narrowed. "They were experimenting with live parasites from Fuselage."

"The things that killed Josephine?"

Tina nodded. Dustin's face hardened. The airship floated in the sky, unmoving. Then, as the two watched, the bow of the ship dipped downwards.

"Took him long enough," Tina muttered as the ship plummeted. "He could've finished faster and helped us fight that dragon."

"Chad boarded the ship?"

Tina grunted in affirmation. A low rumbling roar brought their attentions back onto Lindyss. The golden aura was now circling around her foot, forced down by the purple aura. A miniature dragon head formed and dispersed repeatedly as a purple bat head chased after it, nibbling it and slowly eroding the golden aura. Lindyss' breathing was shallow, her aura visibly diminished compared to the one she showed during her fight against the infected ones.

Metal clanked as an armed demon ran over to Dustin. The demon saluted and said, "We found a severed arm. My partner is keeping an eye on it. We did not engage as per orders."

Dustin nodded. "Lead the way."

Tina raised an eyebrow, but her face darkened when she realized Lindyss was still missing an arm. She glanced at

Delphina who nodded back. The two followed Dustin and the armed demon.

"It's right ahead," the armed demon said. A scream rose into the air, and the three following demons dashed forward, surpassing the armed demon. They arrived in time to see another guard clawing at his own face. Multiple smaller worms were burrowing into the ground. A sword, stained with green blood, lay on the floor beside the guard.

"Dammit," Tina said while growling. She raised her staff into the air and chanted.

Delphina grabbed Dustin and dragged him back. "She's casting absolute zero," she said and bit her lower lip. "Let's hope she finishes before any parasites escape. It'll be a disaster to the whole continent if one of them does." Her eyes drifted to the multiple holes in the ground.

Dustin nodded and placed his hands to the ground. Lines of fire snaked from his fingers and dove into the holes left behind. Delphina clasped her hands together and a barrier formed around herself and Dustin.

Twenty seconds passed before Tina stopped chanting. She slammed the bottom of her staff against the ground, causing a blue sphere of light to flash through the area. Everything the light touched stopped moving, and a layer of ice formed on every surface. The armed demon who led the way arrived just in time for the blue light to wash over him, creating a beautiful ice sculpture.

"Shatter!" Tina shouted and slammed her staff against the floor again. Cracks formed along the ice before it disintegrated. The two frozen guards disappeared into a myriad of ice crystals, leaving no trace behind. Buildings and trees disintegrated, turning into tiny puddles of water. The ground beneath her caved in, leaving behind a crater with no trace of the worms or any of their holes. Delphina's barrier faded away, revealing her and Dustin—both unharmed.

"I think she got them all," Delphina said, surveying the area.

***

Tears streamed down Rella's and Bella's cheeks as they sat underneath a dome of mist beneath a tree. "We should've stopped her," Rella said in between sniffles. Bella nodded and sobbed harder.

Stella sighed as she rubbed her children's backs. Her body tensed and she frowned at the ground. She turned around and slammed her fist against the grass. The earth split open, and a worm, leaking green blood, flew up into the air, trapped by a purple bubble of mana. Stella waved her hand, and the bubble drifted onto her palm. She murmured. "What have we here?"

28

Lindyss groaned as her eyes flickered open. She winced as she sat up and placed her right hand against her forehead. She reached with her left to rub at her eyes, but it wasn't there. Her body stiffened. Her eyes widened as she looked around, taking in the surroundings. She was sitting on a bed in a white room with no windows. A chain led from her left leg to the wall, and mana dampening runes decorated every inch of the room. Vur was lying unconscious on a bed adjacent to hers, his body bound tightly with metal. Chad was sitting on the floor to the right of her with his back leaning against a metal door. His spear was propped up beside his body.

Chad tilted his head to the side. "Finally awake? Sorry about the arm. Tina destroyed it on accident."

Lindyss glanced at her residual limb and nodded. "It's easy enough to fix. No worries. How long was I out?"

"About a week." Chad tapped his spear against the door without sitting up. "Tell Dustin she's awake," he said. Footsteps echoed from outside the room. "How's the basilisk doing?"

Lindyss smiled. "Pretty good. He's a nice guard. The only person I've been bothered by the whole time since I've had him was Vur. He might be getting fat though," she said and frowned. "The civilians of Konigreich pamper him and feed him too much."

Chad chuckled as he stood up and stretched. "You're not going to ask about your situation?"

"I have the general idea. How bad's the damage?"

The door swung open and Dustin, along with Tina and Tafel's grandmother, stepped into the room. "About 25 percent of the city is completely destroyed while another 40 percent is damaged in some shape or form. A lot of people have died, but we don't have an exact number. There's not enough volunteers to help out," Tafel's grandmother said as she narrowed her eyes at Lindyss. "Everyone's afraid the dead aren't actually dead."

Lindyss scratched her nose and nodded.

"Not only that," Tafel's grandmother said, "but every member of the royal family on Zollstock's side has gone missing. The only ones left are my grandchildren and the ones related to Mina by blood."

Lindyss raised an eyebrow. "That wasn't me," she said. Tina's eyes flickered towards Chad.

"Don't look at me," Chad said and shrugged. "I only killed eight of them."

Tafel's grandmother's eye twitched as she glanced at Chad. "You really shouldn't say things like that out loud," she said and sighed. "Luckily for you, my hearing seems to get worse the older I get." She turned back towards Lindyss. "I'll be straightforward. Why did you attack us?"

Lindyss frowned. "I came here to retrieve Vur. Unfortunately, I ran into the fairy queen and lost a fight against her. She put the berserk curse on me, and I accidentally destroyed your capital. Of course, reparations will be paid in full."

"The fairy queen? Why would she be in Niffle?" Tina asked.

Lindyss tilted her head. "She's been locked away in your mana source. You didn't know?"

The demons glanced at each other before shaking their heads.

Lindyss shrugged. "Then it was most likely kept as a secret by the throne," she said and paused. "She's probably the one responsible for the disappearance of the royal family."

"If she was locked away, then how'd she get out?" Chad asked.

Lindyss blinked and pointed at Vur.

"I think we should dispose of him," Chad muttered as he picked up his spear and walked towards Vur. Dustin placed a hand on his shoulder.

"You trust me, right?" Dustin asked, causing Chad to snort. "Then believe me when I say you shouldn't hurt him."

"Whatever," Chad said as he lowered his spear and leaned against a wall. He scowled at Lindyss. "Why'd the queen curse you?"

Lindyss smirked. "We had a little tiff way back when and she never forgave me. That woman can really hold a grudge; it's been over four centuries."

"Four centuries?" Tina asked with a raised eyebrow. "What did you do? Kick her dog?"

Lindyss' face beamed as she smiled. "Killed it, actually, but close enough. I also may or may not have betrayed her and sold her off to the demons."

***

Stella sat cross-legged on a green slime as she giggled at the thirty demons hanging from the ceiling by their feet. She was in a cave with Rella and Bella standing behind her, their eyes downcast and faces pale. The cave was located in a valley teeming with hundreds of fairies, most of which were sunbathing or playing with slimes.

The demons were naked, their bones leaving an outline on their skin. Their cheeks were sunken in and dark bags circled their eyes. Black scabs covered the regions where their nails used to be.

"Isn't this too much?" Bella whispered to Rella.

"No." Stella's voice was soft, but the two fairies behind her trembled and flinched. "Four hundred years. Four hundred years without seeing the sun, living in total darkness. Four hundred years without food or water. I couldn't even die because of the mana they poured into me through that chain." Stella gnashed her teeth together and narrowed her eyes at the chains suspending the demons.

Stella smiled at them. "Let's play a game. I found one of these worms and I really want to see what they can do. The thirty of you are going to vote on who gets the worm. The winner will be kept alive as long as possible as I experiment with them."

Rella and Bella shivered.

Thirty minutes later, a male demon was strapped onto a table underneath all the other demons. The worm floated above him, trapped in a bubble. "I can tell you everything we know about the worm," he said. "Just, please, don't put it inside me."

Stella grinned. "Speak then," she said as the worm thrashed against the wall of the bubble, lunging towards the demon.

The demon gulped. "They're parasites, but they can reproduce and survive without a host. When they infect a host body, the host body becomes extremely resistant to magic. Their ultimate goal is to consume as much mana as possible before reproducing. All the worms are the same level as the parent worm. The smallest piece we've seen grow into a new worm was a tenth of the size of the parent. Thankfully, they're not very strong without a host. We started killing them before they reached level 100. There was one worm that was able to use the host body's spells at level 100 and the next host it infected retained the ability."

Stella nodded and hummed as she drummed her fingers against her knee. "How resistant is extremely resistant?"

"We don't know the exact numbers, but—"

"Then I guess we'll just have to find out," Stella said with a grin.

The bubble holding the worm burst.

***

"Teach me how to fight," Tafel said.

Chad blinked at the kneeling demon princess at his feet. "No," he said and walked around her. The two were in a hallway of the royal castle near the room holding Lindyss.

Tafel grabbed his leg. "Please, please, please, please, please, pleaseeeeee."

"You're annoying. Let go," Chad said as he stopped and pried her fingers off. "Go ask your mother; I'm not a mage."

"I don't want to use magic," Tafel said as she scrambled to her feet. "I want to learn how to fight. With a weapon."

"Are you stupid?" Chad asked as he narrowed his eyes. "You already have six horns and you're not even ten. Your potential for magic is huge."

Tafel bit her lower lip. "I'm not giving up on magic. I just want to learn how to fight too."

"Go ask Doofus then," Chad said as he walked towards a door. "He's teaching at the academy."

"But you're the strongest warrior," Tafel said. "No one's as good as you."

"That's right. I'm the strongest," Chad said as he nodded and opened the door.

"The way you use the spear is amazing," Tafel said as she chased after him. "It's hard for me to see it move. And you beat eight members of the royal family by yourself."

"Of course," Chad said as he smiled. "I've been doing it for years."

Lindyss and Tina were sitting in the room, talking to each other when Chad and Tafel walked inside. Vur was still unconscious in the bed adjacent to them.

"You're also the most handsome person I've seen," Tafel said as her eyes sparkled. "You look so cool in your armor."

Chad chuckled. "Don't I?" he asked as he stuck his chest out and strutted to a chair.

"Creep," Tina said as she rolled her eyes at him.

Chad snorted. "You're just jealous," he said as he sat down. "You know children always tell the truth."

"Especially when they want something from you, right?" Tina asked and winked at Tafel.

294

Tafel's face turned red as she looked away. "He would've agreed after one or two more lines of praise," she mumbled.

"What?" Chad asked as his face snapped towards Tafel. "You were trying to flatter me into teaching you."

"No! Of course not," Tafel said as she shook her head. "I meant everything I said, teacher."

"Who's your teacher?!" Chad asked as he crossed his arms and looked the other way. He sighed. "Kids these days."

Tafel pouted at Tina. "You ruined it."

Tina smiled at her. "Why don't you join Swirling Wind? Ruji's one of the best spellblades out there. You should leave the warrior classes to the simple-minded brutes like our friend here." She gestured towards Chad.

"Fight me."

"See what I mean?" Tina asked. "We'll be going back to Fuselage as soon as Lindyss returns to the south."

"Can I really? What about my mom?" Tafel asked as her eyes widened.

"She has a country to run," Tina replied and grinned. "Don't worry about her. I bet Dustin could convince her. The two seem awfully chummy nowadays."

Tafel looked up and thought about her mother's recent behavior: She smiled a lot more, and her face didn't always look so stern. Tafel nodded. "When are you going back?" she asked, turning towards Lindyss.

"Sera should be here soon. I don't know how long it's going to take Vur to wake up; he wasn't ready to awaken the bloodline. It's possible it may take a few years," Lindyss said and sighed. "At least I'm still able to control his dreams."

Tafel frowned and approached Vur's bedside. She clasped his hand in between hers and closed her eyes. "I'll get stronger. So strong that you won't be able to break your promise to me. I promise. Just you wait."

***

Stella hovered over the restrained demon. "Isn't this amazing?" she asked the upside-down demons above her. "It's been over a month and he's still not dead. He's struggling with the same amount of gusto as he was in the beginning. I really want to see how long it'll take for him to break." She giggled as she prodded the struggling demon with a stick. "I wonder where he gets all this energy from. If he doesn't need to eat, drink, or sleep, then it must be coming from somewhere. Maybe the mana in the vicinity?" She frowned at the unresponsive demons above her. She clapped her hands and a bolt of electricity struck the chains holding them.

"How rude. No one said you could sleep," Stella said as the demons writhed. "Tell me. Am I right?"

The demons wailed as more electricity snaked through their bodies before they fainted again. "Ah, so fragile. Maybe I should remove their eyelids," Stella muttered and shook her head. "Guess I'll have to experiment to find out for myself. Rella! Get me as many bananerry seeds as you can. We're going to plant them around this demon. If the plants closest to it have less mana than the ones further away, then I'll know I'm right."

Rella trembled as she nodded and flew outside.

Stella turned towards Bella and smiled. "Isn't learning fun?"

Bella gulped and nodded with wide eyes.

"I'm glad you agree," Stella said. "You want to learn more too, right? Go round up your sisters and get me more bodies. Demons, humans, animals, elves—no, wait, that'd just be saying animals twice—it doesn't matter. As long as they're alive, I want them all. Of course, don't let anyone know fairies are catching people to play with. We wouldn't want to spoil the surprise too early."

Bella shivered and flew outside.

"Oh, I'm so excited!" Stella squealed as she hugged her shoulders. "I can't wait to see the expression on your face, Lindyss." Stella licked her lips and caressed the thrashing

296

demon's cheek. Her horns pulsed with a red light as her eyes turned red. A mixture of sounds escaped from her throat at the same time, creating a strangled sobbing laughter.

Rella froze at the entrance of the cave and trembled as she dropped a seed.

"Oh, good. You're back," Stella said as she smiled and turned towards Rella. Her horns dimmed as her eyes returned to their normal color. "Let's get these seeds planted now, honey."

29

Sera rested her head on her paws, staring at Vur who was lying on a mountain of mana crystals in a tub. A layer of liquid covered his body but avoided his nose and mouth, allowing him to breathe. Lindyss was standing next to him, drawing a rune on his forehead with her left hand that had been restored earlier by Leila. Her right hand held a blue crystal which emitted rays of light.

"I never expected him to awaken so early," Sera said as she sighed. "I should have been there."

"You couldn't have known, matriarch," Lindyss said while shaking her head. The crystal in her right hand stopped glowing, and she picked up another one. "Awakening amongst elves can take hundreds of years; I've never even heard of a human awakening after being imprinted. It's possible that his awakening is related to the large quantity of fruits he's eaten from the elves' tree."

Sera sighed again and closed her eyes. "You're right. Perhaps I'm the only one to blame since I imprinted him," she said. The cave was silent except for the low hum of the crystals as they emitted light. Sera opened her eyes and blew a puff of smoke at Lindyss through her nostrils. "Guide him with your dreams. Now that he's awakened, he can't continue playing around without thinking of the consequences. Let him know that his actions affect everyone around him. Help him mature."

Lindyss clenched her jaw and shivered as goosebumps rose on her skin. "I will."

***

Vur was standing in a clear meadow with the sun shining directly above him. He shielded his eyes with his hand and squinted, looking around. The meadow extended past his range of sight in every direction. *Where am I?* He closed his eyes and frowned. *Why can't I remember anything?*

"Vur?" A voice from behind him asked.

Vur's eyes snapped open, and he whipped his head around. Tafel was standing behind him, her head tilted to one side. "Are you okay?" she asked. "You said you needed to pee, but it's been over an hour, so I came to find you."

Vur stared at Tafel and knit his eyebrows together. Tafel was holding her skirt with one hand, surrounded by foliage and trees that weren't there a few seconds ago. Her other hand held two round, white objects. He turned around and saw more trees. The meadow he was standing in had disappeared, replaced by a rainforest. He lowered his head and saw a body lying underneath his feet.

"What's that?" Tafel asked, pointing at the corpse underneath Vur. Vur shook his head and squatted next to the body. He flipped it over and gasped. Lindyss' face stared at him with empty eye sockets. Black blood flowed from the corner of her mouth. Vur's chest tightened as he dropped to his knees.

"Auntie!" he shouted and shook her body. He bit his lower lip and put both hands on her chest. Green orbs of light floated around his body and gathered onto his hands. His hands trembled as the light flowed around Lindyss before dispersing, unable to enter her body. "Why won't it work!?"

Vur shuddered, and black orbs of light flowed from the ground into his hands. They circled around the corpse before entering it. A low groan escaped from Lindyss' mouth as she sat up. Her empty eyes continued to stare at Vur, her body unmoving. "Auntie," Vur said as he grabbed her hands. He gritted his teeth and waved his hand in front of her face. "Why aren't you saying anything? Why?" Tears formed in the corners of his eyes. "Tafel," Vur said as he raised his head. "Help me. She's not—" Vur froze as his gaze locked onto the objects in Tafel's hands.

"I know," Tafel said as she smiled, rolling the objects around. A pair of purple pupils revealed themselves to Vur as the objects twirled in her hands. "Because I did it."

Vur's mind blanked as his jaw fell open. His mouth closed and opened a few more times as he tried to speak. Finally, he choked out, "But why?"

Tafel didn't say anything as she grinned at him. "You can't hurt me, remember?" she asked. Her grin widened. "You promised."

Kill. Vur's body tensed, and a black aura in the shape of a dragon crawled out of his back. *What's the matter? Kill her.* The voice of a dragon whispered in his head.

Vur shook his head. "I can't."

Can't? Or won't? She disrespected you. She disrespected US. You're just going to watch your things being taken from you? If you won't, then I will. The dragon's body coiled around his head and slowly sank into his face.

"Stop!" Vur shouted. His body shuddered as a white-hot pain wracked his head. "Who are you!?"

I am you. You are me. We are one, the voice rang out in his head. *Embrace me and we will be strong. A real dragon. Unstoppable.*

Vur's vision went black. When his vision returned, he was lying on his back. The clear-blue sky was all he saw, cloudless. Vur groaned and sat up. The ground was wet, and a body lay by his feet. He looked down. Pools of blood stained the ground, originating from a corpse. "Tafel?" Vur asked with a trembling voice as he reached his hand forward. His fingers were red and dripping. "Tafel. Please." His hand touched her shoulder, but her body disintegrated on contact.

She deserved it. The black dragon crawled out of his stomach.

"No!" Vur shouted. "Why did you do this?"

Me? It was you. The dragon hissed and images of Tafel flashed through Vur's head. She screamed and trembled as Vur

300

tore her apart limb by limb. "You promised," she wailed over and over.

Vur clutched his head and yelled, "Make it stop!"

A chuckle echoed through his head. *What are you crying about? That was just the start. Look around you.*

Vur shuddered as his head rose against his will. Sera lay on the ground, gasping for breath as blood gushed out of her stomach. Grimmy's decapitated head stared at him with accusing eyes. Snuffles lay on his back, unmoving.

Isn't being a dragon great? Anyone who questions your authority will die. Anyone who even thinks of hurting you will die. You are a king!

"Why?" Vur asked as his hands dropped to his sides.

You asked me to, the dragon said as it curled around Vur's body.

"I didn't." Vur shook his head.

But you did. Every time you feel angry, you ask for my help. The dragon's tongue flickered in front of Vur's face. *Don't you understand? You need me.*

"No," Vur mumbled as he shook his head.

But you do.

"No!" Vur growled as he grabbed the dragon by the neck and flung it off his body. "No."

Then prove it. Prove that you're stronger than me, the dragon said and laughed. *I'll bring them all back to life if you win. If you fail, however...* The dragon grinned.

Vur took in a deep breath. Mana surged through his body, but there was no golden glow in his eyes. "I'll show you," he said and lunged forwards.

***

Ten Years Later

Wind blew Lindyss' hair to the side as Grimmy landed beside her. She was sitting next to Vur in an open meadow surrounded by trees made of glowing blue crystals. His body was soaking in a tub of crystal-clear liquid taken from the

Fountain of Youth. "How is he?" Grimmy asked as he lowered a basket of crystals next to Vur's body. Vur had grown considerably taller and his hair reached down past his waist.

"I purified the last portion of aura nearly a year ago," Lindyss said as she took crystals out of the basket and rearranged them around the tub. "He should be waking up soon." She reached for another crystal, but a skeletal hand popped out of the basket, followed by a skull. The skeleton stood up and grinned as crystals rolled off its body. It saluted Lindyss before handing her a scroll. Lindyss sighed as she unrolled the paper and read through its contents. Her eyebrows furrowed, and the scroll burst into flames as she tossed it over her shoulder.

Grimmy studied Lindyss' expression and asked, "Anything wrong?"

Lindyss shook her head. "People are disappearing a lot more frequently. The humans and demons are formally requesting our presence to guard their villages and cities. A whole village disappeared overnight." Lindyss sighed. "That crazy fairy, I wish she would just show herself. She kidnapped nearly five thousand people over the last decade."

Grimmy nodded. "What do you think she's doing?"

Lindyss shrugged. "I know she absorbs all the mana in an area and then moves on. My skeletons found multiple areas with traces of fairies having been there, but everything is dead or dying." She frowned. "I hope Vur would wake up sooner so I can go out there myself."

Grimmy arched his back and stuck out his front claws. He yawned and lowered himself onto the ground. "You're finally healed?"

Lindyss smiled and nodded. "It only took what? Eight centuries?" she asked as she splayed her fingers out in front of herself.

The ground rumbled as Grimmy chuckled. "Give or take a hundred years," he said and raised an eyebrow. "Was it worth it? Do you ever regret it?"

"I can't even tell you how many times I've regretted listening to you," Lindyss said as she stuck out her tongue at him. She lowered her head. "But I think it was worth it." She raised her head and stared Grimmy in the eyes. "Don't think I'm letting you stick another soul inside me ever again though. Seven times was enough."

Grimmy's teeth shone in the sun as he smiled. "You sure? I've acquired a lot more in the two hundred years you spent at the fountain."

"No."

"But look," Grimmy said as he stuck out his front claw. A white fireball sprang into existence and hovered in the air. A golden halo revolved inside of the fire. "It belonged to one of those blessed heroes of light that the humans are so proud of."

Lindyss sucked in her breath. "Where did you get that?"

Grimmy laughed and the flame disappeared. "Get what?" he asked with twinkling eyes. "I'm not sure what you're talking about."

Lindyss snorted and turned back to watch Vur. A few moments passed as Grimmy hummed behind her. "Maybe just one more," she mumbled.

Grimmy's smile widened as he cupped his claw next to his face. "What was that?" he asked. "I couldn't hear you over a fickle person talking."

Lindyss pouted and whirled herself around to face Grimmy. She opened her mouth to speak, but a white flame smacked her in the face and entered her body before she could react. "You!" Lindyss coughed and spluttered. "Couldn't you have at least waited until after Vur woke up?" She clutched her chest and gritted her teeth as her body broke out in sweat.

Grimmy chuckled. "Don't worry," he said. "I can control dreams too. See?" He lifted his claw and poked Vur in the forehead. Black lines appeared on Vur's head and wriggled underneath Grimmy's claw. He lifted his claw into the air, and the lines spread out, crawling along Vur's skin. Vur's body spasmed and floated above the ground. "Hmm...." Grimmy scratched the scales on his chin. "Was that soul too strong?"

Lindyss exhaled through clenched teeth. "Sera's going to kill both you and me if anything happens to Vur," she said as Vur's body trembled and twitched. His muscles expanded and shrank, pulsing in time with his heart.

Smoke puffed out of Grimmy's nostrils. "You worry too much," he said. "You think I would intentionally harm him? Don't forget; I helped raise him."

Lindyss shuddered and closed her eyes. "That's why I'm worried."

***

Vur stood with his arms across his chest, staring at the dragon sitting across from him. The dragon aura sat on its haunches with its head lowered. *You did well,* it said with its eyes downcast. *I suppose I wouldn't mind letting you take control.*

Vur nodded. "I've seen everything you can do, learned all your movements," he said. *Just like Auntie taught me.*

The dragon nodded and shrank its body down to half of Vur's size. It shook its head and sighed as it trudged in front of Vur with its head lowered. As Vur reached down to lift its body up, a black bolt of lightning appeared from the clear sky and struck the aura. It shrieked and shuddered as Vur leapt back and armed himself with Lust.

The dragon growled as solid, black scales grew around its body. A pair of red pupils appeared in its once pitch-black eyes, and multiple rows of white teeth sprouted inside of its mouth. Its body expanded, and a second pair of wings grew out of its lower back while the tip of its tail curled upwards and flattened into a blade. It stopped trembling once its body grew to the same size as Vur.

304

Vur gazed into the dragon's red pupils and widened his eyes. The dragon disappeared. Vur whirled around while slashing with Lust at the same time. The bladed tail struck against the dagger's edge, and Vur's body was sent flying into a tree. He clenched his teeth and let out a hiss as he stood back up, circulating mana through his body.

The dragon disappeared and reappeared in front of Vur, its claw slashing towards his chest. Vur stomped on the ground and earthen spikes shot upwards, impaling the claw and halting its movements. A line of black fire appeared in front of Vur and shot towards the dragon as he swung his arm outwards, mimicking the cerberus' attack from the nagas' arena.

The dragon's tail flickered and smashed against the line of fire, dispersing it. It grinned and lunged at Vur with its free claw. Vur inhaled deeply and exhaled a gray cloud of dust as the claw was about to reach his face. The dragon's grin vanished as its body disappeared and reappeared a few meters away. The gray cloud fell to the ground. When it made contact with the grass, the green blades turned to stone. Vur's mind raced as he sifted through the multitude of blue magic skills he had. He stared at the dragon, a wry smile appearing on his lips once he found a suitable skill.

The dragon crept in a circle around Vur, its body poised to strike. Vur roared and a giant roulette wheel appeared above his head with an image of himself and the dragon on it. The dragon shivered and pounced towards Vur while the wheel spun. Vur crossed his arms in front of his body, encasing himself in a sheen of light. The dragon let loose a barrage of attacks and multiple cuts appeared on Vur's body, but he remained unmoving. He smiled as the wheel slowed. When it stopped, the needle landed on the image of the dragon.

The dragon howled as a spectral grim reaper appeared above its head. The dragon disappeared and reappeared repeatedly, getting further and further away with each successive teleport. The grim reaper stayed in place and raised its bony arm. A suction force yanked the dragon towards the ghastly figure. The dragon whimpered as it struggled in the air, flapping its wings and clawing at the clouds, trying to get away, but it was futile. The reaper waved its scythe once before disappearing. The dragon fell to the ground as its scales fell away and its red pupils disappeared. Its body shrank as the wings on its lower back receded and returned to how it looked before.

Vur walked up to the dragon and grabbed it by its neck. He closed his eyes as a burning sensation ran through his arm and into his body as the dragon faded away. A few moments passed in silence as the dragon's body became more and more transparent.

Vur opened his eyes.

"I told you not to worry," a familiar voice said.

Lindyss snorted. "Welcome back."

"Auntie?" Vur whispered. His voice cracked, and he let out a dry cough. He swept his tongue through his mouth, trying to moisten it. He struggled to get up, but Lindyss poked his forehead with her finger and he fell back into the tub.

"Drink," Lindyss said and placed a goblet against Vur's lips. His Adam's apple bobbed up and down as the liquid flowed down his throat. His torso heated up, and his body tingled as warmth rushed through his limbs.

"Thank you," Vur said. Tears formed in the corner of his eyes as he smiled.

"What?" Lindyss asked as her brow creased.

"I'm happy you're alive," Vur said as he sat up and hugged her, pulling her against the side of the tub. Lindyss' body stiffened and she blinked a few times before placing her hand on his back.

"Did you shrink, Auntie?" Vur asked as he broke the embrace and held Lindyss' shoulders away at arm's length.

Lindyss snorted and flicked his forehead. "Who shrank? You just grew up," she said and brushed his hands off her shoulders. "And don't call me Auntie anymore. It's weird hearing it from someone taller than me."

Vur's brow wrinkled. "Grandma?"

Lindyss smiled at him, and a purple fireball appeared in her hand.

Grimmy laughed before blowing out the flame in her palm. "Now, now," he said as his tail swished. "You shouldn't injure the patient the moment he wakes up. And you are old enough to be a grandma, you know? It's just that your personality hasn't let you get married yet."

Lindyss threw a thunderbolt at Grimmy's face. He ducked and chuckled. "Should you really be throwing spells around with that soul rampaging inside of you?"

Lindyss' face paled as she trembled. She clenched her teeth as sweat formed on her brow.

"Are you alright, Aun—, Grand—, Lindyss?" Vur asked, correcting his words as Lindyss glared at him.

"She's fine," Grimmy replied. "More importantly, how do you feel?" His eyes twinkled as he inspected Vur. He leaned forward and sniffed Vur's body.

"Sore," Vur said as he looked down. "And hungry."

"Let's hunt," Grimmy said and nodded. "Your ribs are showing. We need to fatten you up a bit."

Vur nodded and scrambled up Grimmy's back while Lindyss protested as Grimmy picked her up and placed her on his head.

30

"Tafel's gotten really strong, huh?" Tina asked. She was sitting with four other members of Swirling Wind at a booth in a restaurant.

One of the members, Ruji, sighed as she slashed apart the crab on top of the table with her sword. "It's ridiculous. I get that she has ten horns and all, but it's not fair that she's so good at swordsmanship too," she said and shook her head. "She actually beat me in a fight before she left yesterday."

Delphina patted Ruji's back. "Doesn't that just mean you did a good job as a teacher?" she asked as she grabbed a crab leg.

Ruji made a face as she chomped on her food. "I should've been a time mage subclass too. I wouldn't have lost then."

Another member of Swirling Wind snorted. "You don't know how taxing it is to cast time magic," she said as she ran her fingers through her silver hair. "Tafel can do it to support herself because of her abnormally large mana pool." She sighed and looked up at the ceiling. "Too bad she didn't pick it as her main class. I could have taught her so much more."

"I just never thought the day would come when she would get stronger than me, you know?" Ruji rolled her eyes. "She was such a tiny little thing. I wish I had half her determination."

Tina closed her eyes and rested her cheek on her right hand. She shuddered as she recalled the look in Tafel's eyes when she had told her a reaper was as strong as Vur.

"What are you thinking of, Tina?" Delphina asked.

Tina's eyes opened. "That time she asked us to fight against that reaper alone," Tina said. "How old was she? Thirteen?"

"Yeah," Ruji said and nodded. "She lost so badly that I thought she was going to give up being an adventurer at that very moment. I know I would've."

"But she decided to stop grouping up with us because she'd get more experience solo," Tina said. "And now she's going to challenge a reaper again, three years later."

"You think Stacy is enough to keep her safe?" Delphina asked.

Tina nodded. "Tafel would notice if we all decided to follow her," she said as she pulled a clear crystal ball out of her bag, "and Stacy did promise to project the fight to us."

***

Tafel took in a deep breath and exhaled while opening her eyes. She was standing in front of a rusted metal door. A blue, form-fitting robe made of spider silk was draped over her, and an orange zweihander with black runes pulsating along the surface of the blade was strapped to her back. Her horns throbbed with a dim silver glow in time with the runes on her sword. She stepped forward and pushed open the door. Behind it, there was a circular arena bathed in a purple light. In the center of the arena, there was a single sapling with an apple growing from it. Purple barnacles grew along the walls and spectator areas. Different sections of the arena were in various states of decay.

Tafel drew her sword and closed her eyes. Her horns shone with a dark-green light as she swung the zweihander horizontally. The silence in the arena was broken by a shriek as a blade of wind severed the sapling and left a meter-deep gouge in the wall across from her. The floor around the sapling cracked and trembled. Two sickle-shaped blades erupted from the yellow dirt in front of the sapling, and the tiles around the plant bulged as a large praying mantis head appeared. The broken sapling was attached to its forehead like a horn. The reaper let out a shrill cry that made Tafel wince.

The rest of the praying mantis broke through the floor, and it rubbed its scythes together as it eyed the demon standing across from it. Tafel's horns glowed with a silver light as she raised her hand. Two runes, both resembling clock faces, appeared underneath Tafel and the reaper. The clock underneath Tafel spun clockwise while the clock underneath the reaper spun counterclockwise.

The reaper lunged forward, its two scythes snapping downwards towards Tafel. Tafel grimaced and dashed towards the scythes, twisting her body to avoid them. The reaper's movements were sluggish as if it were fighting underwater, but Tafel's speed had increased. She ran to one of the reaper's legs and swung her sword at its knee joint. An explosion of fire blasted out of the blade once it made contact with the reaper. It flapped its wings and retreated backwards, seemingly unharmed. Multiple wind blades crashed against the same joint before the reaper managed to defend itself with its scythes.

The clock underneath the reaper's body flickered as the minute hand made a full rotation. The reaper rubbed its scythes together and stared at Tafel, wary and waiting. Tafel raised her zweihander and stood unmoving as her horns glowed silver. A faint ring of light appeared beneath both her and the reaper, but a sonic boom resounded as the reaper's body blurred and reappeared in front of Tafel. One scythe pierced through her abdomen, sinking halfway into the floor behind her. The reaper tilted its head as Tafel's body disappeared. A loud crack echoed through the arena as an explosion assaulted its knee, causing it to wobble and fall to the floor.

Tafel grabbed the now-severed leg of the reaper and disappeared, reappearing into the doorway she came from. She slammed the door shut and disappeared again, reappearing a few meters away from the entrance. Cold sweat ran down her back as she shivered. Her breathing was ragged as she sat down, pulling a mana potion out of a bag she left in the corner.

"Isn't this cheating? The dragon boy would be able to follow you out of that room," a voice said from behind her.

Tafel whipped her head around and held her sword in front of her body. She relaxed and let out a sigh. "Hi, Stacy. Did the rest of them come?" she asked as she lowered the sword. A clanging sound echoed through the hall as the reaper smashed its claw against the door, piercing it.

Stacy shook her head. "Nope, just me," she said and pointed an orb at Tafel. "You're being recorded though. Say hello."

Tafel rolled her eyes before drinking another mana potion. She readied her sword, and her body disappeared again. Stacy shrugged and tiptoed to the door, peering through the crack left behind by the reaper.

A few minutes later, Tafel reappeared with another one of the reaper's legs. She sat down and pulled out another potion. "This is definitely cheating," Stacy said and pouted. "Time mages have it so easy with their teleportation."

Tafel stuck her tongue out at Stacy before disappearing again. Even less time passed before she came back with another leg. "Eventually, I'll be able to beat it without having to retreat for mana potions," she said. "But for now, this'll have to do."

***

"Ah, I think I traveled too far south," a fairy said to herself as she crossed her arms and flew through the air. "There's just too much good fruit to eat past the dragons' roost." She sighed as drool leaked from her mouth. Movement beneath her caught her eye.

"What kind of creature is this?" the fairy asked. She hovered above a blue, four-legged creature and tilted her head. The creature had blue wings, pointed teeth, and the body of a boar, but its eyes were reptilian. Blue tufts of down sprouted from its legs: above its hooves but below its knees.

The fairy shrugged and flew in front of the creature while waving her arm. Black tendrils swirled out of her body and enveloped the feathered boar. It squealed as it ran around, trying

311

to escape the smoke before finally collapsing in front of the fairy. The fairy grinned and landed on top of its head.

"Don't worry, little piggy," she said as she rubbed its ears. "The queen will take good care of yo—eh?"

The piglet shuddered and flung the fairy off its head. It dashed forward and grabbed the fairy with its needle-like teeth. It shook its head and rattled the fairy around until she stopped moving. The feathered boar snorted and trotted north towards the dragons' roost, still carrying the fairy in its mouth.

***

"Stella's really gone too far," Lindyss said as she narrowed her eyes at the fairy's corpse. The feathered boar had returned home with prey after a day of exploring. "Coming this far south? She must be looking for a fight."

A high-pitched squeal interrupted her train of thought. Vur was holding the blue boar upside-down by its tail as it flapped its wings and struggled. He poked it with his finger and received a bite in return. "What is it?" Vur asked as he sucked on his bleeding finger.

Prika laughed. "It's your grandchild," she said and grinned. "Just wait till you meet your daughter-in-law. You'd be surprised."

Vur tilted his head and placed the piglet on the ground. It hissed at him before hiding behind Prika's leg. "Does it have a name?"

"Nope. Snuffles can't speak," Prika said as she nudged the piglet with her snout. "Neither can your daughter-in-law. I'm sure they wouldn't mind if you named her."

"Floofykins," Vur said without hesitation and pointed at the piglet. It squealed and rapidly shook its head back and forth.

"Floofykins?" Lindyss asked as she raised her eyebrow. "You're going to name her Floofykins? She's the offspring of a phoenix and a dragon-imprinted boar and you want to name her Floofykins. Can't you think of something a little bit more awe-inspiring?"

312

Vur's body blurred and he reappeared behind the piglet. He lifted her up with one hand. "But she's so fluffy," he said and pointed at the bits of down on her legs. "See? I like Floofykins."

Tears formed in the corners of the piglet's eyes as she whimpered. Lindyss sighed. "Sorry, Floofykins," she said. "He's being stubborn."

Vur whirled the crying piglet around to face him. "Do you really hate it that much?"

She nodded and sniffled. Vur sighed. "Fine," he said. "I'll think of something better." He hummed. "Maybe if I add a title…. How about … Little Miss? Yes, Little Miss Floofykins sounds nice."

The piglet spat a white fireball into his face.

Vur nodded. "It's settled then," he said as he wiped the flames off his eyebrows and smiled. "Henceforth, your name will be The Awe-Inspiring White Flame, Little Miss Floofykins."

Lindyss shook her head and looked at Prika.

Prika shrugged. "Don't look at me," she said. "I kinda like it."

***

A man was standing on top of a blue dragon's head in a courtyard. He wore silver armor adorned with the crest of the human royal family, a pair of lions crossing arms. A black kite shield was strapped to his back, and an orange longsword hung from his waist.

"Prince Rudolph," a man said as he stood at the entrance to the courtyard with his head lowered. "The king is seeking an audience with you."

Rudolph nodded and jumped off of Johann's head, slowing in midair before landing on the ground without a sound. "Very well, you're dismissed," he said to the sentry who saluted and ran off. "Stay here, Johann." The dragon growled in reply and lowered its belly onto the ground.

A few moments later, Rudolph approached the mahogany doors leading to the throne room. "Prince Rudolph," the two sentries said and stepped away while bowing. Rudolph ignored them as he pushed the doors open and walked inside. His father was talking to a man, the pope, who was wearing white robes and a golden tiara.

"Prince Rudolph greets the pope," Rudolph said as he knelt on one knee.

"Rise, rise," the pope said and waved his arm. "No need for formalities when it's just us."

"Rudolph," the king said as he rose from his throne. "I'll get straight to the point. The sacred spirits have decided to give us their blessing to counter the threat of the fairy queen. Too many of our people have gone missing in recent years and the spirits are displeased."

Rudolph's heart beat faster in his chest. "You wish for me to inherit the spirits' will?" he asked as he lowered his head.

"Not quite," the pope answered in place of the king. "The spirits wish to have a full party."

The king nodded. "The spirits will watch over an organized tournament and decide on who to bless. Don't disappoint me." The king narrowed his eyes at Rudolph.

Rudolph trembled and crossed his arm over his chest. "I won't, Father."

"Good," the king said. "The deciding tournament will take place three months from now. I wanted to warn you before you decided to go on an adventure and disappear for another year. Of course, I'll let everyone else know only a week in advance. Use this time to prepare yourself well." He nodded. "You may leave."

"Thank you, Father," Rudolph said and bowed before leaving. He clenched his fists. *Just you wait, Michelle.*

***

Vur sighed as he gazed at the patch of land underneath him. He stood on the branch of a tree that had lost its leaves. The

314

vegetation around him was withered and gray, and there were a few areas where sand was forming. Images of Yella's smiling face appeared in his head as he sat down and hunched over, clasping his hands together. Stella's face superimposed itself over Yella's face and Vur shook his head. He sighed again and stared up at the clouds in the sky.

What are you going to do when you find them?

Vur glanced at the metal chain hanging from his neck. Attached to the other end was the pink lightning elemental. "I don't know. Part of me wants to kill Stella for what she did to Lindyss. But the other part of me knows that Yella loved Stella and she wouldn't want me to hurt her. She gave her life for me."

The lightning elemental buzzed. *Couldn't you say it was Stella's fault that Yella died? If she didn't curse Lindyss, then you wouldn't have gone berserk.*

Vur shook his head and pointed his finger to the sky. "You could blame anyone that way," he said as his finger zigzagged downwards. "It's Stella's fault for cursing Lindyss. It's my fault for not being able to control the dragon inside of me. It's the demons' fault for using the parasites. It's Tafel's fault for running in front of me. It's Auntie's fault for betraying the fairy queen so many years ago. I'm sure Stella is just as, if not more, devastated by Yella's death."

You didn't think that way when you first woke up, the lightning elemental noted.

Vur nodded. "Aunt Leila helped me work through my feelings," he said and clenched his hand. "Nothing is black and white. There's always more."

"Message for Vur!" A skeleton head popped out of a knot in the tree Vur was sitting on. Vur stiffened before he exhaled and relaxed. The skeleton tilted its head. "Why am I in a tree?"

Vur shrugged and helped free the skeleton.

"Thank you," the skeleton said as it dusted flecks of wood off its body. It coughed and cleared its throat. "Our unholy mistress wishes for you to infiltrate the human kingdom. Rumor

315

has it that the humans are holding a competition and the winner gets some sort of blessing. The majority of the positions in the competition are already filled by promising students, but a preliminary competition will be held for the general public to fill in the remaining slots."

Vur frowned. "I haven't found the fairies yet."

"Give me a second as I talk to our mistress," the skeleton said and froze in place. A few moments passed. "Alright, she says that if you win the competition, the reward will help you locate the fairies. Oh, she also wants you to shave your head, change your name, wear a mask, and pretend to be a black mage with a monk subclass until you receive the prize for winning."

"How long do I have to get there?"

"Four days. You better start running," the skeleton said. "The mistress doesn't want you to be associated with dragons or the undead or even falling from the sky because of Exzenter."

Vur's eye twitched. "I guess I should get going then," he muttered. "The prize better be worth it."

"Wait a moment," the skeleton said and pointed at itself with its thumb. "I'll help you shave your head. I'm the best skeleton around for undead haircare and manicures."

Vur's head tilted. "But…"

"No butts. Only heads," the skeleton said as it pulled a knife out of its pelvic bone. "Ready?"

***

Tafel leaned against a dilapidated wall and exhaled. Her sword lay on the ground next to her, covered in green blood. Across from her was the mangled corpse of a praying mantis.

"That's pretty amazing."

Tafel grabbed her sword and faced the entranceway where the voice came from. She released the sword and closed her eyes when she identified the speaker.

"After three months of fighting reapers, you were able to kill one without retreating," Stacy said as she handed Tafel a flagon of water. "How many does this make? Seventeen?"

316

"Eighteen," Tafel said as she opened her eyes and grabbed the flagon. She gazed at the reaper's unmoving body and sighed. "You know … I almost forgot why I wanted to get stronger. Well, not really, but after all these fights … Vur just became a side goal. I haven't seen him in ten years after all. What I feel now is a desire to conquer this continent. Be the best, do what no one else has done. Do you know what I mean?" Tafel made eye contact with Stacy.

Stacy shrugged. "I just do this to support my family," she said. "Drinks from the Fountain of Youth are expensive. I'm not a battle maniac like you and Chad. Just give me a warm fireplace and a nice book to read and I'll be satisfied."

"Battle maniac, huh?" Tafel asked as she grinned and glanced at her blood-soaked sword. She handed the flagon back to Stacy and stood up while stretching her arms out wide.

"Do you want me to get Lucy to transport this one back too?" Stacy asked Tafel as she motioned at the corpse with her head.

Tafel shook her head and smiled. "I'll teleport it to town with us. I think it's time I head back to Zuer."

"Oh? What are your plans?" Stacy asked as she helped bundle up the reaper's corpse.

"Nothing much," Tafel said. "I'll probably just say hi to Vur, maybe fight him. Visit my mom and Dustin. Eat something that's not related to insects, crabs, or worms. Sleep in a real bed. Take a hot shower. Seize the throne. Read a good book. You know, the usual."

Stacy scratched her head. "Err, I'm pretty sure one of those is not like the others."

Tafel nodded. "Yeah, maybe, it's best if I save fighting Vur for later," she said as her horns glowed silver and a ring of white light surrounded the two women standing on the corpse.

"No, no," Stacy said as she shook her head. "I was talking about seizing the throne."

Tafel grinned. "Did I say that? You must've misheard," she said and winked. A pillar of light rose from the circle into the sky, and the demons vanished along with the corpse.

31

"We're about a day away from the capital, young miss."

"Haaa, still so far?" a girl wearing a white dress asked as she exhaled. She had shoulder-length, blonde hair. She was in a caravan with three other people: two men wearing armor sat in the driver's seat while a boy her age sat beside her. His hair was the same color as hers, and he was wearing a gray suit.

"We're already going as fast as we can," the boy next to her said. "Have some patience."

The girl pouted. "If Grandpa would just let us ride the rocs, we would've been there already," she said as she leaned back and stretched her feet forward.

"But you're afraid of heights…," the boy said.

"Shut up!" The girl kicked him with her heel.

"Ow!" The boy grimaced and grabbed his leg. "You better behave yourself when we get to the capital or I'm telling Grandpa. He'll be so mad at you if you get us kicked out because you offended the wrong person."

One of the guards cleared his throat. "Young masters, there appears to be a disturbance ahead. I suspect some bandits are harassing a poor fellow. Should we go around them or pass straight through?"

The boy rubbed his chin. "Let's go around—"

"Straight through!" the girl said and pointed ahead. "I'm not spending another day on these wooden chairs because of some stupid bandits." The boy sighed and shook his head but didn't say anything.

The caravan continued forward until it reached a group of people; five men with machetes stood in front of a masked monk. The caravan slowed down but carried onwards as the bandits made no move to hinder its progress.

"They're not going to stop us?" the girl asked as she leaned over the boy to look out the window. "I wanted to get some exercise before the competition."

One of the bandits waved his arm, motioning for the caravan to hurry forward.

"Wait, why don't they have to pay the toll too?" the monk asked. The monk was wearing a smiling raccoon mask that had narrow slits for eyeholes. "Isn't the toll required for everyone?"

"They're bandits, stupid! There's no toll on these roads," the girl stuck her head out the window and shouted at the group that was now behind the caravan.

"Lillian! Don't stick your head out like that," the boy said as he dragged her back into the caravan. "What if they shot at you?"

Lillian stuck her tongue out at the boy.

"Should we stop to help him?" one of the guards asked. "Monks are good people. They don't—"

Cracking sounds filled the air behind the caravan. Screams echoed through the surrounding area, causing birds to scatter from the nearby trees. The screams were soon cut off by crunching noises. The guards looked at each other while dismounting and unsheathed their swords as Lillian shoved the boy aside to look out the window. She shuddered and fell back in her seat with a pale face. "M-monster," she whispered.

The boy picked himself off the floor and raised the window's curtain. A raccoon's face was smiling at him with blood spatters along its cheeks. The boy screamed and fell backwards onto Lillian.

"Hi! Thanks for telling me they were bandits," the monk said to the trembling pair. "They're dead now. You can stop screaming."

Lillian stiffened and nodded. She opened her mouth to say something, but only a squeaking noise came out.

320

"You killed them?" one of the guards asked, his sword at the ready. He eyed the bloody metal staff in the monk's hand.

"Yeah." The monk nodded. "They tried to stab me after she yelled."

The guard grunted. "I see," he said as he retreated back towards the driver's seat with his sword still out. "We'll be going first then—if that's okay with you."

"Okay," the monk said and strapped the metal staff to his back. He walked back to the bandits' corpses and rummaged through their clothes.

The caravan traveled onwards, and the two teenagers exchanged glances with each other. "That was scary," Lillian said as she bit her lower lip. "When he stood over those bandits and turned to look at me, I thought I was going to die. I've never felt that way before—not even when Grandpa's lion roared at me."

"Do you think he's going to the competition?" the boy asked as he scratched his head. "I don't see why someone that strong would be traveling in this direction by himself. Adventurers travel away from the capital, not towards it."

"Competition?" a voice asked from outside the window.

Everyone in the caravan stiffened and turned to their right. The monk was jogging alongside the caravan.

"Y-yeah," Lillian said after a moment. "The competition for the spirits' blessings."

"Oh. I think that's where I'm going," the monk said and nodded. "Are you going there as well?"

"Umm." The boy's face stiffened as he smiled. "Yeah, would you like a ride?"

Lillian's face paled. "Are you out of your mind?!" she whispered and pinched the boy's side.

"Sure," the monk said as he jumped towards the window and slipped through with ease. "Thanks. I was getting tired of running."

"Yeah, of course," the boy said with wide eyes. "My name is Paul. This is my cousin, Lillian. She doesn't know how to control her mouth, so please don't be offended by anything she says. We're from the Leonis household. What about you?"

"I'm Vurrrr…durr?" Vur said with a questioning tone and nodded. "I'm Vurdurr. I'm not sure what household I come from. Hmm, what was Tafel's last name…? I think it was the Besteck household?"

"Besteck?" Lillian asked as her brow creased. "Isn't that the demon lord's—"

Paul nudged Lillian in the ribs before she could finish her sentence. She glared at him.

"You're really strong," Paul said to Vur and sighed. "I really don't want to compete against you in the competition. I'm a bishop and Lillian's a hunter."

"Why would we compete?" Vur asked as he tilted his head and rested his staff against the wall.

"You're a monk, right? There can only be one winner for the healer position," Paul said. "There's a tank slot, which is most definitely going to be taken by the prince. One healer, three attackers, and one support tank. We'd be competing for the healer position."

"But I'm not a monk. I'm a black mage," Vur said.

The pair stared at Vur's half-naked body that rippled with muscles as he moved.

"What?"

"Yeah. Black mage," Vur nodded. "I cast spells to fight."

Lillian's brow creased as she eyed the bloody metal staff leaning on the wall. It was still dripping onto the caravan's floor. "But—"

"Black. Mage." Vur crossed his arms.

Paul covered Lillian's mouth before she could speak again. "Sorry," he said and smiled. "My cousin can be hard of hearing sometimes. I'm quite relieved we don't have to compete against each other." He reached under the seat and pulled out a bottle

322

of wine. "How about we share a drink? In our household, anyone who shares a drink with us is a friend. What do you say?"

Vur grabbed the glass offered to him. "Sure," he said. "Friends."

***

"He's really weird," Lillian said to Paul as Vur traveled ahead to the competition booth. "Who wears an eye mask underneath a mask? I've never heard of wine referred to as fire water either."

"Maybe he's a half-breed. He did give us a demon's last name after all," Paul said. His eye twitched when Vur knocked over a crowd of people. "Purple eyes would really stand out, so he's most likely hiding those. He's probably been ostracized his whole life because of them. Try to be nice to him, alright?"

Lillian pouted as they followed the trail left behind by Vur. "If you guessed as much, why didn't you kick him out? You keep lecturing me about offending the wrong people, but you want to associate with a demon."

"Demons are slowly being accepted by the populace; that's why the school in Flusia was founded," Paul said. "With our grandpa's territory being so close to the border, making friends with a demon isn't a bad thing to do."

"Whatever," Lillian said. "If Grandpa asks, it's your idea." The two caught up to Vur and stood behind him while ignoring the glares and murmurs from the masses around them.

"Umm," Paul said as he tapped Vur's shoulder. "Did you skip the whole line?"

Vur turned around and tilted his head. "What line?" he asked the throng of people behind him. "No one said anything about a line."

"You should clean the blood off your equipment...," Lillian said as she scratched her head. "Everyone's probably too scared to say anything to you."

"Blood? Oh. From those people I killed earlier," Vur said as he nodded. "I'll clean it before I sleep."

"Next in line," one of the booth members called out.

Vur looked around, but no one stepped forward. "That's us."

***

"Looks like the dragon boy's all grown up," a girl muttered to herself as drool leaked from her lips. She giggled and pushed her way to the front of the crowd as Vur's group left.

"Hey! Watch it," a guy said as he was nudged aside. "You—"

The girl turned around and smiled at him, showing her teeth. She wiped away a strand of saliva with the back of her hand. Her reptilian eyes changed colors every time she blinked. "Me what?" she asked and licked her lips. "I'll be sure to eat you first in the tournament." She giggled at the trembling boy and proceeded onwards to the booth. Her body shuddered and squirmed. *Not now, little wormy. There's bigger prey out there.*

"What's your name?" the man at the booth asked without looking up.

"Stella. Just Stella. What did that boy with the raccoon mask sign up as?"

"A black mage," the man said as he wrote on a piece of paper. "Would you believe that?" He looked up and stiffened when he met Stella's eyes.

"Mmm, I can see that," Stella said as she smiled and snatched the paper out of the man's hand. She laughed as she left.

***

A crowd of demons were sitting around a plaza underneath the royal castle. They were wearing clothes made of silk and sported jewelry that glittered in the sun.

"Don't you think the prince is too young to be the demon lord?" a demon asked the man sitting beside her.

"I don't think he can seize it," the man said as he adjusted the white bracelet on his arm. "Dustin is strong after all. And he's been doing a good job helping the country recover despite his lack of royal blood. It's a shame a lot of the nobles here are stuck in such a narrow mindset."

The chattering of the crowd died down as the main gates of the castle swung open. Dustin stepped out, wearing a purple robe and holding a golden scepter in his hand. "Thank you all for coming today," he said. "As many of you know, the first prince, Gabriel, has issued a challenge for the throne. Normally, this would be done in private, but many of you wanted to witness the results for yourselves because you don't trust me since I am a man of common birth." He glared at the surrounding nobles before continuing. "I have done my best to lead the country, and you can see the results of my leadership for yourself. I hope that after today, no matter who wins, all of you will respect the new demon lord."

The man with the white bracelet stood up and applauded. "Well said! Show them nobles who's boss. Whup him good, Dusty," he shouted. "And you, Gabriel." He pointed at the prince who had appeared at the entranceway. "If you lose, I'm going to increase your training by tenfold!"

The woman next to the man tugged his sleeve. "Doofus! You said you wouldn't embarrass me tonight," she said with a red face.

Doofus cleared his throat. "My apologies for the outburst," he said to the nobles around him. He sat down and crossed his arms.

Dustin smiled and scratched his head before turning around to face Gabriel. He frowned. "Chad lent you his armor?" he asked as his eyes narrowed.

Gabriel snorted. "I guess he just hates your guts, huh?"

Dustin creased his brow. "The fight ends when one of us surrenders or is rendered incapable of surrendering," he said. "Ready?"

325

"Bring it," Gabriel said and clashed his mace against his shield. He sneered. "I'd like to see what you can do against this armor."

Dustin waved his scepter and thirty fireballs condensed in the air behind him before flying towards Gabriel. Gabriel laughed and lowered his helmet's visor before standing akimbo. The fireballs collided against him, setting his armor ablaze.

"You think your measly little fireballs are going to work? All it does is create some smoke," Gabriel said as he laughed. He inhaled a lung full of smoke and started coughing. "Wait. Smoke?" He screamed and stripped off the burning armor. "Time out! Time out!"

Dustin scratched his head. "There's no timeouts, but I'd feel really bad if I continued to attack…"

Laughter rang out over the plaza. Chad was rolling around on the roof of the royal castle, clutching his stomach. "Stupid brat," he said through tears. "You really thought I'd give you my armor for a position in the nobility? I'm richer than all the nobles out there combined."

"You tricked me," Gabriel shrieked as he stood naked and pointed at Chad. "I'll kill you! I'll rip your intestines out and strangle you with them. I'll—"

Gabriel collapsed as a chunk of ice struck him in the back of the head.

"I guess that was pretty anti-climactic," Dustin said. He turned towards the nobles. "It seems we wasted your time."

The crowd broke out into discussion. A clear voice pierced through the murmurs. "Let me have a shot." A demon wearing a veil and blue robe stood up. She walked out of the crowd towards Dustin. Her veil slid down, revealing her deep-purple eyes.

"Tafel?" Dustin asked as his eyes widened. Murmurs flowed through the crowd of nobles.

"That's the princess?"

"Ten horns…"

An orange sword materialized in Tafel's hand as she smiled at Dustin. "Long time no see," she said and removed her necklace. "I'm returning this to you." She tossed it towards him.

Dustin caught it and rubbed the mangled surface. Ten years of fighting had taken its toll. "The good luck charm that I gave you when you were still a kid," he said and smiled. "I guess that means you're pretty confident now."

Tafel nodded and lifted her sword with both hands. "Ready?"

Dustin lifted his scepter and his horns shone with a red hue. A blue layer of light surrounded his body. "Ready," he said. He waved his scepter towards Tafel, but she disappeared. The next second, the layer of light shattered in front of his eyes. A sharp pain bit into the back of his head, and his vision went black.

Tafel stood behind Dustin with her sword propped up on her shoulder. There was a tiny patch of blood on its pommel. "I guess that wasn't very fair," Tafel murmured. "Well, that's what he gets for underestimating me."

A commotion broke out in the crowd as Tafel walked forward and picked up the golden scepter. She stabbed her sword into the ground. "Anyone who has any objections can step forward and fight me," she announced. "I won't be as merciful as I was with Dustin." She passed her gaze over the crowd.

No one stood up.

Tafel nodded and entered the castle, leaving Gabriel's and Dustin's bodies in the courtyard. She sighed as she traversed through the carpeted halls. It was the same place, yet it wasn't. She used to look up to the sets of armor lining the walls, but now she saw them face to face.

Yelling and bickering ensued the moment the castle doors closed behind her, with many voices high-pitched in disbelief. The nobles had been expecting a long drawn-out struggle that would eventually lead to Gabriel's victory as a rightful heir to the throne.

Tafel smiled. *I showed them.*

"Tafel."

Tafel froze and turned her head towards a closed door. She pushed it open and frowned. "Mother," she said, keeping her head level. "It's been a while."

Mina sighed. "I saw your match, if you could even call it that," she said. "You've gotten strong—stronger than I ever was. I'm proud of you."

Tafel creased her brow. She didn't know what to do with her arms as she fidgeted and shifted her weight between her feet. "Thank you?" she asked as she scratched her head. "Hm. I was actually expecting you to yell at me for running away all those years ago."

One side of Mina's mouth quirked upwards as she rose from her seat next to the window. "I didn't pray for your safety every night just so I could yell at you when you returned," she said as she put her arms around Tafel. "Will you forgive me?"

Tafel stiffened and attempted to pull away, but she stopped when she felt the trembling of her mother's body. "I, I don't know," she said as she stood in her mother's embrace, her arms at her sides. "I know that you were trying to protect me from Father, since he turned out to be crazy and all, but it still … hurt." She spat out the last word.

"I know, Tafel. I'm sorry," Mina said, her voice trembling. She released her daughter and held her by her shoulders at arm's length.

Tafel stared into her mother's eyes and bit her lower lip. "I guess we can try again," she said after a pause, "but not as mother and daughter. This time, we're equals."

Mina sighed. "I think I could live with that," she said and smiled. "You're more than qualified to be my equal."

Metal clanking noises echoed through the hall. "Excuse me, my lady," Retter said as he stopped in front of the doorway. Ten years had passed, yet the sentry still looked exactly the same as he did on the day he found Zollstock dead at the throne. "The nobles outside wish to present gifts to the new demon lord."

Tafel frowned. "That was quick," she said as she broke away from her mother.

"I suspect these gifts were prepared for Gabriel once he succeeded in taking the throne," Retter said with his head lowered.

Tafel nodded. "I'll receive them in the throne room." She asked her mother, "Do you want to come too?"

"I'd love to," Mina said as she took Tafel's hand. "Chances are my new son-in-law will be from those pool of nobles."

Tafel snorted. "Fat chance," she said. "There's only one person whom I've found interesting. Everyone else is too boring."

"I guess the bar is set pretty high when the first boy you've ever been friends with had dragons for parents," Mina said and shook her head.

32

The sun was shining. The sky was clear. A mound of unconscious people lay by Vur's feet. Beside him, in the arena, Lillian was motionless with an unnaturally pale face. The crowd of humans surrounding the stage were shocked: some stared with open mouths, others tried to speak but couldn't.

One person lying on the floor in front of Vur coughed up a mouthful of blood. "What kind of black mage are you? You didn't even cast any spells," he said through gasps. "You should be fighting in the warrior bracket."

The crowd broke out into discussion, and soon they were shouting at the referee. Lillian's face flushed as she lowered her head, trying to ignore the crowd's jeers. During the fight, Vur had thwacked everyone with his staff except for her.

"He's trying to avoid fighting the prince, so he slipped into the ranged bracket!" a man shouted as he threw a bottle at Vur.

Vur pointed a finger at the person who just spoke. A bolt of lightning flowed from his chest to his finger before striking the man. The crowd fell silent. "See? Magic," Vur said to the referee. "We qualify for the main tournament now, right?"

The referee scratched his head while looking around. His gaze met with the king's, and the king nodded at him. The referee cleared his throat. "Although there were supposed to be three winners in this preliminary round, there's only two people left standing," he said. "Vurdurr and Lillian have earned the qualifications to compete with the students of the academy in the main tournament." A few students swore and wailed in protest, but the referee ignored them. "The competition for the healers' bracket will be starting shortly."

Vur and Lillian left the stage and met up with Paul who was waiting near some food stands. "Congratulations to the both of you," he said as he offered them kebabs. "Man, I wish you could help me win my bracket too."

"Want to borrow my staff?" Vur asked as he held it out in exchange for the kebab. "It's a really good weapon."

Paul rubbed his chin and grabbed the staff. Vur let go, and Paul's eyes widened as he fell to the ground. "Wha—!? How heavy is this!?" Paul asked as he struggled to slide his hand out from underneath the metal rod.

"I think it was six hundred pounds," Vur said as he tilted his head, chewing on a roasted pepper.

"Is that why the caravan was uneven...?" Lillian muttered to herself as she took a bite from the kebab.

Paul rubbed his arm as he stood up. "I think I'll just use my own staff.... I don't get why us healers have to compete in a free-for-all knockout competition like you guys," he said and sighed. "Well, it's not like the nobles expect us non-students to win anyway. Wish me luck."

"Good luck," Lillian said.

Vur nodded as Paul walked to the edge of the arena. "Can he win?" Vur asked Lillian.

"Nope," she said and tossed the kebab stick away. "He's screwed."

Just as she predicted, Paul lost miserably to a monk who ended up winning the preliminaries. Lillian patted her cousin on the back. "At least you tried, right?" she asked. "Don't worry. I'll be sure to win a blessing for the both of us."

Paul sighed.

"Due to the lack of participants for the warriors' bracket, Stella wins by default." The referee's voice rang out over the field, his voice carried by the wind.

Vur tilted his head. "Why don't people compete as warriors?"

Paul and Lillian glanced at each other. "That's because the prince is counted as a warrior class and he commands a dragon," Paul said. "No one wants to fight against a dragon."

Vur lifted his mask and finished his third kebab. "Dragon, huh?"

***

Two fairies were hovering in a cave that had a layer of clean water covering the floor. Thousands of worms wriggled in the water beneath them as they levitated eggs out of the pool with magic.

"Woah, look at these big ones," a fairy said as she raised a cluster of eggs into the air. She turned to face the fairy next to her. "They're glowing green. Should we tell the queen?"

"You shouldn't disturb the queen right now," the other fairy said. "She's busy mind-controlling her new toy. What if she loses control of it?" The fairy poked the glowing eggs. "Those eggs are really weird though."

While they were giggling and poking the sack, a worm lunged out of the water towards the two fairies. One of the fairies snorted and bunted it away with a mana shield. "Stupid worm," she said and stuck her tongue out at it. "You'll have a host soon enough."

***

"Something doesn't seem right about that warrior," Paul said while shivering. Vur and Lillian were beside him at the edge of the arena, watching Stella leave the platform. She turned towards Vur and smiled, her eyes swirling with different colors. Lillian's and Paul's bodies stiffened as Stella winked at them before walking away.

"Did you know her?" Lillian asked Vur.

Vur shook his head. "The only Stella I know is a lot shorter than her. Like, a whole person shorter."

"Excuse me," a voice said from behind them. A boy, who was half Vur's height, fidgeted and handed him a letter before running away.

332

Lillian and Paul exchanged glances as Vur tore the letter open.

To the winners of the preliminary:

It would please us academy students if you attended a banquet we're holding tonight in the royal courtyard. Be there at eight. We'll be waiting.

"Should we go?" Lillian asked.

Paul scratched his head. "They're only inviting the two of you," he said and made a face. "I don't think either of you know how to behave appropriately in front of those nobles..."

Lillian snorted and Vur crossed his arms across his bare chest.

"Snorting's not ladylike," Paul said. He turned towards Vur. "And do you even have any formal clothes?"

Vur ignored the question. "A banquet should have lots of food, right?"

Lillian nodded. "Those nobles from the capital spend so much on food that it's disgusting," she said. "I love it."

"We're going," Vur said.

Paul sighed and shook his head. "Just try not to offend too many people, alright? And use Grandpa's name liberally. He should still have a lot of influence even if he was given land next to the border."

"Mhm, yes, Mother, I got it," Lillian said as she yawned and waved her hand. "You worry too much. Nothing's going to happen." She tugged Vur's arm. "We still have a few hours before eight. Let's go shopping; you need some clothes." Paul sighed as he followed behind them.

Hours later, Vur and Lillian approached the entrance to the royal castle. Lillian wore a blue dress while Vur wore a black suit with his raccoon mask still on. Lillian presented the letter to the guards at the gate and received directions to the courtyard.

The courtyard was filled with tables that had a multitude of dishes arranged on them: steaming meat, goblets of wine, baked potatoes. Some students were milling around, getting food, but the majority of them were sitting in a circle.

"It's almost eight," a student said, holding a glass of sparkling liquid. "Do you think they'll show?"

"Of course they will," another student said as he leaned back against his chair. "Didn't you see that girl's demeanor on stage? She's definitely a noble and wouldn't pass up this opportunity."

"Should we really scare them with Johann then? We can't let a bumpkin win, but if it's a noble...," a girl said as she shot a glance at the corner of the courtyard. Rudolph was sitting with his arms crossed and eyes closed. He didn't seem to care that Johann was waiting beside the entrance, crouching behind a wall. The blue dragon's head perked up as the sound of footsteps approached from the other side. Johann inhaled, causing his chest to expand. A few students noticed and plugged their ears.

Vur and Lillian stepped past the threshold, entering the courtyard. Johann opened his mouth and roared. A massive breeze, carrying globs of spittle assaulted the duo, causing their hair to fly parallel to the ground.

Lillian shrieked and fell over, scrambling away from Johann's gaping maw. Vur picked his ear with his pinky before glaring at Johann. A golden rune appeared on his forehead underneath his mask, invisible to onlookers. He placed his hands on his hips, copying Lindyss' posture.

Roar? Johann tilted his head and blinked his eyes.

"Sit," Vur said and pointed at the ground. The students' eyes widened. Rudolph stiffened as green runes shone through his sleeves, readying himself to stop Johann in case the dragon lunged. But his concern was unwarranted. Johann shuddered and sat on his haunches while Lillian stared at Vur, her mouth gaping. She was still on the ground, shifting her head back and forth between the dragon and her strange companion.

"Down," Vur said.

334

Johann's tongue flickered in and out of his mouth as he crawled onto his belly.

"Roll over," Vur said and twirled his finger in the air.

Johann barked and rolled over onto his back.

Vur stepped forward and scratched under Johann's chin. "Good boy."

Rudolph's face was frozen from the time Johann sat down, but he regained his senses when Johann sighed in content from Vur's scratches. "What do you think you're doing!?" Rudolph shouted as he rose from his chair and stomped towards Vur. The students fell silent while backing away.

Vur stopped when Johann raised his head to look at Rudolph. "Scratching his chin," Vur replied. "He likes it."

"You!" Rudolph spluttered. "Who do you think you are?"

"I'm Vurdurr Besteck. I came here for the food," Vur said as he patted Johann's snout. Johann scrambled to his feet and sat on his haunches, making whimpering noises. Vur stopped petting Johann and turned his attention to Rudolph. The prince froze and shuddered as a cold aura enveloped his body. His skin crawled, and he couldn't help but take a step back.

"Who are you?" Vur asked, tilting his head.

Rudolph placed his palm against the hilt of his sword and found that it was slick with sweat. "I-I'm the crown prince, Rudolph the First," he said as he tightened his grip on his sword.

"I see," Vur said. He turned around and walked towards Lillian who was still on the ground. Rudolph let out a breath that he didn't know he was holding as Vur extended his hand towards Lillian.

"What are you?" Lillian whispered with wide eyes as she grabbed his hand.

"Hungry," Vur said. "Let's eat."

From a nearby table, Michelle observed Vur and Lillian as they gathered food and found a place to sit. Beside her, there were three other students. "Where do you think he's from?" the girl sitting next to Michelle asked. Students scattered as Vur sat

335

down because Johann had followed him and curled up by his seat.

"The girl's from the Leonis household. I've seen her a few times," a red-haired boy said. "I've never seen the freak before. His table mannerism is proper, so he can't be a bumpkin. Maybe he's an illegitimate child?"

"I've never seen Johann act like that to anyone," Michelle said as she put down her glass. "Not even Rudolph." She glanced at the prince who was sitting alone at a table with his eyes closed.

"You think the prince is angry?" the girl asked. "I know I'd be angry if my lion acted that way to someone else. I feel bad for the peasant girl Rudolph's fighting tomorrow." She sighed and shook her head.

"What about for me?" the red-haired boy asked. "I have to fight that raccoon-faced freak just because I'm the strongest in our class. Sure, the administration's going to rig the tournament and place us top seeds against the non-students, but that really doesn't help me at all."

"You don't matter, Roy," Michelle said and stuck her tongue out at him.

Roy snorted. "You don't have to worry about anything. Everyone knows you're going to win the healers' bracket because of your dad."

Michelle laughed. "You sound jealous," she said and smiled. "Why don't you go make friends with him? He might go easy on you tomorrow."

Roy's brow creased. "You know we invited them to intimidate them, right?"

"And look what good that's done: Two of the winners didn't even show up and now we're terrified of the person we wanted to scare," the boy sitting next to Roy said. "Let's go talk to them. Besides, the girl's pretty cute."

"No way," Roy said as he shook his head. "I'm not going."

Michelle snorted and stood up. "Coward. I'll go."

"Wait, you serious?" Roy asked as he raised his eyebrows. Michelle ignored him as she approached Vur's table. Roy grumbled and rose to his feet, slamming his wine glass against the table. "Dammit. We can't let her go alone."

The other boy and girl followed after exchanging glances. Maybe Vur and Lillian would take it easy on them if they made friends with them.

Lillian sighed as she put her fork down. "Why would they bring a dragon to a dinner party? I nearly pissed myself, and now no one's talking to us. How am I supposed to make connections if every one of them avoids eye contact?" She glanced at Vur who continued to eat. His eyes were covered with a bat-shaped masked while his raccoon mask lay on the seat beside him. Lillian pouted. "Are you even listening to me?"

Vur shook his head and continued eating. He passed a piece of meat to the dragon waiting behind him. He ignored Lillian as she muttered a string of curses and grabbed another piece of steak.

"Is this seat taken?" Michelle asked, placing her hand on the chair beside Lillian.

"Does it frickin' look like it's taken?" Lillian spat as she turned around. Her face turned pale. "Err, I mean, no. It's not, um, taken. You can sit here if you want is what I meant to say." Lillian's heart raced. *I swore at the pope's daughter. Paul's going to throw a fit.*

Michelle smiled and sat down while her friend sat on the other side of Lillian. Roy and the other boy attempted to walk to Vur's side of the table but decided to sit next to Michelle when Johann growled at them while pawing at the ground. Vur cut his steak in half and slipped the bony portion towards Johann.

Michelle's eyes widened as Johann licked Vur's hand and took the piece of meat into his mouth. "I think he really likes you," she said to Vur. "He's never that friendly to anyone."

Vur turned towards Johann. "Is that true?"

Johann nodded and sighed through his nostrils.

"What's your name?" Michelle asked as she retrieved a plate.

"Vurdurr Besteck," Vur replied as he wiped the slobber off his hand. "It's common courtesy to introduce one's self before asking for another's name." The students exchanged glances with each other. It looked like Vur really was a noble.

"I'm Michelle Heilig, the daughter of the pope," she said. She raised an eyebrow. "You've never seen me before?"

"Nope," Vur said and continued eating. "I didn't know there was even a pope."

"Where are you from?" Roy asked as his brow creased. "How can you not know the pope?" He glanced at Lillian. "Is he serious?"

"Huh?" Lillian asked as she flinched, practically jumping out of her seat. "I-I'm Lillian Leonis! I didn't catch your question. What did you say?"

The girl beside her laughed. "See," she said as she poured herself a glass of water. "Now that's a normal reaction to the pope's daughter sitting at your table."

Michelle rolled her eyes while Lillian blushed.

***

"How'd it go?" Paul asked as Vur and Lillian entered the living room of their suite in the inn.

"I don't want to talk about it," Lillian said and walked straight to her room.

Paul tilted his head and turned to Vur. "What happened?" he asked as muffled yells resounded from Lillian's room. He thought he heard a punch against the wall.

"She spilled wine on the pope's daughter," Vur said. "And she used her as a shield to avoid dragon puke." Vur muttered to himself as he walked towards his room, "I shouldn't have fed him those plants…"

Paul sighed. "Well, it could've been worse."

"Oh," Vur said and stopped closing his door. "She also slapped the prince and called him an obnoxious twit before publicly denouncing the behavior of all the nobles present. I think that's it." Vur paused. "No, wait. She cursed at the pope's daughter too." Vur nodded and closed the door.

Paul's face paled. "Wait! You can't just tell me that and not explain what happened," he said as he tried to open Vur's door.

"Tired," Vur said from inside his room. "Going to sleep now."

Paul's shoulders drooped. *What do I tell Grandpa?*

The next morning, three people exited the inn: Two of their faces were haggard with dark circles underneath their eyes. The third wore a mask. Vur's metal staff was strapped to his back, while Paul had left his staff in the inn and carried a bag instead. Lillian had a longbow staff in her hand along with a quiver holding her arrows and a bowstring strapped around her waist.

"Lillian," Paul said.

"Still don't want to talk about it," Lillian replied and shook her head. "I was hoping last night was just a dream. The hangover tells me it wasn't."

The three traveled in silence to the competition area. The stone arena platform was gone, and the spectator seats were pushed outwards, making the center of the area larger. There were fifty stone golems on the grassy field, all of them motionless.

"This wasn't part of the competition," Paul said with a frown. The students were standing around the field, smirking at the trio that just arrived. Spectators murmured in confusion as they filled in the surrounding seats. The referee from yesterday was sitting on top of a golem with his arms crossed. The king's and pope's entourages arrived, and the referee stood up.

"Ladies and gentlemen," the referee announced with his voice amplified through wind magic. "As you can see, there have been some slight modifications to the program. Many nobles have expressed their discontent with the tournament style. After taking their accounts into consideration, the administration has agreed with their views.

"For the ranged bracket, the test is no longer a one-on-one tournament. Instead, the competitors will be tested through these golems. As ranged attackers, it is their duty to stay behind and wreak havoc on the enemy's frontlines. The three winners will be determined by the number of golems they destroy within an hour. This not only tests their strength but also their accuracy and mana management."

Lillian frowned. "Aren't the golems physically sturdy? What if we don't use magic?" she shouted at the referee. Paul sighed as the nobles around them snickered and commented on her interruption.

The referee smirked. "Oh? There's actually a hunter competing as a ranged attacker. I didn't realize we had such a backwater noble who still used a bow. You'll just have to adapt, I suppose." The referee shrugged.

Lillian ground her teeth, and her bow staff creaked as she tightened her grip. Paul put his hand on her shoulder and squeezed. Lillian exhaled and nodded, biting her lower lip. There were traces of tears in the corners of her eyes. Vur frowned.

"As I was saying before I was so rudely interrupted," the referee said while glancing at Lillian, "it's only the person who destroys the golems that gets the points. It doesn't matter if you were the one who weakened it.

"The healer competition is also going to be related to these golems. Once the golems are destroyed, the eight competing healers will restore them. Only restorations on a fully destroyed golem count. The warrior competition will continue as planned once the ranged and healing competitions conclude. I wish you all the best of luck."

The eighteen ranged competitors lined up side-by-side with Vur and Lillian on the rightmost end. Roy was on the leftmost end, his eyes staring straight ahead. The eight healers were on a platform behind the competitors.

The referee climbed off the golem and positioned himself at the side of the field. "You have one hour," he announced. The golems' eyes lit up as their bodies moved. "Begin!"

The majority of the students chanted while a few waved their staves, sending spells towards the golems. The golems dodged and blocked the projectiles with their arms in return. Vur raised his staff into the air, closed his eyes, and chanted in a low hum. Lillian bit her lower lip as she focused mana into her arrow and drew her bow. A loud twanging sound reverberated through the field as the arrow struck a golem, sending cracks through its head. It wobbled, but steadied itself before a ball of ice struck its already cracked head and knocked it over.

The noble next to Lillian snickered. "That's one for me," he said as he raised his staff and chanted again.

A green light enveloped the fallen golem, and its head reformed before it stood up again. The pope nodded his head and smiled at his daughter who had just cast a simple cure spell.

Lillian stomped her feet and nocked another arrow, storing mana inside of it. A lightning bolt struck a golem, leaving a crack in its head. She loosed her arrow at the golem. It flew straight and true, approaching the crack in the golem's forehead. An instant before the arrow made contact, a green light enveloped the golem and mended the wound. The arrow smashed into the golem, but it remained standing.

Lillian wheeled her body around and glared at the healers. One of them grinned and scratched his head. "Oops," he said. "I guess I healed it too early. Better luck next time."

Lillian ground her teeth together and inhaled as she closed her eyes. She turned back around and nocked another arrow, storing mana again. She didn't come all the way to the capital to fail during the competition. Sweat formed on her brow as her face paled. Before she took another shot, the ground trembled underneath her and she paused, turning towards Vur.

"The Lightning God's Fury!" Vur shouted and swung his staff towards the ground. A vortex of air swirled around his body, silencing the whole region. All eyes, competitors' and spectators' alike, widened.

"Aren't all the competitors under twenty-five?" the pope asked the king. The king nodded with his mouth open.

Hundreds of thunderbolts rained down from the sky, obliterating the golems and setting fire to the field. The competitors fell onto their hands and knees as the ground shook from the impacts. The children in the crowd of spectators wailed in their mothers' arms.

"This—," Michelle said before shaking her head and scrambling to her feet. A white aura surrounded her body as she chanted, ignoring the ringing in her ears.

Vur snorted and raised his staff, ignoring everyone's gazes. He closed his eyes as low murmurs escaped from his lips.

"That's monstrous," the pope said as he raised a barrier around himself and the king. "We need to have him."

The king chuckled. "Well, he's clearly going to win."

"That's not what I meant," the pope said as he lowered his voice. "Imagine if a sacred spirit rested inside of his body instead of just blessing it."

The king's eyes narrowed. "Your daughter and my son are part of this too," he said. "I refuse."

"We can let the spirits bless all the winners normally," the pope said as he waved his hand. "Then we wait a year for the spirits to recover and invite the boy back for some other reasons."

The king rubbed his chin as he narrowed his eyes at Vur. "Can the possession fail?"

"The spirits aren't that weak."

A white pillar of light rained down from the sky and crashed into the burning field, removing the fire and recovering the golems' injuries. Their disintegrated bodies reformed, dust particle by dust particle. Michelle gasped and broke out into a cold sweat as she stumbled. Her face was pale, but her lips were drawn into a wide smile.

A ball of lightning formed in the air above the golems, crackling, but not striking. Sweat rolled down Vur's back as more and more balls of lightning manifested in the air. He tapped Lillian's shoulder and pointed at the golems as he continued chanting. Lillian furrowed her brow before loading her bow. The other competitors glanced at each other and proceeded with their own attacks when they realized Vur wasn't going to strike.

Lillian loosed her arrow and cracked a golem. A noble smirked and followed up with a ball of fire. Vur snorted and a lightning ball tore the golem apart before the fireball reached it. The noble glared at Vur who didn't even notice his gaze. Every time a noble was about to destroy a golem, a bolt of lightning would strike it. The only exceptions were Roy, who was able to destroy the golems with a single surprise hit from underground, and Lillian.

Vur ignored the jeers and gazes for a full hour, continuously chanting and forming more balls of lightning. The lightning only dissipated when the referee called time.

"For the ranged competition, first place goes to Vurdurr with a total of 97 golems destroyed," the referee announced. "Second place goes to Roy with a total of 20 golems destroyed. Third place goes to Lillian with a total of eight golems destroyed."

"That wasn't fair!"

The other competitors shouted and booed the referee. Yells of agreement rang throughout the field. Vur crossed his arms as he focused on regaining his breath. Rivulets of sweat ran down his body, soaking the ground beneath.

"Shut up!" Michelle yelled. "All of you, just shut up!" The students froze with their mouths open. Michelle's face turned red, and she let out a cough. "I'm disappointed in every one of you. You should be ashamed. None of you wanted to fight Vurdurr in a one-on-one match, so you petitioned for a group competition where you could gang up on him and Lillian." She put her hands on her hips. "Now you're crying because the two of them beat you. This isn't how nobles of prestigious households should act."

"Well said!" the king said and nodded at her. She smiled back.

The referee cleared his throat. "And the winner of the healer competition goes to Michelle with a total of 83 golems healed." The spectators applauded. "The warrior competition will begin in an hour after the field has been adjusted."

Vur turned to face the competing nobles. "I'm sorry," he said. "It must feel terrible to lose to a backwater noble. My condolences." He turned around and walked out of the field, followed by a smiling Lillian.

"That was amazing. I thought I was going to go deaf," Paul said as he burst out into laughter. "It doesn't matter if Lillian offended every single noble in the capital. You're definitely worth more." He thumped Vur's shoulder. "Let's celebrate; drinks on me."

Michelle cleared her throat next to the trio. "Hi," she said. "Can I come too?"

Lillian tilted her head and creased her brow. "You don't hate me?" she asked as she edged towards Paul.

"It was only a dress," Michelle said. "And a shower got rid of the puke smell."

"Not completely," Vur said.

"Excuse me?"

"Nothing. You're not going to watch the warrior competition?"

"Like I'd want to watch that obnoxious twit," Michelle said as she glanced at Lillian and grinned.

"I mean … if you don't mind…," Lillian said as she scratched her head. "I thought he was your boyfriend, you know, with the way he was acting and all."

Michelle rolled her eyes. "He's not. He's just very…. Ugh."

"Oh," Lillian said as she placed her hands on Paul's shoulders. "This is Paul. He's my cousin." She turned towards Paul. "You should know who she is, unlike someone." Her eyes flitted towards Vur.

"Um, hello," Paul said, his face tinged with a faint red color. "What do I address you as?

"Just call me Michelle," Michelle said and curtsied.

Paul nodded and wheeled around. "A-alright. Drinks, yeah?" he asked as he willed his face to cool down.

Vur said to Lillian, "He seems to be unwell."

Lillian smirked.

33

"Lady Tafel, the young master from the house of Sinnlos has sent you another gift," Retter said as he stood in front of an oak door.

"Again? Didn't I tell him to leave me alone?" Tafel's voice came from behind the door.

"He's very obstinate, my lady. I'm afraid he'll keep pestering you until you give him a chance."

Tafel sighed as she got dressed. She observed herself in the mirror and adjusted her hair before nodding. "Can I execute him?" she asked as she strapped her sword to her back.

"I-I'm just a sentry, Lady Tafel. It would be better to ask your mother that question."

Tafel opened the door and stepped out as Retter moved aside. "You've been in employment since my father was the demon lord," she said and narrowed her eyes at him. "Surely you must have some opinion on the matter."

"As a sentry, my opinion should not hold any weight in the upper echelons," Retter said as sweat rolled down his back. "But if my lady insists on knowing, I think you shouldn't execute him. The Sinnlos family is a major backer of the capital. They contributed a lot to the reconstruction of the city after the zombie incident."

Tafel sighed. "Fine. Tell him he has to obtain three things before he can meet with me: the tooth of an infant dragon, the fart of a unicorn, and the hairs from the eyebrows of a phoenix."

"Understood," Retter said as he nodded his head. "The tooth of an infant dragon, the fart of a unicorn, and the hairs from the eyebrows of a phoenix." His brow creased. "Do phoenixes even have eyebrows?"

"No," Tafel said as she stretched her arms above her head. "I need a vacation from all this demon lord work. Tell my mom to substitute in for me. Thanks." Her horns glowed silver, and she disappeared from the hall.

"But it's only your third day...," Retter mumbled as he scratched his head. He shrugged and proceeded towards Mina's living chambers.

***

Lindyss rubbed her temples and sighed. She was sitting next to Grimmy with her legs dangling off the edge of a cliff. There was still no news on the location of the fairies even with her skeletons and bats searching in full force. Ten years of searching had been fruitless.

"Just relax," Grimmy said as he yawned and flapped his wings. "We can handle anything Stella throws at us." The Awe-Inspiring White Flame, Little Miss Floofykins squealed as she was displaced and slid off Grimmy's back.

Lindyss sighed again and leaned back onto her arms. She frowned as she sensed a vortex of magic forming behind her. "Didn't I tell Exzenter not to follow me?" she asked as she lobbed a small fireball over her shoulder without looking back.

Lindyss' eyes narrowed, and she tilted her head as the fireball shot back towards her, almost burning her hair. She turned her head around. "Sorry," she said to the ten-horned demon. "I thought you were someone else."

Tafel lowered her sword. "Hi, Auntie."

"Tafel?" Lindyss asked as she raised an eyebrow. "You've grown." A blue blur darted past Lindyss towards Tafel.

Tafel's body flickered, and she grasped Floofykins by one of her hind legs. "This is...?" Tafel asked as Floofykins snarled and snapped at her arm.

"Vur's granddaughter, The Awe-Inspiring White Flame, Little Miss Floofykins," Lindyss said. "Her mother's a phoenix."

Tafel flipped Floofykins onto her back and tickled her belly. "Let me guess. Vur named her."

Lindyss' lips quirked upwards. "It was that obvious, huh?"

Tafel nodded as Floofykins squealed in protest. For a while, only Floofykins made any sounds.

"You're not going to ask about him?" Lindyss asked, leaning against Grimmy's belly.

Tafel bit her lip. "Should I?" she replied as she tossed the protesting Floofykins up and down. "He never contacted me this whole time."

"He was comatose for ten years," Lindyss said as she observed Tafel's face. It froze. "He woke up three months ago and wanted to look for you, but I persuaded him not to."

Tafel knitted her eyebrows and frowned. "Then I guess I can't be too angry at him," Tafel said after a while and sighed. "Is he alright?"

Lindyss nodded and caught Floofykins as she flew into her arms. "He was really miserable about the whole 'almost killing you' incident," she said as she preened Floofykins wings. "Most likely still is. I sent him to the human kingdom to vent a bit."

"Is that fine?" Tafel asked and raised an eyebrow.

"He'll be alright."

"I meant for the humans."

"Oh. Probably. If there's an incident, I can always play the 'you stole a dragon's baby' card," Lindyss said and smiled. "Are you going to go look for him?"

Tafel lowered her head. "I'm not sure what I would say if I met him."

"How about, 'hi, my name is Tafel. You almost killed me before. Please take responsibility.' That sounds good, right?" Grimmy asked and grinned.

"No!" Tafel protested and shook her head. Her face turned red. "Actually, that might work…"

Grimmy chuckled. "Of course it would. I wouldn't have suggested it otherwise."

348

Lindyss nodded. "His personality hasn't changed too much after all," she said to Tafel who was drawing circles in the ground with a stick. "You seem unsure."

"I'm not sure if I'm strong enough to not be a burden. What if someone dies for me again?" Tafel sighed. "I trained a lot at Fuselage. I'm stronger than Dustin and a few members of Swirling Wind, but Vur was stronger than them ten years ago. I was pretty confident in my abilities before coming back," she said and glanced at Grimmy. "But seeing a dragon again just reminds me of how small I actually am."

The ground trembled as Grimmy laughed. "Everything's small when faced with a dragon," he said and puffed up his chest.

Lindyss snorted and smacked Grimmy's side. "Would you like to fight against me?" she asked Tafel. "I can tell you how close or far away you are from Vur."

Tafel raised her head. "Really?"

"Of course," Lindyss said and stood up while stretching. "I won't be going easy though."

Tafel flashed her teeth and unsheathed her zweihander. "I wouldn't have it any other way."

Grimmy placed Floofykins on his head and took a few steps back. "Use the new soul I gave you," Grimmy called out to Lindyss. She made a face.

"We'll see," Lindyss said. "Ready?"

Tafel nodded as she exhaled and tightened her grip on her sword. "Ready."

Lindyss stamped her foot, and a spear of earth shot out of the ground underneath Tafel. Tafel slid backwards and slashed her sword downwards, breaking the earthen spear and sending a blade of wind towards Lindyss. Lindyss waved her hand and a wall of air disrupted the wind blade. Tafel disappeared and Lindyss whipped her body around, crossing her arms in front of her chest.

Tafel's blade cut towards Lindyss, but a black layer of mist on Lindyss' arms absorbed the slash. The mist rumbled as if it was boiling, and spikes emerged from the darkness, shooting outwards at Tafel. A chill ran down Tafel's spine as she held her breath and disappeared again, this time, materializing in the air above and behind Lindyss. A chain made of shadows rose out of the ground and wrapped itself around Tafel's ankle as Lindyss whirled around, blocking the blade with her arms. Tafel's body jerked backwards as the chain whipped her towards the ground. She tried to teleport, but the chain flashed with a black light and her spell failed. She summoned a cushion of air behind herself an instant before she slammed into the ground.

Tafel exhaled sharply and gritted her teeth as the chain dragged her along the ground. The runes on her sword glowed with a white light, and she slashed it against the chain before rolling backwards and dodging a fireball flying towards her. The chain dissolved into a black liquid that merged back into Lindyss' shadow.

Lindyss raised an eyebrow. "Nice sword," she said as thirty purple balls of fire materialized and circled around her body.

Tafel grunted and stabbed her sword into the ground. A blue snake emerged from the sword's edge and slithered towards Lindyss, leaving a trail of ice behind it. Tafel dragged her sword through the ground as she ran in a circle around Lindyss, surrounding her with snakes. Lindyss ignored them and threw lightning bolts at Tafel as the purple fireballs defended her from the ice autonomously.

Tafel weaved through the lightning and raised her sword above her head. The runes lit up with a purple light as a green layer formed along the edge of the blade. Lindyss raised her arms, ready to defend herself from a wind-blade, but an explosion resounded above Tafel's head, accelerating the blade downwards. The blade shrieked and the tip of the sword vanished, reappearing directly in front of Lindyss, connected by a portal in the air.

Lindyss enveloped her arms with a black mist to block, but the blade vanished again, entering another portal. It exited from a portal behind Lindyss and struck her back, leaving a line of blood. Lindyss grimaced and tried to channel mana to her wound but failed. *Silenced!*

Tafel teleported in front of Lindyss and swung her sword, using the flat of her blade. Lindyss exhaled and a sword made of light appeared in her hands while a white halo rose above her head. The white blade passed through the zweihander, freezing it in place, before stopping in front of Tafel's neck. Tafel froze and swallowed. The blade of light disappeared a moment later.

Grimmy smiled. "You used it after all."

Lindyss faced her head the other way, ignoring him.

"How?" Tafel asked as she wiped the sweat from her forehead. "I thought I won when I managed to hit you with the silencing slash."

"It was a good attack," Lindyss said and nodded as a layer of green light appeared on her back, mending the wound. The halo above her head dispersed. "But unfortunately for you, I developed an attack that works through all kinds of silence."

"You developed it? Stealing my credit," Grimmy said and snorted. "Isn't she mean?" He rolled his eyes towards Floofykins.

Lindyss ignored him again. "I think you would still lose against Vur," she said. "He awakened the dragon bloodline in his imprint. Magical attacks, like your silence, have minimal effects on him now. Your blade sped up by the explosion might be able to catch him off guard and injure him, but everything else was too weak. You could avoid him with your teleports, but you'll run out of mana first."

Tafel sighed and sheathed her sword. She stuck her hand in a portal and grabbed Floofykins. The blue boar squealed as she struggled, flapping her wings, but Tafel snuggled her into her chest. "What class are you?" she asked Lindyss.

Lindyss smirked. "That's for me to know."

"And me," Grimmy said as he yawned.

34

"Hey. These aren't done yet?" A fairy with purple hair hovered above four writhing humans. She turned towards the fairy beside her. The other fairy looked like an identical twin except for her green hair.

"Ah. We were short three worms, so I split one into four," the green-haired fairy said and scratched her head. "Logistics error higher up in the chain, it's not our fault." She shrugged.

"Ehhhh." The other fairy grumbled and pouted. "That means we have to wait here for another twelve hours. I'm going to go check on the two primaries. Maybe they'll be ready."

"I checked on them yesterday. They still haven't converted," the green-haired fairy said and grabbed the other fairy's ankle before she could fly away.

"Still?" The purple-haired fairy leaned back and sat on the air. "It's been almost a decade."

"Yeah, well, their birthflower's gone missing a few centuries ago," the green-haired fairy said and crossed her arms. "It's not too surprising that the process is taking forever."

An orange-haired fairy flew into the cave from above. "What's taking so long?" she asked. She saw the squirming humans. "Oh. Did you misplace the worms again?"

"It wasn't me this time!"

"Ah, whatever. I don't want to track them down," the orange-haired fairy said as she yawned and sat next to her sisters. "The queen's too busy to notice. What's a few missing worms anyway? We can let the tertiaries handle it."

***

A human guard marched through the streets. He looked up at the sun and sighed. *Just a few more hours and I can watch the competition with my kids,* he thought. *It'll probably be over by then. Man, no one would dare to rob the nobles' houses anyway. Why am I even here?* He hung his head and dragged his feet through the empty streets. A sobbing sound caught his attention, and he looked up while facing towards an alley.

There was a girl leaning against a wall while hugging her shoulders. She was hunched over, and her body shook as strangled sobbing noises escaped through her lips.

"Hey!" the guard called out and entered the alley. "Are you alright?"

The girl continued to shake as her face snapped towards him. Her eyes were snake-like and shifting in colors.

"Aren't you that warrior girl? Stella?" the guard asked as he squatted beside her. "Did something happen at the competition?" He put his hand on her shoulder. "Ah, right. You had to fight the prince. It's understandable to be scared after that." The guard sighed while shaking his head. "But isn't it too early for the ... eh?" His words froze.

Stella smiled at the guard as his hand fell off her shoulder—along with his arm. The guard looked down. Blood gushed out of the stump that was once his arm. He shrieked and fell backwards, clutching his residual limb. A red blur shot out of his severed arm towards his face, but it stopped before it collided with him, revealing a worm wriggling in front of his nose, its body thrashing in the air.

Stella chuckled as she grabbed the other end of the worm with her left hand. A hole, leaking black liquid, could be seen on her forearm. Her right hand was holding a sword that dripped with the guard's blood. "So that's why I felt like I was losing control," she said as she lifted the worm above herself and ripped its head off with her teeth before swallowing. She continued to consume the remainder of the worm in a similar fashion. "Naughty little worm. Splitting yourself in half to try to overtake my body." She smiled at her belly before turning towards the guard who was staring at her with wide eyes.

354

"I think you've seen too much," Stella said and smiled at him. "You did help me though. Promise me you won't say anything?"

The guard nodded his head as tears formed in his eyes. "I didn't see anything," he said as his voice quavered. "I swear. My arm just fell off on its own."

A crunching noise echoed through the alley. "Too bad," Stella sang. "I don't trust humans." She smacked her lips and grinned. "I should play with the prince before they disqualify me. Wouldn't want to be late." She left the alley while licking the blood off her sword, oblivious to the two worm-sized holes left in the wall behind her.

***

Rudolph waited at the center of the stone arena with his arms across his chest. Johann was lying on the grass behind him with closed eyes, a bubble of snot extending from his snout. The referee stood outside the stage, looking at the sundial on the ground.

"She probably ran away," someone from the spectator seats said and grumbled.

"Just move on to the next match," another person said. "We all know who's going to win anyway."

"Stella still has two minutes to show up before she automatically forfeits the match," the referee said, ignoring the murmurs from the crowd.

"I'm here. I'm here," a voice called out. "I just needed to get a snack to pick myself up." Stella brushed past the crowd and walked onto the stage.

Rudolph frowned. "Are you injured?" he asked, staring at her foot. It was covered in blood.

"Ah." Stella smiled as a strand of saliva leaked from her lips. "I must've stepped on a tomato in the market place. I'm perfectly fine." Her figure blurred, and she appeared in front of Rudolph, staring into his eyes. "See?"

Rudolph's eyes widened as he took a step back.

Stella giggled as she took a step forward. "Why don't you call your dragon onto the stage?" she asked as she took another step forward.

The referee cleared his throat. "Fighters to their positions, please."

Stella grinned and sauntered back to her side of the arena. "I'm telling you now," she said. "If you don't call him up, you won't have a chance to later."

Rudolph narrowed his eyes. "We'll see about that," he said and equipped his sword and shield.

"The first person to force the other to surrender or renders the other incapable of surrendering wins. Soul destroying techniques are forbidden. Violators will be punished by death," the referee said. "Begin!"

"You aren't going to draw your sword?" Rudolph asked as he raised his eyebrow.

Stella's body blurred. "Don't need it," she said from behind him as she launched him forward with a punch.

Johann roared as his back flashed with a green light. His massive head glanced around as he rose to his feet.

Rudolph tumbled through the air as he struggled to orient his body. Stella appeared above him with one leg raised. She whipped it downwards, smashing her heel into Rudolph's back like an axe, sending him straight towards the floor. The impact cracked the platform, and a green ripple of light flowed through his body. Johann let out another roar and scrambled onto the stage as two green marks shone on his back and belly.

Rudolph snorted as he lifted himself off the ground. There wasn't a single scratch on his body. He narrowed his eyes and took in a deep breath.

Stella cocked her head to the side. "Sturdy, aren't you? I wonder what would happen if I killed your fake dragon first." She smirked and dashed towards Johann, her body turning into a blur. Johann swung his paw outwards and smacked Stella head-on. She flew backwards and rolled a few times before
356

standing back up. A thin line of blood trickled through a cracked scale on Johann's claw. Stella coughed out a wad of coagulated blood, containing miniscule green orbs, into her hand and dashed at Johann.

Once again, Johann deflected Stella with the same motion and Stella repeated her tumble before climbing to her feet. Rudolph and Johann closed in on her from her left and right sides. She ran two steps towards Johann before changing directions towards Rudolph and kneed him in the head before he or Johann could react. Rudolph fell onto his back, and Stella stomped onto his nose, but she was unable to leave a mark. A green light flashed on Johann's snout, causing him to bellow and lunge at Stella. She spat on Rudolph's face. "Coward."

Rudolph's face contorted as he swung his sword, but Stella raised both of her hands, retreating backwards. "I surrender," she said and kicked Rudolph towards the charging dragon. Johann dug his claws into the ground and caught Rudolph with his mouth before glaring at Stella who stuck her tongue out at him. The spectators, who had been silent since the first punch, broke out into a commotion.

"The prince won, but it feels like he lost…"

"What was that speed?"

"Honey, you should recruit her as a bodyguard."

Stella whirled around on her heels and stepped off the stage. Her body blurred and she disappeared before the referee even announced her loss.

***

A student was sitting on a balcony overlooking the arena. He held a cup of tea in his hands. Beside him, his greatsword was propped up against the banister's rail. His metal helmet rested on the hilt. *If I were in Rudolph's position,* he thought and shuddered. He shook his head. *No point thinking about it. She's out of the contest.*

"Hello, Trent," a feminine voice said from behind him.

The student stiffened and whirled around. "You," he said with wide-eyes and glanced at the arena before turning back towards the girl. "Weren't you just there?"

"I was," Stella said and stepped forward. "And now I'm here." She placed her hand under the student's chin and tilted his head up. "Let me borrow your body for a bit," she whispered and locked lips with him. His eyes widened before he relaxed and lifted his hand to her face while moving his left hand to her waist. His body stiffened mid-motion. Seconds later, his eyes shook in their sockets as his body twitched and thrashed about.

Stella collapsed on top of the twitching student. His eyes closed as a shudder ran through his body. When he opened his eyes again, they were serpentine and swirling with a myriad of colors. He stood up and wore the helmet that was on the sword, lowering the visor. He snapped his fingers, and a black fire enveloped Stella's body. A few moments passed and only an ashy residue remained.

35

Vur walked alongside Paul who was holding onto Lillian's left hand. Lillian's right arm was linked together with Michelle's by their elbows. "You have a pretty high tolerance," Paul said to Vur as he led the girls around a signpost. He shook his head as the girls giggled.

"Isn't their tolerance just too low?" Vur asked. The four of them were following a sentry towards the temple.

"Hey," Michelle called out. "Hey. Mr. Sentry. Hey. Who won the warrior competition?"

"The prince won first-place. Trent won second-place," the sentry said as he continued marching.

"Ah, that stupid egg. I was hoping someone would kick his ass," Michelle said and stumbled. She giggled and looked at Lillian. "You did a pretty good job."

Paul sighed. "I can't believe she only had two glasses of wine. Has she never drank before?"

The sentry cleared his throat. "She *is* the pope's daughter," he said as the group arrived in front of the temple. The sentry nodded at the two guards standing in front of the door before he turned around and speed-walked away.

"Well, he seemed to be in an awful hurry to get away," Michelle said as she staggered up the steps, supporting herself with Lillian's arm.

"It's because you're embarrassing," Vur said and shrugged.

"You're embarrassing!" Michelle pouted. "Everyone was only staring because of your mask."

The two guards looked at each other before opening the door and stepping aside. Paul passed Lillian's hand to Vur and nodded while saying, "I'll be waiting right here."

"What? You're not coming with us?" Michelle asked as she struggled against Lillian. "Come 'ere."

"Only winners are allowed to enter the temple," the guard to their right said. "He can't enter."

"That's not fair," Michelle whined. "He's a good healer; he just couldn't compete in the main competition because the preliminaries weren't fair."

"But then I would have lost to you," Paul said and scratched his head as Vur tugged the two girls through the door.

"Oh. Right." Michelle giggled.

The guards closed the door as Paul sighed and shook his head.

Inside the temple, the pope was waiting in front of an altar, facing the six winners of the competition as they approached and came to a halt in front of him. A golden fire burned in a bowl on the altar, emitting a thick yellow smoke that converged towards the ceiling of the temple.

"The six of you have proven yourselves worthy of receiving the blessing of our god," the pope said and spread his arms.

"God?" Vur asked while tilting his head. "I thought we were here to be blessed by spirits."

"You are," the pope said as he raised an eyebrow. "Did you not know that our god is the collective whole of our spirits? When we leave our mortal coils for the last time, we become one with our god and our god becomes one with us."

"He was raised in isolation, Father," Michelle said and sniffled. "Can you imagine not living with other people? He must've been so lonely." She sobbed and hiccoughed, burying her face in her hands.

The pope's brow creased, and he frowned at his daughter but kept his mouth shut. "I understand now," he said to Vur and sighed. "You poor soul. You've never been enlightened or baptized by their aura before." The yellow smoke behind the pope thickened and swirled in the air above the group. Rays of golden light shone down from the yellow cloud and bathed the seven people in the room with a soft glow.

Seven gasps sounded out at the same time as the group shuddered. Vur lost feeling in his legs and his knees buckled, but he managed to stay standing by taking a step forward. The pope fell to the floor and prostrated himself. Michelle fell next, followed by the prince, and then Roy. Lillian let out a moan and also prostrated herself while Trent shuddered and panted, still standing with his hands on his knees. A line of saliva dripped out of his mouth before he fell to the floor on one knee. Veins bulged outwards on his forehead.

Chills coursed through Vur's body, eliciting goosebumps all over his skin. His muscles relaxed, and his shoulders drooped. He was about to fall when a roar rang through his head, causing his whole body to tense. Underneath his mask, a dark rune appeared on his forehead and a black aura rushed through his body, devouring the golden specks floating in his blood.

A DRAGON DOES NOT KNEEL!

Vur's eyes narrowed underneath his mask as he straightened his back and crossed his arms, sticking his chest out. He raised his head and glared at the glowing cloud, letting the waves of light wash over him. A smile appeared on Trent's lips when Vur's posture changed, but everyone else remained prostrating on the ground with their eyes closed, oblivious to their surroundings.

Time passed and the light dimmed before fading away. Trent wiped his hands on the back of his pants as he stood up. Lillian's body shuddered as her eyes opened. She climbed to her feet and glanced at her palms, an odd expression on her face. Roy rose at the same time as Rudolph. Michelle stood up next, her steps no longer unsteady and her face no longer flushed. The pope stood last. He smiled.

"Did you feel that? Our god coursing through your bodies," the pope said. He made eye contact with everyone, but his gaze stayed on Vur. "Would you like to become a member of our church? The same pleasure runs through your veins every time you follow their will. This is only a small fraction of the true god." He gestured at the cloud above the group.

"It felt nice," Vur said and nodded. The pope's smile widened. Vur snorted. "But it's not for me."

The pope's face froze. "Ah, truly regrettable," he said and nodded. His gaze passed over the six winners once more. "All of you are welcome to join us at any time."

"Is it over?" Lillian asked as she bit her lip. "That was the blessing?"

The pope shook his head. "That was just a simple scan spell. Each of you will enter one of the rooms"—he gestured towards the doors behind himself—"for your blessing. I cannot accompany any of you." The yellow cloud split into six streams of smoke and flowed through the doors behind the pope. The winners exchanged glances with each other except for Vur who had already started walking towards a door when the cloud split. The doors closed behind the six without a sound once they entered the rooms.

Vur tensed as the yellow smoke swirled around his body before it rushed to the center of the room, condensing into a humanoid figure. A man's face formed, but the rest of the body remained as smoke.

The man clicked his tongue. "You have a very unique body," he said. "We're not quite sure whose blessing you should receive." The face disappeared, but it was soon replaced by a woman's.

"You have a tremendous amount of mana and physical strength," the woman said and sighed. "If only I had as much strength as you did…" The face blurred as it was replaced by another woman.

"What's your preferred weapon?" the new woman asked Vur.

"It doesn't matter," Vur said. "Anything I can hit or stab with."

"You've never had formal training in any discipline?" the woman asked as she raised an eyebrow. Vur shook his head. "That's a surprise. The other people you came with were all well-trained."

Vur shrugged and crossed his arms. "I'm different."

The woman chuckled. "Yes, we could tell. You're the first person who hasn't kneeled to us after witnessing our splendor. Ah, this is truly difficult."

"What kind of blessings do you give?" Vur asked. "Can you just give me a list to choose from?"

The woman's face was replaced by a mustached man's. "Insolence!" the man said as his mustache flared upwards. "We tailor fit our blessings to each individual. This isn't a food stand where you can pick and choose what you want!"

***

The pope smiled as a stream of smoke flew out of a room. The volume of smoke was similar to the amount that entered. The door opened and Roy stepped out.

"What blessing did the spirits grant you?" the pope asked.

Roy smiled as a circular rune appeared on his forehead. He held out his hand and a yellow orb floated above his palm before lengthening until it became a staff. "They said it would amplify my spells' effects and decrease the amount of mana it takes to cast them," he said as he admired the etchings on the staff. The pope nodded his head.

Another stream of smoke flew out of a different room. This time, only half of the volume that entered appeared. The door opened and Michelle stepped out. The pope's body tensed before his smile widened. *50%,* he thought. *They used half the energy to bless her.*

Three more streams of smoke appeared, and Rudolph, Trent, and Lillian returned to the altar room. Lillian conjured a bow and arrow in a similar manner as Roy. Tears appeared in the corners of her eyes as the bow pulsed in her hand.

"We're just waiting for one more," the pope said as he gestured at Vur's door, "and then the party will be complete."

Ten minutes passed with everyone testing their new blessings. "Should it be taking this long, Father?" Michelle asked.

The pope frowned and shook his head. "No. Usually a spirit takes interest in someone and forms themselves with the smoke to grant their inheritance. That's what happened with all of you, right?"

The group members nodded. Lillian paced back and forth as another ten minutes passed. "Can we open the door and check on him? What if something happened?"

"We can't. Only the spirits can open the doors," the pope said. "I'm sure nothing—" The door opened, causing the pope to stop mid-sentence. *The spirits used all the energy?* he thought as Vur entered the altar room.

Vur burped. A wisp of smoke, shaped like a mustache, slipped out from under his mask and rose into the air. The six people before him stared at the mustached-shaped smoke wisp as it floated towards the ceiling.

Lillian's mouth dropped open. "You ate a god?" she asked. "What the actual fu—"

Vur burped again, and another wisp of smoke leaked out of his mask. "Excuse me," he said and cleared his throat. "I didn't eat him on purpose. He just kinda got swallowed. And it was just part of him, right?"

"I-I don't understand," the pope said with a pale face. "What have you done!?" His eyes widened as his hands grabbed the sides of his head.

"Isn't he still there?" Vur asked as he pointed at the ceiling. The cloud of smoke condensed and pressed itself into a corner. Vur scratched his head. Was it scared of him?

"How dare you!" The pope roared as a white rune shone on his forehead. A ball of light emerged from his hand and took the shape of a two-handed battleaxe. A silver light rushed up his arms, solidifying as it traveled to his shoulders. "Even death cannot pardon you for what you've done!" His irises disappeared as his eyes glowed with a yellow light. He braced himself to swing.

"Dad! Wait!" Michelle yelled as she ran towards Vur. The pope swept his axe to the side, knocking Michelle over with sheer wind pressure. She tumbled along the ground and stopped when she crashed into the wall.

"Shatter!" the pope shouted. His loose white robes disintegrated as a wave of heat poured out of his body. Cracks formed in the air, distorting the axe's image as it swung downwards towards Vur. Vur shifted his body back, dodging by a hair's breadth. The pope bared his teeth as the axe slammed into the ground, creating a web of fissures that radiated outwards.

Vur tilted his head. A second later, his masks shattered into pieces, revealing his golden eyes. The ring that saved his life in the nagas' arena more than ten years ago split in half and dropped to the floor. Lust's blade disintegrated, and its hilt fell from its sheath.

Vur frowned at the fallen hilt. "You shouldn't have done that," he said as his eyes narrowed. His knees bent and his shoulders hunched over as he swiped his right hand horizontally. A black dragon claw, interlaced with bands of golden scales, materialized in the air a few meters in front of him. It raked towards the pope who blocked it with his axe's haft. Vur slammed his left hand into the ground as the pope was sliding to the right from the previous impact. Another claw materialized above the pope and rushed downwards, forcing the pope to his knees. The pope's gauntlets absorbed the damage from the blow even though the attack struck his back and head.

Fractures formed along the armor on his forearms, but they disappeared a moment later as a white light covered them.

Vur's frown deepened, and he alternated slamming the ground with his right and left hands. A barrage of dragon claws rained down on the pope. The pope's face turned red, and the veins on his neck bulged as he raised his axe above his head while he struggled to stand. More and more cracks appeared on the silver armor as if the regeneration couldn't keep up with the destruction.

"Stop! Both of you, stop!" Lillian shouted as she raised her bow. The tip of her arrow shone as bright as the sun, blinding everyone in the room. A final crashing noise resounded through the chamber before it fell silent. The light dimmed, revealing a single figure in the center of the room. Vur stood with his forearms shielding his eyes. The pope was on his knees in front of the wall across from Vur. A human-shaped web of cracks was imprinted on the surface behind him. The golden light in the pope's eyes shone brighter as he lunged forwards, swinging his axe towards Vur.

"Stop!" A wall of yellow smoke rose up in front of the pope, halting his forward movement. The smoke converged into a human-shaped figure which placed its palm on the pope's forehead. The golden light in his eyes dimmed as his irises returned.

"Grandfather," the pope whispered as his eyes focused on the golden spirit. "I—"

A slap echoed through the room. "I didn't raise you like this," the spirit said as it retracted its hand. The pope touched his cheek and lowered his head, his eyes wide.

The spirit turned to face Vur. "Forgive my grandson," he said. "He was too impulsive. His devotion to us clouded his rational thinking."

Vur paused before nodding and standing up straight. "I know that feeling," he said as an image of Yella flashed through his head.

The pope raised his head and frowned at Michelle who was standing with the support of her staff, guilt clouding his heart. He winced before lowering his head again, staying silent. After a moment, his eyes widened and his head snapped upwards to stare at Vur. "You're the dragon child!"

"What's going on?" Lillian asked as her grip on her bow and arrow tightened, pointing in between Vur and the spirit. The pope opened his mouth to speak but stopped when his grandfather sighed.

"A portion of Lady Solandra's soul entered your body, granting you the blessings of increased perception and the right to manifest her weapons," the spirit said to Lillian as he pointed at her bow. He gestured towards Vur. "We tried to do the same with this young man, but there's a monster living in his soul. It latched onto Sir Edward and consumed most of him along with every other soul in that room. We only know this because a tiny bit of the collective soul returned to us and relayed what occurred."

"What are you going to do to him?" Lillian asked with a quavering voice, arrow still nocked. Vur frowned and crossed his arms across his chest.

The spirit shook his head. "You needn't worry. It's not his fault that a monster is living inside of him," he said. "There's no permanent damage done to us; it's not even a minor inconvenience."

"Why do you call it a monster?" Vur asked as he bared his teeth. His eyes narrowed. "It's my mother's imprint."

The spirit stroked his chin. "I'm afraid it's not that simple," he said as his gaze fell on the pope. He looked back at Vur. "I assume you were imprinted by a dragon."

Vur nodded.

"What was inside you wasn't a dragon, at least, not one that we've ever seen," the spirit said. "It had horns shaped like a demon's, four wings, and a blade attached to the end of its tail. Unleash its aura and you'll see."

***

Lindyss frowned as a chill ran down her spine. She stopped etching runes on the tree in front of her and turned around.

"What's the matter?" Tafel asked. Her body was covered with sweat as she poured mana into the tree. Lindyss had asked her to help set up a few spell formations. Tafel didn't know what they did, but she complied anyway.

"It's Vur. He unleashed his awakening," Lindyss replied and knit her eyebrows. Grimmy's eyes opened as he smiled.

"What exactly does that mean?" Tafel asked as she wiped her brow with her sleeve.

"Either he's really, really angry, or he's in dire straits. It's a lose-lose situation no matter which you pick," Lindyss said.

"I'm coming with you," Tafel said.

"Me too," Grimmy said as his wings flared outwards. Floofykins growled on top of his head and mimicked him, spreading her wings. "I want to see my newest modifications in action."

"Alright," Lindyss said. A pair of skeletons gathered the fallen magical equipment that she had lying around. Tafel stood behind Lindyss, taking one last look at the trees she helped inscribe.

"How are we getting there?" Tafel asked. Grimmy and Lindyss turned to look at her.

Grimmy tilted his head. "What do you mean? You're teleporting us. Obviously."

"What? Me?" Tafel asked. Her lips parted as her eyes widened. Were they serious?

"Of course," Lindyss said as she dragged Tafel by her arm to Grimmy's side. "Who else? It'd take too long to fly there."

"But I don't know where we're going...," Tafel said as she bit her lower lip. "And I've never teleported a dragon before. I don't have enough mana to do that."

"It's fine," Lindyss said. "We'll pour mana into your body while you set up the spell. We want to teleport about 2,000 kilometers in that direction." Lindyss pointed to the northeast.

"I really don't think this is a good idea," Tafel said as she took a step backwards.

"What's the worst that could happen?" Grimmy asked as he stretched his front legs. "That wacky human does it all the time."

"We could end up hundreds of meters underground and suffocate," Tafel said as she took another step backwards. "We could end up hundreds of meters above ground and—"

"Fly. Because I'm a dragon," Grimmy said as he grinned. "If we teleport below ground, we'll dig. If we teleport into the water, we'll swim. If we teleport into lava, we'll … well, you'd probably die, but I'd be fine."

"I am very much against dying," Tafel said as she lowered her head.

Lindyss raised an eyebrow. "Don't you want to save Vur? How can you hope to walk alongside him if you can't even reach him? If ever a time came when Vur needed you to save him and we weren't around to help, what would you do?"

Tafel ground her teeth. "Alright," she said and clenched her hands. "I'll do it."

***

"W-what is this?" Lillian whispered. She was sitting with her knees folded under her; her hands were on the floor, supporting her body from behind. Her head was tilted upwards with her lips parted and eyes wide. Cold sweat rolled down her back, and she gulped. Michelle, Roy, and Rudolph were in similar positions as Lillian, their backs to the walls. The pope was kneeling with his body shielded by the spirit standing over him. Trent stood in front of Rudolph with a grin plastered on his face.

"Amazing," Trent whispered while licking his lips as his body shuddered.

Vur stood in the center of the room with his eyes closed. Waves of black light cascaded out of his body, washing over the inhabitants of the room. A layer of black mana obscured the finer details of his body. Scales formed along the aura, and two pairs of wings sprouted from his back. The pair on his shoulders looked sharp and dragon-like while the ones above his waist were rounded and similar to a fairy's. A bladed tail extended from his coccyx, and claws covered his hands and feet. The aura around his head took the shape of a dragon with a pair of horns growing from his temples, similar in shape to the ones Yella had. The faintest hint of a golden mustache glowed below his nostrils. His golden slit eyes opened and shone through the dark aura.

The spirit in front of Vur sighed. "It's really no wonder why you were able to consume us so easily," he said. Vur glanced at his hands before craning his neck to inspect his wings. The spirit walked in a circle around Vur. "We've seen hundreds of elves unleash auras during the wars, but we've never seen any that looked like this. There've also been a few of us who have been imprinted, but we never managed to awaken at all."

Shouts sounded outside the temple, and shrieks echoed through the air as the ground shook. Dust rained down from the temple's ceiling as cracks spread down the walls. Rays of light pierced through the room as the roof was ripped away, revealing a black dragon's face.

"Eh?" Grimmy blinked his eyes. "Why aren't you killing anything?"

Lindyss peaked over Grimmy's snout. "Maybe he just finished transforming? It always takes a while the first time," she said. "Let's wait a bit and see."

Grimmy nodded while sitting down. "Right," he said and placed the roof back on top of the temple as if he was covering a pot with a lid. He looked down at Paul who was sitting in a puddle of urine near Grimmy's feet. The other humans in the vicinity were in the midst of hiding or running away.

370

"What are you looking at?" Grimmy asked as a wisp of smoke drifted out of his nostrils. "Never seen such a handsome creature before?" He lowered his head towards Paul, squinting at him. "Why aren't you running?"

"M-my f-friends a-a-are t-there," Paul said with a pale face as his shaking arm pointed towards the temple.

"Oh?" Grimmy tilted his head. "I guess you're not too bad of a human. Good thing I didn't squish you on accident. You should do something about wetting your pants though. It's not very manly." Grimmy's tail thumped against the floor as he sighed. "I wish Vur would hurry up. I really want to see how he uses that leviathan tail." He lay on the ground with his belly on the road, staring at the door to the temple.

Tafel hugged Floofykins as she paced around in front of Lindyss on the steps. Paul purified his robe and cleaned up the mess he made, but he was still sitting on the floor since his legs wouldn't stop trembling.

"U-uhm." Paul squeaked. "Wasn't there a pact made a long time ago forbidding dragons from entering the capital?"

"Hah?" Grimmy squinted his eyes at Paul.

"I'm sorry!" Paul squealed as he covered his head with his arms and curled up into a ball.

Lindyss scratched her head. "Yeah, there was something like that, wasn't there?" She rummaged through her bag. "I think I still have it somewhere here..."

"What?" Tafel asked as she stopped pacing and looked up. "Why would you have that?"

"Because I wrote it?" Lindyss raised an eyebrow. She pulled a rolled up piece of laminated paper out of her bag. "Why else? And it's just a copy so it doesn't matter if you burn it." She glared at Grimmy who shut his mouth and swallowed the flames on his tongue.

"Let me see that," Grimmy said as he held out his claw. Lindyss placed it on his palm. He scanned the document and nodded. "There's no issue with me being here then." Grimmy

371

grinned at Paul who was still hiding his head. "It clearly says, 'Dragons will not invade any human establishment that has a scion of the royal family.'"

Paul's shoulders were hunched over as he peaked up at Grimmy's face. "But the prince is—"

"Dragons. Plural. I am a singular dragon," Grimmy said as he passed the document back to Lindyss. "I see no issues with my presence in the area." He blinked at Lindyss. "You knew."

Lindyss smiled. "Of course. I wrote it."

"What other loopholes did you include?" Grimmy asked as he reached for the paper again.

"Those are for me to abuse," Lindyss said as she stuck out her tongue and incinerated the paper before Grimmy could grab it, "and—for the sake of the human race—for you to never find out."

The door to the temple creaked, and Tafel stiffened. A few moments passed with no other noises, and she exhaled while looking down at Floofykins who tried to bite her nose. "Why is this so nerve-wracking?" she asked as she held Floofykins in front of her face. She sighed. "I'd rather fight three reapers at the same time." Floofykins tilted her head and squirmed in her grip.

Tafel frowned at Lindyss. "Is she not imprinted?" Tafel asked as she parted the fur on Floofykins forehead, ignoring the boar's protests.

"No," Lindyss said and offered Floofykins a piece of roast pork. "Snuffles is a male, so he has no instincts whatsoever to imprint his offspring. And her mother didn't have an imprint."

"Somehow that feels wrong."

"Well, phoenixes never existed on this continent until 800 years ago. They came at the same time as the humans from Fuselage," Lindyss said and looked up at the sky. "They were as arrogant as dragons and vied for the top spot in the ecosystem. So the dragons wiped out the phoenixes, but spared their eggs, effectively leaving their race as strong as wyverns."

Lindyss sighed and shook her head. "A lot of dragons died during those hunts."

Tafel frowned at Floofykins who looked bloated. "I meant it felt wrong to feed a boar pork, but that's also pretty messed up," she said. "Why'd the phoenixes leave Fuselage?"

"Same reason why the humans did," Lindyss said as she turned towards the door of the temple. "To survive."

"They never told us why humans moved to this continent. We always started history lessons at the time of landing 800 years ago," Paul said, his voice barely above a whisper. "I feel like I heard something I shouldn't have."

"Then keep it to yourself," Grimmy said and snorted. "What are you, a child?"

"But something this huge—. I'm sorry! Please don't eat me!" Paul shrieked as Grimmy glared at him. He prostrated himself in front of Grimmy. "You're right, O wise one. I shouldn't have questioned you. Forgive this unappealing, stick-thin human who definitely tastes like sour milk and expired eggs."

The temple door swung open, and Vur walked out with his aura gone. He froze as he met Tafel's gaze. The two stared at each other without moving while creaking sounds came from Floofykins as she squealed and struggled to flee Tafel's tightening grip.

"Tafel?" Vur asked.

Tafel nodded as she released Floofykins. She inhaled and approached Vur, stopping when she was in front of him. "You almost killed me," she said with her hands on her hips.

Vur flinched. "I—"

"Take responsibility," Tafel said with a red face. "You brute."

Vur blinked and nodded as he wrapped his arms around Tafel. "I'm sorry." Nothing else was said, but those two words were the only ones Tafel needed to hear. The two stood motionless with their ears resting against each other's.

"Now kiss!" Grimmy said. He chortled. "She actually said it." He grinned at Lindyss. "You owe me a meal when we get back."

Lindyss sighed. "I'm disappointed in you, Tafel," she said and shook her head. "I thought you'd be more refined. Do you know how much effort it takes to feed a dragon? And ... those two aren't even listening to us."

The rest of the people inside the temple walked up to the entrance and froze, unwilling to take another step. Paul met Lillian's and Michelle's eyes. Michelle stared at Grimmy with her eyes wide and mouth open like a girl finding out her parents bought her a puppy.

'What's going on?' Lillian mouthed to Paul. Paul shook his head, and his eyes flickered towards Grimmy. A white light formed a line of words above his head with the words, "Don't move. ← He's scary." It disappeared again when Grimmy turned his head to find the sudden source of light. Paul lowered his head, avoiding the dragon's gaze.

Before anyone could say anything else, a sharp yell split the silence. Green runes flashed along Rudolph's arms and body. He shrieked as he clawed at his skin with his nails. Tafel and Vur broke away from each other, frowning at the prince. He writhed on the floor as blood leaked out of and coalesced along the runes, erasing them from existence. He screamed, "Johann! Something's happening to Johann!" The prince gasped and shuddered as his eyes rolled upwards. After a few more moments of twitching, his body stopped moving.

36

"Who's this Johann?" Grimmy asked as he poked the unconscious Rudolph. His snout crinkled, and he turned away. "Such a bad-smelling contract magic."

"Johann's the big blue pupp—dragon. He's Rudolph's contracted beast," Michelle said. She lowered her head at Vur. "Please, you have to help him. Johann really respects you and you're really strong. I don't think Geralt can save him if he's in danger." A chill rolled down her spine as someone snorted.

"Who are you?" Tafel asked as she narrowed her eyes at Michelle. Her grip on Vur's hand tightened.

"I'm Michelle Heilig, daughter of the pope," Michelle said with a slight curtsy. "You are?"

"Tafel Besteck," Tafel said, her eyes sweeping over the group by the temple's entrance. "Vur's fiancée. Oh. And the current demon lord." Every human's body stiffened except for Vur.

Vur blinked. "You're my fiancée?"

"Am I not?" Tafel asked as she glared at him. "Don't you remember what we promised each other when we were little?"

Vur smiled and gazed into Tafel's eyes. "Then I guess you are." He pulled her closer to his body.

"Ahem, ahem." Lillian cleared her throat. "Johann. Danger. Help? Yes, no?"

"No."

Everyone stared at Grimmy.

"Aren't you a dragon? How could you abandon your own kind?" the pope asked as he stepped forward.

The ground underneath Grimmy's claws shattered. He snorted and lowered his head to look down on the pope. "You humans stole a dragon egg and now want our help when you can't control it? What a joke." Smoke creeped out of Grimmy's mouth. His eyes narrowed. "Don't ever forget your place, human."

Vur frowned. "Johann was nice to me," he said to Grimmy. "We should at least check what's happening to him."

Grimmy blinked his eyes and chuckled. "Alright," he said. He winked at Lindyss. "Looks like he's all grown up; this is the first time he's ever disagreed with me." He scooped Vur and Tafel onto his forehead while Lindyss climbed onto his claw with Floofykins. His eyes flickered to the pope. "Of course, I'll be expecting a reward for this. And I'll be taking it whether you like it or not." He leapt into the air.

"The royal castle!" Michelle yelled from the ground. "Johann's staying at the castle!"

***

Randel slammed his fist against the armrest of his throne. "What do you mean Johann is rampaging?" he asked the sentry who was on his knees before him. "Bring Exzenter to me, immediately!"

"Yes, Your Majesty," the sentry said. He stood up and sprinted out of the room without looking back.

Randel exhaled and clenched his fist. The words of the pope echoed in his ears, 'Imagine if a sacred spirit rested in his body instead of blessing it.' His eyes narrowed, and he raised one hand. "Bring the pope here. I need to ask him a few questions."

Gale saluted. "Yes—"

"Your Majesty!" A sentry burst through the doors. "A black dragon has appeared outside of the temple along with the Corrupted One! They're currently sitting outside doing nothing, but that can change at any moment. The pope is still inside the temple with the winners."

Randel's face paled. "When Exzenter arrives, tell him to stop Johann with Geralt and his men. Johann must be subdued and not killed," the king said to the sentry. He whipped his head towards Gale. "Come with me."

Randel and Gale left the throne room, leaving the sentry to deliver the message to Exzenter. "Where are we going, Your Majesty?" Gale asked as the two descended down a spiral staircase.

"The Vault of the Spirits," Randel said as he led Gale into an unlit corridor. He opened a plain wooden door at the end and stepped inside. Glowing white crystals littered the floor and illuminated the room.

Gale's eyes widened. "These are…"

"Correct," Randel said as he picked up a crystal. It looked similar to the one the pope had lit on fire to summon the yellow smoke at the altar. "The pope is the capital's strongest defender with these crystals in his hand; however, he's cornered by a dragon and can't access them." Randel's gaze locked onto Gale's. "It's up to you—the archbishop closest in line to becoming the next pope—to call upon our ancestors to defend the capital. I will try to negotiate with the Corrupted One, but if things cannot be settled peacefully, then you are our last hope."

Gale shuddered. "I understand, Your Majesty," he said and lowered his head. "I will do my best."

"Of course. I expect nothing less," Randel said and removed the ring he was wearing. He passed it to Gale. "This ring will shatter if I die." Randel stared into Gale's eyes, hesitating. In the end, he patted Gale's shoulder and left the room.

Outside, Randel went to the royal stables to acquire a horse. He rode towards the royal castle's exit, but before he could leave, a shadow blotted out the sun and landed behind him. His face paled as the horse threw him off and bolted away. The king dusted himself off and gulped as he turned around. A black dragon smiled at him.

"Grimmy, you almost squished the king," Lindyss said. "No amount of loopholes in the contract would've changed that."

"Well, he's still alright, yeah?" Grimmy asked and gestured towards the trembling king. "See, just a little shaky and frightened. Maybe his pants are soiled, but that's it. He'll be fine."

The king took in a deep breath and stuck out his chest. His knees knocked together as he asked, "May I know what you are doing in my kingdom?"

Grimmy blinked. "Sightseeing."

"S-sightseeing?"

"Yup, but then we encountered the prince who wanted us to help him with his Johann problem," Grimmy said. "He promised to give us the royal treasury as payment."

"That's…"

"What? Does the royal family renege on their deals?" Grimmy asked as he leered at the king. "I think I understand how they came into power. It'd be a shame if something were to happen to them."

"F-fine. The royal treasury for your assistance," the king said through gritted teeth.

Grimmy smiled while Lindyss sighed.

***

Charon sneezed as he dusted off a book. "It feels like I'm forgetting something," he mumbled to himself. "Like, future of the world important…" He frowned and stepped to the window, staring off into the horizon almost as if he was seeing past the ocean and into Fuselage. "Well. If it was that important, then I wouldn't have forgotten it." He turned his attention back to the book as he scratched his naked legs.

***

Geralt stood outside of Johann's courtyard with a contingent of soldiers behind him. His face was dark. Though he had failed to subdue the skeletons of Konigreich, the king still trusted him with important tasks. Like suppressing a dragon. By his side, Exzenter was drinking mana potions.

"How do we stop him?" a soldier asked, his face pale. In the courtyard ahead of him, Johann was clawing the floor and bellowing into the air. His wings quivered as he struggled to fly, but he kept crashing against the ground before he could get a meter into the air. His claws left parallel rifts in the ground as he pulled himself off the floor over and over again.

Geralt snorted. "This is why I told the king to keep a closer watch on this beast," he said as he tightened his grip on his sword and shield. "We'll hamstring it. Cut the tendons in its legs and wings. The first phalanx will be responsible for keeping its attention on them while the rest of us focus on its limbs." He raised his voice. "Understood!?"

"Y-yes, sir!" the soldiers behind him shouted. Their orange swords shone in the sun as they trekked through the entrance to the courtyard.

Exzenter narrowed his eyes at Johann. Wind swirled around the time mage's feet as he chanted. A giant clock's face appeared underneath Johann's body and counted down in reverse. "He's slowed," Exzenter shouted to Geralt. "Luckily he's not resistant to magic like most dragons."

Geralt grinned as he circled behind Johann and slashed towards the dragon's hind leg. Johann's tail blurred and slammed into Geralt's body, flinging him against the wall. His bones cracked as he coughed out a mouthful of blood. "Dammit, Exzenter!" Geralt roared. "You said he was slowed!"

Exzenter scratched his head. "I did use slow though," he said and frowned. "Unless I cast haste? I wouldn't make such a rookie mistake. Hold him off as I cast a stop spell."

The soldiers ground their teeth as they took a step back and readied their shields. They flew through the air as Johann smacked against them with his claws and tail. A few unlucky ones were torn to shreds by the dragon's teeth. Cuts gradually accumulated along Johann's legs, leaking bright-red blood. A worm crawled out of a particularly large wound and lunged towards a soldier.

"What the hell is this?!" The soldier bunted the worm with his shield and bisected it with a single slash.

"Watch out! It's still moving," the man next to him said. The front half of the worm flew towards the soldier's face before he could raise his shield.

"Stop!" Exzenter shouted. The worm froze in mid-air, and the soldier hacked it to pieces. Johann let out a bellow, unaffected by the time magic.

"Magic's not working on him!" Geralt shouted, flecks of blood flying from his mouth. "Regardless, we can still stop him. He's wounded and our white mages will be here to heal us soon. We'll win in a battle of endurance. Keep it up!"

Johann's body shuddered as his eyes closed. He stopped moving as Geralt's men advanced and hacked at his legs, severing his tendons.

Geralt laughed. "I guess it gave up knowing it would lose. Kill these worms, men. I don't know what they are, but they're disgusting me."

Johann's eyes snapped open. The bleeding flesh on his wounds wriggled and writhed. They grew and expanded outwards, the severed muscles and tendons stitching themselves back together. Johann bellowed and flapped his wings, no longer struggling and thrashing.

"This...," Geralt said as his brow creased. "Fall back! Everyone, fall back!"

Johann roared and slammed his claws onto the ground. A storm of lightning rained down on the soldiers, eliciting pained cries and shrieks. He swiped his claws towards the ones who were lucky enough to avoid the bolts. Green blades shot out of his claws, cutting into the soldiers.

"He's using magic," Exzenter said with wide eyes. "That's impossible—he's not imprinted. What's going on here?" Wind swirled around Exzenter as his body disappeared. He reappeared on a roof and fell over backwards. "It's you?"

"Hello, Exzenter," Lindyss said. "Running away?"

Grimmy was sitting on the roof with Lindyss, Tafel, and Vur. They watched Johann fight against the soldiers, crushing what remained of them.

"We're not fighting that," Grimmy said. "Forget the treasury; I'm rich enough."

Vur frowned. "But—"

"No buts. We came to assess the situation, and the situation is bad," Grimmy said and stretched his neck. "He's resistant to magic and can cast spells. I would stop him if that was it, but he's seriously infected by those parasites. I refuse to get close to something like that."

Lindyss nodded. "I'm sure the humans have some safeguards to deal with extreme threats," she said. "Let them handle it. There's no need to sacrifice ourselves. I do wonder where those worms came from though." She narrowed her eyes. "The demons brought over a batch from Fuselage. I wouldn't be surprised if the humans did the same and something went awry. You reap what you sow. We're leaving."

"Wait!" Exzenter said. "Please, help me stop him."

Lindyss frowned. "Didn't you hear any of what I said? We're not risking our lives to clean up someone else's mistake."

"You won't be at risk," Exzenter said and lowered his head. "Please. I just need you two to feed mana into me so I can perform a largescale area teleportation spell."

"He's resistant to magic, did you forget?" Lindyss asked. "Where would you even teleport him to?"

"I'll teleport him to Fuselage," Exzenter said. "As long as I teleport the whole space around me, he'll be included in the spell, regardless of resistance. I just need more mana."

Grimmy raised an eyebrow. "You're sure? You'll be stuck on Fuselage too, you know? With an angry dragon at that."

Exzenter nodded. "I swore an oath to protect the kingdom. If I ran away now, then I wouldn't be able to live with myself." He knelt on the floor and lowered his head towards Lindyss and Grimmy. "Please."

Lindyss sighed. "The humans don't deserve someone like you," she said and shook her head. "We'll help." She slid off of Grimmy's head and grasped Exzenter's hand. Grimmy placed the tip of his claw on Exzenter's head. Vur and Tafel exchanged glances with each other before grabbing Exzenter's other hand. The time mage's veins bulged as his hair fluttered, streams of mana flowing into him. Blood dripped out of his pores, leaving a layer of red on his body.

"Thank you," Exzenter said through clenched teeth. "Save my room in Konigreich for me. I'll be back." His bloody body disappeared from the four's grasp and reappeared on top of Johann. A moment later, the courtyard vanished, leaving a crater in the ground. Wind howled as it rushed in to fill the empty void.

***

"Crap!" Charon shouted as his book dropped to the floor. "I was supposed to stop myself today!" His naked body vanished and reappeared on the roof behind Lindyss' group. His eyes narrowed as his gaze landed on the crater. "Well, damn. I screwed up." He sighed.

The four turned around to face him. "What do you mean you screwed up?" Lindyss asked the naked man. "And what are you even doing here?" Her brow furrowed. "And where's your clothes?"

Charon let out another sigh and shook his head. "I was supposed to stop myself from teleporting Johann to Fuselage. It's too late now. The fact that I'm still here is proof of that. Ah, I really messed up."

"Speak clearly, you crazy old man," Grimmy said as he flicked Charon's forehead, causing the frail man to tumble and roll over backwards.

Charon rubbed his forehead. "I am Exzenter," he said as he picked himself off the floor. "I didn't just teleport Johann to Fuselage. I brought him back in time too." Charon raised one hand as Lindyss opened her mouth. "Hear me out before you

382

speak, please. The humans fled from the continent of Trummer 800 years ago because of me.

"After I brought Johann to Fuselage, I teleported as far away as I could. I got away from him, but the soldiers who came with me weren't as lucky." Charon sighed. "You'll have to forgive me if I forget a few things; it's been over a thousand years and a lot has happened since then. I encountered the city of Verderb after wandering around Trummer. There were a lot of interesting creatures there: phoenixes, manticores, behemoths, giant praying mantises. Well, they're still there but just corrupted and all wiggly. The plants there were huge and plentiful with great restorative properties. Oh, there was so much to learn." Charon coughed. "Ah, I'm getting sidetracked.

"Anyways, I managed to convince the citizens of Verderb that Johann was a threat, and they responded. The king sent out waves of soldiers to stop him. Their weaponry was much more advanced than ours, but they didn't rely on magic as much— only faith. They fought an endurance battle with Johann and destroyed all the replicating worms and their hosts. Eventually, the region they contained Johann in was drained of mana and he, along with the parasites, became progressively weaker.

"The king ordered the destruction of Johann and all the worms, but one of the princes had other plans. He pretended to follow the king's orders and buried Johann's body in a casing of orichalcum while keeping the worms for himself. By that point, the worms were so weak that they couldn't fully control a human body even after digging inside of them. He planted them in anyone who opposed him and used their madness as an excuse to have them executed or locked up."

Tafel frowned. "You didn't stop him?"

Charon creased his brow. "If I had known back then what I know now, then we wouldn't be in this position," he said and scratched his chin. "I was also a bit preoccupied with all the new species of animals and plants around me, but that's beside the point. That prince became king and used the worms to

383

ensure the security of his reign. Eventually, it became the collective secret of the upper echelons. One day, someone messed up and the worms were set free, starting from the center of the capital. It spread outwards, and no one could stop it since the king had undermined the strength of the kingdom to ensure his own sovereignty. People panicked and cities fell. The beasts on Trummer became infected when they ate humans or other infected beasts.

"Eventually, humanity was backed into a city on the coast, Fuselage. The only reason it held was because of the crystals— I call them Spirit Tears—which were able to maintain a barrier against the worms. They're the same crystals the humans use now to summon their ancestors' spirits, by the way. I set up a portal and had the non-combatants flee to this continent along with a few commanders who I knew were strong enough to establish a foothold against the elves. I established rules for teleporting to and from Fuselage to ensure the worms wouldn't be able to travel to Zuer, but I must've failed somewhere along the way because, clearly, worms made it across and infected Johann."

Vur tilted his head as his brow furrowed. "So the worms that infected Johann ... were the ancestors of themselves?"

"Precisely," Charon said and nodded. "If I didn't teleport Johann to Fuselage, then the worms would never have existed, thus eliminating the need to teleport Johann to Fuselage. But I was too late to stop myself."

"Aah," Tafel said and exhaled. "I don't get it. Where does that put us now?"

Lindyss crossed her arms across her chest. "We have to find out where the worms are coming from. The last outbreak was when I almost destroyed Niffle and the demons released the worms, but that was ten years ago," she said and frowned. "How is it that only Johann became infected? What happened here?"

"Vur! Help..."

The group standing on top of the roof peered over the edge. Lillian was lying on her belly, hanging over a horse's saddle. A trail of blood was left behind as the horse moved forwards. Vur frowned and jumped off the roof, landing in front of the horse. He placed his hand on Lillian's back, and a breeze encircled her, illuminating her wounds with a green light.

Lillian sat up with tears streaming down her cheeks. "Paul... Michelle...," she said as her voice cracked. "They're dead. Y-you have to resurrect them before their souls leave their bodies. Please."

"What happened?" Vur asked as he grasped Lillian's arm. "Weren't you near the temple?"

Lillian's body trembled as she shook her head. "It was Trent. He used some sort of magic to make the spirit disappear, and then he knocked the pope out. He killed Michelle and Paul after you four left," she said through sniffles. "He almost killed me too, but my grandfather's ring helped preserve my life. Trent took Rudolph and the pope. I tried to find a healer, but everyone had already fled the area because of the dragon."

"I'll save them," Vur said and turned towards Grimmy. "I need a ride."

Grimmy glanced at Lindyss before scooping her up along with Charon and Tafel. "We can figure out the worm thing later; let's save Vur's friends first."

Lindyss frowned as they flew towards the temple. "The only resurrection magic I know is reanimating the dead." She poked Tafel. "I don't suppose you know any?"

Tafel shook her head.

"I can do it," Vur said. "I learned it from Juliana when she thought she killed me."

***

A fairy with magenta-colored hair was sitting outside of a cave, eating a berry. Metal bars with blue runes covered the cave's entrance. Two fairies were lying face down in the makeshift prison with shackles attached to their ankles and wrists. The magenta-haired fairy raised her head as an amber-haired fairy approached her from the skies. "Oh? I'm off guard duty already?" she asked as she placed the rest of the berry into her mouth. She stood up and stretched her arms above her head.

"Any change?" the amber-haired fairy asked as she landed in front of the entrance.

"Nope. They haven't moved since I got here."

"They're not dead, right?" the amber-haired fairy asked as she peered through the bars at the red and blue-haired fairies lying on the ground. They looked dead.

"Not possible. They couldn't die even if they wanted to," the magenta-haired fairy replied as she glanced at the chains holding Rella and Bella. They were pulsating with a sky-blue light. "Have fun watching over them." She laughed and flew into the air.

The amber-haired fairy snorted and sat in the chair as the other fairy disappeared into the distance. A crack formed beneath the fairy's chair, and she tilted her head before inspecting her feet. A worm shot out of the ground and pierced through her abdomen before she could react. Her body convulsed as she opened her mouth to scream, but no sounds came out. She lay on the floor, twitching for a few moments, before she stood up with unfocused eyes. She turned towards the cave entrance with saliva leaking from her mouth.

Rella was awakened by the sounds of crunching metal. Her eyes fluttered open. A fairy was crouched over her arm, eating the chains of her manacles. A shiver passed over her body, and the eating fairy froze. Saliva dropped to the ground as she stared at Rella. A long moment passed before the fairy continued to chew on the chains. Rella's lips cracked as a corner of her mouth twitched. *A chain has more mana than me, huh?* Her eyes shut as she lost consciousness.

37

Rella opened her eyes. Her lips cracked when she inhaled after peeling her tongue off the roof of her mouth. *I'm alive?* Her head flopped to the left. Bella was lying next to her, unmoving. Rella groaned as she sat up. The remaining bits of her manacles that hadn't been eaten fell off her wrists with a clinking sound.

"Bella," Rella said and leaned over the blue-haired fairy's body. She shook her sister's shoulders. "Wake up, Bella. Please, wake up." She took her fingers and placed them along Bella's neck, feeling for a pulse. After a moment passed, she heaved a sigh of relief. Though faint, there was still a heartbeat. Rella removed her hand and glanced around.

The metal bars with the runic inscriptions that had previously blocked the entrance to the cave were gone—only a faint trace of metal residue remained. The chains and manacles on the two fairies' bodies were reduced to a similar state of decay. Rella picked up her shattered manacle. There were teeth marks on the broken edges. The image of the amber-haired fairy eating the chains appeared in her head, and a chill ran down her spine.

"R-Rella?"

Rella whipped her head around and stared at Bella. "Bella! We have to get out of here," she said and helped Bella to her feet.

"We're free?" Bella asked. Her eyes widened. "Is this a trap?" She shoved Rella over and retreated backwards until her body collided with the cave wall behind her.

"You stupid nit!" Rella said as she picked herself off the floor. "I'm not a trap. One of the tertiaries messed up and got infected by those worms."

Bella shivered. "You know what happened the last time we tried to escape," she said as tears formed in the corners of her eyes. "I don't want to go through that again."

Rella crossed her arms over her chest. "This is the only chance we're going to get," she said. "I saw the infected tertiary with my own eyes. Come on." She extended her hand towards Bella.

Bella trembled but took Rella's hand.

Rella nodded. "Let's go. We need to tell someone about the worms. We have to find Vur. He can stop Mom."

***

"Where's Roy?" Vur asked Lillian. He was standing over Michelle in the altar room, wiping the sweat off his brow. Behind him, Paul let out a groan as his eyes twitched. Grimmy had lifted the roof of the temple off the building and was peeking inside. Tafel held Floofykins in her lap as she watched Vur work, unwilling to take her gaze off of him.

Lillian shook her head. "I don't know where Roy went. Trent attacked me after Paul and Michelle." She clutched her shoulders and shuddered.

"Who's Trent?" Lindyss asked as she inspected the altar in the temple. She took the bowl that held the remains of the crystals used to summon the spirits.

"He was one of the winners of the competition," Lillian said. "He was the second-place warrior."

"Did you notice anything strange about him?" Lindyss asked as she rummaged through the rubble.

Lillian shook her head. "I never met him before, so I wouldn't know. And we didn't see the competition either because we were ... preoccupied. He seemed normal—wait. His eyes. When he stabbed me, they looked like Stella's."

The rock in Lindyss' hand turned to dust as she made a fist. "Stella?" she asked, narrowing her eyes at Lillian.

Lillian took a step back and gulped. "Yeah. Stella was a warrior in the competition, but she lost in the first round. Her eyes were reptilian and they kept changing colors. It felt like they could see through to your soul."

The floor underneath Lindyss shattered. "I see," she said with a tight smile. "This may be a bigger problem than I thought."

"What do you mean?" Charon asked. He had 'borrowed' a set of priest robes to cover his naked body.

"The queen of the fairies kidnapped the pope and the crown prince," Lindyss said. "And somehow, the crown prince's dragon gets infected by parasites at the same time." Lindyss chewed on her lip.

"So the fairy queen has access to the worms?" Charon asked with a frown. His brow creased. "Didn't you sell her off around four centuries ago? I vaguely remember taking part in that."

Lindyss nodded. "That's the problem. I wouldn't put it past her to breed the worms and unleash them all over this continent. We'll have to let the humans, demons, and elves know about this. I don't suppose you have a way of stopping the worms?"

Charon nodded. "I do, in fact," he said and stroked his chin. "You can squish them easily as long as they don't have a host."

"And if they do have a host?" Lindyss asked with a raised eyebrow.

Charon shrugged. "Tear them apart with orichalcum."

"Isn't that what they did in Trummer when Johann first arrived?"

"Correct."

"And now Trummer is completely overrun except for Fuselage, right?"

"That is also correct."

"Goddammit, Exzenter. What the hell have you been doing for the past millennium?" Lindyss asked as she kicked the time mage. "You seriously banked the future of the world on you stopping yourself?"

Charon made a face. "It was a good bet; after all, I got to spend a thousand years studying to my heart's content. If I was going to stop existing after I stopped myself, then, of course, I wanted to know how everything in the world worked. What would you have done if you knew you were going to vanish after a thousand years?"

Lindyss sighed. "Get out," she said and rubbed her temples. "I don't need your existentialist nonsense right now. Bring the king and his advisors to Konigreich. A meeting needs to be held."

"I can bring the demons," Tafel said as she stood up.

"Alright," Lindyss said. "We will—" She stopped talking and frowned.

Tafel tilted her head. "Did something happen?"

Lindyss creased her brow. "A squad of skeletons was just eliminated by a group of infected fairies. Stella's making her move. She was hiding right under our noses on the border between the three nations. My bats located a series of underground caves that must've been hidden with illusion magic."

"Infected fairies? Like by the worm things you were talking about?" Lillian asked.

Lindyss nodded.

Lillian's face blanched. "The Leonis household is stationed on the border. My grandfather's there."

"Then we better hurry," Lindyss said.

* * *

The pope opened his eyes. A pair of speckled reptilian irises stared down at him. "Finally awake?" a feminine voice asked through Trent's mouth. "I was wondering how long you were going to sleep for."

The pope tried to sit up but found himself unable to move. His body was strapped to a table, bands of orange metal wrapped around his wrists, ankles, neck, and chest. "You're not Trent," the pope said as his body shivered. A breeze rolled over him, and he realized he was naked.

"What makes you say that?" Trent asked, his voice still high-pitched and lilting. "What makes a human a person? What makes Trent Trent? His body? His thoughts?" A silver knife glinted in Trent's hand as he traced its edge along the contours of the pope's body.

"You!" The pope narrowed his eyes. A white rune appeared on his forehead and webs of light appeared on his body.

"Oops," Trent said as the knife's blade disappeared into the pope's torso. He flashed a smile. "Can't have you doing that right now."

The light on the pope's body faded as the rune disappeared. He coughed as a trickle of blood leaked out the corner of his mouth. He grunted. "Who are you?"

Trent licked his lips as he turned his back on the pope and selected another knife from the table behind him. "I'm just a nobody," he said. "Forgotten for a few centuries. Completely and utterly forgotten." His eyes reddened as he stabbed the knife downwards, leaving a gouge in the table. He whipped his head around to face the pope, eyes wide. "But not for long. Soon, no one will be able to forget my name." He crouched and pulled a bucket out from underneath the table.

The pope's eyes shifted downwards. His skin crawled. There was a mass of wriggling worms devouring each other inside the bucket. A groan escaped from his mouth as he asked, "Why?"

Trent smiled at the worms as they wriggled just underneath his face. "Why? No real reason," he said and gently rocked the bucket. "Maybe revenge against the person who took everything from me."

"I never did anything to you," the pope said. His eyes widened as Trent reached into the bucket and pulled out a worm. "I can help you."

Trent sauntered over to the pope with the worm's body thrashing against his arm. "You're right. You didn't do anything to me," he said and nodded. The pope let out a slow exhale. "Just like everyone else. They completely ignored my existence, content with me being the sacrifice. No one spoke up. No one did anything. Just. Like. You."

The pope shrieked as the worm entered the sole of his foot and crawled towards his heart. Trent stared, expression unchanging, as the pope's body convulsed and thrashed against its bindings. Trent turned his head away from the pope and locked his gaze onto a figure in the corner of the room.

"Did you enjoy the show, little prince?" Trent asked with a smile. Whimpers slipped out of Rudolph's mouth.

"Don't worry," Trent said as he walked up to Rudolph. "I'll give you a chance to live." He pinched Rudolph's nose and flicked a green orb down the prince's throat when he opened his mouth to breathe. Trent placed his hands against the chains holding Rudolph down and shattered them. Rudolph coughed and shoved his fingers down his throat, trying to force whatever Trent had him eat out, but no vomit came up.

"Run. The egg will hatch if you're too slow," Trent said and took a step back. "It'd be such a tragedy if the crown prince slaughtered his own citizens in cold blood."

***

Vur and Tafel stood next to each other on top of Grimmy's head. Lillian, Paul, and Michelle were hanging in the air, held up by one of the black dragon's claws. Lindyss was flying in front of Grimmy, a pair of translucent batwings sprouting from her back. They were hovering in the air above the Leonis household's territory. Soldiers were rushing out of a castle towards the surrounding farmlands. A sea of flames blazed in the westernmost tip of the farms, heading east towards the castle.

Lillian's eyes glowed with a white light as she scanned the land beneath her with magic. "I see Grandpa!" she shouted and pointed towards the wave of soldiers rushing towards the fire. Her eyes narrowed. "He's fighting against a group of fairies. I have to help him!" She scrambled up Grimmy's claw and steadied herself as she conjured a white bow, nocking an arrow made of light.

Paul squinted and shielded his eyes from the sun with his right hand. "Can you really hit them from here? Grandpa barely looks bigger than an ant."

Lillian released her arrow in response. It screeched as it ripped apart the air, homing in on the dust-sized fairy below. It left behind a trail of light like a shooting star across the night sky.

Lindyss raised an eyebrow as the arrow struck its target. "Not bad," she said as the arrow pierced the fairy's body, pinning it to the ground. The soldiers in front of the fairy froze before looking up, following the trail of light. "It's a shame they're resistant to magic." Lindyss shook her head as the fairy ripped the arrow out of its stomach while standing up.

Lillian's grandpa stepped forward and beheaded the fairy before it could take to the air. A worm lunged out of the fairy's carcass towards him, but he punted it away with his shield. Another arrow of light flew through the air and struck the worm's body, disintegrating it with a white flame.

"It seems like the humans can take care of themselves," Grimmy said as he flew closer to the combat area. A few of the humans were casting water-oriented spells to douse the burning farms while the armored men fended off the fairies. Arrows of light knocked the fairies in the air to the ground, preventing them from escaping the swords. A rune formed on Michelle's forehead as she chanted a spell. A few moments later, pillars of white light rained down on the battlefield, healing the humans and blinding the fairies.

"The infected ones haven't used magic yet," Lindyss said, flying alongside Grimmy. She rubbed her chin with her hand. "I wonder why. Maybe this is a weaker breed of worm? If that's

393

the case, you can leave the three humans here while we head to the underground fairy city."

Grimmy nodded. "You hear that, kiddies?" he asked the three humans standing on his claw. "I'm going to drop you now."

The trio screamed as the foundation they were standing on vanished, causing them to plummet towards the earth. Lindyss conjured a cushion of air beneath them, stopping their descent inches away from the ground.

"We're going to find Stella?" Vur asked. His hands closed and tightened into fists.

Lindyss nodded. "Ideally, she'd be unprepared because she's currently possessing someone." Her eyes narrowed. "I'm not letting her get away this time."

Vur frowned. "Is she really a bad person?" He gripped the lightning elemental hanging on the end of his necklace. "When I helped free her, she gave me Sparky as a present. And she really cared about Rella, Bella, and…" Vur paused and bit his lower lip.

Tafel took Vur's hand into her own. "Even if she was nice," she said, making eye contact, "it doesn't pardon her for what she's done. I only became the demon lord a few days ago, but I've read a lot of reports about missing people. She's kidnapped over a thousand demons and humans in the past ten years. And with this worm business, I don't even want to think about how many are dead or wish they were dead."

Vur sighed and nodded. "I just want to know why she suddenly changed from nice and caring to evil and cursey after Auntie showed up." He frowned at Lindyss' back. "What exactly happened between the two of them?"

Lindyss continued to fly forwards without pause, and Grimmy took a sudden interest in studying his nails.

***

Rella and Bella flew over an open plain with a white layer of mist encasing their bodies. Multiple tunnel entrances perforated the field below. "The illusion's gone," Bella said with wide eyes.

Rella nodded. "I told you it wasn't a trap. Someone really messed up."

Bella squinted and raised her hand over her eyes, shielding them from the sun. "That looks like a dragon," she said and tugged on Rella's arm while pointing at the sky.

"What? Dragons don't fly this far north," Rella said and squinted at the clouds. Her neck craned forward as she peered at a black dot in the distance. "Maybe it's a roc?" She shook her head. "It doesn't matter. We have to get out of here before they get things under control and notice we're gone."

Bella kept her eyes locked on the sky while continuing to fly forwards. "That's definitely a dragon," she said as the dot got closer. "It's most likely Grimmoldesser. Maybe he noticed the worm outbreak?"

"Do you think we should fly up there and meet him?" Rella asked. "He might know where Vur is since he's a dragon and all."

"Ehh!?" Bella asked as her eyebrows shot up. "Are you crazy? We're barely the size of one of his teeth. He'd kill us over something small like if our voices were too high-pitched for him."

Rella bit her lip. "How else are we going to find Vur? He could be anywhere. We don't even know if he's alive or not."

Bella released Rella's arm and stopped moving.

Rella turned her head and frowned. "What's wrong?"

"Would Vur even listen to us?" Bella asked as her shoulders drooped. "We asked him to help free Mom, and then Mom went and cursed the Corrupted One. I know that the Corrupted One stole the Fountain of Youth from us and that she was the reason why Mom was locked up in the first place, but Vur didn't know that. He called her Auntie." Bella lowered her head as tears formed in the corners of her eyes. "He helped us and we hurt him. Ye-Yella knew that."

Rella placed her hands on Bella's shoulders. "Vur said we were his friends and he didn't need a reward for helping us," she said and tilted Bella's body to look her in the eye. "What we need to do now is let Vur know what Mom is planning, so he doesn't regret becoming friends with us in the first place. Yella was better than the stereotypical fairy who befriends people for mischief. We can be too."

Bella focused her gaze on Rella's eyes. She wiped away her tears with the backs of her hands and nodded. "When did you become so mature?" she asked as she embraced her sister. "It makes me look bad as the oldest."

Rella snorted as she pulled away. "You're only older by a fraction of a second," she said and crossed her arms. "Now let's go confront that dragon. Of course, the oldest should go first." Rella motioned for Bella to fly ahead of her.

***

Tafel sucked in her breath. "This is huge," she said with wide eyes. "How did no one ever notice for ten years?" She was crouching next to Vur and Lindyss, peering over Grimmy's snout at the plains below. "The tunnels practically span the whole area between our nations."

"They had a massive illusion set up," Lindyss said and frowned. "Not only that, but they also relocated repeatedly once they drained an area of all its mana. This is the best place for them to set their base and sow chaos with the worms. But I don't understand why the fairies infected themselves to initiate the attack."

Grimmy circled over the plains, scanning the ground below. "What's the plan? Should I just burn it all down? Pour some lava in the holes and cover the top with hellfire?"

Lindyss nodded. "That might be the best course of action," she said as she stood up and rubbed her chin. "We should cover all the entrances except for the one you're pouring the lava through."

396

"You're going to kill all the fairies?" Vur asked and knit his brow. "Didn't you say killing fairies brings bad luck?"

"It does," Lindyss said as she narrowed her eyes at the tunnel entrances. "I killed a fairy once and now the world might be ending because of that."

"But you shouldn't kill them all. There are some good fairies too," Vur said.

Tafel squeezed his hand. "Yella saved my life, and her sisters weren't bad people despite their initial curses." She frowned at Lindyss. "We can't just slaughter them all—not when there can be others like them living in those caves."

Lindyss sighed. "Both of you are too young for this," she said and shook her head. "If it makes you feel any better, the fairy queen plays a major role in the emotional and physical states of her children. If she thinks torturing babies is fun, the rest of the fairies will agree. Stella's gone crazy, and her mental state should be reflected in all the fairies."

"That's not true!"

A voice came from behind them. Rella's and Bella's figures appeared as the mist surrounding them dispersed. "You're the crazy one," Bella said as she hovered in the air with her hands on her hips. She lowered her head and glanced at Vur's face before shifting her gaze to his toes. "Hi, Vur."

"Rella? Bella?" Vur asked and tilted his head while taking a step forward. "You two look abnormally thin."

"Your face is abnormally thin," Rella said and stuck her tongue out at him. A lightning bolt flew through the air.

"Eep!"

Rella ducked her head, avoiding the bolt. "What was that for!?" she asked and shook her fist at Lindyss whose finger was emitting smoke.

Lindyss crossed her arms over her chest. "You heard what I said. Prove to us you're not under Stella's influence."

Bella and Rella glanced at each other. They landed on Grimmy's forehead and kneeled while lowering their heads.

"You're awesome!"

"Amazing!"

"I hope you live long and prosper!"

"For a hundred thousand years!"

"Your mastery of black magic is beyond our understanding!"

"And the fact that you can use so many skills from so many different classes—"

"Alright," Lindyss said as a vein bulged on her forehead. "Enough, enough. I believe you; Stella would never allow anyone to lower her head to me. Why aren't you under her influence?"

"We relocated our birthflower a long time ago," Rella said as she stood up. "Mom can't control us without it."

Bella nodded. "It was Yella's idea." She looked at Vur and Tafel while pouting. "You've gotten a lot taller. You too."

"We can save the reunion for later," Lindyss said and waved her hand to stop Vur from moving forward. "For now, tell us about the situation inside."

38

"Bella and I were imprisoned for nearly ten years, but we managed to pick up some gossip here and there," Rella said as she scratched her head. "I'll start from when Mom captured one of those worms from the demons' capital. She wanted to experiment with them after seeing their destructive power while fighting against you, so she abducted the rest of the demons' royal family members."

Bella shivered as she hugged her shoulders. "She tortured them," she said, her voice quavering. "It was horrible. She hung them upside down by chains and had them vote on who to infect with the worms. They were terrified. I've never seen Mom act that way before."

Lindyss and Vur frowned while Tafel's face blanched. "Well, that's to be expected," Lindyss said with a sigh. "She was imprisoned and used as a mana source for over four centuries. What else happened?"

Rella and Bella exchanged glances. "She came back and overthrew the secondaries' and tertiaries' queens. She seized all their birthflowers and ordered everyone to set up the tunnel system. Afterwards, she had us kidnap humans and demons who wandered into our illusions," Rella said as she stared at Lindyss' feet. "Bella and I refused, so she imprisoned us for being bad children who didn't listen to Mommy."

"Ahem," a voice said from underneath Grimmy's wing. "I couldn't help but overhear something about secondary and tertiary queens?" Charon's head peeked out, and he climbed Grimmy's scales before standing behind the fairies.

Lindyss furrowed her brow. "And what exactly are you doing here?"

"Now, now," Charon said as he raised his arms in front of himself, "don't be mad. I did everything you asked me to before coming along." He grinned at the fairies. "I've never had a chance to study fairies before—such elusive creatures. Come, tell me about these queens."

"But," Rella said and glanced at Lindyss, "there's more important things."

"Nonsense," Charon scoffed. "Knowledge is power. Nothing is more important than knowledge."

Lindyss sighed. "You continue telling me about what happened," she said towards Rella. She pointed at Bella. "You go entertain the crazy old man."

"Eh?" Bella asked as she pointed at herself. "No wa—"

Rella shuddered as Bella was dragged away by Charon. "Anyways," she said and cleared her throat. "We heard a lot of conversation between the fairies who watched over us. They've been breeding the worms in pools saturated with mana and letting them infect the humans and demons they kidnapped. Just very recently, one of the fairies screwed up and the worms infected at least one fairy who freed us—most likely by coincidence."

"So it wasn't a planned attack," Lindyss said and thought about the Leonis household's farmland. She nodded. "Why didn't Stella stop them? I don't believe she was unable to."

"She locked herself in a room and told everyone not to disturb her," Rella said. "That can only mean two things since she didn't come out to quell the commotion: she's focusing on a long-distanced mind-controlled target, or she's making seeds for new birthflowers."

"It's the mind control," Lindyss said. "Her objective was most likely to bring the humans' ancestors' powers or pope back here. If we can use this opportunity to eliminate her while she's in someone else's body, then we wouldn't have to resort to genocide."

"Are there any uninfected humans or demons?" Tafel asked.

400

Rella nodded. "Most of them are just locked up because they'd be too hard to store if they were infected. I heard some fairies complain about having to deliver them food."

"That makes things more problematic," Lindyss said. "It's hard enough to deal with Stella on her own turf without having to worry about collateral damage. Do you know how many captives there are?"

"No, but there should be no less than a thousand," Rella said. "Mom wanted the tunnels to be big enough to house over ten thousand humans."

"How do they feed that many people?" Tafel tilted her head and muttered. "Could I use their methods for my people?"

Rella's face turned green. "You don't want to know. You really don't."

Vur raised an eyebrow. "Cannibalism?"

Rella turned her head away.

"Forget it," Lindyss said. "Can you draw a map of the place with all the important locations we have to look out for?"

Rella heaved a sigh of relief as she faced Lindyss while avoiding Tafel's gaze. She raised her hand and drew on the air with blue lines of mana. "These were the original plans for the tunnels," she said as a web of mana came into view, "but I don't know how much has changed over the years. Over here is where they imprisoned Bella and me. The fairies' living quarters are over there. Their birthflowers are beneath Mom's chambers, which are down at the lowest level, with the worm pools a passage away. The captives are supposed to be stored over here."

"It looks like a mixture between an ant colony and a beehive," Charon said as he rubbed his chin while peering over Rella's shoulder. "Very interesting."

"I understand the layout," Lindyss said, ignoring Charon's comment. "It looks like we have three objectives: take down Stella, eliminate the worms, and free the captives."

"Can you save the birthflowers too?" Bella asked. "It'd be bad if they were damaged during a battle. A fairy can be reborn as long as their birthflower is still alive."

Vur's eyes widened. "Then Yella?" he asked. "You said—"

"No," Rella said in a low voice and shook her head. "She gave her soul to you. She can't come back."

Vur's shoulders drooped.

Rella flew up to him and kicked his bicep. "Stop looking so droopy," she said and pouted. "She gave her life for you. You have to live yours to the fullest now. For her. It's the least you can do."

Tafel squeezed Vur's hand. "Me too," she said and sighed. "Yella wouldn't have died if I didn't act so rashly. We owe it to her to save her sisters."

Vur nodded, eyes still downcast.

"Then it's settled. Charon and Bella will free the captives. Tafel will move the birthflowers with Rella. Vur will kill the worms," Lindyss said and clenched her hand. "And I will take care of Stella."

"I think you're forgetting someone," Grimmy said with narrowed eyes.

"What are you going to do?" Lindyss asked. "You'd never fit in the tunnels. They're only big enough to transport humans." She patted his head and smiled. "Just wait here like a good boy, alright?"

Grimmy snorted and growled. The passengers riding on his body screamed as he dove towards the ground. He crashed against it, shattering the earth like a black meteorite, causing plumes of dirt and grass to shoot into the air. Screams whistled out of the tunnels and into the air around them, the field sounding like a discombobulated church organ. Grimmy roared and stomped his claw against the ground, causing a cave-in underneath him. "I'll wait right here," he said as he shook his passengers off, "but I'm not your dog."

"Ah." Lindyss sighed as she fixed her ruffled hair. "It was just a joke. Dragons and their pride." She clicked her tongue and glared at everyone else who was on the ground with their faces pale. "Well, what are you waiting for? Go on. We all have jobs to do."

"Yes!"

They shouted and rushed down the closest tunnel entrance as Lindyss and Grimmy watched them from behind. Grimmy flicked her forehead. "I have to watch my appearance when we're in public, you know?"

"I know," Lindyss said and stuck her tongue out at him before entering the tunnel herself.

***

"Huh?" Bella muttered and rubbed her eyes. "Weren't we just here?"

Charon peered through the layer of mist surrounding his body and traced his hands on the tunnel wall. He hummed and rubbed his chin after sniffing the residue on his fingers. "This looks exactly like the passage we were just in. Then again, everything looks the same down here."

Bella sighed. "As long as we keep going downwards, we'll have to find those prisoners."

"You're right," Charon said and nodded. His hands flickered, and a silver light appeared underneath the duo. "I cast haste on us; we don't want to be the last ones to finish, right?"

Bella flew through the tunnels, leading the way while maintaining her invisibility on herself and Charon. They traveled without stopping, passing bustling fairies, until they reached a fork in the cave that split off into two directions.

"That way," they said at the same time. The two of them were pointing in opposite directions.

"Who's the fairy here!?" Bella asked while pouting. "We're going this way. My fairy instincts are telling me I'm right."

Charon peered down the tunnel he wanted to enter before he sighed. "Alright. Your way it is then." Nothing good would come from arguing with a fairy. He heard the rumors about their curses.

The two crossed through multiple forks with Bella guiding them each time. Charon held a notebook in his hand, scribbling in it while looking up every so often. "This is odd," Charon said as he flipped back to the previous page in his book.

"What is?"

"We've been encountering fewer and fewer fairies as time's gone on. It would make more sense to encounter more fairies because the prisoners were supposed to be close to the fairies' living chambers."

"Are you stupid?" Bella asked as she placed her hands on her hips and pointed her chin at him. "Did you forget Grimmoldesser crash-landed against the ground? Of course all the fairies would be rushing outside to see what's going on." The two approached a tunnel entrance that was twice as wide as all the others. Bella nodded and sped up. "See? We're here."

Charon scratched his head as he followed behind the blue-haired fairy. A bright-purple light greeted them when Bella pulled open a door at the end of the passage. Multiple translucent, purple spheres were floating in the room. Flowers grew towards the spheres, blanketing the ground, walls, and ceiling. The room extended as far as the eye could see.

Charon raised an eyebrow. "The fairies converted the prisoners into flowers? Very interesting. I had entertained the idea of transforming a creature from one kingdom to another, but I never succeeded."

Bella ground her teeth together. "Okay," she said and furrowed her brow. "Maybe I wasn't right. But we're clearly the first ones here, so it's our duty to transport the birthflowers out." Her hand shielded her eyes as she scanned the room. "And knowing Mom, there's most likely some kind of guardian that will appear the moment we touch a flower. Ah. There it is; it looks like a giant spider. How do we do this?"

"That's easy," Charon said as he wiped his hands on his robe.

"You can kill that thing without hurting the flowers?" Bella asked with wide eyes. "I would never have guessed."

"Of course not," Charon scoffed. "I'll just teleport the whole room to Konigreich. Then we let Lindyss deal with the guardian at her leisure."

Bella stared at Charon with half-closed eyes and tilted her head. "Do you even see how large this room is? How are you going to teleport the whole thing?"

Charon chuckled. "Just watch," he said as he placed his right hand inside his mouth. A cracking sound came from his jaw, and his face contorted. He pulled out a bloody blue tooth. A gale swirled around him, blowing outwards. He chanted in a low voice, causing a silver light to spread out from his feet, crawling along the insides of the room while coating the flowers in a soft glow. A torrent of blue light flew out of the tooth in Charon's hand, pouring onto and entering his body. The silver glow crawled along until it encompassed the whole room.

The spider guardian twitched and sprang to its feet. It hissed at the duo at the entrance, but the glow vanished before the guardian could do anything, and the room disappeared, leaving a gaping void in front of Bella and Charon.

Charon fell to his knees and dragged his body towards the wall. "Ever since that day I had to borrow other people's mana to teleport a dragon," he said as he wiped his brow with his sleeve, "I decided to store mana inside one of my teeth over time. A thousand years, to be precise." He leaned against the wall. "Give me a few minutes to recover."

Bella alighted in front of him, landing on his knee. "Thank you," she said and knelt, touching her head to his robe. "Really. Thank you."

"Raise your head, little one," Charon said. "Humility doesn't suit you. A child should act like a child."

Bella raised her head and pouted. "And a crazy old man shouldn't be so reliable," she said. "Who do you think you are?"

Charon laughed. "Come," he said and patted the space beside him, "finish telling me about queens and birthflowers."

***

Grimmy yawned as a cluster of five fairies approached him. A layer of obsidian separated his body from the ground as he lay prone. Thousands of fairy heads at the tunnel entrances peered at him, their bodies too afraid to exit.

"O mighty Grimmoldesser," the fairy at the front of the cluster said. "May I ask what brings you here?" Her body trembled in the air as the dragon's gaze pierced through her.

Grimmy's wings flared outwards, and the fairies let out cries as their bodies were blown backwards. "Do I need a reason?" he asked. His reptilian red eyes locked onto the trembling fairies. They were larger than the fairies' bodies.

"No! Of course not!" the fairy said and lowered her head to the ground. "Forgive my impudence."

Grimmy snorted and closed his eyes before resting his head onto his front claws.

"W-we'll be taking our leave now," the fairy said as she inched backwards. "Forgive our disturbance."

"Wait," Grimmy said as one of his eyes opened.

"Y-yes?"

Grimmy smiled. "I want a snack. Get me something. *All* of you." The surrounding fairies in the tunnels shuddered as a chill ran down their spines and gripped their hearts. "If I'm not full by the time I eat all your offerings, then I'll make up the difference in fairies. No humans or demons. They're too squishy and watered down."

Murmurs rose up into the air. The fairies in the tunnels glanced at each other.

"What are you waiting for?" Grimmy growled. The obsidian underneath his claw shattered as he raised his head.

"Eep!"

406

Thousands of fairies streamed out of the tunnels into the air, spreading outwards into the surrounding areas.

Grimmy yawned again and lowered his head.

***

"This way!" Rella pointed. The mist surrounding her body followed her arm.

"We just came from there," Tafel said and frowned. "You're lost. Admit it."

Rella pouted. "It's not my fault the witch rushed us all in here," she said and landed on Tafel's head. "Why don't you do something instead of complaining then?"

"Watch me," Tafel said as her horns glowed green. She closed her eyes, and a sphere of wind radiated outwards from her body. The wind howled through the tunnels, forcing the few fairies lingering around to lose their balance and tumble on the ground. A minute passed.

Tafel opened her eyes as her horns dimmed. "This way," she said and pointed. "I found the captives, but no signs of Charon or Bella. I couldn't locate the birthflowers either." She sprinted down the tunnels, weaving past the leftover fairies with Rella clutching her horns to prevent herself from falling off.

The two traveled passed numerous caves and passages until they reached a massive archway with three fairies playing cards in front of it. Tafel approached them, still cloaked by Rella's invisibility spell, and drew her sword. She stabbed it between the fairies. A snake made of smoke sprang out of the sword and swallowed the trio before disappearing, leaving behind three sleeping fairies.

"It's here," Tafel said and sheathed her sword as she entered the archway. She walked through the dark passage with Rella flying next to her and rounded a bend. A soft, blue light greeted the two. In front of them was a steep cliff, leading to a pit that contained thousands of bodies. The walls were peppered with blue stones that faintly illuminated the captives. They looked sick underneath the dim glow. Tafel wrinkled her nose and held back the urge to vomit.

Rella pinched her nose as tears sprang to her eyes. "This smells so bad," she said, her voice nasally. "Are they even alive?"

Tafel frowned. "I can't teleport this many people," she said and stepped towards the edge of the cliff. She drew her sword and held it in front of her chest. An orange flame blazed into life on its blade while the mist surrounding her and Rella dispersed. Whimpers rose from the bottom of the pit as the gazes of the captives were drawn to the flames like moths.

"Is there anyone who can be counted as a leader amongst you all?" Tafel asked. Her voice thundered in the ears of the captives. Some of them shook. "I may be able to free you all, but there needs to be order."

Instantly, a cacophony of noise resounded from the pit: people shouted, begged, cried. Someone shouted, silencing the crowd. The captives' heads turned towards the furthest region of the pit. A man staggered his way to the front, stepping over the living and stepping on the dead.

"My name is Opfern," the man said. "I am the Baron of Blod. Who are you?"

"Tafel Besteck," Tafel said. "The current demon lord." More murmurs rose up, but they were silenced by a gesture from Opfern. The demons on the right half of the pit looked up in admiration and puzzlement. The humans on the left half trembled and muttered to each other.

"How do you plan on saving us?" Opfern asked as he gestured towards the people in the pit. "None of us can use magic. The fairies take them away first. Many people here haven't lifted a weapon in their lives."

"How long have you been here?" Tafel asked, ignoring Opfern's question. Sweat rolled down her back as her gaze roamed over the crowd of people staring up at her like frightened kittens in a box.

408

"Five years," Opfern replied. His stare drilled into Tafel. "How are you going to save us?"

Tafel frowned. "How do the fairies bring you out of this pit?"

"A group of them come and levitate us with magic," Opfern said. "The ones they take never come back."

"I understand," Tafel said as the flames on her sword disappeared. "I need to consult with my allies before I can proceed." She turned around and walked back towards the entrance, ignoring the screams and cries echoing through the cave behind her as she rounded the corner.

Rella shuddered. "Can you save them?" she asked as she raised a barrier of mist around their bodies.

Tafel bit her lip but didn't reply. Rella opened her mouth to speak, but the sounds of fluttering wings cut her off. The two pressed their backs against the tunnel wall as a group of thirty fairies flew past them, all of them carrying baskets. "Why do we have to do all this work while those three slackers sleep on the job?"

"Hush. Don't act as if you've never slept on the job either."

"I don't want to hear that from you of all people."

"Huh, aren't the fodder awfully noisy today?"

Tafel raised an eyebrow at Rella. 'Food?' she mouthed.

Rella shrugged in reply. Thuds sounded out as the baskets crashed into the crowd of people. The fairies flew back, passing Tafel and Rella before stopping to pick up the three sleeping fairies.

"Hurry, hurry. Don't want to stay here for too long," one of the fairies said as she looped one of the sleeping fairies' arm over her shoulder. The group disappeared from Tafel and Rella's view. Screams and shrieks echoed through the tunnels.

"Oh, it's already starting. Why did the queen tell us to do this though? Can't they get out through magic?" one of the fairies asked.

"Don't question the queen. And those were the weakest worms—they can't use magic."

Tafel and Rella had dashed out of the mist barrier towards the edge of the cliff as soon as the screams had started. Their eyes widened at the sight below. Hundreds of people were thrashing on the ground while others were running to the sides of the pit. The baskets lay scattered amongst the crowd with their lids off to the sides. A few worms slithered through the throngs of people, searching for those who weren't already infected. Only a few men were stabbing bloody bones at the worms and twitching people.

"It was you!" Opfern roared as his gaze locked onto Tafel and Rella. He held a rib with a squirming worm impaled on the other end. "You killed us! The fairies never did this before. Not until you came." He pinned the worm to the ground and stomped on it until it stopped moving.

"N-no," Tafel said as she took a step back. "I didn't. It wasn't me." She unsheathed her sword and took a deep breath as she approached the edge of the cliff.

"Stop!" Rella said and pulled on Tafel's robe. "You can't. There's too many."

"If not me, then who?" Tafel asked as she jerked her robe out of Rella's grip. "I've fought thousands of worms and infected ones in Fuselage. I can do this." Tafel's sword glowed red as she leapt into the pit, plunging her sword into the chest of a man who was thrashing against the ground.

"I'm sorry," Tafel said as the man stared into her eyes, terrified. White flames enveloped her sword and burnt the man to ashes. She climbed to her feet and whirled towards the next person, her sword cutting everything in its path.

Rella fell to her knees and bit her lip. She clasped her hands together. *Please let her be alright*. Her eyes closed as she chanted. A black mist rolled out from underneath her feet and formed a wall behind her, blocking out the sounds of slaughter. *I won't let anyone interfere. This is the most I can do.*

410

The white flame danced along the bottom of the pit, casting grotesque shadows on the walls. It traveled in a spiral fashion, sometimes cutting towards the sides, sometimes bending towards the center. Tears streamed from Tafel's eyes as her sword passed through humans, demons, and worms alike.

"Why?" she asked as her voice cracked. Her movements flowed like water as she slipped through the crowd, leaving a trail of ashes behind her. "Why are they spreading so fast?" Every time she thought it was over, more screams would echo from a different region in the pit and she'd charge over. The worms entered their hosts and left behind a fraction of themselves before exiting again, seeking the next victim. Others burrowed into the ground and reappeared, striking at the captives on the other side of the pit from Tafel.

Time passed.

Rella opened her eyes and stopped chanting. The room was silent even without her magic. She stumbled as her stomach sank. She climbed to her feet and peered over the edge, flinching at the soft sobs trickling into her ears. Tafel was sitting in the center of the room with her face buried in her knees, arms hugging her legs. Her sword was beside her, resting on a layer of ash. A group of thirty survivors were sitting with their backs pressed against the walls of the pit, their mouths and eyes wide open, their gazes locked on the demon lord.

***

Lindyss stood in front of a fork leading to three different passages. A trail of unconscious fairies marked the path she traveled to get there. "Looks like the fairy's map was a little off," she mumbled to herself as she closed her eyes. A few moments later, she opened them and entered the leftmost passage. Her eyes narrowed. *I should reach Stella if I follow the highest concentration of mana.*

A quartet of fairies appeared in her line of sight as she rounded a bend. She flicked her wrist and a shadowy hand shot out of the ceiling towards the fairies. Their eyes widened as the shadow expanded and slammed them into the ground before they could move out of the way.

Lindyss stepped over their bodies and continued down the path. She passed through more and more tunnels as she proceeded deeper into the caves, encountering and forcing a few fairies into the ground without hesitation. Eventually, she came to a halt in front of a doorway with a black golem sitting in front of it. A purple orb was embedded in its rectangular chest, spreading a web of lights through its body.

The golem didn't react as Lindyss raised her arm and conjured a spear of ice in front of herself. It rotated in the air, kicking up the dust on the ground before flying towards the golem. Moments before it hit its target, an explosion occurred behind the spear, speeding it up—a technique she stole from Tafel. The spear pierced the golem's core as if it were butter, causing the golem to topple over. Lindyss frowned as a sword made of white light appeared in her hand. She approached the golem, and black tentacles sprang from her shadow to probe it.

Too weak, she thought after confirming it was disabled. *It wasn't even facing the right way.* She stepped over the fallen golem into the corridor behind the doorway. The floor was steep and became steeper still until the path leading down was nearly vertical. She pushed open another door at the bottom and raised her hand in front of her eyes as a green light assaulted her vision. Groans and roars reached her ears as well as a few fairylike gasps and squeaks.

Lindyss stiffened. Inside the room, there was a gigantic pool filled with green water. Its diameter spanned over a hundred meters. Underneath the surface, thousands—maybe hundreds of thousands—of worms swam and wriggled, making it impossible to see the bottom. Baskets filled with green spheres lined the edge of the pool while dozens of humans and demons were standing with their wrists and ankles bound by chains attached to the walls. Fairies hovered in front of the captives, but they had all turned around at the sound of the door opening, confusion plastered on their faces.

Lindyss reacted first, and lightning bolts flew out of her hands towards the fairies. One fairy managed to evade, but in the next moment, she was pierced by a spear that emerged from her own shadow. Lindyss shook her head after confirming the room was clear of fairies. "So it looks like the golem was made to keep things in, not out," she said to herself as she approached the green pool. "I guess I'm responsible for disposing of these since Vur isn't here yet." Her head turned towards the fettered prisoners. Saliva ran down their mouths as they struggled against their chains, straining their necks towards Lindyss.

Lindyss snorted as she backed away from the pool and placed her hands on her hips, facing the prisoners. "You might be resistant to magic," she said as she stomped her right foot against the ground. A wall of earth rose up in front of the captives before pressing towards them. "But I can squish you to death." Squelching noises and shattering sounds echoed through the room as the moving wall crushed the infected prisoners, manacles and flesh alike. The expression on Lindyss' face didn't change as black blood oozed through the earthen wall.

"How can you use geomancy?" a voice asked from behind Lindyss. She turned around. There was a red-haired fairy lying on the ground with a hole in her stomach—the fairy that managed to evade the initial lightning salvo. Lindyss ignored the fairy's question and placed a finger on the fairy's forehead. A green light enveloped the fairy, healing her wounds. The fairy's eyes widened. "White magic too? What are you?"

"You're a primary fairy, aren't you?" Lindyss asked. "First one I've seen since I entered this place. You're going to lead me to Stella after I dispose of these worms."

The fairy gasped when she heard Stella's name. "You're the Corrupted One! You dirty witch! You lousy lemon-eyed snot drinker!" She rose to her feet and launched herself at Lindyss,

413

but the elf snapped her fingers, and the fairy's body stiffened before falling towards the ground.

"Call me what you want," Lindyss said as she walked towards the pool, turning her back on the stunned fairy. "I did what I had to do. Now be a good little child and wait for me to finish cleaning up your mess."

***

"I've come with an urgent message for the king!" Trent rode a horse, shouting as he approached the gates of the royal castle. "It concerns the pope and the missing prince!"

The two guards standing in front of the gate exchanged glances before addressing the oncoming horse. "Please dismount," one of the guards said. "We'll bring you in right away. The king has given orders for us to take anyone with information about the pope and prince directly to him. As a safety precaution, you must leave your weapons and armor behind."

Trent nodded as he dismounted and stripped himself of his equipment. He raised his head and passed the guards his items. His eyes were pure white with no traces of irises or pupils. "I just came from receiving my blessing from the spirits," Trent said, taking a step back as the guards' eyes widened. "They'll return to normal in a few hours."

"Understood," the guard said and relaxed his posture. "You must be Trent then? This way." The guard opened the gate and walked ahead.

"Yes," Trent said with a strange smile. "I'm Trent."

The guard stopped in front of a metal door. "The king is inside his study on the second floor." He knocked twice before opening the door and gestured for Trent to go in.

"Thank you," Trent said as he nodded at the guard and stepped inside the room. It was filled with bookshelves and contained a spiral staircase leading upwards positioned in the center of the room. The door closed as Trent climbed halfway up the stairs. As soon as his head appeared on the second floor,

414

a spear stabbed downwards from behind him, piercing through his spinal column at the base of his neck. His body twitched, and he coughed out a mouthful of green blood before collapsing.

"You're up, Siz," a voice said. "Charon told us to be wary of worms and to incinerate the body."

"I know," a feminine voice said as Trent's body went up in flames. "Let's tell the king."

***

In the center of a dark chamber, a diminutive figure was sitting with her legs crossed. Her eyes flew open and blinked a few times, revealing a pair of irises that shifted colors with every blink. Stella stretched her arms above her head and cracked her neck. "Ah," she said as she rubbed her temples, "that wasn't very nice of them. Well, it was fun while it lasted." Her body stiffened. "Oh?" Her head turned to the side. "I know you. It's been a while, dragon boy. How've you been?"

Vur stood at the entrance to Stella's chambers with his eyebrows furrowed.

"Care for a cup of tea?" Stella asked and waved her arm. A teapot that was resting on a table in the corner of the chamber sprouted legs and waddled towards the fairy. Two teacups hopped after it. Stella gestured at a cushion across from her. "Have a seat."

"You're not going to fight me?" Vur asked as he approached the cushion.

"Why would I? You were the one that freed me after all. If you were someone else, I'd dissect you in a heartbeat," Stella said as Vur sat down on the cushion. She raised an eyebrow. "You seem awfully relaxed for someone who was expecting a fight."

"And you seem awfully cohesive for someone who's supposed to be insane," Vur said and shrugged as the teapot vomited out a fountain of clear liquid into the two cups. "Why did you imprison Rella and Bella? They helped free you too."

415

Stella smiled. "Imprisoning them was the only choice I had. And I'm not insane, not at all. Is that what they're saying about me?" She pulled out three green orbs from a bin and dropped them into her teacup. "Would you like some? They're quite chewy. I call them tapioca. Such a nice sounding word, don't you agree? Taa-pee-oh-kah." She giggled as she brought the cup to her lips and took a sip.

"I don't eat bugs," Vur said as he shook his head and picked up the cup in front of him. He sniffed it and tilted his head. "What's in this?"

"The tears of orphans boiled with the crushed dreams of the just departed. It's good for the soul," Stella said as she chewed on one of the eggs. A miniature worm popped its head out of her mouth as she spoke, but she slurped it back inside before it got away. "So what made you come visit little old me? You got here pretty quickly considering the fact you were in the human capital not too long ago."

"I got lost," Vur said as he took a tentative sip from the cup. "I was supposed to get rid of the worms, but I ended up here instead. I guess that means Auntie got lost too since she's not here."

Stella's horns glowed red as her eyes narrowed. Her hands clenched, and the cup in her hand squealed before it shattered. "You really did come here with her then." After a moment passed, she sighed as the pieces of the cup crawl back together. "It's not fair. Why does that backstabbing butt-cow get all the nice things?" She pouted and crossed her arms over her chest as her horns dimmed.

Vur stayed silent as he took another sip of tea. "Why did you attack her? After I freed you, I mean. Even if I was hungover, I could tell you were genuinely happy to see Rella, Bella, and Yella again," he said, his gaze locked on the tea's surface. "What happened between you two in the past? Is it really so bad that you have to try to destroy the continent to get back at her?"

416

Stella tilted her head. "She never told you?" she asked as she poured herself another cup of tea. "Well, that's to be expected. If I was a backstabber, I wouldn't want my allies to know either. Do you want the long version or the short version?"

"The long version."

Stella nodded and closed her eyes. "I'll need to cast an illusion to keep that wrinkled tomato preoccupied." A line of smoke flowed from Stella's hands out the door. "That should do the trick," she said and gazed into Vur's eyes. "You're a blue mage; Rella told me. I can teach you a truth curse that you can cast on me."

"You'd go that far?" Vur asked, raising his eyebrows.

"Fairies are notorious for lying," Stella said and lowered her head as a crooked smile appeared on her lips. "I want you to believe me."

Vur nodded and the two exchanged curses.

Stella took a deep breath. "I come from the first generation of fairies. We were born from the flowers that sprouted from Aeris' body when she was buried. There were twenty flowers, one for each of us. We decided to part ways and establish our own colonies. I was lucky and discovered the Fountain of Youth. My siblings were less fortunate and eventually passed on. Their offspring were later incorporated into my colony with the condition of surrendering their birthflowers to me. It was lonely at the top," Stella said and sighed as she stirred her tea. "Fairies had developed a bad reputation from the start with our pranks and tricks. The other races learned not to trust us, and I was always suspected when I wanted to converse with them. As for my own children, how can you become friends with someone whose life belongs completely to you? It's not the right dynamic for a meaningful friendship.

"Lindyss, that banana-nosed outcast, was my first friend. At least, that's what I believed up to the moment I was imprisoned. We first met when she came to the fountain and got trapped in

417

my illusions. She told me she was looking for a cure to her condition, and I yielded after listening to her story. She was lonely, never had any parents. Her adoptive mother, which wasn't even an elf, was killed by a bear. A dragon, Grimmoldesser, was bored and decided to plant the elder lich's soul inside her body because she didn't want to be weak anymore. When her batty bloodline awakened, it conflicted with the lich's soul and her body almost fell apart. She needed the power of the fountain to stay alive which is why I allowed her to stay.

"It was pleasant. We used to explore the region together. I'd show her places she'd never been. She showed me some of the more dangerous regions occupied by dragons," Stella said as she popped another worm egg into her mouth. After chewing, she washed the remains down with the rest of her tea. "She was too interested in the humans. By that time, our continent had been at war with them for close to four hundred years. There were times where I'd leave the fountain and preoccupy myself for weeks to make seeds for more birthflowers while Lindyss did her own things. I didn't know her 'things' involved selling me to the humans.

"One day, after I had just finished making a fresh batch of seeds, an army of humans were waiting for me. Even when I was under the cover of my illusions, they knew I was there. And they let me know, using Lindyss' name to bait me out of hiding, saying she sold me out." Stella ground her teeth. "I didn't believe them until after they captured me. I was too weak to resist and my guardians were slain by an ambush. I used a truth curse on them and interrogated them as we fought. Lindyss really did betray my trust in her. They managed to defeat me and locked me up on the spot, demanding for me to give up my powers or they'd hunt down every single fairy and present me their heads. I refused, believing the rest of the continent would fight against the humans for my children—if only because of a mutual enemy.

418

"Even though I refused, they managed to extract my powers from me, but I infused as much of it with my hatred and bitterness as I could. The results of the forced extraction were obvious, and the group of humans who took my power and drank tea made out of my children's birthflowers gained immense magical powers compared to the other humans, but they sprouted horns and became demons. They were ostracized by other humans, but they were a sizable group and managed to hold their ground, establishing a city around my place of imprisonment." Stella trembled. "They kept me weak, unable to do anything. A spell formation in the room would absorb all the mana in my body, twice a day. Another chain would forcibly inject mana into me to keep me alive.

"The worst part was they kept their word." Stella's horns flared up, bathing the room in a red glow, and the teacup in her hand shattered once again with a pitiful mewl. "Even if Lindyss did betray me, the least she could've done was keep my children safe. With every head the humans brought, I could feel a part of me dying. It made my heart ache; the pain was unbearable. They would bring my children in front of the door and rip their heads off while they were still conscious. They'd tell them that it was my fault. That I was the reason why they were going to die so pitifully. I could feel my children's fear within the room, and I'd see it on their heads moments later when they'd be teleported inside, faces still contorted in a silent scream with tears streaming down their cheeks. I couldn't even save their heads because the rats would eat them, yet I still tried every time. I tried, but it never worked!" Tears streamed down Stella's cheeks as she took in deep breaths. "There was a long period of time where they stopped. I was thankful for it, but then they brought hundreds of fairies at once. It was then that I vowed to torture the humans and everything they held precious if I were to ever be set free."

Vur's eyebrows furrowed as he frowned and scratched his cheek.

Stella blinked and her horns dimmed. "Not you, of course. I could tell there was something different about you, something dragonlike. You brought me a feeling of awe and fear rather than resentment and undying hatred. I understood when Bella told me you were imprinted by the matriarch. Everything has an innate sense of respect and a healthy dose of fear for dragons—those that don't are dead." Stella smiled. "It's a nice feeling that you bring, comforting. And it's gotten even stronger since I last saw you ten years ago. It helps keep my head clear. More tea?"

Vur nodded and the teapot vomited into his cup. "You don't know why Lindyss betrayed you?"

Stella shook her head. "It doesn't matter. What's done is done. No reason of hers can ever allow me to forgive her. Do you think I'm wrong?" She tilted her head. "Am I a villain?"

"No. I don't think so," Vur said. "Might makes right. I know Mom and Grimmy have slaughtered countless people out of anger—Dad too. It's the dead people's fault for being too weak. They wouldn't have died if they were stronger."

Stella smiled. "I had a feeling you'd understand me."

"But," Vur said and sipped his tea, "that doesn't mean I don't feel bad for the people you've killed."

Stella raised an eyebrow. "Well, aren't you unexpectedly kind? I didn't expect you to be so sympathetic to the plight of the humans."

Vur shrugged. "They have families. People care for them and feel sad when they lose them just like you did when you lost your children. I realized it in the dream Lindyss placed me in for ten years: how much it hurts to lose people who are close to you. The sense of loss eating away at your heart. I must've watched Tafel, Mom, Auntie, Grimmy, Yella, and everyone else die hundreds of times because of my weakness." He sighed. "You'd think it'd hurt less after the first few times, but it doesn't. It hurts just as much, if not more."

Stella frowned and stared at the reformed teacup in her hand. Images of her fallen children replayed themselves in her head. A tear sprang to the corner of her eye which she quickly wiped away. She pouted at Vur. "Don't act so moral and righteous now, you hypocrite," she said. "The food you eat has family too, you know? What about all the bear cubs that'll never see their mother again because you got hungry?"

"That's different," Vur said. "Killing to eat is necessary for me to continue living to keep my family happy. Killing to make others sad is just not nice."

"I'm not killing just to make others sad," Stella said and crossed her arms. "Although it is a nice bonus. I'm getting revenge for my children."

"You've already avenged them," Vur said. "I know you captured the demons' royal family. The other humans did nothing wrong."

Stella looked down. The two sat in silence as they drank their tea. A strong wave of magic brushed over them and sent goosebumps down their arms.

"Hey," Stella said, eyes still downcast. Vur looked up from his empty cup. "If I die, will you take care of my children?" She raised her head. "They did nothing wrong."

Vur nodded. "I will."

Stella smiled and held out her hand. A white rose bloomed from her palm, its roots wrapping around her arm. "A reward," she said and extended it towards Vur, "for accepting my task."

"I don't need a reward for helping a friend," Vur said and shook his head.

"Then a favor," Stella said and brought the flower closer to Vur. Vur extended his hand, and the flower's roots crawled onto his palm, wrapping themselves around his arm. They crawled along his body until the rose migrated over his heart. "Take care of me in my next life, okay?"

Vur patted Stella on the head and nodded before standing up. The mist blocking the door dispersed as he approached it.

He walked past the door and rounded a bend. A figure grabbed his arm.

"You're not going to fight?" Lindyss asked, staring at the rose on Vur's chest.

Vur shook his head. "It's your fight," he said and gazed into Lindyss' eyes.

Lindyss furrowed her brow but let go of his arm, leaving behind a bloodstain. The blood didn't belong to her or Vur. She passed Vur and continued down the path until she reached Stella's chambers.

"Friend, huh?" Stella said to herself and smiled as Vur vanished around the corner. "There's just one more person I have to get rid of to avenge my children." She glared at Lindyss who appeared at the entrance to the room. "You."

***

Vur sat with his back against the tunnel wall. He shook as vibrations ran from the rocky surface into his body as explosions and crashes resounded in the room behind him. He raised his head at the sound of approaching footsteps. Charon was walking towards him with Rella and Bella sitting on his shoulders. Tafel was further behind, dragging her feet with her gazed locked on the floor ahead of her.

"Hmm." Charon hummed and rubbed his chin. "We've accomplished the tasks we set out for. Why do you two look like we lost?"

Rella and Bella flew off of Charon's shoulders and hovered in front of Vur. "Is that—?" Rella asked and stared at Bella with wide eyes. The flower blooming on Vur's chest seemed to wave at them, its petals swaying even though there was no wind.

"It is," Bella said and gasped. She clutched her chest. "He feels like how Mom used to before she got taken away."

Vur ignored the fairies and frowned at Tafel. She had taken a seat across from him, her back pressed against the wall of the tunnel. Her knees were bent in front of her chest, and her head was buried in her knees with her arms hugging her shins. Vur

422

stood up and brushed past the fairies before sitting down beside Tafel. He placed a hand on her head and smoothed out the tangles in her hair.

The two fairies exchanged glances before tugging on Charon's sleeve. He shrugged. "I'm going to watch the battle," he said as he took a step towards the chamber's entrance. A flood of lava rushed out and nearly engulfed him. He cleared his throat. "Never mind then. I will not be spectating."

The group waited in silence as the ground continued to tremble and the walls continued to shake. Dust sprinkled from the ceiling. Rella and Bella had draped themselves over Vur's shoulders, admiring the rose on his chest but not daring to touch it. Vur's hand was still in Tafel's hair. Neither of them had said anything. Charon worked on clearing the hardening lava away.

An hour passed in this fashion. The rose on Vur's chest shone with a golden light before dimming. The rumbling in the tunnels stopped. Lindyss walked out of the chamber's entrance with her hair frayed and charred, the clothes she wore in tatters and dried blood caking her body. There was no expression on her face.

"Is it over?" Charon asked as he peeked his head into the entrance. There was nothing to see. A pile of rubble had blocked off the opening to Stella's room.

"Yes," Lindyss said. She glanced at Vur and Tafel before walking away. "It's over."

39

"Exactly what is this?" Grimmy asked as he flew through the sky. Lindyss and Vur were sitting on his head with Rella and Bella sitting on Vur's shoulders. A swarm of fairies flew behind Grimmy, blotting out the sun for the people on the ground. "I feel like a mother duck with her chicks in tow."

Lindyss snorted. "Blame the new fairy king over here," she said and placed her hand on Vur's head. "They'll be following him like moths to a flame until the queen is born."

Vur scratched his cheek. "At least there's plenty of space for them in Konigreich, but we'll have to defeat the guardian for their birthflowers first."

"That shouldn't be an issue," Lindyss said. "It's probably disabled if it's a construct, or it'll submit to you if it's biological. I do wish Charon teleported the room somewhere more convenient though." A vein appeared on her forehead.

"Where'd he put it?" Bella asked, peeling her eyes away from the rose.

"On top of his tower in Konigreich. Literally." Lindyss sighed. "I just hope a breeze doesn't tip it over. My skeletons have been telling me about the panic it induces every time it wobbles."

"Ah," Bella said and lowered her gaze. "And here I was thinking he looked pretty cool when he teleported the whole room away."

Silence fell over the group save for the chatter of the swarm behind them.

"I should've gone with Tafel," Vur said as he looked up at the sky.

"And bring this many fairies back to Niffle?" Lindyss asked as she gestured behind herself. "Not happening. I have a feeling she doesn't want to see any fairies for a long time."

***

"What does it mean to be the demon lord?" Tafel asked. She was sitting on the edge of her bed with her hands clenched into fists on her lap. Her head hung as she stared at the floor, dark circles underneath her eyes. Dustin and Mina were sitting on chairs across from her.

Dustin frowned. "Tafel? What happene—"

"Answer me!" Tafel's voice cracked when she yelled. She raised her head and glared at the duo across from her. Tears threatened to fall from her eyes.

"Calm down, Tafel," Mina said. "We're just worried about—"

"It's just one question. If you're not going to answer it," Tafel said in a low voice as her horns glowed silver. She shouted as a circle appeared underneath Dustin and Mina, "Then get out!" Their bodies disappeared along with the chairs and carpet.

Tafel panted, glaring at the exposed marble floor in the center of the room. She threw her body across her bed and buried her face in her pillow. A minute passed before the door to her room creaked open by an inch.

"Excuse me," Retter said and rubbed his nose. "I couldn't help but overhear—" He shut his mouth when Tafel raised her head and glared through the crack in the door with puffy eyes. "A demon lord is the demon who holds the respect of the people." Retter gulped and pushed the door open further. "Whether by power or charisma."

Tafel sat up and pointed at her desk's chair. "Sit."

Retter nodded and took a seat. "The demon lord is the one who guides the direction of the kingdom. She is the one who makes the important choices: to go to war or seek an armistice, to abolish laws or to create new ones. Everything a demon lord

425

does is to ensure the continuation of the demon race. I don't know what happened to you to make you—"

"I killed people," Tafel said. Tears rolled down her cheeks. "Thousands of people. Humans. Demons. Men. Women. Children." Her voice cracked as her tears dripped from her chin.

Retter's brow furrowed as he frowned. "That—"

"I'm a monster." Tafel lowered her head and stared at her palms. The setting sun colored her hands red. Like blood. "Aren't I?"

"No," Retter said. His armor clanked as he kneeled by the side of the bed. "I've fought in too many battles to keep track of before I became a sentry in the royal castle. I've seen my fair share of monsters—you're not one of them. All I see in front of me is a scared child who feels remorse for what she's done. Monsters don't feel remorse."

Tafel sniffled and raised her head. She turned away from Retter's sincere gaze. "I'd like to be left alone."

"Understood," Retter said and saluted as he stood up. "Let me know if you need anything." He left the room and closed the door. He sighed as soft sobs echoed in the room behind him.

***

Michelle and her mother were standing over an open white sarcophagus. They were wearing black dresses, uncharacteristic of the pope's family. "This isn't real, right?" Michelle asked. "Tell me it's not true." She grabbed her mother's hand. "Mom?"

"I'm sorry, Michelle," Marissa said and hugged her daughter. Lines streaked down her face where her tears had ruined her makeup. "I'm sorry."

Michelle's body trembled. "How?" Her arms hung by her side. Inside the sarcophagus, there was a blanket. The top was peeled back, revealing the pope's mostly burnt face. "Dad's the strongest. He's blessed by the spirits. He talked to me just a few hours ago. He can't be dead." Michelle broke out of her mother's embrace and kneeled beside the side of the sarcophagus, clasping her hands together while chanting. A

426

white light enveloped the burnt corpse but dispersed without any effect. She chanted again and again to no avail as tears sprang to her eyes while her mother cried silently behind her. "I promise I won't be bad anymore: I won't drink. I won't run off and disobey you. I'll pray twice as much without complaining." Her voice quavered, and her hands turned white from gripping the side of the sarcophagus. "So please, Dad. Get up. Please, get up."

"Michelle…" Her mother hiccupped and placed her hand on her daughter's shoulder.

Michelle flinched as her mother's hand made contact. "Who did it?" she asked and gritted her teeth as she wiped her tears away with the backs of her hands. "Who?"

"It was me."

Michelle whirled around and glared at the doorway. The human king was leaning against the door's frame with his shoulders slouched, his crown lopsided. "I gave the order to have him killed. If you want to blame someone, then blame me. It is my duty to protect the people as the king, and I did what had to be done." *Forgive me, Rudolph.*

***

"It's been a month since the last worm outbreak," Gale said. He was standing in front of an altar dressed in the white robe that represented the pope's station. "I think it's safe to say we have fully exterminated them, Your Majesty."

"Good. But we must maintain vigilance," Randel said with a sigh. After seeing Michelle and her mother in the basement of the temple crying over their lost family member, his own loss felt even greater. His purple robes had grease stains decorating the sleeves and belly. Dark circles surrounded his eyes while wrinkles lined his forehead. Bits of food were entangled in his beard by the corner of his mouth. "And how are your duties as the pope? Are you able to handle them?"

"Yes, Your Majesty," Gale said and nodded his head once. "However, I think making Michelle a bishop may be a bit too

much for her to handle. Her father just passed away and she—
"

"Work conquers sorrow," Randel said and waved his hand. "It's best to keep her busy to distract her from her loss."

Gale swept his gaze over the king's unkempt body. *Are you really one to say that?* "Pardon my abruptness," he said and lowered his head, "but how are you doing now that Rudolph is gone? Isn't it about time we hold a proper funeral for him?"

"I'm fine, Gale," Randel said as his eyes narrowed. "The country requires me to be strong. Holding a funeral at this moment, after our people have been terrorized by the worms, would be inappropriate. When we recover, we'll hold a national holiday to honor the dead. We know that the worms can lie dormant for up to two months from our sources in Fuselage. We'll construct a memorial as a reminder of our resilience then."

"I understand."

"More importantly," Randel said as he leaned against his scepter, using it like a cane, "have you figured out the effects of the formation?"

Gale shook his head. "It seems like something that only the popes have knowledge of, but unfortunately, the knowledge wasn't passed on to me. I think it's best to leave it alone; however, I have noticed a marked decrease in the amount of mana surrounding it. It's most likely due to us burning the crystals from the vault to aid us in eliminating the worm-infested hosts. Let's hope nothing too catastrophic occurs when the formation runs out of energy."

***

Vur was sitting on top of the head of a giant purple spider facing Lindyss who was sitting on its butt. The two were surrounded by the fairies' birthflowers in the room Charon had teleported back to Konigreich. The purple spheres illuminating the room were now golden and splotches of gold decorated the purple leaves of the flowers.

428

The spider's body tensed as the walls around them trembled and the floor wobbled. Faint screams could be heard outside of the room, coming in from the newly added windows. Lindyss sighed and channeled her mana as a whirlwind swirled around the earthen block, stabilizing its position above the narrow tower.

"That's the third earthquake in a month," Lindyss said and looked out a window. People were running about, ducking underneath shelters made of bear skeletons. "We're really going to have to figure out what to do about this room."

Vur didn't respond as he played with the hairs near the spider's eyes. It was furry like a tarantula. He raised his head. "You said that you were going to tell me why once I beat Mr. Skelly in a war," he said and crossed his arms over his chest. "I won."

Lindyss raised an eyebrow. "You really beat him? Let me ask." She closed her eyes and an image of the undead skeleton leader appeared in her head. *Did Vur beat you in a mock war?* A moment passed, and Lindyss chuckled. "Sorry, Vur. Mr. Skelly says, 'he technically didn't beat me. He used his soldiers to win against my soldiers, so it can't be said that he, as a person, beat me. I did not lose. Skeletons never lose.'" Lindyss smirked. "You'll have to try again next time."

"That's not fair," Vur said and pouted.

"Skeletons never fight fair," Lindyss said and laughed. "And stop pouting. You've been hanging around the fairies too much."

"Then how am I supposed to make you tell me?" Vur asked and knit his brow. Why had Lindyss betrayed Stella?

"You don't," Lindyss said and brushed her hair behind her ear as she stood up, "so stop asking. It's a boring story anyway and a certain dragon would probably kill me if I told you."

"Who?"

"Your mother."

Vur tilted his head. "Grimmy?"

Lindyss burst out laughing before she walked away, careful not to step on the flowers on her way out.

***

"The nightmares again?"

Tafel nodded and plopped herself down onto her grandmother's bed. Her grandmother sat up with a groan and wrapped her arms around Tafel.

"You poor child," her grandmother said and rubbed her granddaughter's back. "Maybe you should take that strange creature for a walk."

"Strange creature?" Tafel asked and broke away from her grandmother's embrace.

"Yes," her grandmother said and pointed at a winged creature sitting on Tafel's head. "That one. The thing on your head. Have you not noticed?"

"On my head...?" Tafel asked as she raised her hand. She squeezed something soft. The creature squealed before hissing and ruffling her hair with its hooves. "Floofykins? How did you—, I don't understand. What? When did this happen?" Tafel sighed and held Floofykins in front of her face. "Well, you're Vur's granddaughter after all, so I can't really judge you by normal standards."

Floofykins stuck her tongue out before waving her hooves at Tafel. "Alright," Tafel said. "I'll walk you. Do you want to come, Grandma?"

Her grandmother shook her head. "I'm getting too old for midnight strolls with winged pigs."

Floofykins coughed once. Then she coughed again. And again. When Tafel thought she was done, Floofykins hacked up a hairball with a piece of paper sticking out of it. Tafel wrinkled her nose as she brushed away the stiff fur and read the letter:

Dear Tafel,

  Don't   *be*   *sad.*

Love,

Vur

430

"Ah, young love," her grandmother said, peeking over Tafel's shoulder. "You should clean that up before you store it, or it'll stink up all your other love letters."

"Grandma!" Tafel said as her face heated up. "This isn't a love letter!" She paused. "I think..."

"Mhm." Her grandmother lay back down. "And I'm an elf. Now go walk that pig before it pees on my bed."

Floofykins stuck her nose into the air and snorted.

40

In the royal gardens, two figures walked side by side: one demon, one winged pig. Tafel wore a silken bathrobe along with fuzzy, pink kitten-slippers. A cold breeze blew past, causing her to sigh and pull the bathrobe around her body tighter. A full moon hung in the sky, illuminating the plants and flowers decorating the road. Floofykins stopped next to a metal fence and raised one leg. The metal hissed and corroded as she marked her territory. Tafel's eyes widened as the metal bubbled and the fence collapsed in on itself.

"You're pathetic."

Tafel whirled around as Floofykins stopped mid-stream and turned her head towards the sound. Gabriel was standing behind them with his arms crossed over his chest. The moonlight glinted off of his light-blue armor, made from actual mithril instead of the fake armor Chad had given him last time. An orange morning star hung by his waist. The prince glanced at Floofykins and sneered before tilting his head up to look down on Tafel.

"Gabriel," Tafel said and crossed her arms.

"Didn't you hear what I said? You're pathetic. A loser. How could someone like you become the demon lord?"

Tafel snorted and turned around. "Let's go, Floofykins," she said to the snarling birdpig. "Trash like him isn't worth the effort."

"Oh?" Gabriel asked and chuckled. "And I suppose those thousands of innocent people were? I guess the demon lord only knows how to slaughter the weak and helpless."

Tafel froze mid-step. Floofykins tilted her head and nipped at Tafel's fingertips.

"You thought nobody would know? What a joke. You left too many survivors." Gabriel sauntered towards his sister. "It was easy for me to find out and that's after Dustin tried to hide it. I imagine it wouldn't be too hard for your dragon-boy lover to find out since the humans aren't trying to defend you at all. I wonder what he would think about a girl who slaughtered thousands of people in cold blood. It's like a match made in heaven—a monster falling in love with another monster." Gabriel grinned.

Tafel's body trembled. Her sword materialized in the air in front of her. "Shut up."

Gabriel breathed down the back of her neck. "Make me."

Tafel's left hand grasped the hilt of her sword, and she swung it while spinning around to face Gabriel. Gabriel raised his mace and blocked the blow. He was forced to take three steps to the side to steady himself. Floofykins hissed and spat a fireball at Gabriel's feet, causing him to swear and leap backwards. "Stupid mutt."

"What's your problem?" Tafel asked as she stabbed her sword into the ground. "I knew you were stupid, but I didn't think you'd be this stupid. You know you're weaker than me. Why provoke me?"

"Me? Provoke you?" Gabriel asked and chuckled. "No. That's not how the nobles will see it. After all, you killed Lamach earlier tonight and now you came to attack me. Bloodthirsty princess who's slaughtered thousands—including hundreds of innocent children—returns home and kills one brother while the other narrowly escapes with his life. That'd make a great story, eh?"

Tafel's eyes narrowed. "You killed Lamach?"

"Not me," Gabriel said with a smirk and shook his head. "You did. I don't use a sword after all."

"I suppose you're doing this so you can become the demon lord once they try to overthrow me? Which family is backing you? What makes you think I won't kill you here?"

Gabriel laughed and threw his mace to the side. "Can you do it, sister?" he asked with a smile and spread his arms to the side. "Take that sword and run it through my heart like you did to those countless innocents. The nobles won't care if you kill me, but the citizens will panic. They'll think, what if I'm next? If the demon lord is willing to kill her own brothers, what's to stop her from killing us?"

Tafel raised her sword and pointed it at Gabriel. The image of a child's face stricken with fear superimposed itself over her brother's. Tafel's hand trembled as she took a step forward. Childish screams resounded in her head, begging her to stop. She listened. Her sword slipped out of her hand as she hung her head and trembled while gritting her teeth. Floofykins whimpered and licked Tafel's hand while pushing her thighs with her hooves.

"That's what I thought. Pathetic." Gabriel walked over to his mace and hung it by his waist, doing his best to keep his body from trembling.

Floofykins growled at Gabriel and dashed towards his leg. She bit clear through his greave and shin bone, causing him to fall over and howl. Floofykins snarled and spat the bloody glob onto his face. Her wings flared outwards, and she pawed at the ground with her hoof like a bull before a charge.

"I'll kill you!" Gabriel howled as he grabbed his mace and swung it at Floofykins. She caught the shaft of the mace with her mouth and bit down. A crack formed on the orichalcum weapon before it broke completely. Gabriel stared at his now-headless mace before his brain registered pain in his unhurt leg. He screamed. Floofykins spat out another bloody glob and tackled Gabriel's chest, knocking his head against the ground—stunning him. She raised one leg and peed over his stomach before snorting and trotting back to Tafel's side. Grimmy had once told her to not eat humans. Now Floofykins knew why. They tasted terrible.

Tafel hugged Floofykins who rubbed her snout against Tafel's face, leaving bloody trails on her cheeks. "I want to see Vur," Tafel said with tears forming in the corners of her eyes. Her horns glowed silver, and the two disappeared, leaving behind a moaning demon prince with bubbling armor.

***

"Vur."

"Yes, Mom?" Vur asked as he sat cross-legged in front of Sera. The two were resting in a moonlit glade with fairy birthflowers carpeting the ground. The dragons had given him a space in the roost to plant the birthflowers; though, Grimmy took objection with Vur's new gardening hobby.

"I have a task for you," Sera said as she gazed at Vur with her golden eyes. "I can sense your grandfather's beginning to wake up. I want you to become the king of the humans; it'll be a nice present for him to celebrate his awakening."

"Oh," Vur said and nodded. "Why would it be a good present though?"

"Well," Sera said and raised her head to look at the stars in the sky, "he did try to wipe out the human race when they first invaded. However, something happened and he told us not to kill them before he went to sleep, but conquering them with you as the king should make him happy."

Vur scratched his head, which was starting to be full of hair again after having it shaved off by Lindyss' skeleton. "I don't really get it, but okay. I'll do it. Does it matter how?"

Sera shook her head. "Just try not to kill too many of them. That'll ruin the purpose of making you king," she said. Vur nodded. "You have around a decade or two at the current rate of his awakening." She unfurled her wings. "You can continue planting your flowers now. I love you. Take care."

"Bye, Mom," Vur said and waved as Sera flew out of the glade. He dug a hole in the ground, and a skeleton walked over, handing him a flower. He planted it and packed soil around its stem before nodding. Vur's body froze for a split second before he turned around with a smile. "Hi, Tafel."

Tafel had teleported behind him with Floofykins in her arms. "Good evening, Vur," she said with her eyes downcast. She raised her head as a tear streaked down her cheek. "Hold me?"

"What's wrong?" Vur asked as he stepped forward and embraced Tafel. Floofykins squealed in protest and slipped out from between the two. Tafel shook her head and rested her chin on Vur's shoulder. Her body trembled as she silently sobbed and wrapped her arms around Vur.

An eternity passed in silence before Tafel stopped trembling and leaned her upper body away from Vur. "Would you hate me if I did something bad?" she asked, staring into his eyes.

"Well, it depends on...," Vur said and stopped himself as Tafel's gaze shifted downwards and to the side. "No. I wouldn't."

"Really?" Tafel asked as she lowered her head. "What if you walked into a room and I was in the middle of killing a bunch of helpless children?"

Vur placed a finger underneath Tafel's chin and tilted her head upwards. "Then I'd ask if you wanted any help," he said.

Tafel avoided Vur's gaze. "But—"

Her eyes widened as Vur leaned forward and kissed her on the lips. Her body tensed for a second before she closed her eyes and reciprocated. Moments passed. Tafel broke away from Vur and stared at his chest, her cheeks flushed. "Learn to read the mood...," she said in a soft voice. "Jeez."

Vur smiled and shrugged as Tafel shook her head and sighed. "Feel better?"

"Mm."

"Good."

Four skeletons popped out of the ground and formed a makeshift bench with their bodies. Tafel sat next to Vur and Floofykins crawled onto her lap.

436

"Hey," Vur said. "Just wondering, but what did you do to become the demon lord?"

"Hm?" Tafel leaned her head against Vur's shoulder. "I beat up the previous demon lord in front of a bunch of nobles."

"I see."

"Why?"

"No particular reason."

***

"Vur? What are you doing here?" Paul asked with wide eyes. "And Ms. Besteck… I didn't think either of you would show up for the memorial."

Lillian stood next to Paul—frozen—with an ice cream cone on the floor in front of her. Vur and Tafel were standing in the center of a plaza filled with a countless number of humans giving them a wide berth. "I-it's been a while," Lillian said and lowered her head, lamenting over her fallen treat.

"Hey," Paul whispered and nudged Lillian. "Why are you being such a stranger?"

"I'm not being a stranger," Lillian hissed back. "We don't really know his fiancée after all."

"What are you two whispering about?" Vur asked and tilted his head. "I heard that the king was supposed to make a public appearance today in front of a lot of important people, so I decided to take a look."

Tafel blinked a few times and frowned as she thought back to a certain question Vur randomly asked her one night.

"Oh. Yeah," Paul said. "The king's declaring a national holiday out of respect for the ones who died during the worm outbreaks." He lowered his voice. "Rudolph and the pope were amongst the first casualties. Lillian and I were worried about you; you disappeared on us and we never heard from you again."

"Do you guys want to move somewhere less conspicuous?" Lillian asked. "It feels like everyone's staring at us."

"Everyone *is* staring at us," Paul said.

Tafel tugged on Vur's arm. "Can we move out of the crowd?" she asked with a tremble in her voice. "I don't like it."

"Our grandpa's back there," Paul said as he motioned in a vague direction. "We can go watch the memorial with him. He's not too fond of crowds either."

The sea of people parted as the group of four made their way out of the plaza. "What've you been up to for the past two months?" Paul asked as they headed towards a secluded corner.

"And what's with the flower tattoo?" Lillian asked as she pointed towards Vur's chest.

Vur looked down. Stella's birthflower had sunk into his skin and left an outline of a rose with its roots wrapped around his body. "A friend gave it to me," he said. "As for what I've been doing... making babies, I guess. It feels nice. I've also remodeled a mountain to make it more hospitable for my children."

Lillian's face turned red as she stared at Tafel whose face turned an equal shade of scarlet. Paul slapped his hand on Vur's shoulder and gave him a thumbs up.

"Vur...," Tafel said and glared at the dragon boy. "Can you not say such ambiguous things? People will take it the wrong way."

Paul cleared his throat as the group arrived in front of his grandfather. "Well, I don't think that was very ambiguous. What other meaning could that possibly have?"

"What are you talking about?" Grandpa Leonis asked and raised his eyebrow. "You must be Vur. I've heard a lot about you from Paul and Lillian." His eyes narrowed as his gaze landed on Tafel's horns. "And this young lady is?"

"Vur's fiancée who's sleeping with him before their marriage," Lillian said in one breath and stared at her toes.

Tafel stomped her foot. "We're not!"

"We aren't?"

"Not in the way she's talking about!" Tafel's face turned an even brighter shade of red.

438

"What's going on here?" Grandpa Leonis cupped his hand and whispered to Paul.

Paul cupped his hand and whispered back, "I don't know, but she's the demon lord, so we probably shouldn't tease her too much."

"Demon lord!?" Grandpa Leonis shouted and swiftly covered his mouth with his hands. A few people at the edge of the plaza turned their heads.

"It's in name only," Tafel said as she took a deep breath and closed her eyes. "I let my mom handle everything."

"I see...," Grandpa Leonis said and nodded. He placed his hands on Paul's and Lillian's heads. "You two have made yourselves some very interesting friends. I'm surprised, considering how ... special you are." He smiled at Lillian.

"Hey!" Lillian said and crossed her arms. "Don't make fun of me! It's not nice."

A cannon shot resounded through the air, and the murmurings of the crowd died down.

"Looks like it's starting," Paul said as he shielded his eyes from the sun with his hand. Gale and his entourage of bishops came into view from the northern side of the plaza followed by the king and his accompanying soldiers a few paces back. "I see Michelle. It looks like she became a bishop since we've last seen her."

"So she's getting even further out of your league is what you're saying?" Lillian asked as she elbowed Paul's ribs. "You have to step your game up. Look at Vur; he's walking straight for—, wait. Why's he walking that way? Hey, Vur? Uh, Ms. Besteck?"

"Call me Tafel, please. I'm younger than you two," Tafel said as she sighed. "Vur's going to cause a huge commotion any second now. I shouldn't have brought him here."

Grandpa Leonis burst out laughing. "I wonder what surprise that boy's going to show us," he said as the crowd parted and made way for Vur.

Gale stopped in his tracks when Vur walked in front of him. Vur tilted his head and squinted at Gale's face. "I know you," Vur said and rubbed his chin. "You're one of the volunteers that the skeletons brought." He turned away from Gale's blanching face and waved at a bishop behind the new pope. "Hi, Michelle."

"Vur?" Michelle asked. "You have to stand with the crowd. You're not supposed to pass the line by the guards."

"What line?" Vur asked. "No one stopped me." The guards standing near the line behind him scratched their cheeks and whistled, pretending not to notice.

The king frowned as the group of people in front of him stopped in their tracks. "Why'd you stop?" he asked and walked to the side of the bishops. His eyes widened when he saw Vur. "You!"

"There you are," Vur said and smiled as he walked around Michelle. He amplified his voice with wind magic. "I've come to seize the throne. Prepare yourself."

The king froze. "Huh?"

The crowd burst out into a commotion. Tafel slapped her forehead with her palm and sighed. Paul and Lillian stared ahead with their mouths gaping. Grandpa Leonis broke out into a booming laugh.

A flash of light emanated from the tattoo on Vur's chest and blinded the crowd. When they regained their vision, Vur was standing over the unconscious king with the royal crown on his head and golden scepter in his hand.

"That was easy," Vur said and walked back the way he came. "Oh, wait a moment. Paul wanted to be a bishop..." His eyes focused on the bishop standing next to Michelle. "Your build is the most similar to his."

Tafel squinted her eyes at Vur in the distance. "Is he stripping a bishop?"

"You're asking the wrong question," Paul said as he regained his composure. "Did he just assault the king?"

440

"I mean," Lillian said and rubbed her chin, "he did eat a god. Assaulting the king isn't as bad, right?"

Shouts and screams composed of many mixed emotions echoed through the air as the king's entourage encircled Vur. They readied their weapons as the bishops chanted. A few nobles in the crowd equipped their swords as well.

A black rune appeared on Vur's forehead. He snorted before shouting, "Kneel!"

Waves of energy poured out of his body and washed over every person present. Chills rolled down their spines as their legs turned to jelly while some people fainted outright. Everyone—except for Tafel—fell onto their knees with sweat pouring out of their bodies. With one word, Vur had silenced the capital.

"Does anyone object to me becoming king?" Vur's voice boomed throughout the plaza. Silence reigned as the people remained unmoving. Ten seconds passed.

"We object," a feminine voice said, breaking the silence. A golden spirit formed in the sky above the people.

"Wait, he's the one who ate Sir Edward," a different feminine voice said.

"But we still have to stop him," the spirit said in a male voice.

"I'm not dying for something like that," another voice said. "It doesn't matter who ends up as king."

The spirit cleared its throat. "We give the new king our blessing!"

"..."

Tafel sighed and closed her eyes.

Vur retracted his aura and smiled at the crowd before walking back to his group. The crowd broke out into whispers as they regained their strength.

"King? Him?"

"Is this real?"

"The spirits accepted him. It's my first time seeing them in person."

One man, wearing a white suit with an eagle crest on his shirt pocket, shoved aside the man beside him. "I can't accept this!" he shouted towards Vur who was making his way past him in the crowd. "Someone like you can't become king!"

Vur tilted his head and turned towards the man. "Oh? Then why didn't you say anything earlier when I asked if there were any objections?"

The man gritted his teeth. "That's because....," he said as his voice trailed off. "It doesn't matter. What's important is that, at this very moment, I refuse to accept you as king."

"As king, I deny your refusal," Vur said and continued walking towards Tafel.

"What's wrong with all of you?" the man shouted as he whirled around and gestured at the people in the crowd. "How can you just accept this!?"

A few nobles murmured in assent and nodded. The commoners exchanged glances with each other and avoided the man's gaze. "This doesn't change anything for us," one man with a straw-hat said. His pants were ragged and torn at the ankles. "The crown could change hands to a pig and our quality of living would be the same."

"How can you say that?" the man with the eagle crest asked and slapped the commoner. "The king cares about all his people! Letting someone like him"—he pointed at Vur's back—"become king will ruin the nation. I bet he doesn't know the first thing about running a country!" He shouted at Vur, "Do you know who I am!?"

Vur turned his head and narrowed his eyes. "Are you important?"

The man puffed his chest out. "Yes! I'm Raffgier, head of the Ruhr household! The amount of wealth and power I hold is second only to the royal family. There's no one who hasn't heard of me."

442

Vur nodded. "In that case, I declare Raffgier a traitor and strip him of his noble title and land. You," he said and pointed at the man with the straw-hat. "You're now the head of the Ruhr household."

"Eh?" both the noble and the commoner asked.

"You can't do that, Vur," Tafel said. She had teleported next to him during the commotion.

"Why not?" Vur asked and tilted his head, ignoring the flustered Raffgier.

"You just can't! It doesn't make sense," Tafel said as she sighed. "You're breaking the order of things. Apologize to the king and give that poor bishop his clothes back."

"Don't want to," Vur said and crossed his arms, hugging the bishop's clothes tighter. "I'm king."

The crowd fell silent as Tafel and Vur stared at each other.

"You can't just declare yourself as king," Tafel said.

"I just did. I performed a coup d'état."

"A coup can't be done by a single person!"

"Why not?"

"Because a single person can't … fight against a whole nation," Tafel said. Her voice trailed off as she hung her head.

"But I can," Vur said and tilted his head.

Tafel opened her mouth to speak but shut it a second later. She sighed. "You're right," she said after a pause. "But it still feels so wrong."

Vur smiled and wrapped his arms around Tafel. The people in the crowd exchanged looks with each other, but no one said a word as they ruminated over everything that transpired.

"Can… can I keep my land?" Raffgier asked.

"No. You're a traitor," Vur said without looking up. "Anyone else wish to express their displeasure about their new king? No? Good."

"Vurrrr," Lillian cupped her hands over her mouth and shouted from behind the crowd. "Can I be a duchess?"

"Hm? Sure, why not?" Vur replied back with his voice amplified by wind magic.

Lillian beamed at her cousin and grandfather. "I'm so glad we became friends with him."

Vur cleared his throat. "Since a lot of people are gathered here today," he said as he released Tafel, "I'd like to declare today the day of my coronation. I'm also renaming the nation to Konigreich the Second." He adjusted the crown on his head. "There. I just coronated myself." He waved his hand at Gale. "You can carry on with the memorial and what not now."

Gale's body twitched as he was broken out of his stupor. "Y-yes. Of course."

Vur grabbed Tafel's hand and led her towards the cushioned seat which was reserved for the king.

"You're just going to go with it?" Michelle whispered to Gale.

Gale nodded. "Of course. He gained the approval of our god," he whispered back. "If I don't listen to them, then who else would I listen to?"

"Hey," Vur said out loud. "Are you around, golden thingy?"

"Um, Your Majesty," Gale said as he dipped his head towards Vur. "The spirits don't just appear when called for."

Vur snorted. "If you don't come out, then I'm going to eat you the next time I see you," he said towards the sky.

Five seconds passed before a golden outline materialized in the sky. Smoke gradually filled the interior and a feminine sigh rang through the air as a frowning face appeared in the smoke. "Yes?"

"Nothing," Vur said and waved his hand. "I just wanted to see if you were there."

A vein appeared on the woman's forehead as she smiled at Vur.

***

Lindyss dropped her knitting needles. "Vur did what?"

Mr. Skelly cleared his throat. "He performed a coup and became the king of the humans."

"Why would he do something like that?" Lindyss asked and picked up her fallen woolen article. "It's not really an issue, but it would've been nice to know he was planning something like that."

"Perhaps he was bored?" Mr. Skelly asked and cackled.

"That really may be the case. Well, this works out pretty well," Lindyss said and rubbed her chin. "If Tafel's the demon lord and Vur's the humans' king, then the continent is pretty much united. I just hope he doesn't break anything important. Our spies did mention something about a weakening spell formation, correct?"

"Yes," Mr. Skelly said. "Unfortunately, the humans don't know what it does either. I don't get why they don't just ask their god."

"They wouldn't exhaust their energy just to answer a few measly questions," Lindyss said and snorted. "They have their pride, you know?"

41

Vur's eyes shot open as a short scream woke him up from his dreams. He sat up and wrapped his arms around the sitting figure in his bed. "Tafel."

Tears fell off Tafel's face, staining her silken pajamas as she let out muffled sobs. Her body shuddered, and she buried herself in Vur's embrace. "It's not just a dream," she said, her voice cracking. "I can still hear them blaming me. Cursing me."

"Really?" Vur asked. "Can you see them?"

Tafel shook her head. "I can sense them. It wasn't always like this," she said. "It started when we came to the human capital."

Vur frowned. "Hey, golden thing. Get out here."

A sigh echoed through the room as a shimmering gold light appeared at the foot of their bed, bathing the dark room with a soft glow. "Do you need us to fetch you water again?" a distorted voice asked as a female face started to form.

"No. Actually...," Vur said and tilted his head. Tafel pinched him. "Never mind. Can you see any other spirits in the room?"

The golden figure nodded. "There's a ton around you two. They seem very resentful. Very dark and depressed looking."

"Did you see them before?" Vur asked as he narrowed his eyes.

The figure scratched her cheek. "Err.... No?" she asked. The rune on Vur's forehead shone with a black light, counteracting the spirit's glow. "I mean yes! Yes! Please stop glowing like that."

"Why didn't you say anything earlier?" Vur asked as his rune dimmed. "They've been here for a while, haven't they?"

"We noticed them the first time we saw the demon girl," the spirit said. "It's not our responsibility to take care of a demon. Human souls wouldn't possess someone like that unless they really resented them during their death. If anything, she deserves it."

Tafel's nails dug into Vur's back as her body tensed. Vur glared at the golden spirit. "Get rid of them."

The spirit took a step backwards. "We can't do that," she said and took another step back. "It's not within our capabilities. Honest." She raised her hands above her chest. "Please don't eat me."

"Why?" Vur asked. "Aren't you a bunch of spirits mashed together? Why can't you take them too?"

"Mashed is such a crude description…," the spirit said and hung her head. "There are certain requirements for spirits to join us; these spirits don't satisfy them. They've already attached themselves to a corporeal object, and they're filled to the brim with resentment. You'd have to placate them and convince them to leave the demon girl alone."

"How?" Tafel asked. Her eyes were red and puffy, but at least the tears had stopped.

"Well, it depends. What did you do to them?" the spirit asked as she flew closer to Tafel and made grabbing motions at the air around her. "We're a bit curious. We haven't seen such resentment since the village massacres."

Tafel bit her lip.

"If you did do something similar to a massacre, then there's not much that can be done," the spirit said as she made a releasing motion and flew back to the foot of the bed. "They'll haunt you until you die, and then they'll try to consume your soul."

"Can't we just force them to leave?" Vur asked.

The figure snorted. "Do you know a necromancer?" she asked. "Just finding one is like finding a needle in a haystack and you want to have him cooperate with you?"

Tafel and Vur stood outside of a wooden door with the golden spirit floating behind them. "Go inside and wake the person up," Vur said to the spirit. Tafel gripped Vur's hand.

"Why me?" the spirit muttered as she passed through the door. "Even relegating me to be a humanoid rooster now."

Tafel and Vur disappeared in a silver flash of light and reappeared outside of the castle-like building. Tafel asked, "Should we really wake Auntie up like this?"

"It'll be fine," Vur said as the two backed away from the building.

A thunderbolt, that was as wide as a person was tall, struck the building and turned the night into day for three seconds. A terrified wail echoed through the air as the golden spirit rushed towards the sky through the hole left behind by the lightning. A massive hand made of hellfire shot out after her. She let out another shriek and dove towards Vur and Tafel. "Save me!"

Vur nodded. "Wait right here and I'll stop it," he said. The spirit hid behind them, and the black flames approached the trio on the ground. Vur squeezed Tafel's hand and she nodded. Her horns flashed, and the two of them disappeared, leaving the spirit behind.

The spirit whimpered as the flaming hand grabbed her, burning away her body until she was the size of a small bean. "Never again," she said as golden tears streamed down her cheeks. "I never want to see him again. Someone else can deal with him."

In the castle, Lindyss' was standing by the window with bloodshot eyes, glaring at the spirit in her spell's grasp. A vortex of black flames surrounded her body. She snorted and the flames dispersed. Moments later, Tafel and Vur appeared in her room.

"Hi, Auntie," Vur said with a smile.

Lindyss kicked him. "Auntie my ass. I told you to call me Lindyss," she said. "And don't send flamboyant glitter spirits

448

to wake me up ever again. I'll destroy it for real next time." She crossed her arms and plopped onto her bed. "What do you need?"

"Tafel has a lot of spirits haunting her," Vur said. "The golden thing said that a necromancer could get rid of them."

Lindyss nodded. "I can, yes," she said. "I just need a suitable host for each spirit." She closed her eyes and shuddered. A wave of mana washed over Vur and Tafel. After a minute passed, Lindyss opened her eyes with a frown. "There's too many spirits following you—at least five hundred, but I'm guessing a lot more. I can't get an accurate count."

"What's a suitable host?" Vur asked.

"A corpse or skeleton without a soul lingering nearby," Lindyss said. "I don't have that many spares, and animal bodies won't work either unless they were imprinted during life."

"Then we have to kill people to get rid of resentment caused by killing people?" Tafel asked and furrowed her brow.

"Eh? Just go raid a cemetery or two. Maybe ten," Lindyss said and smiled. "I'm pretty sure the humans entomb all their clergy."

"Isn't that wrong?" Tafel asked and bit her lip. "It'd be like blaspheming the dead."

"It's fine. They're dead," Lindyss said and waved her hand. "And Vur is king after all."

* * *

Vur, Tafel, and Lindyss stood in front of a one-story building. Its walls were smooth and painted white, pillars adorning the sides with vines and leaves sculpted on them. The door was made of a light-blue metal that reflected the moon. Tombstones were propped up around them, marking the end of a person's journey.

"Do you have the key?" Lindyss asked.

Vur shook his head. "Keys are unnecessary," he said and pushed on the door. The wall next to the doorknob cracked and shattered as the mithril-plated door swung open. Tafel sighed as pieces of the wall fell to the ground. The trio stepped inside the dark room. Upon entry, a light flashed and a golden spirit appeared.

"Intruders will be—," the spirit's voice trailed off. It opened its mouth and a trembling male voice came out, "What are you doing here, Your Majesty? Only members of the clergy may proceed beyond this point."

"Says who?" Vur asked and tilted his head. The spirit took a step backwards and gulped.

"It was decreed long ago by us," the male spirit said. "All the bodies preserved in this mausoleum may not be defiled. Each person entombed here had the qualifications to join us as god."

"It's not like you need your bodies anymore," Lindyss said with a smile. "Is it just your pride speaking? Nothing is eternal. Thinking you can preserve your bodies forever, so naïve." She shook her head.

The spirit glared at Lindyss and crossed his arms. "What do you intend on doing here?" he asked and narrowed his eyes. "An elf doesn't have the qualifications to be in the cemetery, much less the mausoleum." It snorted at Tafel. "A demon has even less of a right to be here."

"They're with me," Vur said and took a step forward.

"You also do not belong!" the spirit said with a shout. He thumped his arm across his chest and a golden tower shield materialized in his hand. "I, Sir Magnus, am the designated guardian of this place! Do not underestimate me. While I was alive, I was able to deflect the attacks of a phoenix. Now that I'm dead, I'm even stronger with the help of my comrades. The others may call you god eater, but I'm not afraid." His knees knocked together as he trembled.

Lindyss snorted. "So tell me," she said as the air around her crackled, "how strong am I compared to a phoenix?"

"Come!" Sir Magnus shouted and slammed his shield against the ground. A web of golden light spread out from the shield and enveloped the room.

Lindyss closed her eyes and spread her arms out to the side. Rumbling sounds filled the air as a vortex of wind surrounded the mausoleum while red clouds formed in the sky, crackling with black electricity. Dust rained down from the ceiling as the walls shook. Sir Magnus gritted his teeth as goosebumps formed along his body.

Vur tugged on Lindyss' arm, and the vortex stuttered. "I thought the corpses had to be intact," he said. "Why are you trying to destroy them too?"

Lindyss' eyes opened as the red clouds dispersed. "Oh. I forgot," she said and scratched her head. "I think I'm still a little grumpy since someone interrupted my nap."

Magnus cleared his throat. "So, you're leaving?" he asked, still bracing his shield. "Please?"

"Hmm? Of course not," Lindyss said as she pulled a bat skeleton out of her pocket. "I wonder how strong this minion will be if I use a spirit that was qualified to be a god." A shadowy tendril shot out of the bat skeleton and wrapped around Sir Magnus.

"What is this?" Magnus asked as he tried to grab the tendril. His hands passed through it. "Necromancy!? You're the Corrupted One!"

Lindyss smiled. "I'll be using your spirit to reanimate a corpse," she said as the tendril dragged Magnus towards the bat skeleton.

"This is impossible! I'm a god!" Magnus said as he dug his shield into the ground, attempting to break away. "You can't do this!"

"Sure I can," Lindyss said as the bat skeleton opened its mouth and sucked Magnus inside, shield and all. "The living will always be stronger than the dead." The skeleton flew on top of Lindyss' head and buried itself in her hair.

Tafel tilted her head. "Do you always carry a bat skeleton around with you?"

"Of course. You don't?"

"N-no," Tafel said and shook her head. "I've never found myself in a situation where I thought, 'I could really use a bat skeleton right now.'"

"Then you haven't been in too many situations," Lindyss said as she pulled another bat skeleton out of her pocket. "You can have this one. You never know, it may save your life one day."

Tafel raised an eyebrow. "Thanks, I guess?"

"I don't get one?" Vur asked.

"No. I doubt you'd ever be in a situation where your life was threatened," Lindyss said as she walked deeper into the mausoleum. "There's a stairwell going down. I'll use the spirits around Tafel to reanimate the corpses as we go."

"They won't try to kill me?" Tafel asked as she held Vur's hand and followed after Lindyss. A single torch illuminated the spiral staircase.

Lindyss shook her head. "They'll be under my control," she said. She pointed at the skeleton in her hair. "See how obedient this bat is?"

"Mm. This place is massive," Tafel said as she gripped Vur's hand tighter. Rows upon rows of sarcophaguses surrounded them on a marble floor. Each sarcophagus had a crystalline cover that revealed a pristine corpse resting on red silk within. Plaques with epitaphs hung on the foot of each sarcophagus.

Lindyss nodded. "According to that spirit from earlier, there should be corpses from before the humans landed on this continent," she said as she placed her hand on a sarcophagus and gazed at the corpse within. "I wonder how long it took Charon to transport all of this over here."

The group walked in a spiral pattern, reanimating each corpse along the way. The zombies lay unmoving with their

452

eyes open. An hour passed in this manner, but they had only reanimated half the corpses.

"It's fine if we just leave them here and have them pretend they're dead," Lindyss said. "There must've been a thousand bodies, but I still can't get an accurate sense on the number of spirits haunting you." She poked the skeleton on her head. "Is there another floor?" It chirped and nodded. "Well, we still haven't fully gone through this floor. We'll hit the way down eventually."

***

Gale's eyes widened as he sat up in bed. Sweat soaked the back of his shirt. "What is this feeling?" he asked himself as he shivered and looked around his room. He had moved into the previous pope's living quarters in the temple after he was promoted. He climbed out of bed and lit a torch while equipping himself with his staff. The halls were silent; the only sounds were his padded footsteps and ragged breaths. He muttered to himself, "The basement?"

He made his way to the bottom of the temple, finding nothing amiss along the way. He stopped in front of a mithril door and gulped as he retrieved a key from his necklace, unlocking the door. The door screeched as he pushed it open. A baleful aura washed over him, causing his knees to tremble and his teeth to chatter.

"The formation?" he asked. "How? What's happening?"

The once white runes that were engraved on the floor were cracked with black spots dotting them. Wisps of dark smoke rose out of the cracks, condensing into a ball at the center of the room. Gale slammed the door shut and dashed down the hall. "I need to get to the vault. This can't be good."

***

"And we're done with this floor. Nearly all the spirits have hosts now, just a couple left," Lindyss said as she exhaled and sat down on top of a sarcophagus. A ball of water materialized in her hand, and she took a sip. "I need a break."

453

"Thank you for doing this," Tafel said and lowered her head. She raised it again and looked around. "This place was really expansive, wasn't it? It makes you wonder how much time the humans have spent making it."

Vur nodded as he sat down next to Lindyss. "There's still another floor," he said and pointed at a stairwell in the corner of the room. "How long have we been here? I'm getting sleepy."

"About six hours," Lindyss said. "Two hours per floor." She stood up and stretched her arms above her head. "Let's take a peek at the fourth floor. Some of the epitaphs are really interesting."

"You've been reading them?" Tafel asked and raised an eyebrow. She glanced at the plaque attached to the foot of the sarcophagus closest to her. "Here lies Lady Poe, the first person to scale Mt. Berg. Passed away at 80 years old when she tripped over a chicken." Tafel frowned. "Are these real?"

Lindyss chuckled. "They are," she said. "You just chose one of the less heroic ones to read."

"Here lies Mr. Ratsel," Vur read aloud. "The only thing we know about him is his name, but he must have been important if I was asked to make a plaque for him. –Plaque Maker Josef."

"…"

"Well, the other four thousand were interesting, okay?" Lindyss crossed her arms and marched towards the stairwell. Vur and Tafel exchanged glances before following after her. The trio descended down the stairs, leaving footprints in the dust. At the bottom, there was a pair of double doors with two armored statues standing at the sides, facing each other.

"This wasn't here for the other floors," Lindyss said and examined the lock on the door. She hummed as she rubbed her chin and fiddled with the runes surrounding the lock. The door remained closed. She pointed at the keyhole and said, "Vur. Key."

Vur took a step forward and kicked the lock. Metal screeched as the doors were torn off their hinges, and a plume of dust erupted as the doors fell to the floor with a clang, causing the three to cover their faces. Lindyss waved her hand, and a fireball materialized in the air in front of her, illuminating the darkness ahead. The room was tiny with a single glass coffin resting upright in the center. A purple carpet lined the floor, and words were inscribed around the walls, leaving no white space.

Lindyss gasped as her body froze mid-step. Her eyes were locked on the figure in the coffin ahead. Vur tilted his head and blinked at the young man's preserved body resting behind the glass. "Do you know him?"

Lindyss' hands clenched into fists, but she didn't respond. Her body trembled as she took a step forward, eyes never leaving the corpse. Vur frowned and reached for Lindyss' arm, but Tafel grabbed his wrist and shook her head. She brought him to her side and put a finger to her lips as Lindyss took slow steps towards the coffin.

Vur opened his mouth, but Tafel placed her finger on his lips without taking her eyes off Lindyss. She shook her head again. Vur sighed while turning away from Tafel.

Lindyss placed her hand against the glass coffin. A single tear rolled down her cheek and dropped to the floor. After a few minutes passed, she sighed and wiped her face as she turned around, displaying a slight smile that didn't reach her eyes. "Let's go," she said and brushed past Vur. "We'll dig up a few corpses in the cemetery outside and place the rest of the spirits in those."

"You're not going to reanimate him?" Vur asked, taking one last glance at the man in the coffin before he followed after Lindyss.

"No," Lindyss said as she trekked up the stairs. The fireball flickered out of existence, returning the room to darkness. "He deserves to rest." The trio remained silent as they climbed to the third floor. Lindyss turned around and waved her arm, causing a wall of earth to seal off the stairwell.

"Who was he?" Tafel asked as the group made their way out of the mausoleum. She looked at her toes as she walked. "If you don't mind me asking, that is." She squeezed Vur's hand as Lindyss continued to walk in silence. A minute passed.

"Here lies Vincent the Dragonslayer," Lindyss said, her voice steady. "If any man deserved to join our ancestors in the afterlife, then it would be him. Unfortunately, he paid the greatest sacrifice for the sake of humanity." She fell silent.

"Dragonslayer?" Vur asked.

"He didn't actually slay any dragons," Lindyss said and gritted her teeth. "He was the one who injured the patriarch and forced him to sleep."

"My grandpa?"

"Yes."

"How?"

"With a sword."

"What kind of sword?"

"Orichalcum."

"He used an orichalcum sword to injure Grandpa?"

"Yes."

"Did he use magic?"

"No."

"Was he that strong?"

Lindyss snorted and didn't reply. Tafel tugged Vur's arm as he opened his mouth to ask another question. Vur frowned. "You're acting strange, Auntie. Are you on your period?"

"Die." Lindyss whirled around and threw a black lightning bolt at Vur's face. "What do you know about periods, you brat? And call me Lindyss!"

A black aura enveloped Vur's hand as he caught the lightning bolt. He beamed at Lindyss, and the black lightning crackled before dispersing. "That's better. A mad Auntie is better than a sad Auntie," Vur said. "Maybe I should tell Grimmy that you were sad today."

"If you tell Grimmy, I'll kill you and feed your soul to a squirrel," Lindyss said and ruffled Vur's hair. She smiled with her eyes narrowed into crescents. "And then I'll feed the squirrel to Tafel. Understand?"

Tafel's face blanched. "He understands," she said and covered Vur's mouth with her hand.

"But seriously," Vur said as he pulled Tafel's hand away from his mouth. "How was he that strong?"

Lindyss sighed. "Resentment," she said as she turned back around and headed towards the mausoleum's exit.

"Resentment?"

Lindyss nodded. "If the humans' god is made up of spirits who must have certain qualifications, then what happens to the spirits who fail to join? Surely you don't expect every commoner and villain to become a god. People would just kill themselves if that was the case," she said. "That man chose to harbor all the spirits who failed to become god and gained immense power, but he lost himself in the process." She sighed as she pushed open the door leading outside. A sliver of sunlight shone on her face.

"Then where are all the spirits now?" Tafel asked.

Lindyss shrugged. "The humans probably sealed them away somewhere..." Her voice trailed off as Mr. Skelly's words came back to her. She mumbled, "Weakening formation?"

***

"The formation's been stabilized."

Gale was kneeling on the floor while a golden spirit stood in front of him with its arms across its chest. A white crystal emitted yellow smoke underneath it, flowing into the spirit's body. The runes on the floor beneath them were completely golden; there were no signs of the black spots that had existed before. The cracks had been repaired, and an extra layer of golden light laminated the floor.

"You did well in informing us, Gale," the spirit said and nodded. "We've been too preoccupied with the new king and surveillance in the outskirts of the kingdom."

"Thank you for the praise," Gale said, still kneeling. He hesitated before speaking. "If you don't mind me asking, what exactly does this formation do?"

The spirit sighed. "I suppose you have the right to know as pope," it said. "Let me ask you a question. What happens to an animal after it dies?"

"It stops moving," Gale said and nodded.

The spirit blinked. "Obviously! I meant what happens to its soul?" Gale opened his mouth, but the spirit stopped him. "Wait. Judging from your previous answer, I'll have to start with an even more basic question. What is a soul? What is it made of?"

"The soul is a person's essence," Gale said and frowned as he rubbed his chin. "Is it made of mana?"

"Close," the spirit said. "The soul is the energy that generates mana. Every person's soul differs in power which causes different constitutions between people. Now, what happens to an animal's soul when it dies?"

"It disperses into the surroundings, right? That's why people level up."

"Incorrect," the spirit said and sighed while shaking its head. "The education system truly is failing. The residual mana is what disperses; the soul remains intact. How do you think resurrections work if the soul disperses?"

"Err."

"Never mind that," the spirit said and sighed again. The crystal underneath it dimmed as it released a noticeably lower volume of smoke. "I'm running out of time, so I can't hold your hand all the way to the answer. Listen up! Not all souls are equal. Some get tainted as they go through life, whether by evil thoughts or outside measures. As god, we only accept the purest of souls; however, the tainted souls still linger: some are

458

reanimated as undead, some are eaten by certain beasts, and others are reincarnated and given a chance to become pure again. This formation seals the souls who are beyond hope." The spirit's image flickered as wisps of smoke trailed out of its body. "Don't touch anything and let us know if it weakens again."

"I understand," Gale said and scratched his head. "I do have one last question."

"Speak," the spirit said. Its feet blurred and turned into smoke, followed by its calves.

"Why do I need a crystal to summon you but King Vur doesn't?"

"He summons a powerless version of us. The crystal provides us with a medium through which we can apply our strength," the spirit said. Half of its body was gone.

"Doesn't that mean you can stop your dispersal right now?" Gale asked and tilted his head. "You'll just be powerless, but still here, no?"

The spirit cleared its throat as it scratched its nose. "That is.... We're very busy," the spirit said and nodded as its neck disappeared. "Have to do god stuff, y'know? If every Jack and Jill could summon us at will, we'd never get to have any fun— err, important stuff done."

"But..." Gale sighed as the spirit disappeared completely. The dim crystal on the floor cracked and dissolved into dust.

42

Raffgier wrung his hands together while gritting his teeth. He was sitting at a circular table with three men standing before him. They hung their heads, staring at their toes. A banner with an eagle crest hung above the four men, and a bloody straw-hat lay in the corner of the room.

"What do you mean the poison was ineffective?" Raffgier asked as he slammed his fist against the table. "How incompetent are you fools? I paid you quadruple the normal costs, and you come back with no results. Explain yourselves."

"There's not much to explain, Sir Raffgier," the man on the far left said as he raised his head. "I personally handed the king the goblet with the striped snake's venom inside of it. He drank all of it in one gulp, but nothing happened. I later applied the venom to a passerby who died almost instantaneously."

Raffgier snorted. "Then you should have tried again," he said as he leaned back against his chair. "Doesn't your organization guarantee the death of anyone for the right price?"

The man in the middle sighed. "Sir Raffgier, we've already helped you reclaim your land and noble title, not to mention the previous deeds we've done for you," he said and rubbed his bald head. "You should already know we're the best around. The target is a little more difficult. We'll need more time."

"I don't have time," Raffgier said and ground his teeth together. "Who knows when that brat will decide to check on my household and find that I'm back in power? I don't care what you have to do. If you can't kill him, then turn the people against him. Kill a few bishops and frame him. I don't care; just get him off the throne. Do you understand me?"

"We understand," the man in the middle said and nodded. "It wouldn't be good for us either if we lost our biggest customer."

"Good. Don't disappoint me again. Call Julia in here on your way out," Raffgier said as he exhaled and clasped his hands together. The three men nodded and exited the room. Raffgier closed his eyes and tilted his neck towards the ceiling.

"You called for me?" a feminine voice asked.

Raffgier's eyes snapped open. "Yes. I want you to get in contact with all the nobles who are discontent with the king"— his eyes narrowed—"demons too. Surely not all of them are satisfied with such a young, female demon lord. Rope them in with treasures. Spare no expense on the gifts; we want everyone to cooperate."

A chill ran down Julia's spine as she lowered her head. "I understand, Sir Raffgier. It will be done."

***

In the royal dining room of the castle, Vur was sitting across from Tafel with a table filled with food between them. Vur was shirtless with his crown resting on an empty chair beside him. Tafel was wearing a purple sleeveless dress that stopped at her ankles. Vur made a face as he swallowed his drink and sniffed the empty goblet.

"Was it poisoned again?" Tafel asked as she eyed the liquid in the goblet by her plate. She sighed and put her fork down as Vur shrugged. "You shouldn't drink it if it is, you know?"

"Sometimes it tastes nice," Vur said as he rinsed his mouth with a conjured ball of water. "And you know it won't hurt me." He glanced at the rose tattoo on his chest. Its roots pulsed with a slight purple glow.

"But still, it makes me uneasy," Tafel said and frowned. "You go through ten assassination attempts a day. There's no need to take unnecessary risks. Why don't you do something about the people targeting you?"

"They'll give up eventually," Vur said as he cut his steak. "It's a waste of effort. My problems tend to go away if I ignore them long enough. The attempts are already starting to lessen."

Tafel sighed and shook her head. She nibbled on a piece of bread and leaned back in her chair. She remained silent as Vur ate, a small smile appearing on her lips as Vur brought a cube of meat to his mouth with his fork.

"What?" Vur asked after he swallowed his food.

"Nothing," Tafel said and giggled. "I was just thinking back to the first time you ate with my parents. You've gotten better at not breaking things."

Vur stuck his tongue out before focusing his attention on his steak. "I've gotten better at a lot of things."

"Oh? Like what?"

Vur rolled his eyes. "Like everything."

Tafel smiled as she placed her bread down. "I suppose that's true," she said and leaned forward. "You've gotten better at controlling your emotions and thinking before acting. Although your common sense hasn't improved one bit."

Vur shrugged. "I think my common sense works well. It's everyone else's that doesn't make sense."

"Mm. You're right. Everyone else is clearly wrong," Tafel said and nodded. She rested her chin on her palm. A moment of silence passed as Vur chewed on his steak. "Hey."

"Yes?"

Tafel's cheeks flushed. "When are you going to marry me?" Her gaze lowered to the food on her plate. "Because, you know. We're almost seventeen and all," she said in a soft voice. "Most girls are married when they're sixteen."

Vur blinked a few times. "I thought you didn't want to get married young," he said and scratched his head. "Didn't you want to be an adventurer?"

"What does being an adventurer have to do with marrying young?" Tafel asked and raised her head. "There are plenty of married adventurers."

462

"I don't know," Vur said and rubbed his chin. "I just assumed you wanted to explore the world before you got married."

"I can still explore the world," Tafel said and crossed her arms. "And it'll be more fun if you came along too. This is why I said you have no common sense. Jeez."

Vur slowly nodded his head. "I see," he said and wiped his mouth with a napkin. "Then let's get married. How do we do that?"

Tafel froze. "Um. I'm not too sure on the details myself," she said and stared at her hands. She nodded. "Let's tell our parents first."

Vur swallowed the rest of the food on his plate in one gulp. "Alright," he said and nodded. "We should go see my parents first before they decide to sleep for a few months." The two stood up and left the room, leaving the dishes behind.

A boy with a suit flinched as the door opened and Tafel and Vur stepped out. "Y-you're done eating, Your Majesty?" the boy asked with wide eyes. His face was slightly pale.

Vur nodded. "You can clean up now."

The boy lowered his head and nodded.

"Hey," Tafel said. "Don't you think he's acting suspicious? He's probably the one who poisoned you, you know?"

Cold sweat rolled down the boy's back as he froze in place.

Vur shrugged. "I know, but it doesn't matter," he said and held Tafel's hand. "He's just the messenger. Let's go before it gets too dark." The two walked down the hall, ignoring the frozen boy. Only after Vur and Tafel rounded a corner did he dare blink.

***

Julia stood across from Raffgier's table with her head lowered. Raffgier's face was red and veins bulged on his forehead. "You're saying none of the nobles want to join forces with me?"

Julia nodded. "They accepted the gifts at the start, but eventually all of the gifts were returned," she said. "They requested we not ask them again in case they're mistaken for colluding with a traitor."

Raffgier's armrest splintered as his right hand clenched into a fist. "What is the meaning of this?"

Julia pulled a stack of letters out of her bag and passed it to Raffgier. "All the nobles who were originally receptive to the idea have attempted their own assassinations and failed. To quote Sir Klug, 'I refuse to fight against an enemy that drinks poison like water and uses a sword like toilet paper.'"

Raffgier ground his teeth as he read through the letters.

"Not only that," Julia said with her head still lowered, "but the assassins' guild has refunded us fully. They said that after further investigation, they've come to the conclusion that it's best not to anger him due to his background. The full report is within that stack of letters.

"Also, we've received reports from multiple sources saying skeletons have been delivering food to the poor ever since Vur removed the soldiers stationed on Konigreich's borders. We've been unable to gain the support of the nobles, and Vur has gained the support of the masses."

Raffgier's face blanched as he read letter after letter. He sighed and rubbed his temples. "Take all the gifts we sent to the nobles and consolidate them," he said after a while. He crossed his arms and nodded.

Julia raised her head. "Understood," she said. "Who's the recipient?"

"We'll send it to the king. A spy says he's planning on having a wedding," Raffgier said as he leaned back into his chair. "If you can't beat them, join them. Who knows, I might be able to gain more benefits from Vur than I did from Randel."

Julia smiled. "I'll have it ready to be sent at a moment's notice."

***

"Hey, Mom," Vur said as he stepped inside of a cave. Tafel followed behind him with Floofykins in her arms. Moonlight shone into the cave from behind the two, illuminating a small mountain of blue scales ahead of them. The mountain twitched and stirred, revealing a pair of golden eyes.

"Vur. You're back," Sera said and yawned, revealing rows of foot-long teeth. A tiny puff of smoke trailed out of her nostrils. She eyed the lopsided crown on Vur's head. "You're already king? It doesn't feel like I've slept for that long."

Vur nodded. "It was easy," he said as Sera used her claw to straighten his crown. "Is Dad around? I wanted to talk to both of you."

Sera grunted and swished her tail, thumping it against a wall of golden scales hidden behind her. A snorting sound came out of the wall, followed by a mumble, "Just two more months." Lips smacked and snoring sounds followed. Sera thumped her tail against Vernon's back again.

"Huh?" Vernon's eyes shot open. His nictitating membrane flickered a few times as he raised his head. "Oh. Long time no see, Vur. Is that Tafel? You're both less tiny now."

"Vur wants to speak with us, pay attention," Sera said as she crawled onto her haunches. Vernon stretched his front paws forwards and arched his back before crawling next to Sera. Tafel gulped and squeezed Floofykins tighter, using the winged boar as a charm of bravery.

"I want to marry Tafel," Vur said.

The two dragons blinked and stared in silence as if they were waiting for more. A few seconds passed. Sera tilted her head, and Vernon yawned while asking, "That's it?"

"Yes," Vur said and nodded.

The two dragons exchanged glances. "Then marry her?" Sera asked as she tilted her head the other way. "Is someone stopping you? Do I have to destroy everything they hold precious?"

Vur scratched his head. "No. No one's stopping us," he said. "It's just that Tafel said I had to talk to you two first before we could get married." He skillfully redirected the two dragons' gazes towards his future wife.

"Y-yeah," Tafel said and nodded as Floofykins squealed from her tightening grip. "Usually the parents want a say in their children's marriage partners…"

Sera snorted. "Humans and their weird traditions," she said and crawled back onto her belly. "Isn't it enough for Vur to kill all his potential rivals? Why do we have to do anything?"

Tafel's face blanched while Vernon grinned and nuzzled Sera's neck with his snout.

"Is that what Dad did?" Vur asked.

Vernon chuckled and shook his head. "It was your Mom who claimed me," he said and focused his gaze on Tafel. "Don't let anyone steal Vur from you now."

Tafel nodded with her face still pale. "I won't," she said and raised her chin. "Does this mean you approve of me?"

"We'll approve of whomever Vur chooses," Sera said and rested one finger on Vur's head, ruffling his hair. "Does this mean you're going to hold a human wedding?"

"Or demon," Tafel said and breathed a sigh of relief. "It doesn't matter really. It'd be great if you two showed up. I'll be sure to prepare a lot of food."

Sera smiled. "If my child decides he wants to have a wedding, then I suppose it's my duty to show up," she said and retracted her claw from Vur's head, "even if I think it's silly. If Prika comes back from her journey, I'll let her know. She always had an odd fascination for the romance of humans."

"Thank you," Tafel said and smiled. "I'll send a message with the details later on. We still have to talk to my mom about this."

Sera grunted and lowered her head onto her claws. She yawned and snapped her jaws shut. Her eyes closed, and she drifted off to sleep while Tafel and Vur made their way out of the cave.

A silver light enveloped Tafel and Vur as their bodies disappeared from the cave entrance, but Floofykins escaped from Tafel's arms and crawled onto Sera's head before she was transferred too. After multiple teleports, the duo reappeared in a hallway with an oak door in front of them. Tafel took a deep breath and knocked on the door. "Mom? Are you awake?"

"Tafel!? Just a minute," Mina's voice said from behind the door. Tafel and Vur exchanged glances as they waited. Vur squeezed Tafel's hand. The door creaked open, and Mina stepped out, closing the door behind her. Her face was slightly flushed while her hair was disheveled with her pajama buttons mismatching. She flinched at Vur, but regained her composure and clasped her hands behind her back, nodding while asking, "What is it, Tafel?"

Tafel lowered her head and wrung her hands. "Can we go inside? It's a bit sensi—"

"I want to marry Tafel," Vur said and wrapped his arm around Tafel's shoulder. "Give me your blessing."

Tafel froze with her mouth still open as her face heated up. Mina also froze, staring at Vur with wide eyes. Silence ensued.

A voice broke the silence. "Mina? Is everything okay out there? I suddenly felt uneasy."

Tafel blinked a few times as she regained her senses. "Is that Dustin?" she asked. She gasped and raised her head to inspect her mother's clothes. She hadn't noticed their condition at first because of her own nerves. "Were you two...?"

"No!" Mina said and shook her head, causing her hair to become even more disheveled. "We were just discussing ... demon lord things. Since you're never home after all."

Tafel opened her mouth but closed it again before nodding.

"I'm marrying Tafel," Vur said and stared into Mina's eyes. "My parents already agreed."

Mina shivered as a chill ran down her spine. She sighed and closed her eyes. "I had a feeling this would happen one day," she said. "If that's what Tafel wants, then I can't refuse. Thank you for letting me know." She smiled at Tafel. "Am I invited to the wedding?"

Tafel paused before nodding. "I'll let you know the details later. We still haven't really decided on anything," she said and scratched her head.

Mina chuckled. "You should go see Prim. She's very good at planning weddings. I bet she'll be delighted to see how you've grown."

"We'll do that," Tafel said and curtsied. "Enjoy the rest of your night."

"Have fun discussing war tactics in bed with Dustin," Vur said.

Mina's hand stopped mid-wave, and she let out a sigh as Tafel and Vur walked down the hallway. She opened the door and walked back inside, glaring at the man on the bed. "You should've stayed silent."

Dustin scratched his head.

***

"Everything's so expensive," Tafel said and frowned as she placed a magazine on her lap. A picture of a white wedding gown was on the cover page. After discussing with Prim, they had gone to a few more places announcing their plans. Their final stop was the royal gardens in the humans' castle. Tafel wanted to plan things in an uncluttered space. "Everything's handmade by elves. I'd have to use all the earnings I made in Fuselage if I want to buy even half of these things."

"Who gave you that magazine?" Vur asked and tilted his head as he leaned back on the bench. A stack of letters lay on the empty space next to him. "And why don't you just use the money from the treasury?"

"Auntie gave it to me," Tafel said and sighed while tilting her head up towards the sky. "And we can't use the money from any of our treasuries. That's for the country."

Vur scratched his nose. His gaze shifted to the side. "Right. Of course. For the country."

Tafel stared at him. "Don't tell me you—"

"Hey, there's a letter from someone named Raffgier," Vur said as he picked up the letter on top of the stack.

"Raffgier.... Isn't that the noble who you bullied?" Tafel asked. "Why's he still using his family's stamp?"

Vur shrugged. "Dunno," he said as he tore open the letter. He read through it and raised an eyebrow. "He's begging for forgiveness and wants to cover all the costs of the wedding."

Tafel's eyes sparkled. "All of them?" she asked and snatched the letter out of Vur's hands. She smiled and flipped the letter over, looking for a backside. "I want everything on the catalog."

"And you say I'm the bully."

"He offered," Tafel said and hugged Vur's arm. "Hurry up and forgive him."

"Alright," Vur said and snapped his fingers. A skeleton popped out of the ground and saluted. "Tell Raffgier he's forgiven and give him this catalog. Tell him to buy everything and send it to the royal castle."

"As you wish," the skeleton said and bowed before it jumped into the hole it previously made.

The two stared at the broken ground. "About that royal treasury," Tafel said, her voice trailing off.

"Royal treasury? Did the humans have one of those?" Vur asked. "I think it was empty before I became king. Definitely."

"Vur."

"Yes?"

"You're a terrible king."

"Yup."

Tafel sighed. "I'm not letting you make any administrative decisions when we get married."

"But I like flipping coins."

Tafel fell silent. Her brow furrowed. "Please tell me that's not how you make decisions regarding your country."

"That's not how I make decisions regarding my country."

"Are you just saying that because I told you to?"

"Yes," Vur said.

Tafel clasped her hands together and closed her eyes.

"What are you doing?" Vur asked.

"Praying for your people."

***

Michelle yawned as she signed a piece of paper with a quill. She didn't know bishops had so many administrative duties—it felt like weeks since she had last rested. She was about to grab another piece of paper when a short, pig-like squeal pierced her ears. The paper dropped to the ground as she whirled around and pressed her face against the window. A small smile appeared on her lips before she dashed out of the room.

"Hey, what's going on?" Michelle asked as she stepped around a pillar, entering the temple's courtyard. Paul was standing by a bench with a flowery envelope in his hand. There was a skeleton-sized hole in the ground next to him. Michelle walked next to the culprit who made the squeal and peered over his shoulder. "I heard a strange noise, so I decided to check it out."

Paul shrugged. "I'm not sure," he said and scratched his head. "I was practicing some sermons when a skeleton popped out of the ground. I tried to banish it, but it just threw a letter at me and ran away. It's directed at the pope."

"We should cleanse it then open it. Maybe it's a trap," Michelle said with a nod. A white light enveloped the envelope before fading away. "Well, it looks like it wasn't cursed. Open it."

Paul frowned and tore the envelope open. A letter lay inside. "Should I read it? It's just a normal letter. Maybe it's confidential."

Michelle snatched the letter out of his hand and read it. She gasped. "Vur's getting married to Tafel and wants Gale to officiate for them," she said with wide eyes. "Do you know what this means!?"

Paul scratched his head. "What are you getting so excited for? We already knew they were engaged."

"Yes, but that was before Vur became king!" Michelle waved the letter in front of Paul's face. "The human king is marrying the demon lord! This is huge! Let's go tell Gale!" Michelle grasped Paul's hand and dragged him towards the temple while sprinting.

The two arrived in front of a room with a pair of black double doors. Michelle let go of Paul's hand and knocked. She kept knocking on the door until it creaked open, revealing Gale's bleary-eyed face. "What's going on? It's not even seven yet."

"Vur's marrying the demon lord!" Michelle said and smacked Gale's face with her hand as she extended the letter towards him. "Oops. Sorry. I didn't mean to hit you."

Gale rubbed his nose and retrieved the letter from Michelle's hand. He frowned as his eyes scanned the page. "I'm not sure if this is a good idea," he said as he rubbed his chin. "It's only been around two months since he became king. There's no way people will approve of this. For now, keep this a secret."

"What do you mean won't approve?" Paul asked and crossed his arms. "He's been king for two months and no one's tried to assassinate him yet. That must mean he has some form of approval, right? Besides, he's been delivering food to the poor and hungry for the past two months. According to Lillian, the citizens love him. Although I do wonder how he's funding that."

"Urgent news!" A teenager, wearing a white robe, ran down the hall towards the trio. "Your Holiness. Seniors," he said and nodded at the three. "The king has announced he's going to have a wedding with the demon lord. Thousands—maybe millions—of skeletons are marching through the nation and announcing it through song. I think this may be the first time everyone's awake before seven in the morning."

Gale let out a sound that suspiciously sounded like a whimper before he fell to the ground and curled up into the fetal position. His hands covered his ears as his body rocked back and forth.

"Err…" Michelle tilted her head before smiling at the boy. "I think it's best if you let the other clergy know too."

The boy stopped gawking and nodded. He took one last look at the quivering pope before turning around and dashing off.

"Gale?" Michelle asked as she poked the crying pope with her foot. "Are you alright?"

"No more singing. No more singing," Gale mumbled through sobs. "Please. Have mercy."

Michelle and Paul looked at each other with their eyebrows raised. Michelle knocked his hand away from the letter and picked it up. "I get dibs on officiating."

43

Tafel stood in front of a mirror with her arms out to the sides. Prim was behind her, fussing over the white wedding dress that clung to Tafel's body. The one-horned maid smoothed out the cloth on Tafel's torso before she stood up straight and smiled.

"You look beautiful," Prim said as she circled around the demon lord. "I always knew I would help you wear a wedding dress, but I never would've thought you'd be the demon lord. Your mother must be proud."

"You think so?" Tafel asked as she twisted from side to side, observing the dress ripple in the mirror.

"I know so," Prim said with a nod as she reached for the veil hanging on the rack next to her. "I bet your father would be proud too if he was still around."

Tafel snorted and rolled her eyes. "Yeah, if he wasn't busy torturing people."

"Don't snort. It's not ladylike," Prim said and combed Tafel's hair before setting the veil on her head. "I watched your father grow up; in fact, I was his etiquette teacher. He wasn't always evil. Or, maybe, he was but really good at hiding it." She sighed.

Tafel frowned as Prim slapped away her hand when she tried to adjust the veil in front of her face. "Can we not talk about him?" Tafel asked. "I hardly even remember him."

"Of course." The two fell silent as Prim adjusted the white veil.

"Wear these," Prim said and placed a pair of light-purple heels in front of Tafel. She nodded as Tafel followed her orders. "You look great."

"Thanks, Prim," Tafel said as she took a few steps. "For everything."

Prim chuckled. "Just doing my job," she said with a smile. "I'll teach your children too when the time comes. I bet you two would make cute babies."

Tafel's face flushed. "You don't care that he's a human?" she asked, avoiding Prim's eyes.

"Ah," Prim said with an exhale. "I've seen too many things to be shocked by a human marrying a demon."

"Honestly, I thought you'd be more against this marriage," Tafel said and lowered her head.

"Why? Because I'm an etiquette teacher?"

"Well, yes. But you're also kind of old," Tafel said. Prim glared at her. "Old-fashioned, old-fashioned. Not old." Tafel fidgeted and clasped her hands.

"Cheeky brat," Prim said and sighed. "Haa. Time really does fly. It seems like only yesterday when I was helping your mother change your diapers."

***

"Are you sure this is right?" Vur asked as he tilted his head and looked in the mirror. Rella and Bella hovered in the air behind him, grinning from ear to ear with red faces.

"Of course! Of course!" Bella said while gasping. "Trust us! There's no way we'd make a fool out of our king, right?"

Rella burst out into laughter as tears streamed down her cheeks. "You look beautiful, Vur. Absolutely stunning," she said as she rolled around in the air.

Vur frowned at the frilly, white dress adorning his body. "I'm pretty sure the bride is the one that's supposed to wear the dress."

"No, no," Bella said and shook her head. "That's for olden times only! Times have changed while you were comatose! We're entering a new era. Everyone knows that the groom also wears a dress. The books you've been reading are way toooo old."

474

"Right," Rella said and nodded. Her body shook as she gasped for air. "Now you just have to wear this wig and everything will be perfect!" She held up a bright-red wig with shoulder-length hair.

"I refuse," Vur said and crossed his arms over his chest. "I think my hair is an appropriate length."

Rella sighed as she dropped the wig. "Well, I'll take what I can get," she said and grinned. "Let me trim some edges and apply some hairpins."

"And this dress won't be complete until you have breasts," Bella said with a nod. "I can illusion those up for you. And here, these heels totally match your outfit."

Vur frowned as he stared at the pink heels in front of his feet. Bella tugged on his dress. "What are you waiting for? Tafel's going to be wearing heels too, you know? What if she ends up taller than you?"

"Makes sense," Vur said and slipped on the shoes as flecks of his hair drifted in the air.

"How about some earrings?" Rella said as she put away her scissors. "I think a tiny diamond stud would suit you perfectly. Actually"—Rella hid a needle behind her back as Vur glared at her—"we probably shouldn't poke any holes in you."

Rella and Bella flew in a circle around Vur. "I'm almost jealous of how pretty he looks," Bella said and frowned.

"He's still missing something," Rella said and rubbed her chin. "I know! Get the primer. He needs some blush." Rella nodded and picked up a bottle of foundation.

"What are you going to do now?" Vur asked as he eyed the bottle in Rella's hand.

"Some wizardry," Rella said and giggled. "Just trust us and don't ask any more questions. Close your eyes too. Everyone's going to be speechless with awe by the time we're done with you."

'You're sure he's not going to kill us, right?' Bella mouthed as she applied the primer to Vur's face.

'It's okay,' Rella mouthed back as she waited for Bella to finish. 'No one's going to say anything because they'll be too scared to criticize him. Remember that donkey tale about the king who went around naked that Mom used to tell us?'

Bella nodded as she placed the primer back on the table. 'I think it's best if we stay away from him for at least a hundred years afterwards though,' she mouthed as she got the blush ready.

"Are you done yet?" Vur asked.

"No!" Rella said. "Stop talking. I almost smeared your face."

***

Gale sat in his room with his feet propped up on his desk. His robes were discarded on the bed behind him, and a mug of ale was on the stool next to him. He scratched his naked belly and sighed as he closed his eyes with a smile.

"Ahem."

Gale's eyes shot open as he scrambled to get his feet off the desk. His head whipped around, searching for the source of the noise.

"Up here."

Gale raised his head. A golden spirit's face floated just below the ceiling.

"Weren't you attending the wedding?" Gale asked as he covered his crotch with his hands.

"Yes, but we were conducting a final round through the temple to make sure everything was in order before we went," the spirit said in a monotonous voice. "So far, we only found one thing out of place. You."

Gale's face reddened as he lowered his head. "I'm not good with skeletons," he mumbled. "I can't attend the wedding. It's just not possible."

"That's fine," the spirit said. "Carry on with what you're doing. We'll be going now. If any problems arise, call us back right away with a crystal. The capital is surprisingly void of any humans. Except for you."

"I understand," Gale said, still not looking up.

"Good," the spirit said as it dispersed.

Gale sighed and propped his legs back up on the desk. He grabbed the mug next to him and took a swig. "Nothing's going to happen," he said and burped. He shook his head as his body shivered. "Damned skeletons."

Below him, in the temple's basement, a crack formed on one of the runes in the sealing formation.

***

"Where's Vur?" Lindyss asked Paul. The two were outside a small building on top of a hill. To the north, there was a sea of people surrounding an altar with a single red line splitting the crowd down the middle. They were waiting in the fields where the fairies had set up their base, but the holes had been filled in earlier by skeletons.

"H-he's over there," Paul said and pointed with a trembling finger at a building to the south. "Two fairies came by and said they had something really important that needed to be done before the wedding started."

The door behind Paul swung open, and Lillian stepped outside wearing a pink dress and no shoes. "Did you see my heels?" she asked. "I swear I left them next to the door."

Paul shook his head as Lindyss flew towards the building he pointed to. He let out the breath he was holding. "I swear," he said and clenched his hands, "I'll never get used to Vur's relatives. They're the kind of people you hear about in tavern songs."

"Hey. I'm a hero too, you know?" Lillian stuck out her chest. "I was blessed by Lady Solandra, remember? And I'm also a duchess, you plebian."

"You haven't done anything though," Paul said and shook his head. "It's not the same. She's the Corrupted One: the person who guards over the Fountain of Youth, the person who established the treaty between our nation and the wilderness, the person who founded a kingdom by herself through necromancy."

Lillian smacked his shoulder. "I thought you liked Michelle," she said. "Why do you sound so infatuated with Lindyss? Don't tell me you've fallen for her too."

"What?" Paul asked and furrowed his brow. "Don't be stupid. She just makes me feel so small. I would still be some backwater noble if it weren't for Vur. And look at that mountain"—he pointed towards a mountain in the southeast—"over there. Those are real dragons. Those"—he pointed towards the west—"are real elves and dryads. And I've never even seen or heard of anything like those snake people to the south. There are so many things I would never have encountered if I hadn't met Vur."

"Eh, I suppose you're right," Lillian said and scratched her head. "I wouldn't have won that competition if it weren't for Vur. But that just means we're blessed with really good luck, right? That's a strength in itself."

"Only you would count good luck as one of your strengths," Paul said and shook his head. "Luck's not something you can rely on. You'll run out one day when you need it most."

"Hey," Lillian said and slapped his back. "Don't say something so ominous to me, you jinx. Don't you know this is how death flags are raised in stories?"

Paul exhaled and rubbed his back. "This is why you have to rely on luck," he said. "You're always reading stories instead of learning something practical."

***

Rella giggled as she capped her lipstick and tossed it onto the table. "All done," she said and beamed. "You can open your eyes now. Twirl around and look at your back too."

Vur frowned as he stared at himself in the mirror. "What did you do to my face?"

"Wizardry! We already told you this," Bella said and placed her hands on her hips. "Tafel's going to love how you look."

The door behind the trio swung open. The two fairies froze, including their wings, but they somehow managed to stay in the air. Lindyss furrowed her brow when she met Vur's gaze through the mirror. "Sorry. Wrong room," she said and closed the door. The fairies' wings flapped again as they glanced at each other.

The door opened again. "Vur?" Lindyss asked with a frown. "What the hell are you doing?"

Vur tilted his head. "What do you mean?" he asked. "You told me to wear this."

"Flee?" Bella asked Rella.

"Flee!"

The two fairies managed to dart outside the room before two tendrils shot out of Lindyss' shadow and sealed their movements. "Explain," Lindyss said as the tendrils squeezed the sisters.

"We were wrong! Please don't kill—"

The fairies' wails were silenced as their mouths were gagged. "Rella and Bella told me you wanted me to change clothes," Vur said as he frowned at the struggling fairies.

"So you changed into a dress?" Lindyss asked, raising an eyebrow.

Vur nodded. "They said you wanted me to coordinate better with Tafel to make her wedding special."

"And you believed them?"

"Of course. I have no reason not to."

"What do you two devils have to say for yourselves?" Lindyss asked as she smiled at the two fairies who were now hanging upside down in front of her. Her lips were smiling, but her gaze sent chills down their spines.

The two fairies' eyes grew as big as saucers, and their lips quivered. "We were wrong! Please forgive us," they wailed. "It's our nature to play pranks and we haven't tricked anyone in years. We couldn't help it! You'll forgive us, right?" They sniffled as they twisted their bodies to stare at Vur with puppy eyes.

Vur sighed.

"They must've known the consequences of their actions," Lindyss said. "Feel free to punish them."

"We didn't!" Rella said and shook her head. "We never considered the consequences. We didn't think we'd get caught. We were just going to hide for a few centuries until his anger cooled off."

Vur opened his mouth, causing the two fairies to shut their eyes. "I'm disappointed in you two," he said and picked them up, dispersing the shadowy tendrils. They hugged each other and trembled in his palms. "But I'm not going to punish you."

"Huh?" Bella and Rella asked at the same time while opening their eyes. "Really?"

"Dragons don't lie," Vur said. "I know all too well how it feels to give in to your instincts. Luckily, no harm was done. Next time, you should prank someone who can't retaliate."

Rella and Bella hugged Vur's face. "You're the best king ever."

"I know, but for some reason, Tafel disagrees," Vur said and sighed. "Now do something about my breasts. It's weird having them block my vision when I look down."

Lindyss sighed before smiling as the fairies undid their work. "I'll have a skeleton deliver an appropriate garment for you to wear. It's a good thing I decided to check up on you before the wedding started; I had a feeling you'd botch it somehow. You have fifteen minutes to get ready before you walk down the red carpet with Tafel. Normally, the groom would wait at the altar, but you two are special. It'd be more meaningful if a human and demon walked together with their arms linked." She glared at the fairies. "Don't mess with him anymore or else." She drew a line across her neck with a finger.

"Now I have to make sure Floofykins didn't eat the rings." She closed the door behind her as she left.

***

The sun shone down on a white archway with silver double doors. To either side of the archway, there was a wall of mist that obscured the view of the guests on the other side. Vur waited in front of the silver doors while fiddling with his glossy red tie. He wore a black suit with dark-gold cuffs and a white collared shirt underneath. The makeup had been washed off earlier, and his pink heels had been replaced by black leather dress shoes. A ripple in the air beside him caused his suit to flutter.

Tafel appeared next to him. She shielded her eyes from the sun with her right hand over her veil. "Tafel," Vur said and extended his right hand. "You look nice." She smiled and grasped his hand with her left.

"You look nice? That's it?" a voice asked from underneath Vur's suit. His suit's shoulder bulged as Rella crawled out from underneath his collar. "Your vocabulary needs some improvement. At the very least, you should describe her as beautiful or stunning."

"Yeah," Bella said and crawled out from the other side. "She spent hours to look like that and the best thing you come up with is nice?" She pouted at Tafel. "Say something to him."

"But I do look nice, don't I?" Tafel asked and glanced at her dress. "And I know Vur's trying; his nice is a normal person's beautiful. More importantly, why are you hiding in his clothes? You should be waiting with the other guests."

Bella and Rella glanced at each other before darting back within Vur's sleeves. "No one's here except for some talking lint," a muffled voice said before falling silent.

Tafel sighed. "Shall we go?" she asked and faced the double doors. Her heart pounded as she squeezed Vur's hand tighter. Vur pulled Tafel closer, and she wrapped her arm around his. A muffled squeak sounded out from Vur's sleeve.

"Are you nervous?" Tafel asked.

Vur shook his head and took a step forward. He pushed open the doors with his free hand and stepped through the archway, Tafel clinging to his side. The noisy field fell silent as the doors creaked open, their sound amplified by wind magic. A red carpet extended from the doors towards an altar that was nearly a mile away. The crowd was cleanly divided: the demons on the left side of the carpet and the humans on the right. The elves were located behind the altar with the humans and demons who were from Konigreich.

The earth trembled as thousands of skeletons' skulls popped out of the ground between the legs of the spectators. They inhaled at the same time—despite their lack of lungs—and sang in a choir-like manner, surprising everyone around them. Hundreds of fairies flew up into the air, holding onto a silk screen with a projection of Vur and Tafel for the whole crowd to see. As the duo walked down the aisle, a dryad, cloaked by fairy magic, followed behind them, causing flowers to grow from the ground they stepped on.

The crowd maintained their silence as their leaders made their way down the aisle with their heads held high. A chilling pressure emanated from the mountain in the distance as the dragons residing there fully displayed their auras, watching the child they raised. The children in the crowd didn't fidget, and the babies didn't cry. The only sounds that could be heard were the angelic voices of the skeletons and the faint fluttering of fairy wings.

Twenty minutes passed in this manner before Vur and Tafel arrived at the altar where Michelle was waiting with a book spread open on a pedestal. A golden light surrounded the altar as a glowing sphere with eyes hovered in the air above it. As Vur and Tafel ascended the steps towards Michelle, Floofykins darted out of the silver double doors with a red pillow that had tooth marks on one corner strapped to her back. Two rings lay on top of the pillow: one gold and one silver. The crowd raised

482

their eyebrows and one demon, Gabriel, directly fainted at the sight of the blue creature trampling the flowers.

"Welcome, everyone. We are here today to witness the union of His Majesty, Vur Besteck, and Her Highness, Tafel Besteck," Michelle said, her voice amplified through wind magic. The singing of the skeletons gradually faded away. "This is not just a unity between the two nations they represent, but more importantly, it's the union of two people who are in love with each other.

"Everyone present today was invited to this ceremony to bear witness to this miraculous event. You are here to listen to the vows that these two will exchange and forever be their witness. Will all of you do everything in your power to support this matrimony? If so, please respond, 'We will.'"

"We will." The ground shook as everyone, including the skeletons, responded at the same time. Grimmy roared and belched a breath of black fire into the air above the crowd, nearly burning the fairies.

"And you, Vur Besteck and Tafel Besteck, have you come here today with the intention to be legally joined in marriage?"

"We do," Vur and Tafel said, holding hands.

Michelle nodded. "Repeat after me," she said and began to speak.

"I, Vur Besteck, do take you, Tafel Besteck, to be my wife, to have and to hold from this day forward, for better, for worse, for richer, for poorer, in sickness and in health, to love and to cherish, until we are parted by death."

"I, Tafel Besteck, do take you, Vur Besteck, to be my husband, to have and to hold from this day forward, for better, for worse, for richer, for poorer, in sickness and in health, to love and to cherish, until we are parted by death."

"May I please have the rings?" Michelle asked and glanced at Floofykins who was panting and lying on her stomach. Floofykins shook her head and ran behind Tafel's legs. "Please?" Floofykins shook her head again. A small laugh

483

escaped from Tafel's lips as she picked the rings off of the red pillow and handed them to Michelle.

"These rings serve as a reminder of your eternal love. A circle has no beginning; a circle has no end. May your love forever be as unbroken as a circle. Vur, you may place the ring on Tafel's finger and repeat after me," Michelle said.

"Tafel Besteck, with this ring, I join my life with yours," Vur said and slipped the silver ring onto Tafel's finger.

"Now Tafel."

"Vur Besteck, with this ring, I join my life with yours," Tafel said. Her hands trembled as she slid the ring over Vur's knuckle.

"Vur and Tafel, in the presence of everyone in the three kingdoms (except Gale), you have spoken the words and performed the rites which unite your lives. By the power vested in me, I pronounce you husband and wife. You may now kiss the bride!"

Vur raised Tafel's veil and gazed into her eyes. The two smiled before they embraced each other. A golden light shone down on them from the sphere in the sky, bathing the two in a soft glow. The audience cheered.

Lindyss sighed as she leaned back against Grimmy's forehead, watching the two snog each other.

"Are you upset that the bishop didn't ask if anyone objected?" Prika asked from beside her with a grin. "I bet you would've and stole Vur from under Tafel's nose."

"I'm not upset," Lindyss said with a snort. "I'm just starting to feel old."

Prika laughed. "You're almost a thousand years old and you're just starting to feel old now?"

"Shut it," Lindyss said and scowled. "He's really all grown up now, huh?"

44

"So quiet," Gale mumbled to himself as he lay on his bed with his arm draped over his forehead. His face was flushed, and an empty wooden keg lay on its side on the floor nearby. "It's nice." He let out a sigh and closed his eyes before rolling onto his side, causing his bed to shake. He grunted.

"I must've gained weight," he said and yawned before scratching his naked belly. The bed shook again. "Stop shaking." He thumped the bed with the back of his hand. A minute passed with only Gale's rhythmic breathing breaking the silence.

An ear-piercing screech rang through the room.

Gale let out a groan. "Stop," he said and covered his ears with his pillow. "That's too loud." The bedframe rattled as one of the legs supporting the bed splintered, causing the mattress to tilt.

"Dammit, bed!" Gale yelled as he rolled onto the floor. "You never listen!" He clambered to his feet and placed his hand on his nightstand for support. He tilted his head and stared at the broken bedframe before narrowing his eyes and kicking it.

Gale swore and clutched his toes while hopping around before he crashed into the empty keg and fell over backwards. He whimpered as a familiar feeling built up in his throat. A torrent of acidic-smelling alcohol sprang out of his mouth and painted the carpet in front of his face. He attempted to stand up, but his knees buckled and he fell onto the pile of vomit.

Gale sighed as he rolled over onto his back and stared up at the marble ceiling. "It's alright. Everything's fine," he said and closed his eyes. "Only a bad dream."

Gale's chest rose and fell as ten minutes passed in silence. He shivered and clutched his shoulders as his eyes moved from side to side underneath his eyelids. Whimpers escaped from his lips as his body spasmed in the puddle of puke. "No. No more. Please."

While Gale suffered through his nightmares, the runic formation in the temple's basement emitted multiple colors, alternating between dark purple and light yellow. The walls shook and dust rained down from the ceiling. Creaking noises echoed through the room as the floor twisted and bulged, causing cracks to form on the surface of the runes.

Ear-piercing screeches split the air every time a rune gained enough cracks to shatter into pieces, revealing a pitch-black surface underneath. A mist, which smelled like rot and morning breath, streamed out of the surface, coalescing into a sphere above the formation. As time passed, more runes shattered and the sphere continued to grow, gradually taking a humanoid form.

A pair of eyelids formed as the last runes disintegrated. The floor became less opaque as more and more mist joined the humanoid figure. When the floor cleared, revealing a mirror-like surface, the humanoid figure's eyes shot open. The temple shook as the figure yelled, "I'm free!"

The figure cackled as it spread its arms up towards the ceiling. "Come at me!" it yelled and spread its legs apart. "I know you're there, you stupid piss-colored orb!"

It waited with its arms spread out for thirty seconds. "Seriously. Come," it said and frowned. "I've been biding my strength for a few centuries. I'd like to see you try to seal me now." There was still no response. It put its arms down.

"Hello?"

"..."

The figure scratched its head before walking towards the door. It hesitated before kicking the lock, causing the metal to erode. The door creaked open as the figure stood with its arms raised in front of its body, ready for a fight. "I know; you're waiting to ambush me, aren't you? Well, bring it on," it said and puffed out its chest as it stomped up the stairwell on the other side of the door. It reached another door at the top of the steps and eroded it away in a similar manner. It peeked its head out of the doorway and looked both ways before stepping into the hall.

"There's not even one guard?" It swiveled its head around a full 360 degrees without moving its body. It crossed its arms over its chest and frowned. "I bet you're laughing at me right now, aren't you?"

The figure snorted as it stomped down the hallway, leaving a trail of eroding footsteps in the carpet. It wandered through the whole floor, unable to find traces of any humans. "You think I need a body to cast magic, so you had everyone leave, huh?" the figure asked as it placed its hands on its hips. "Well, you're right. Come out and fight me like a spirit, mano-a-mano."

It waited in the middle of the hall, standing akimbo. "Please?" it asked as its shoulders drooped. It waited with a lowered head. "Can you at least talk to me? I haven't had decent conversation for at least a hundred years."

It sighed as its pleading was answered by silence. "I guess I'll go to the holy tomb and possess a corpse," it said and cocked its head. "It might not be as good as possessing a live person, but you don't want your bodies to be desecrated, right? You better come out and stop me if you don't want me to do it."

It walked outside of the temple and headed towards the cemetery. It frowned as it passed through empty streets. The city was completely silent except for the whistling of the wind. "Could some kind of disaster have happened?" the figure asked as it rubbed its chin. "Maybe the humans were wiped out and that's why the formation was abandoned? But the city is still intact; what could've happened here?"

It entered a few houses along the way towards the cemetery, but the only organisms it found were rats and cockroaches.

Finally, it reached the cemetery with the mausoleum at the center. "If I remember correctly, that stuck-up Magnus guy is the guardian. He wouldn't abandon his post unless something really terrible happened."

It walked past the rows of tombstones and kicked open the door to the mausoleum. "Yo, Magnus," it said, voice echoing through the chamber. "You here?"

"..."

"I got a delivery for you."

"..."

The figure sighed and sat down at the entranceway. "Maybe the parasites devoured everyone," it said and buried its head in its hands. "Wait. That can't be right. The plants are still fine and the mana levels are still high." It raised its head and nodded before clenching its hand into a fist.

"For now, I need a body," it said and walked towards the stairs leading down. "Then I can use some magic to locate people. I'm really going to do it. This is your last chance to stop me." It waited and shrugged before opening the door and descending the stairs.

It rubbed its chin when it saw footsteps in the dust. "Someone's been here recently," it said and smiled. "That must mean the world hasn't ended yet."

It whistled and sauntered over to the nearest glass sarcophagus. "They weren't grave robbers," the figure said as its head swiveled around, taking in the view of the tomb. It wandered around the floor, looking at each preserved corpse.

"Ah, perfect," it said and nodded at the well-built body in the sarcophagus beneath it. "Now I just have to press this over here and slide this glass off." The glass lid shattered as it crashed to the floor.

The figure smiled as it stepped on top of the side of the sarcophagus and reached down to touch the corpse's face. The corpse's eyes shot open. The figure froze as the corpse blinked at it and smiled.

488

"HOLY DRAGONBALLS!" the figure yelled and punched the corpse in the face. "AAAAHH! MOTHER OF GOD! IT'S STILL MOVING."

The figure fell over backwards and scrambled to its feet. It froze as the sound of glass scraping against stone filled the air and thousands of sarcophaguses opened.

"Mommy!"

It bolted towards the stairs and dashed up the steps, five at a time. It slammed the door shut behind it and lowered the latch. Its body shook as it trembled and sat on the floor before burying its face into its hands. "I feel so lonely."

After a while, the dark humanoid figure picked itself off its feet and left the mausoleum. It sighed as it wandered down the streets of the human capital, dragging its feet as it walked, leaving behind two parallel lines of dust in the road. It shuddered and shook its head as it recalled the zombies chasing after it in the mausoleum.

"Maybe it's just an isolated incident," it said and nodded as it raised its head to look at the sun. "It must be. The town's still in pristine condition. I really do wonder where that self-proclaimed god went. You hear me, you imposters?"

Its question was answered with silence as a tumbleweed blew past its feet. It hung its head and sighed again. "I guess I'll have to go to the temple and break a few of your crystals. I'll make you show yourselves and explain everything to me." It kicked a rock in front of its feet, reducing the stone to a pile of dust.

It headed back towards the temple it was sealed in, drawing funny faces on all the buildings along the way. It entered the temple doors and rubbed its chin. "I've already wandered around the first floor and haven't found any crystals," it said and tilted its head. "I guess they're held upstairs then." It nodded and pumped its fist as it headed towards the stairwell.

"So what do you think happened?" it asked out loud while walking.

"A zombie outbreak is the most likely scenario. The humans lost the war and their dead was converted into minions for the necromancer."

"Please don't say such ominous things to scare me like that."

"But I'm you. Ignoring that, what do you think happened?"

"I'd like to believe that they found a way to cleanse Fuselage and everyone returned peacefully."

"I didn't realize I was such a pansy. Those centuries of isolation really took a toll on me, huh?"

"Nah. It couldn't have. I'm still perfectly sane."

"Sane people talk to themselves?"

"It's fine as long as no one responds."

"…"

"See. Perfectly sane. Of cou—"

A snore interrupted the figure's conversation with itself. It froze mid-step and held its breath. A few seconds later, another snore resounded through the stairwell. The figure let out a gasp as a few shadowy tears dripped from its eyes. "I'm not alone!"

It sprinted up the rest of the stairs and ran towards the source of the snoring. It stopped in front of a pair of double doors and placed its ear flat against the wooden surface. Snores, interrupted by whimpers, reverberated through the wood. The figure pressed its hand through the door and eroded the lock.

The door swung open without a sound, and the figure stepped inside. Gale lay on the floor with his body covered in his own vomit. The figure frowned and pinched its nose as it approached the sleeping pope. "Psst," the figure whispered and nudged Gale's shoulder. "Hey."

Gale whimpered. "Stop, you damned skeletons," he said and turned over. "Leave me alone!"

The figure froze. "Skeletons?" it asked and held its breath. It fell backwards, landing on its butt. It crossed its arms as its brow furrowed. "Could he be a survivor? Was there really a zombie outbreak?" It raised its head to stare at the naked man covered in his own vomit.

"If I possess him, then I'll really be all alone," the figure said and shook its head. "I can't let that happen. I can't just rudely wake him up either; I need to make a good impression." The figure snapped its fingers as a lightbulb shone over its head. "I'll sing a song for him to wake up to!"

It cleared its throat and sucked in a deep breath. It closed its eyes, opened its mouth, and sang a dirge in a low tenor. Gale stopped snoring as his body stiffened. His eyes shot open, and he screamed like a little girl. "Never again!" he yelled and threw a ball of white light at the black figure.

The figure opened its eyes in time to see an expanding ball of holy energy fly towards its face. The energy smacked it in the forehead and slid downwards like a snowball. The figure spluttered as Gale chanted. "Wait, wait," it said and waved its arms in front of its body. "I'm not going to hurt you; I swear. And that exorcising spell won't work on me; I'm not an undead."

Gale stopped chanting and rubbed his bleary eyes. He blinked a few times at the humanoid figure. "You're trying to trick me again!" he said and gritted his teeth. "I saw what you did to Opfern! Don't think I'm so easily fooled. What do you want from me this time, you undead rascal?" He stood up and edged towards his staff, located next to his broken bed.

"So it's true then," the figure said and sighed as it wiped the holy energy off of its face. "The undead really have taken over."

Gale froze and tilted his head. "Huh?"

"Where did all the humans go?" the figure asked. "The capital's empty. You're the first person I've found."

"The skeletons took them all away," Gale said and moaned. He placed his hands on his temples. "I feel sick."

"The skeletons? What do you mean?"

"You don't know about the skeletons? They were everywhere," Gale said with his eyes shut tight. "Where've you been? Wait, no. Who are you?"

"I'm, uh, just a normal person," the figure said and nodded. "Yeah. Perfectly normal. Can you tell me more about these skeletons?"

Gale furrowed his brow and frowned. He looked down and wrinkled his nose. "I smell terrible. I need to take a bath to clean myself and clear my head," he said and gathered his robes and towel. He walked towards the door and stepped past the sitting figure but stopped himself. He glanced at the smoky fellow that suspiciously looked like an evil version of his god and froze. "Are you...?"

"Yes?" the figure asked and raised its head. "Coming with you? If you don't mind, sure."

Gale broke out into a cold sweat as his face turned pale. "Yeah," he said and nodded. His hands trembled. "Feel free."

"Tell me more about the undead," the figure said as it walked behind Gale towards the bathroom. "Why did they round up all the humans?"

"They were kidnapping people to force them to attend a wedding."

"Forcing people to attend a wedding?" The figure's brow furrowed. "Don't tell me they're going to be used as a blood offering. I think we should get out of here before they discover us."

"What?" Gale asked and almost dropped his towel. "What do you mean?"

"Undead are scary. Who knows what they plan on doing," the figure said and shook its head. "Chances are, we're going to be the only ones left once they're through with their barbaric ritual. Don't you think we should escape together before they discover us?"

Gale fell silent. "Are you afraid of the undead?"

"Me? Afraid? No way," the figure said and raised its chin. "I would never be afraid of something as lame as a zombie."

"There's a ghost behind you," Gale said and pointed over the figure's shoulder.

"Where!?" the figure shouted and leapt behind Gale while glancing backwards. When it saw nothing there, it glared at Gale. "You tricked me."

Gale shrugged. "I could've sworn I saw one. What were you saying about the undead? They weren't scary?"

The figure frowned and crossed its arms. "Don't give me that," it said. "I know you're frightened of skeletons. You almost pissed yourself in your sleep while screaming about them."

Gale shuddered.

The figure nodded. "Just as I thought," it said. "We should get out of here as soon as you finish your bath. We'll go to Fuselage and look for survivors there. There must be some people who survived that didn't escape to this continent."

"I'm not sure that's a good idea…"

"Nonsense. I'll take parasitic worms over an undead apocalypse any day. Trust me," the figure said and thumped its chest with its fist. "You and I. We'll be friends forever."

***

The humanoid figure carried a black sack as it walked alongside Gale who carried a similar bag. The two were on a trail in a forest, heading north, away from the human capital. The figure was humming while swinging its arms, the complete opposite of its reluctant travel buddy who hung his head and dragged his feet.

"Hey," the figure said as it stopped humming. "You never told me your name. I can't keep calling you 'hey' or 'you' this whole time."

Gale sighed and kicked a pebble. "My name is Gale."

"Gale," the figure said and rubbed its chin. "Interesting name. Then you can call me Breeze. We'll be the two wind brothers. Yeah, I like the sound of that."

The only response was the crunching of leaves underneath Gale's feet as the two walked along the path. Breeze whistled as he stretched his arms towards the sky.

"Where are we going?" Gale asked.

"To Fuselage, of course. That was the plan, right?"

Gale frowned. "But the portal to Fuselage is towards the northwest, not the northeast. Aren't we going the wrong way?"

"Don't be silly. We'll probably run into civilization towards the northwest. I'm not going to risk encountering another zombie. Once we hit the coast, we're going to build a raft to sail across the ocean."

"Is that really going to work?"

"It is. You're a laborer of sorts, aren't you? You should know how to build a raft."

"Why would you think I'm a laborer? I'm the pope. I've never built anything in my life."

"What?" Breeze asked and raised his eyebrow. "No way. I found you in a pile of your own vomit with an empty keg of alcohol next to you. You should come up with a better lie if you don't want to do manual labor. If you really were the pope, then I'd have to kill you in case you decide to summon that golden boy." Breeze patted Gale's shoulder, eroding away part of his jacket.

Gale's face blanched. "Yeah," he said and chuckled as sweat rolled down his back. "You got me. I can definitely build a raft. Leave it to me."

Breeze smiled, revealing his pointy, black teeth. "Great," he said. "I'll be counting on you. The sooner we build that raft, the sooner we can get away from these damned undead."

The two continued down the path, eventually exiting the forest and entering an open plain. Breeze squinted his eyes and stared down the horizon. "The shore's over there. We'll have to assemble the raft here and carry it to the coast."

The two reentered the forest to gather materials for the raft. Breeze cut down trees by eroding away their trunks while Gale gathered vines to tether the logs together. "Why are you so afraid of the undead?" Gale asked as he attempted to lash two ill-fitting logs together.

"Me? Afraid of the undead?" Breeze asked. "We've already been through this. I'm not afraid of anything."

Gale sighed. "Why do you want to go to a different continent to get away from the undead then?"

"That's easy. The undead are totally creepy and unnatural," Breeze said as he dragged another log over to Gale. "Don't you think so? If they're dead, then they should stay dead and not bother the living."

Gale stared at the mass of tormented souls in the shape of a human. "Yeah. I guess you're right," he said, enunciating each word. "It would really suck to wake up to an undead being serenading you while you're hungover. I can't even fathom how terrifying that'd feel. I completely understand where you're coming from."

"I'm glad you understand me so well, brother," Breeze said as he passed Gale another vine. "We should speed things up before night falls. I bet the undead will be more active at that time."

45

Vur held Tafel's hand as the two sat next to each other on a cushioned seat in a wooden carriage which had an undead horse pulling it along. A glowing sphere of light hovered in the air in front of the two, illuminating the small cabin. The full moon was visible through the window of the carriage.

Tafel sighed and closed her eyes as she rested her head on Vur's shoulder. Her face was slightly flushed as her fingers traced the veins along the back of Vur's hand. Vur smiled and rested his head on top of Tafel's.

"This is degrading. Absolutely degrading," a voice said from the golden sphere in the air. "I refuse to do this. I will not be used as a lamp for two love puppies. I have important things—"

Vur glared at the glowing sphere while emitting some of his aura. The voice stopped talking as the sphere trembled in the air.

Tafel exhaled and snuggled closer to Vur. "I wish today would never end," she said. A tear formed in the corner of her eye.

Vur squeezed her hand in response.

"I love you," Tafel whispered and raised her head.

"I love you too," Vur said as he gazed into Tafel's eyes. The two leaned closer to each other before locking lips.

The golden sphere flickered and disappeared. "That's it; I'm leaving," a voice said. "I hope you overexert yourself and die while you make babies. You're never going to see me ever again. Have fun on your honeymoon. Goodbye." The snogging couple completely ignored the god as it left.

Back in the Vault of the Spirits, the white crystals simultaneously shattered, filling the room with a golden smoke. The smoke condensed into a shining golden figure. It gnashed its teeth as it stomped out of the vault.

"First he eats me, then he uses me as a maid. Finally, he degrades me and turns me into a lamp!?" The spirit screamed in frustration as it punched a hole into the wall beside it. "I'm through with him! I'll run away to Fuselage. If he chases me there, then I'll run back here! I'd like to see him try to catch me."

The figure's ear twitched, and it froze. "The formation's been broken," it said and creased its brow. It hesitated in the hall. "Eh, screw it. That guy is way too troublesome for me to deal with. The king can play with him instead. I'll spend my days in leisure." The figure nodded as it continued out of the building.

***

Vur and Tafel climbed outside of their carriage as the undead horse collapsed into a pile of bones. They had stopped in front of a city in the desert with stone walls and metal gates. A naga guard eyed them while gripping his poleaxe tighter. The sun reflected off the axe, revealing a layer of runes on the blade.

"We don't take kindly to strangers here," the naga said in snaketongue as he advanced towards the duo. A torch lit up behind him, causing a clamor to erupt on the city walls. Multiple nagas appeared with their bows in hand and their arrows nocked.

"Tell your chieftain the devourer is here to take him up on his offer," Vur said back in snaketongue and crossed his arms over his bare chest. The naga frowned before signaling towards the city wall with his free hand. A lamia nodded in return and slithered off into the innermost parts of the city.

"You can understand them?" Tafel asked Vur as she shielded her eyes from the sun, squinting at the nagas on top of the city walls.

Vur nodded. "Auntie took me here when I was younger. She sold me to the coliseum and had me fight to make her money," he said and scratched his head. "It's been a while since I've spoken snaketongue though."

"She sold you?" Tafel asked and raised an eyebrow. "Why am I not too surprised? Now I know why she'd send us here as a part of our honeymoon."

The metal gate behind the naga guard screeched as it opened, and the chieftain came out, looking unchanged despite the decade that had passed. He wore a silk vest and had dozens of golden necklaces adorning his chest. A cerberus followed behind him with its heads held high. Its legs were as tall as the naga next to it, and its heads were wider than a human body. One of the heads glanced at Vur out of the corner of its eye and let out an involuntary yelp. The cerberus dashed ahead of the chieftain and lay prone in front of Vur while letting out tiny whimpers.

Tafel's eyes widened as Vur reached forward and petted the beast's middle head.

The chieftain sighed as he slithered around the beast and faced Vur. "Greetings, devourer," he said and lowered his head. "I didn't expect to see you so soon after your ceremony with your mate."

"We're exploring the continent and just happened to pass by," Vur said. "Then I remembered your offer of hospitality and decided to take you up on it."

"Of course," the naga said and smiled bitterly. "Come. I'll show you around our city."

"It's so cute," Tafel said as the cerberus licked her hand when she approached to pet it. "I've never seen anything like this before. It makes me wonder what lies even further south."

"We'll find out soon enough," Vur said as he shot a glance at the cerberus. "But for now, let's enjoy ourselves here. The antlions taste really good."

"Oh, joy," Tafel said and wiped the slobber onto the cerberus' face, "more bugs."

***

Michelle frowned as she wandered around Gale's room. A human-shaped stain that smelled like vomit and alcohol was in the middle of the carpet. "Where could Gale have gone?" she muttered to herself as she rummaged through his closet, looking for any hints. "Don't tell me he actually dissolved into a puddle of vomit."

A knocking sound echoed through the room, causing Michelle to jump and knock over a pile of clothes. "Michelle? Are you in there?" Paul's voice asked from the other side of the door. "The Corrupted One has a message for all the bishops."

"I'm here," Michelle said as she dusted herself off and opened the door. "Message?"

Paul nodded. "The bishops are gathering in the central room of the temple right now," he said. "Let's go." The two headed towards the gathering spot.

"Greetings, ye holy peeps," a skeleton wearing a top hat said as the duo arrived. "Welcome, welcome. Make yourselves at home." The group of twenty bishops frowned as they glanced at each other from across the tables. Paul raised an eyebrow but remained silent as he and Michelle took their seats.

"I have a proposal for all of you from our lord and resurrector, the Corrupted One," the skeleton said as it bowed and swept its hat off its head while bringing it to its chest. It raised its head and made eye contact with the bishops. "Join us and become bishops of our religion."

The bishops fell silent. "What?" one of them asked as he stood up. "Are you joking with us right now?"

"No. I'm being absolutely serious," the skeleton said as its eyes glowed purple. Lindyss' voice rang out of the skeleton's mouth. "Your god and pope ran away from their responsibilities; I'll be taking over. It's up to you whether you want to join me or not." The skeleton smirked.

Paul threw his hand up into the air. "I'll join," he said and scrambled to his feet. He walked over to the skeleton who nodded at him.

"Paul!" Michelle said and furrowed her brow.

Paul shrugged. "Vur ate a god," he said. "I wouldn't be surprised if it actually did run away after that, and Gale's already been missing for a week."

"Smart man," the skeleton said as its voice returned to normal. Its eyes stopped glowing, and it readjusted its top hat.

"Don't you worship our god?" Michelle asked. "Why did you even become a bishop if you're so easily swayed?"

Paul scratched his head as the other bishops glared at him. "Well, Vur kinda just made me one," he said and glanced at his feet as he took in a deep breath. "And, quite frankly, I like you, and I wanted to get closer to you."

The skeleton laughed and placed its arm around Paul's shoulder as Michelle's face turned pink. The other bishops' faces turned weird as they muttered amongst themselves. "Just one of you?" the skeleton asked when it finally stopped laughing. "Well, that's one more than what I expected."

"Won't you come too, Michelle?" Paul asked, his face slightly flushed.

"I refuse," Michelle said and crossed her arms.

Paul frowned. "Didn't you tell me how much you hated being raised as the pope's daughter?" he asked. "There's a chance to leave now, but you won't take it?"

Michelle shook her head.

The skeleton let out a sigh as it patted Paul's back. "She probably feels obligated to take up her father's duties," it said. "Don't worry. I got this." The skeleton walked towards Michelle and placed its mouth next to her ear. It whispered something before pulling its head back and winking at her. "We know more about you than you think. Want to join us now?"

Michelle bit her lower lip and furrowed her brow. She sighed. "Alright," she said and hung her head. "Count me in." Her ears burned as the other bishops stared daggers at her.

The skeleton grinned. "Excellent. Any more volunteers?"

***

A young child was kneeling by his bedside with his hands clasped together. His eyes were closed, and his head was tilted towards the ceiling. "God, if you're out there, please give me a sign. Something. Anything."

A few seconds later, a skeletal hand popped out of the floor next to the boy, grasping a wooden sign that read, "Here you go." On the bottom of the sign—in fine print—a message read, "From your newest local god, the Corrupted One."

The boy opened his eyes and fell backwards.

That night, everyone's prayers were answered by skeletons to the best of their ability.

***

Lindyss stood in a cave with her hands on her hips, looking up at a pile of crystals. Her skin was tinted blue by the light they emitted. Grimmy lay on the ground next to her with his eyes half-open.

"What are you going to do with all these mana crystals?" Grimmy asked as he clawed at the mountain of glowing blue stones. "Can I eat some?"

"No," Lindyss said as a horde of skeletons walked into the cave, each one carrying a basket filled with crystals. "Where do you think the energy comes from to power over a million skeletons?"

Grimmy snorted. "I know how much mana it takes. You clearly have a whole lot extra," he said as he split the pile down the middle. "This much is required to maintain the undead for a few weeks. This much is extra."

"Well, those extras are used to help the patriarch recover faster," Lindyss said as she picked up a crystal. "He's going to wake up in a few months at this rate. I should've forced that god out of here earlier, so much wasted mana." She shook her head.

Grimmy tapped his claws against the ground. "What about that spirit who injured the patriarch?" he asked. "Wasn't the god suppressing it? Now that it's gone, won't that thing cause problems?"

"It's already been freed," Lindyss said and dropped the crystal in her hand. "The sealing formation was broken a while ago. I'm guessing it won't take any action against us seeing as it hasn't already. In any case, the best thing to do would be to wake the patriarch as soon as possible to deal with any potential threats."

Grimmy sighed. "Fine," he said and curled up into a ball with his eyes closed. "I won't eat any crystals then. I bet they tasted sour anyway."

Lindyss rolled her eyes. "You can have them after the patriarch wakes up," she said and patted Grimmy's snout. "Now quit sulking."

"Who's sulking?" Grimmy asked as his eyes shot open. "I'm just contemplating."

"About what?"

Grimmy chuckled. "About what the patriarch would think when he wakes up," he said and grinned. "You know how much of a stickler he is for order. Vur's personality is the embodiment of everything that annoys him."

Lindyss let out a laugh and smoothed her dress before she sat down, leaning against Grimmy with her knees in front of her chest. "Says the person who gave him that personality. I'm looking forward to it," she said and smiled. "You don't think he'll do anything too drastic, right? I haven't interacted with him enough to know how he'll react."

Grimmy grunted. "No clue," he said and yawned, "but I'm sure Sera won't let him hurt Vur if that's what you're worried about."

"I hope you're right."

"Of course I'm right," Grimmy said. "Remember that time when Vernon rolled over in his sleep and knocked over a mountain with the patriarch's favorite fruits?"

"No."

"Oh. I guess that was a few thousand years too early for you, huh?" Grimmy asked and blinked. "Well, Sera stopped him from punishing Vernon too heavily. Of course, Vernon was never the same after that and gained a newfound respect for his wife."

"Respect for the matriarch or fear of her father?" Lindyss asked as a skeleton handed her an apple. She bit into it and closed her eyes.

The ground shook as Grimmy thumped his tail against the earth and laughed. "Fear of Sera," he said and grinned. "She convinced the patriarch not to punish Vernon, but she found out that the plant she was raising for a few centuries was crushed by the mountain right before it could bear fruit. She whupped him good."

Lindyss shuddered as a bead of sweat formed on her forehead. "And I fed her child to a miro," she said. She paused and stared at her half-eaten fruit. "Wow. That was stupid."

"Very," Grimmy said with a smile. "But it's alright. If you died, I would've reanimated your corpse for you."

"Thanks," Lindyss said and rolled her eyes. "I guess even death won't let me escape from you, huh?"

"Nope. You'll always be my little elf."

Lindyss smacked one of his scales. "I'm telling your wife," she said and paused. "Where's she been anyway?"

Grimmy yawned. "She flew back to the eastern continent to visit her family."

"Oh," Lindyss said and nodded. "Didn't you promise you'd take me there?"

"Yeah, but you were all, 'oh, the sunlight burns and is going to kill me' for the longest period of time," Grimmy said and snorted.

"That was your fault, asshole," Lindyss said and chucked the apple's core at a nearby skeleton. It knocked its skull off. "I'm all better now, no thanks to you."

Grimmy laughed. "Alright, we'll go after the patriarch wakes up. I haven't seen Leila's family in a long time; I should visit."

***

Vur and Tafel sat on a towel with an ocean-side view in front of them. The sky, sea, and sand turned red as the sun began to set. A few humanoid fishmen stood on either side of the two, fanning them with giant leaves. Their scales were blue, and a shark fin protruded from their backs. Their eyes bulged out of their heads, and their mouths had rows of razor-sharp teeth.

"I wonder what's on the other side of the ocean," Tafel said as she squeezed Vur's hand.

"Want to build a boat and find out?" Vur asked and raised an eyebrow. "We can."

Tafel laughed. "No," she said and rested her head on Vur's shoulder. "It'd be much easier if a roc or dragon carried us over." She sighed and closed her eyes. "Should we head back soon? We've traveled as far south as we could go."

"We could go further if we build that boat," Vur said and furrowed his brows.

"No. No boats," Tafel said. "I get seasick. Tina had us travel across a lake in Fuselage by boat once, and I couldn't even stand up."

"A lake's water is still though, isn't it?"

"That's the point. No boats."

"Alright," Vur said and sighed. A fishman flinched and offered him a glass of pink liquid from a platter in its hands. Vur waved his hand, and the fishman retracted the cup. "I wish we could understand what they're saying. At least the lizard people spoke some snaketongue."

Tafel grunted in reply as she hugged his arm. "Before we go back..." she said. Her face turned slightly red as she

504

whispered in Vur's ear. Vur nodded and shooed away the nearby fishmen as Tafel lay down on the towel.

A few fishmen children were hiding behind a tree, peeking at the couple on the beach. "What are they doing?"

"I think they're wrestling?"

"Weird creatures are weird."

"Definitely."

The sun set.

46

Vur, Tafel, and Lindyss walked through a bush and approached a cliff wall. A dragon-sized tunnel led downwards at the base of the cliff. The ground was shattered, and the trees nearby were uprooted and lying on their sides. A few boulders laid on the ground, having fallen from the top of the cliff.

"This is where your grandpa sleeps?" Tafel asked as she held Vur's hand and squeezed. "Why's everything in ruins?"

Vur shrugged and looked at Lindyss. Her face was pale and her palms were slick with sweat. "Are you scared?" he asked and raised an eyebrow.

"Of course," Lindyss said and kicked Vur's butt. "Who wouldn't be? Let's keep going; the dragons are waiting inside."

The trio passed through the field of ruin and entered the tunnel. Tafel summoned a flame to illuminate the path ahead. They traveled through winding tunnels, passing by no signs of life—not even a speck of moss. "It's so ... empty," Tafel said and shuddered as they followed the clawed footprints embedded in the ground.

Lindyss nodded. "The patriarch absorbed all the mana in the surroundings to recover faster," she said. "It's no surprise that nothing can grow here."

After walking for fifteen minutes, the group arrived in a chamber. Icicles hung from the ceiling, and a layer of frost covered the walls. A pile of glowing blue crystals lay in the corner of the room. Sera, Vernon, Grimmy, Prika, and Leila were sitting on their haunches in a semi-circle around a sleeping green dragon. Snuffles, his wife, and Floofykins were on top of Sera's head.

"You're back," Sera said as her eyes flickered towards the approaching group. "I'm glad you made it in time to see your grandfather wake up."

"How do you know he's waking up?" Vur asked.

Sera let out a low chuckle. "Your grandfather always sneezes three times in his sleep before he wakes up," she said and smiled. "He already sneezed twice. You can tell from all the broken trees outside."

"Oh," Vur said and nodded. "It's like how Prika always says, 'I want a mate' before she wakes up."

"Hey!" Prika said and frowned. "I don't do that. Right?" She looked at the other dragons. They avoided her gaze.

"Actually…," Leila said. Her voice trailed off. "You do."

Grimmy nodded. "Every single time," he said. "Really loudly too."

Prika blinked and tilted her head. She sighed. "I can't tell if you guys are bullying me or not," she said and puffed out her cheeks. "I d—"

A torrent of wind swirled in through the tunnels and knocked the dragons over. The green dragon's back rose by ten meters as the air rushed into its nostrils. The ground trembled while icicles rained down from the ceiling. The wind continued to roar past the group for a solid minute before it stopped.

Lindyss paled and slammed her arms against the ground, causing a bulwark to rise in front of the green dragon's face. The dragon's mouth opened, sucking in even more air. Its nose twitched, and Lindyss summoned another wall of earth as the surrounding dragons turned around and braced themselves. The green dragon's nose twitched again.

An explosion. That was the only way to describe what happened. The green dragon's body deflated in an instant as all of the air was expunged from its body in a fraction of a second. The walls of earth disintegrated, doing nothing to impede the shockwave as it traveled outside. Rumbling sounds echoed through the chamber, and the remaining icicles shattered before touching the ground. Outside, every bird within a 50-mile radius cawed and scattered into the air.

Vur dug out a ball of earwax and looked around. "Is everyone okay?"

The dragons shook their heads like dogs shaking off water and crawled back onto their haunches. Tafel peeked out from behind Vur's back. "A little deaf, but I think I'll be fine when the ringing goes away."

The green dragon sniffled a few times before its eyes shot open. Its mouth widened as it yawned, and it twisted its head towards its tail, causing creaking noises to emerge from its body as it stretched. "That was a good nap," the dragon said and sighed as it stretched its front claws forward while arching its back.

"Patriarch." The other dragons sat with their heads lowered, staring at the ground in front of them.

"Oh?" The patriarch raised an eyebrow. His gaze roamed over Leila. "There's a new addition to the family. Where'd you come from?"

"The eastern continent," Leila said, her head still lowered. "You can call me Leila, Patriarch."

The patriarch made a face. "Eugh," he said and stuck out his tongue. "Then you probably know Kondra. I hate that woman. Is she still kicking?"

Leila nodded. "The matriarch is still alive and well."

"Tch. Such a shame," the patriarch said. "Well, welcome to the clan." His gaze shifted towards Sera. "Sera."

"Yes, Father," Sera said and raised her head.

"What is that?"

"What is what?" Sera asked and tilted her head.

Floofykins screeched in protest as she flapped her wings and scrambled back up Sera's scales.

"The … thing," the patriarch said and pointed at Floofykins. "I've never seen anything like it."

508

Floofykins hissed and spat a fireball towards the patriarch. It collided against his snout and dispersed without leaving a mark.

"Ah," Sera said and nodded. "This is your great-great-granddaughter."

The patriarch blinked with furrowed eyebrows. "My what? Did you mate with a pig?"

Snuffles oinked and snapped his jaws at the patriarch.

"Was it this one?" the patriarch asked as he lifted Snuffles with his claws. "Kinda small, don't you think? There's no way you could've fertilized an egg with him."

"You've misunderstood, Father," Sera said as she held out her claw to retrieve Snuffles. "This is your great-grandson. And this phoenix is your great-granddaughter-in-law."

The patriarch dropped Snuffles into Sera's claw. His shoulders drooped, and he sighed while shaking his head. "You know, back in my day," he said and raised his head towards the ceiling, "species only mated with their own species: phoenixes mated with phoenixes, boars mated with boars. Ducks mated with chickens…. Ducks don't count. You youngins are too progressive these days. Alright"—he lowered his head and narrowed his eyes at Sera—"where's my grandchild if these are its offspring."

Sera's gaze flickered towards Vur. "Vur," she said. "Come here."

The patriarch frowned as Vur walked towards him while holding Tafel's hand. "Please tell me he's at least an elf that looks freakishly like a human," he said, pointing at Vur. He pointed at Tafel. "And she's an elf that happens to have horns."

"I'm a dragon," Vur said and stuck his chest out. His imprint glowed as he opened his mouth and roared.

The patriarch blinked at Vur before turning back to Sera. "Explain."

Sera blinked back. "He's a dragon," she said with a straight face. "And your grandson."

"I see," the patriarch said and nodded. "Then what's the girl?"

"Your granddaughter-in-law," Sera said.

The patriarch nodded and frowned at Grimmy. "Did my daughter hit her head on something?" he asked. "Maybe she ate the wrong kinds of mushrooms for dinner?"

Grimmy chuckled and raised his head. "If the squirt says he's a dragon, then he's a dragon," he said and smiled.

"Vernon," the patriarch said and whipped his head towards the golden dragon. "What is he?"

Vernon raised his head, and a bead of sweat rolled down his forehead. His gaze shifted between the patriarch's piercing stare and Sera's smiling face.

"I, I," Vernon said as his body shuddered. "I'm an ostrich." He dug a hole in front of himself and buried his head in the ground.

"What the hell is going on!?" the patriarch roared and whipped his head towards Prika. His eyes narrowed. "Prika."

Prika whistled while looking towards the ceiling. She inched towards the exit while avoiding eye contact. When she reached the exit, she turned towards the patriarch. "He's a dragon," she said and dashed out of the chamber before he could say anything in return.

"Leila?" the patriarch asked and raised an eyebrow.

"I...," Leila said and bit her lip. She turned her head away. "I've only just recently came back from visiting my family."

Sera beamed. "Three of us said Vur's a dragon," Sera said and patted Vur's head. "And two of us declined to answer. So 100% of the ones who responded said he's a dragon. I think it's safe to conclude that Vur is indeed a dragon."

Sweat formed on Lindyss' brow as she tiptoed towards the exit. *Goddamn dragon logic. I'll get killed if I stay here,* she thought and slipped into the tunnel.

"Mama's so smart," Vur said and nodded.

Tafel stared at Vur. "So it wasn't Grimmy who removed your common sense," she mumbled.

"Sera. Do you really expect me to accept a human as one of us?" the patriarch asked as he sat on his haunches.

"I'm a dragon," Vur said. The patriarch ignored him as he continued to stare at Sera.

"We've all already accepted him," Sera said and matched the patriarch's gaze.

A minute passed in silence as the two dragons stared at each other. The patriarch sighed and looked away first. "Alright, alright," he said. "You win."

Sera smiled. "I'll tell you all about him," she said as she walked over to her father and curled up next to him. Vernon's head popped back up from underground, and Prika peeked her head into the chamber from the tunnels with a squirming Lindyss in her claw.

"Let's gather round," the patriarch said. "I want to hear about everything that I've missed."

Everyone stared at Sera after they formed a circle. "I guess I'll start then," she said and smiled at Vur. "I'll start from when the humans forced you to—"

"Start with me!"

Sera sighed. "Alright."

"It all began when the humans stole my egg…"

Afterword

Thanks to Simon T Andreasen for supporting me on Patreon.

If you liked the story, feel free to check out my website at www.virlyce.com.

A second book is planned for the future.

Thank you for reading!

Made in the USA
San Bernardino, CA
01 February 2018